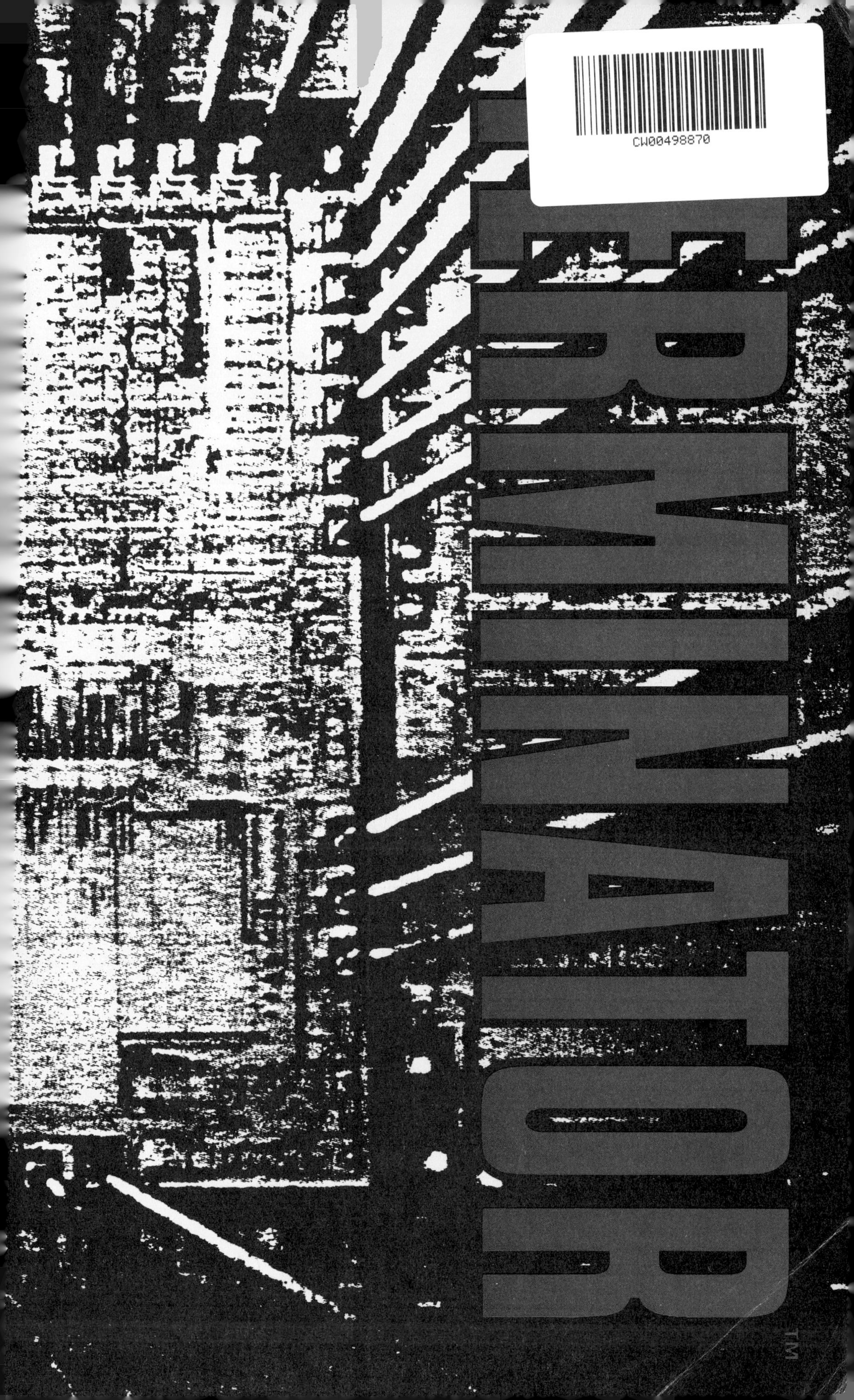
TERMINATOR
TM

TERMINATOR:
T E M P E S T

ISBN 1 85286 393 5

Published by Titan Books Ltd., 58 St. Giles High
St., London WC2H 8LH, by arrangement with
Dark Horse Comics, Inc., USA.
First British Edition: July 1991.

2 4 6 8 10 9 7 5 3 1

PRINTED IN CANADA

TERMINATOR:
TEMPEST

JOHN ARCUDI
WRITER

CHRIS WARNER
PENCILLER

PAUL GUINAN
INKER

KAREN CASEY-SMITH
LETTERER

CHRIS CHALENOR
RACHELLE MENASHE
COLORISTS

JOHN BOLTON
COVER

DIANA SCHUTZ
SERIES EDITOR

JERRY PROSSER
COLLECTION EDITOR

STEVEN BIRCH
JERRY PROSSER
COLLECTION DESIGN

1

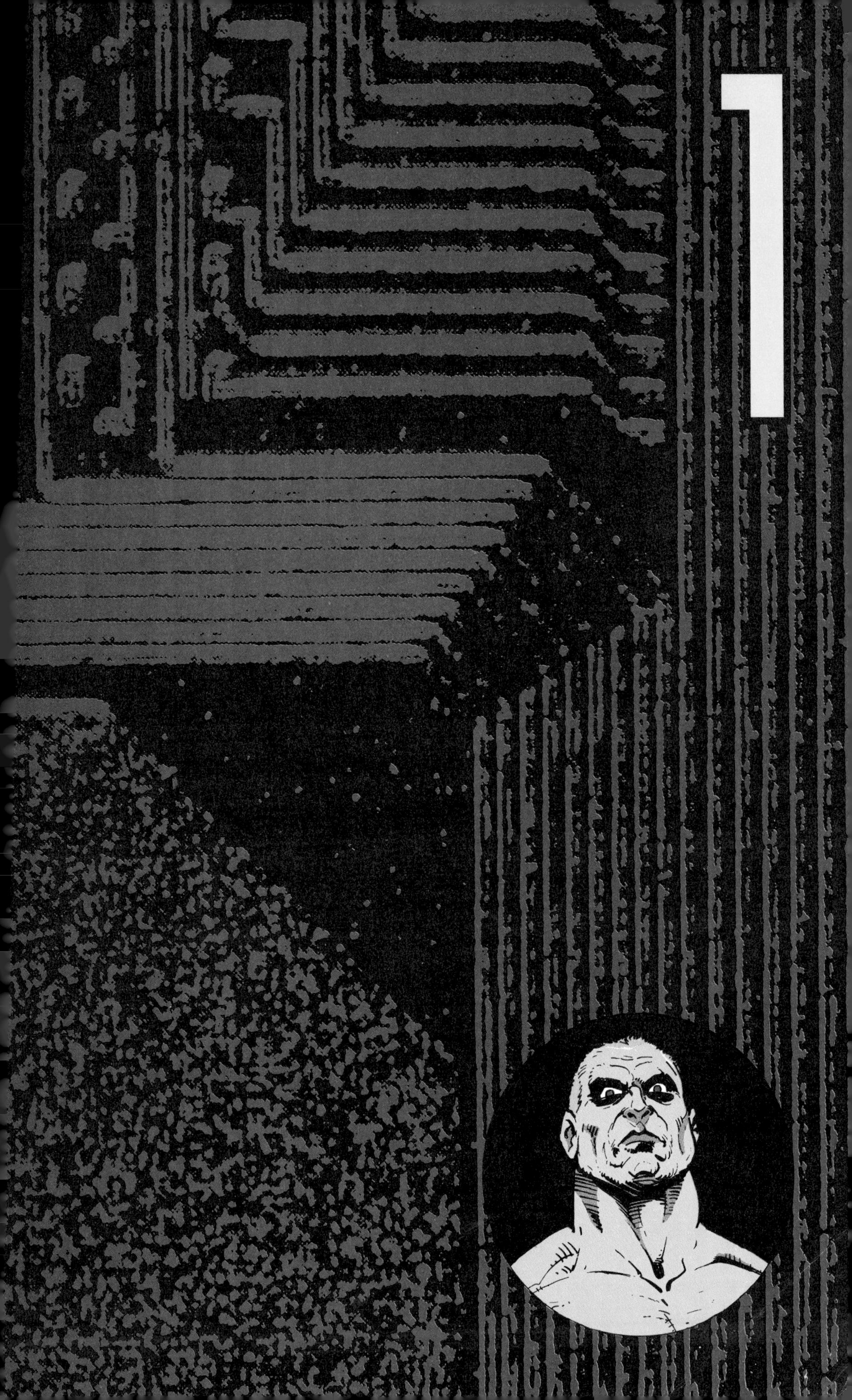

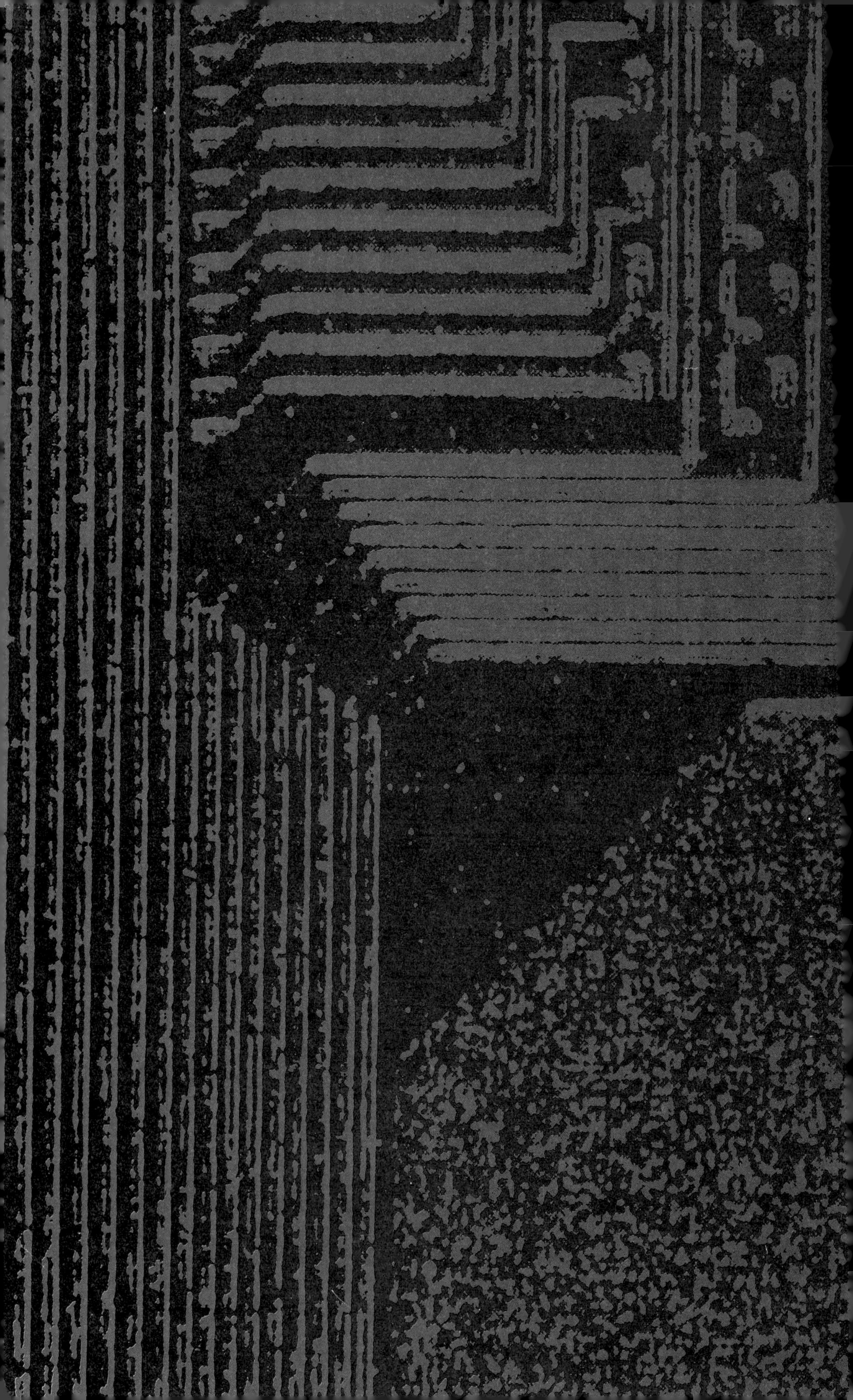

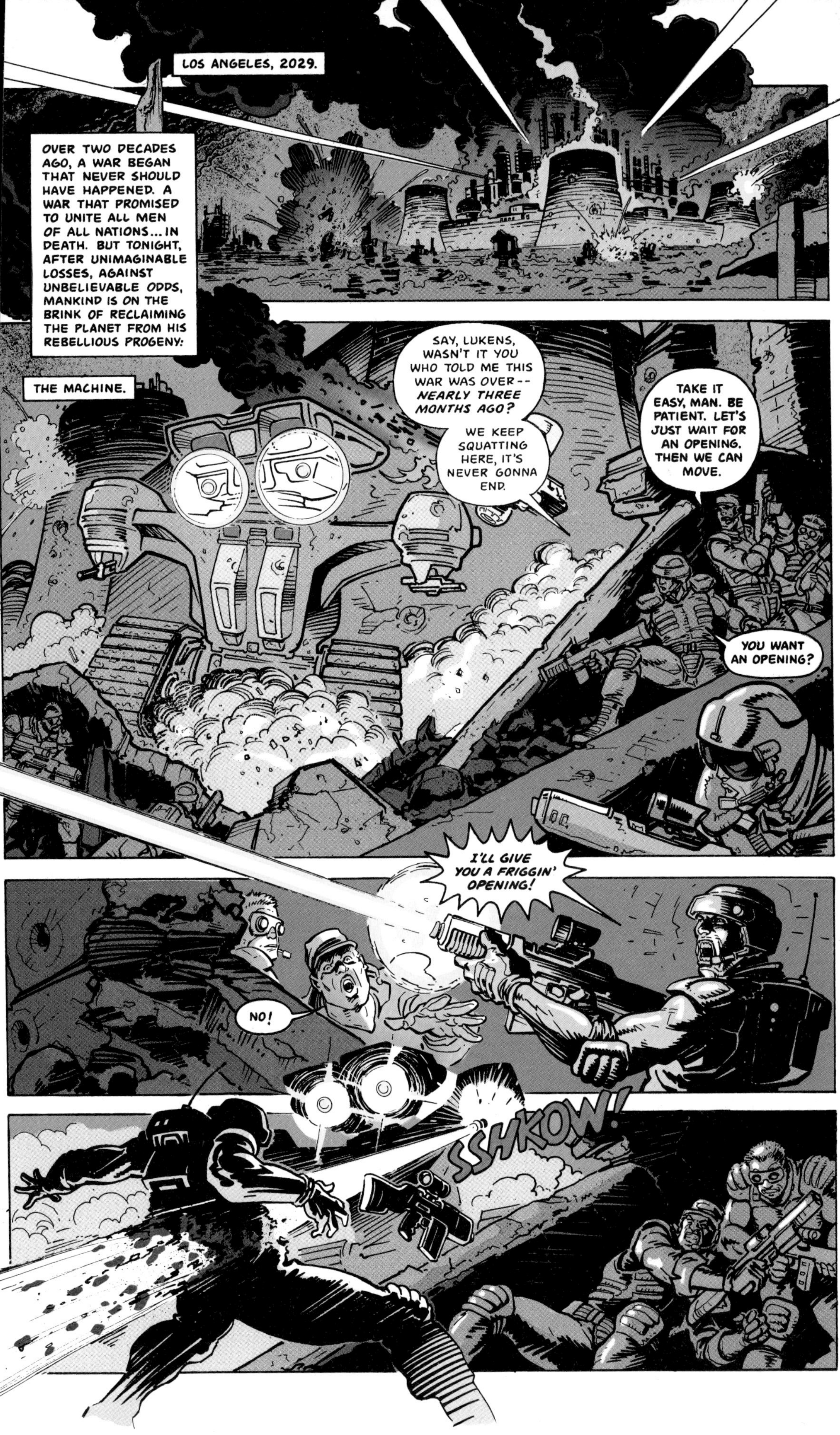
LOS ANGELES, 2029.
OVER TWO DECADES AGO, A WAR BEGAN THAT NEVER SHOULD HAVE HAPPENED. A WAR THAT PROMISED TO UNITE ALL MEN OF ALL NATIONS... IN DEATH. BUT TONIGHT, AFTER UNIMAGINABLE LOSSES, AGAINST UNBELIEVABLE ODDS, MANKIND IS ON THE BRINK OF RECLAIMING THE PLANET FROM HIS REBELLIOUS PROGENY:
THE MACHINE.
SAY, LUKENS, WASN'T IT YOU WHO TOLD ME THIS WAR WAS OVER-- NEARLY THREE MONTHS AGO?
WE KEEP SQUATTING HERE, IT'S NEVER GONNA END.
TAKE IT EASY, MAN. BE PATIENT. LET'S JUST WAIT FOR AN OPENING. THEN WE CAN MOVE.
YOU WANT AN OPENING?
NO!
I'LL GIVE YOU A FRIGGIN' OPENING!
SSHKOW!

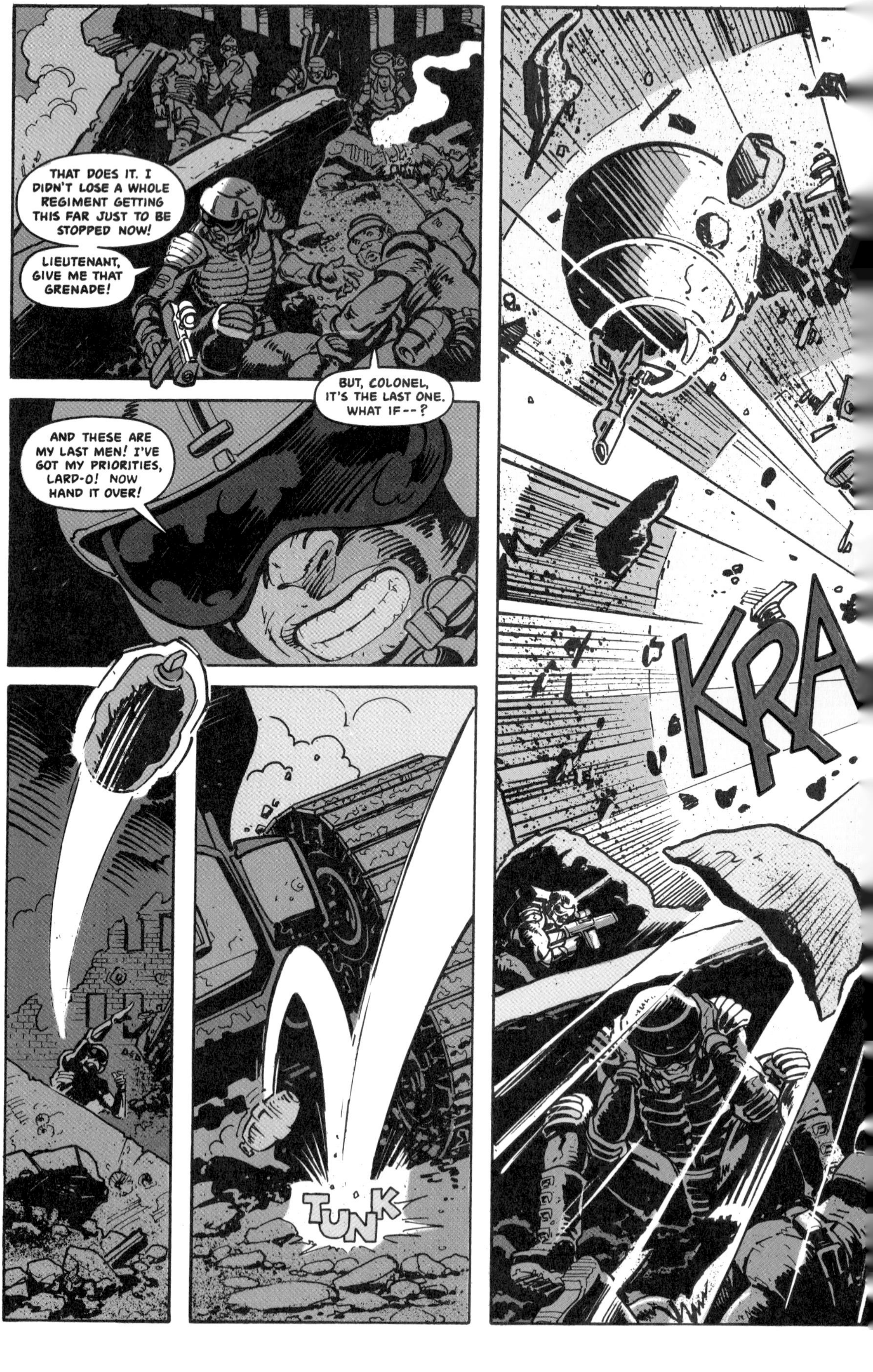
THAT DOES IT. I DIDN'T LOSE A WHOLE REGIMENT GETTING THIS FAR JUST TO BE STOPPED NOW!
LIEUTENANT, GIVE ME THAT GRENADE!
BUT, COLONEL, IT'S THE LAST ONE. WHAT IF--?
AND THESE ARE MY LAST MEN! I'VE GOT MY PRIORITIES, LARD-O! NOW HAND IT OVER!
TUNK
KRA

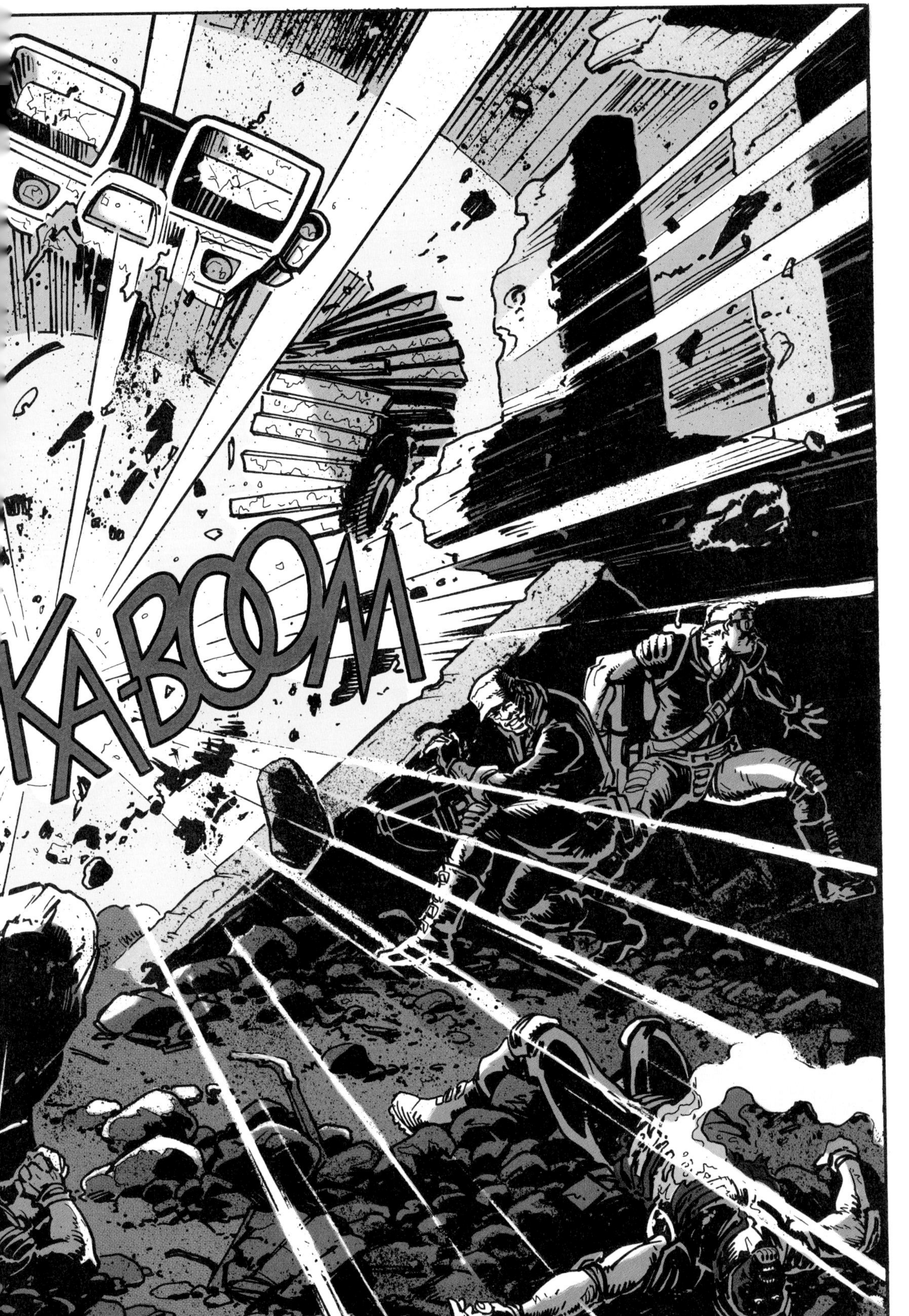
KA-BOOM

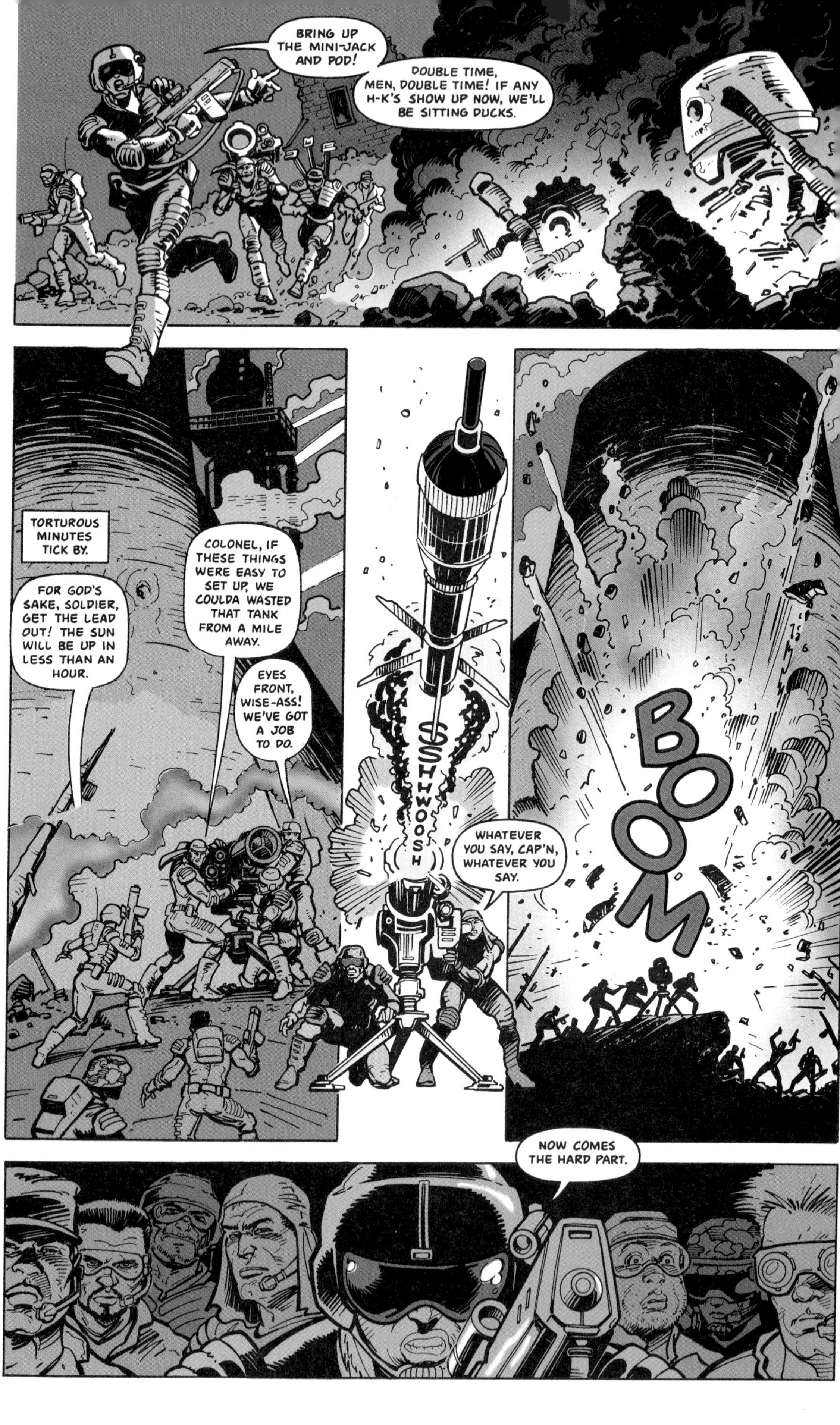

BRING UP THE MINI-JACK AND POD!
DOUBLE TIME, MEN, DOUBLE TIME! IF ANY H-K'S SHOW UP NOW, WE'LL BE SITTING DUCKS.
TORTUROUS MINUTES TICK BY.
FOR GOD'S SAKE, SOLDIER, GET THE LEAD OUT! THE SUN WILL BE UP IN LESS THAN AN HOUR.
COLONEL, IF THESE THINGS WERE EASY TO SET UP, WE COULDA WASTED THAT TANK FROM A MILE AWAY.
EYES FRONT, WISE-ASS! WE'VE GOT A JOB TO DO.
SSHHWOOSH
WHATEVER YOU SAY, CAP'N, WHATEVER YOU SAY.
BOOM
NOW COMES THE HARD PART.

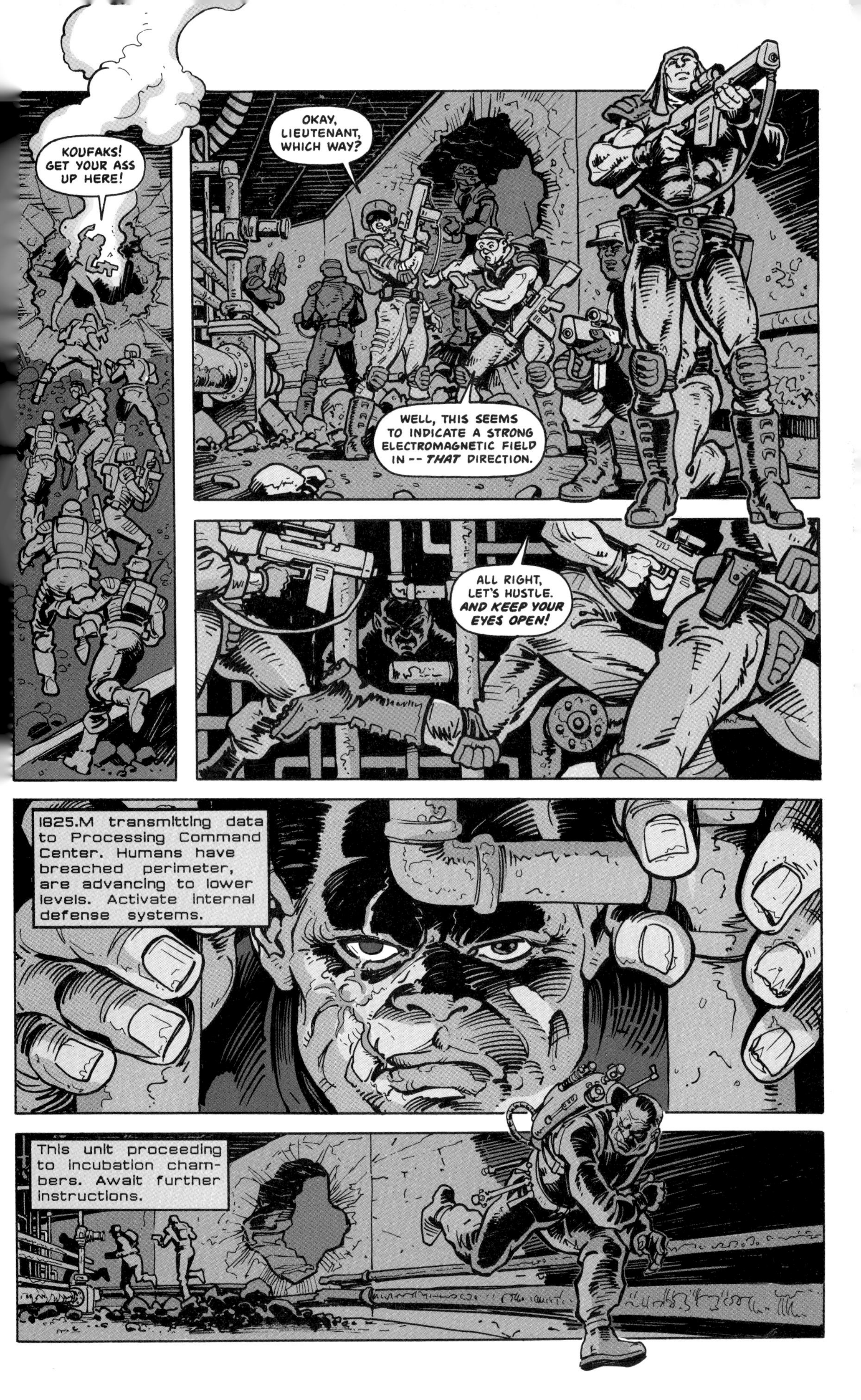
KOUFAKS! GET YOUR ASS UP HERE!
OKAY, LIEUTENANT, WHICH WAY?
WELL, THIS SEEMS TO INDICATE A STRONG ELECTROMAGNETIC FIELD IN -- THAT DIRECTION.
ALL RIGHT, LET'S HUSTLE. AND KEEP YOUR EYES OPEN!
1825.M transmitting data to Processing Command Center. Humans have breached perimeter, are advancing to lower levels. Activate internal defense systems.
This unit proceeding to incubation chambers. Await further instructions.

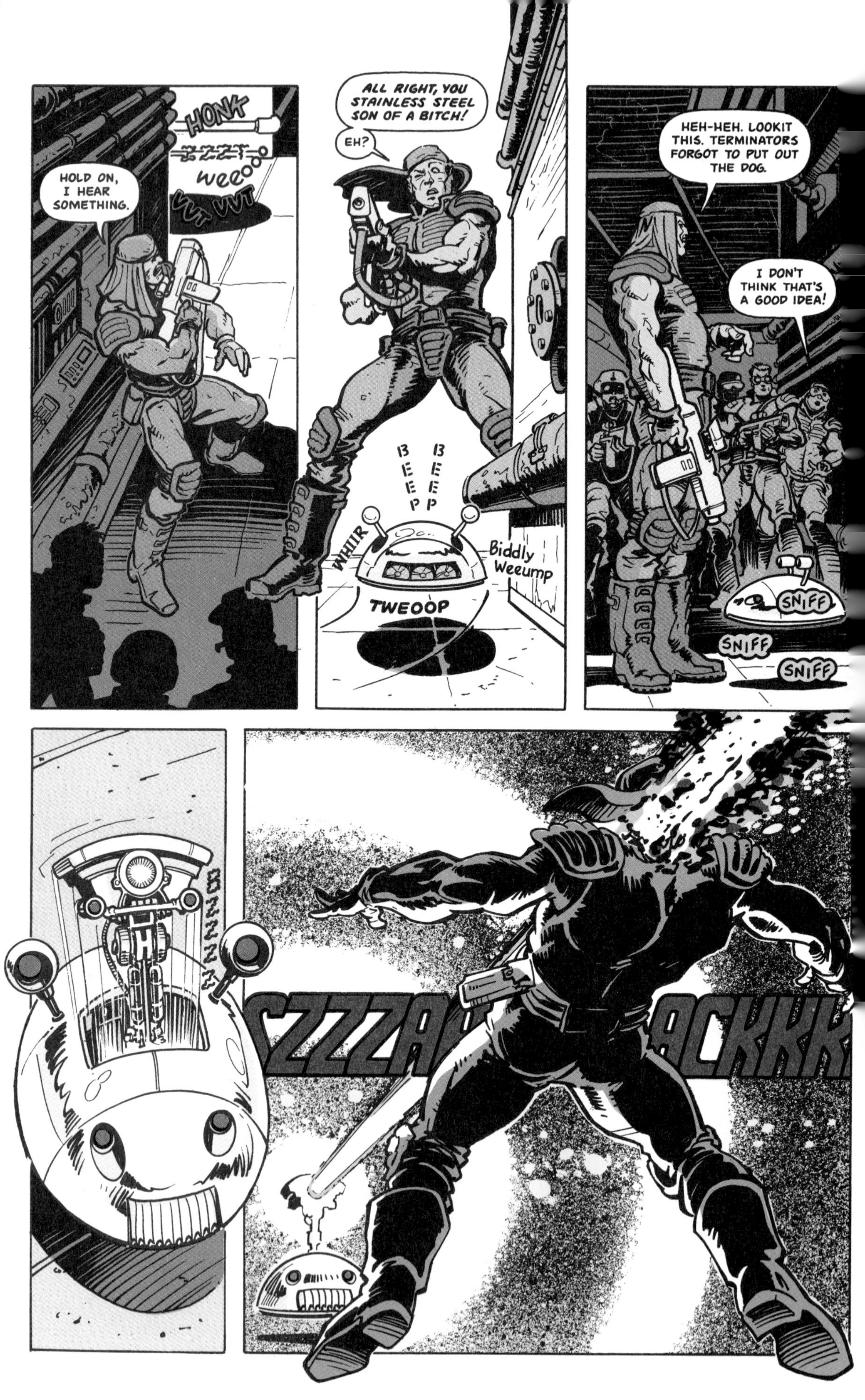
HOLD ON, I HEAR SOMETHING.
HONK
weeooo
VVT VVT
ALL RIGHT, YOU STAINLESS STEEL SON OF A BITCH!
EH?
BEEP
BEEP
WHIR
Biddly Weeump
TWEOOP
HEH-HEH. LOOKIT THIS. TERMINATORS FORGOT TO PUT OUT THE DOG.
I DON'T THINK THAT'S A GOOD IDEA!
SNIFF
SNIFF
SNIFF
SZZZA
ACKKK

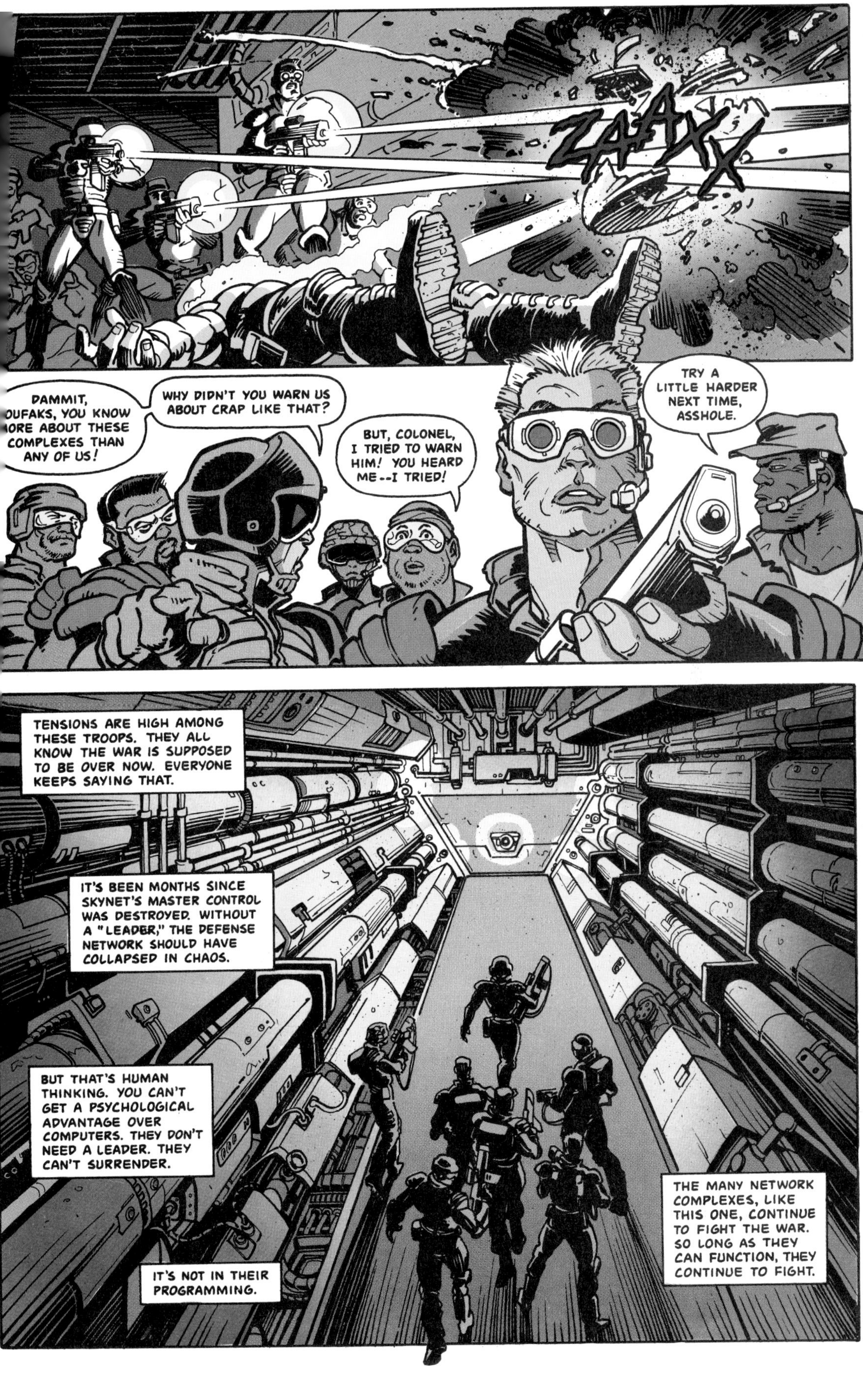
ZAAXX
DAMMIT, OUFAKS, YOU KNOW ORE ABOUT THESE COMPLEXES THAN ANY OF US!
WHY DIDN'T YOU WARN US ABOUT CRAP LIKE THAT?
BUT, COLONEL, I TRIED TO WARN HIM! YOU HEARD ME--I TRIED!
TRY A LITTLE HARDER NEXT TIME, ASSHOLE.
TENSIONS ARE HIGH AMONG THESE TROOPS. THEY ALL KNOW THE WAR IS SUPPOSED TO BE OVER NOW. EVERYONE KEEPS SAYING THAT.
IT'S BEEN MONTHS SINCE SKYNET'S MASTER CONTROL WAS DESTROYED. WITHOUT A "LEADER," THE DEFENSE NETWORK SHOULD HAVE COLLAPSED IN CHAOS.
BUT THAT'S HUMAN THINKING. YOU CAN'T GET A PSYCHOLOGICAL ADVANTAGE OVER COMPUTERS. THEY DON'T NEED A LEADER. THEY CAN'T SURRENDER.
IT'S NOT IN THEIR PROGRAMMING.
THE MANY NETWORK COMPLEXES, LIKE THIS ONE, CONTINUE TO FIGHT THE WAR. SO LONG AS THEY CAN FUNCTION, THEY CONTINUE TO FIGHT.

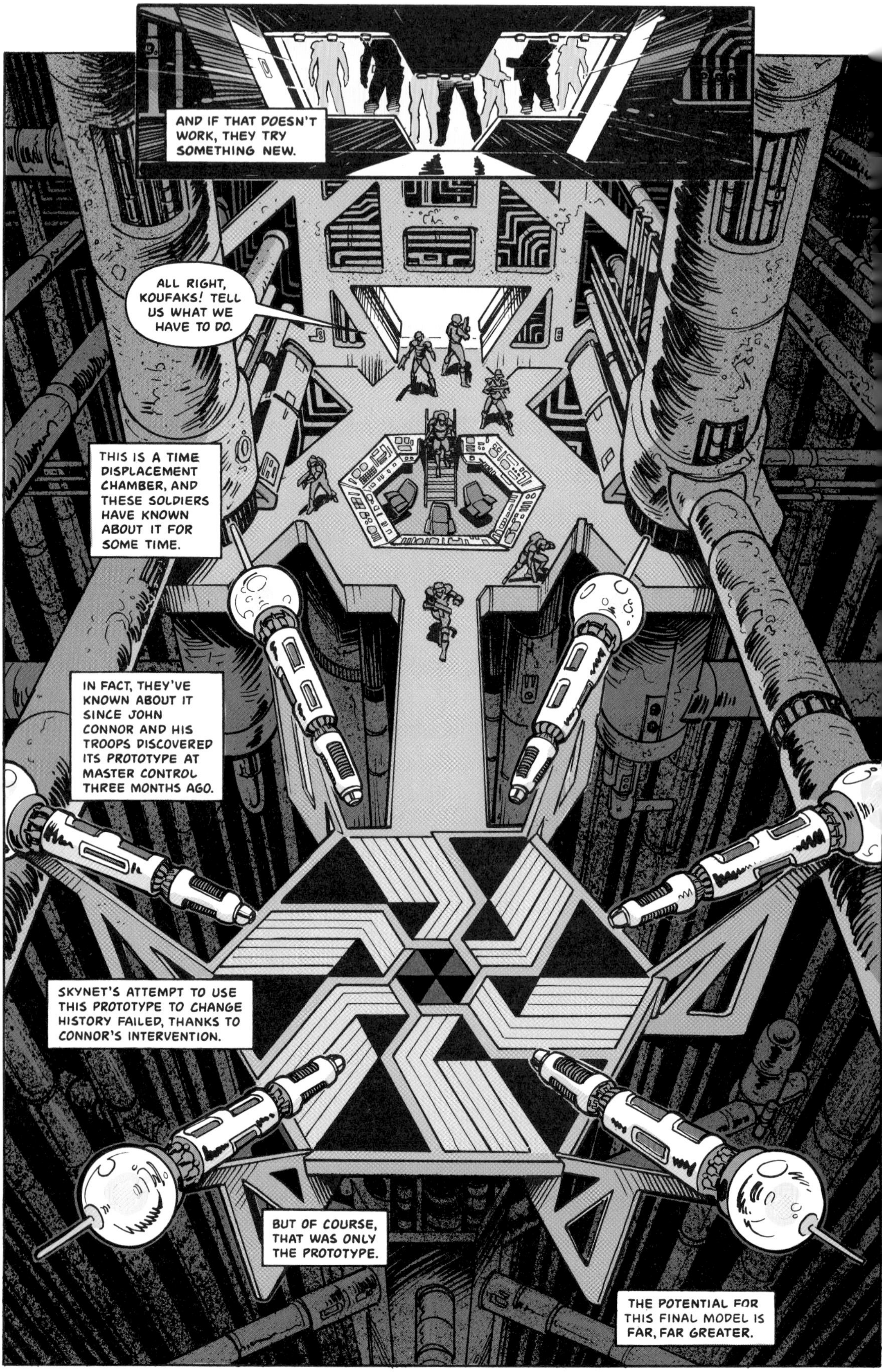
AND IF THAT DOESN'T WORK, THEY TRY SOMETHING NEW.
ALL RIGHT, KOUFAKS! TELL US WHAT WE HAVE TO DO.
THIS IS A TIME DISPLACEMENT CHAMBER, AND THESE SOLDIERS HAVE KNOWN ABOUT IT FOR SOME TIME.
IN FACT, THEY'VE KNOWN ABOUT IT SINCE JOHN CONNOR AND HIS TROOPS DISCOVERED ITS PROTOTYPE AT MASTER CONTROL THREE MONTHS AGO.
SKYNET'S ATTEMPT TO USE THIS PROTOTYPE TO CHANGE HISTORY FAILED, THANKS TO CONNOR'S INTERVENTION.
BUT OF COURSE, THAT WAS ONLY THE PROTOTYPE.
THE POTENTIAL FOR THIS FINAL MODEL IS FAR, FAR GREATER.

DEEP IN THE BOWELS OF THE COMPLEX, A SILENT FIGURE "SPEAKS" WITH ITS SUPERIOR.

Processing Command Center transmitting to 1825.M. Tissue generation incomplete. Do not attempt activation.

Immediate action imperative. Time Displacement chamber has gone on-line.

This unit is not adequately equipped to defend it.

This unit requires assistance.

ALL COMMUNICATION ENDS. BOTH COMPONENTS KNOW WHAT MUST BE DONE.

THE COMMAND CENTER ENERGIZES ITS DEFENSE RESERVES.

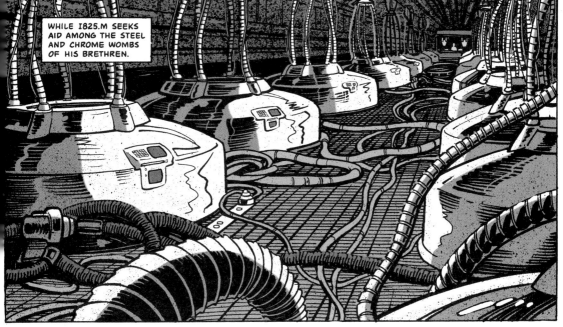

WHILE 1825.M SEEKS AID AMONG THE STEEL AND CHROME WOMBS OF HIS BRETHREN.

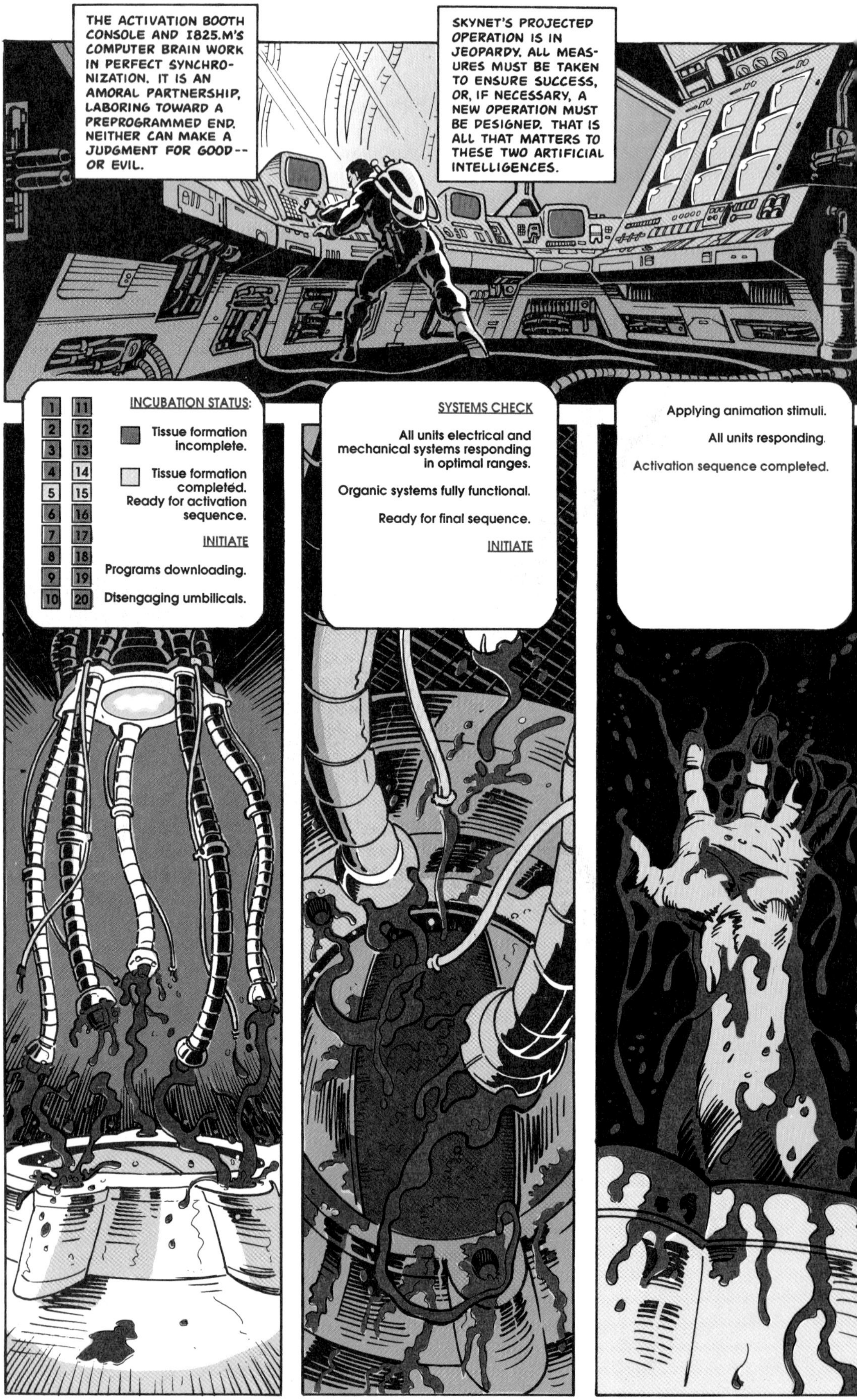
THE ACTIVATION BOOTH CONSOLE AND I825.M'S COMPUTER BRAIN WORK IN PERFECT SYNCHRONIZATION. IT IS AN AMORAL PARTNERSHIP, LABORING TOWARD A PREPROGRAMMED END. NEITHER CAN MAKE A JUDGMENT FOR GOOD -- OR EVIL.
SKYNET'S PROJECTED OPERATION IS IN JEOPARDY. ALL MEASURES MUST BE TAKEN TO ENSURE SUCCESS, OR, IF NECESSARY, A NEW OPERATION MUST BE DESIGNED. THAT IS ALL THAT MATTERS TO THESE TWO ARTIFICIAL INTELLIGENCES.
1 2 3 4 5 6 7 8 9 10
11 12 13 14 15 16 17 18 19 20
INCUBATION STATUS:
Tissue formation incomplete.
Tissue formation completed. Ready for activation sequence.
INITIATE
Programs downloading.
Disengaging umbilicals.
SYSTEMS CHECK
All units electrical and mechanical systems responding in optimal ranges.
Organic systems fully functional.
Ready for final sequence.
INITIATE
Applying animation stimuli.
All units responding.
Activation sequence completed.

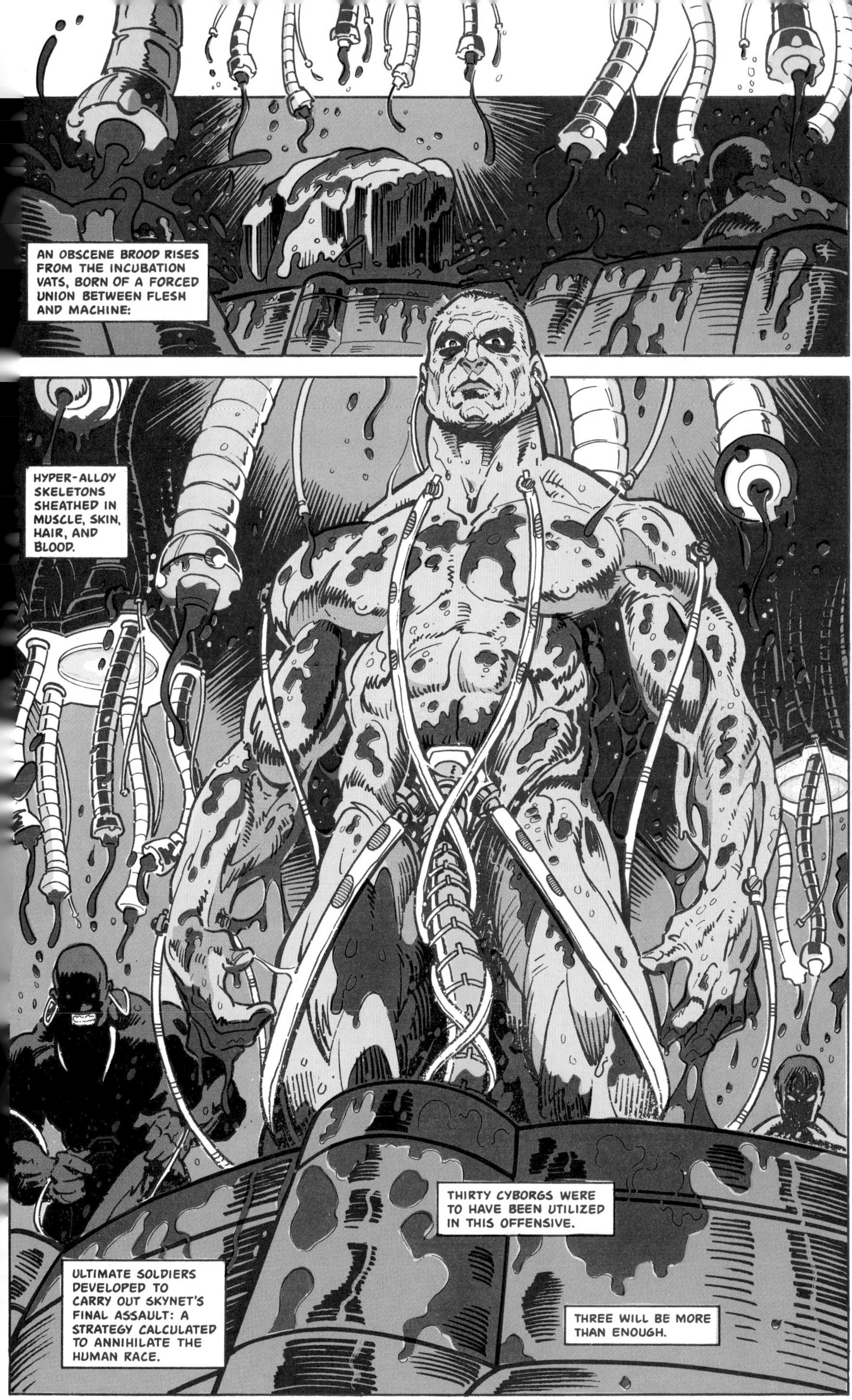
AN OBSCENE BROOD RISES FROM THE INCUBATION VATS, BORN OF A FORCED UNION BETWEEN FLESH AND MACHINE:
HYPER-ALLOY SKELETONS SHEATHED IN MUSCLE, SKIN, HAIR, AND BLOOD.
ULTIMATE SOLDIERS DEVELOPED TO CARRY OUT SKYNET'S FINAL ASSAULT: A STRATEGY CALCULATED TO ANNIHILATE THE HUMAN RACE.
THIRTY CYBORGS WERE TO HAVE BEEN UTILIZED IN THIS OFFENSIVE.
THREE WILL BE MORE THAN ENOUGH.

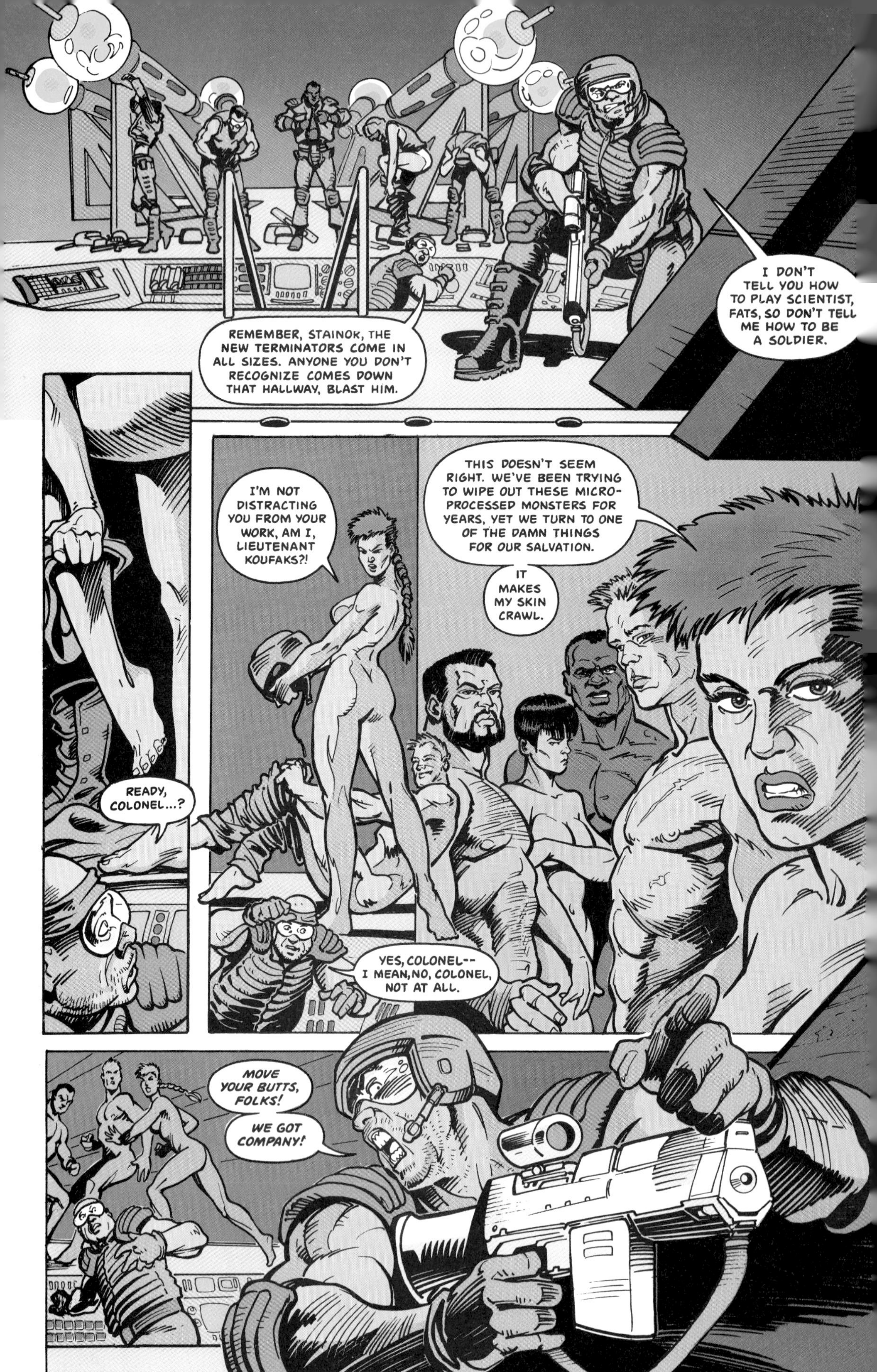
REMEMBER, STAINOK, THE NEW TERMINATORS COME IN ALL SIZES. ANYONE YOU DON'T RECOGNIZE COMES DOWN THAT HALLWAY, BLAST HIM.
I DON'T TELL YOU HOW TO PLAY SCIENTIST, FATS, SO DON'T TELL ME HOW TO BE A SOLDIER.
READY, COLONEL...?
I'M NOT DISTRACTING YOU FROM YOUR WORK, AM I, LIEUTENANT KOUFAKS?!
YES, COLONEL-- I MEAN, NO, COLONEL, NOT AT ALL.
THIS DOESN'T SEEM RIGHT. WE'VE BEEN TRYING TO WIPE OUT THESE MICRO-PROCESSED MONSTERS FOR YEARS, YET WE TURN TO ONE OF THE DAMN THINGS FOR OUR SALVATION.
IT MAKES MY SKIN CRAWL.
MOVE YOUR BUTTS, FOLKS!
WE GOT COMPANY!

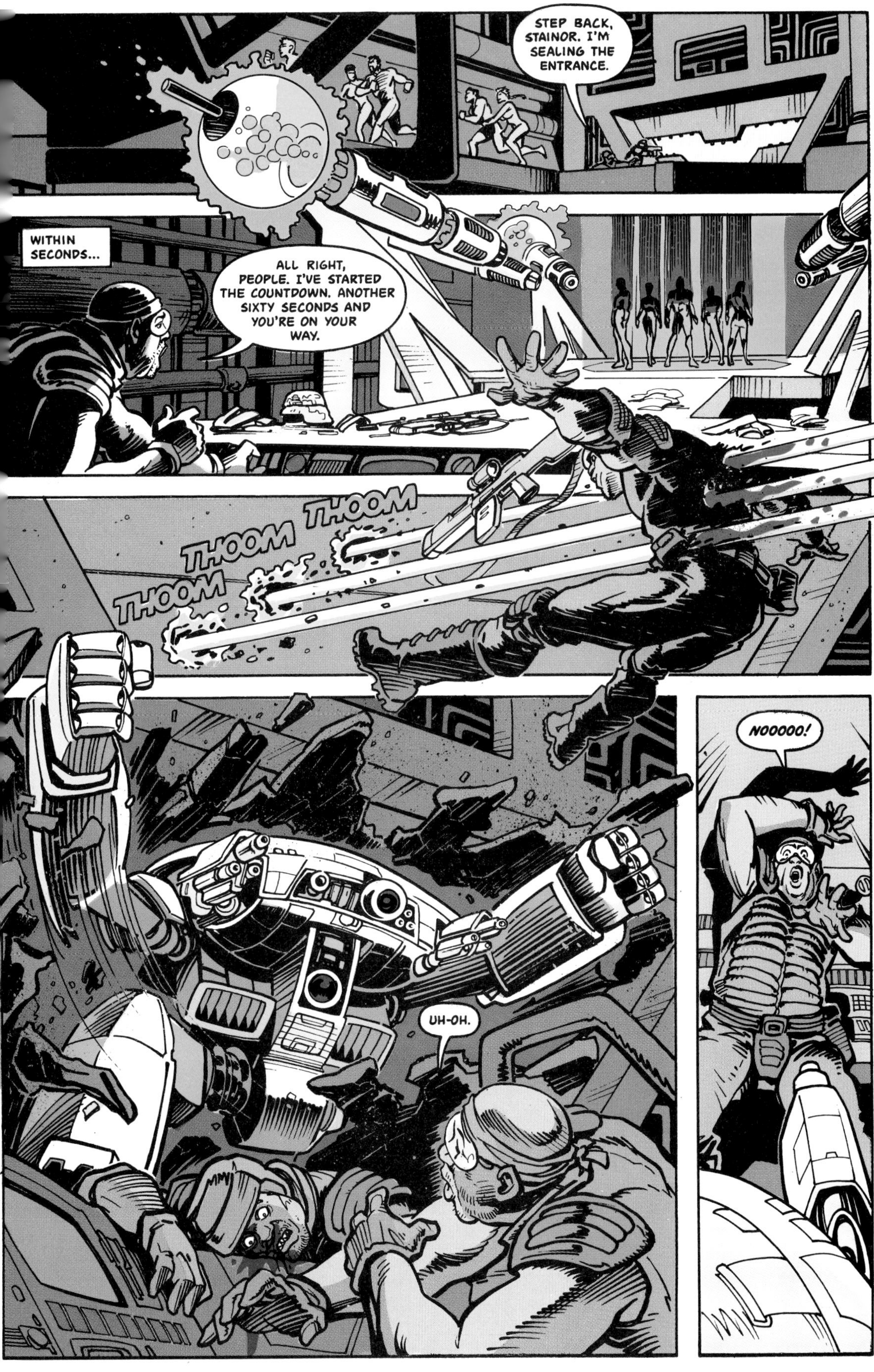
STEP BACK, STAINOR. I'M SEALING THE ENTRANCE.
WITHIN SECONDS...
ALL RIGHT, PEOPLE. I'VE STARTED THE COUNTDOWN. ANOTHER SIXTY SECONDS AND YOU'RE ON YOUR WAY.
THOOM THOOM
THOOM
UH-OH.
NOOOOO!

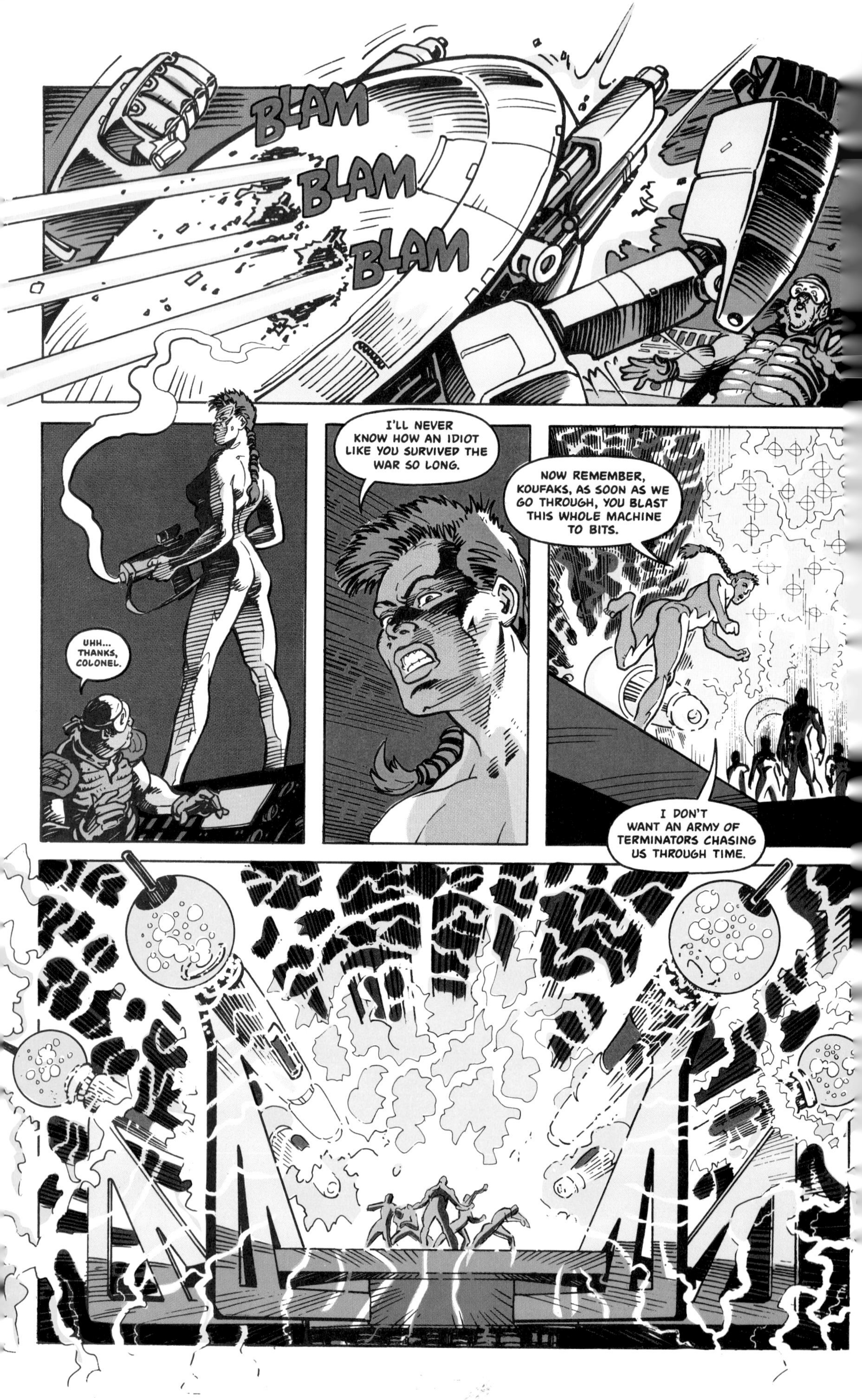
BLAM
BLAM
BLAM
UHH... THANKS, COLONEL.
I'LL NEVER KNOW HOW AN IDIOT LIKE YOU SURVIVED THE WAR SO LONG.
NOW REMEMBER, KOUFAKS, AS SOON AS WE GO THROUGH, YOU BLAST THIS WHOLE MACHINE TO BITS.
I DON'T WANT AN ARMY OF TERMINATORS CHASING US THROUGH TIME.

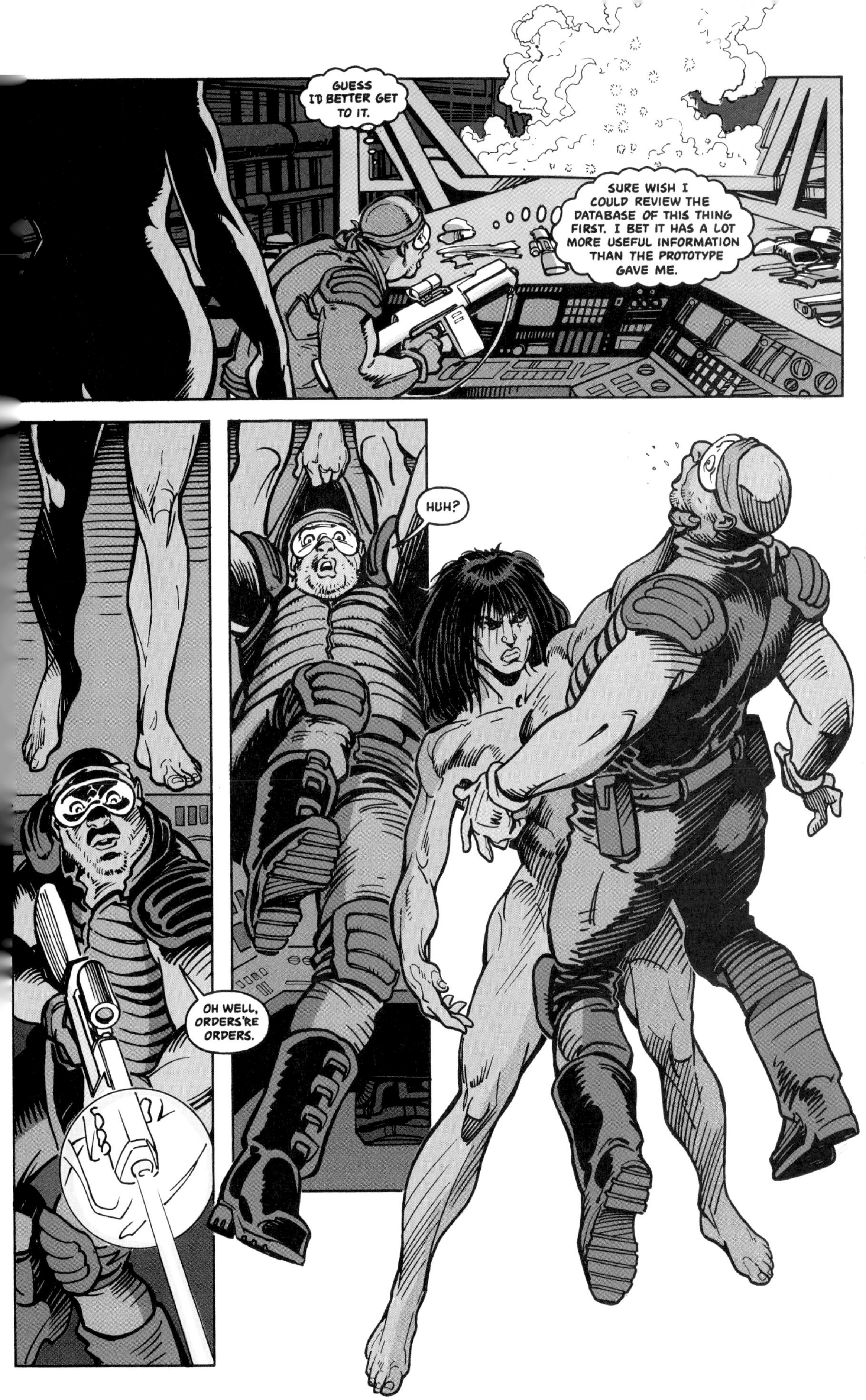
GUESS I'D BETTER GET TO IT.
SURE WISH I COULD REVIEW THE DATABASE OF THIS THING FIRST. I BET IT HAS A LOT MORE USEFUL INFORMATION THAN THE PROTOTYPE GAVE ME.
OH WELL, ORDERS'RE ORDERS.
HUH?

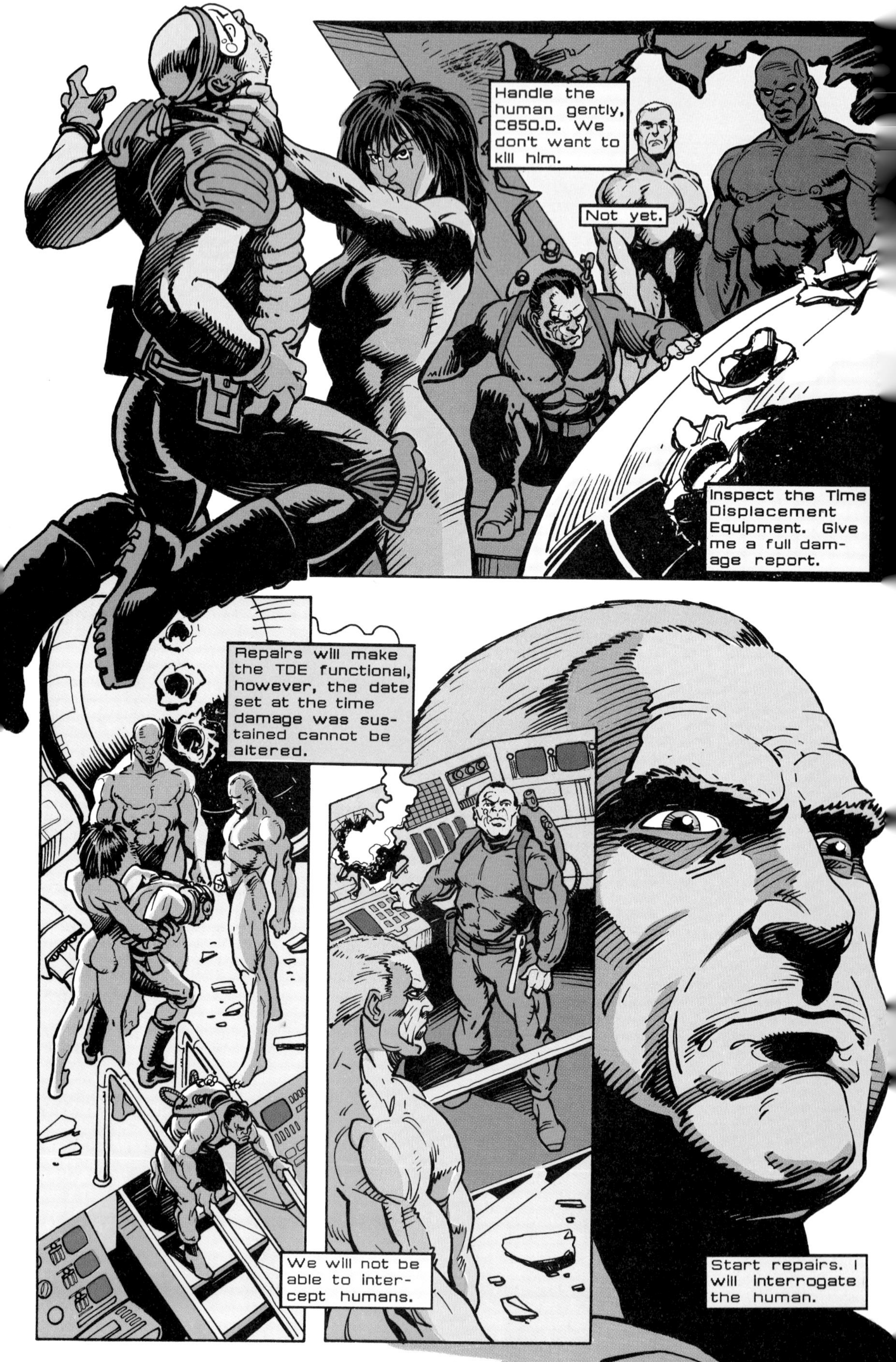
Handle the human gently, C850.D. We don't want to kill him.
Not yet.
Inspect the Time Displacement Equipment. Give me a full damage report.
Repairs will make the TDE functional, however, the date set at the time damage was sustained cannot be altered.
We will not be able to intercept humans.
Start repairs. I will interrogate the human.

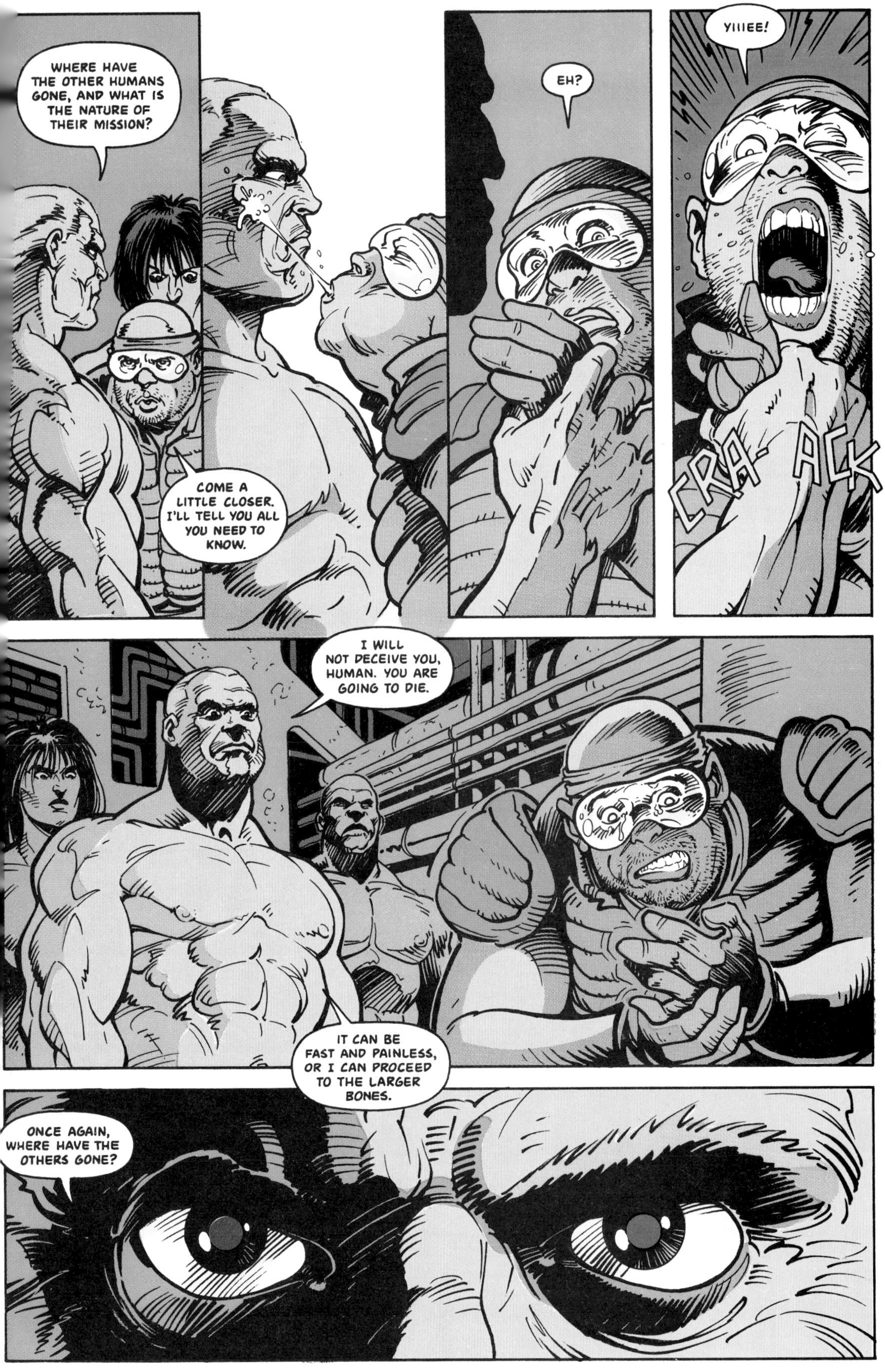
WHERE HAVE THE OTHER HUMANS GONE, AND WHAT IS THE NATURE OF THEIR MISSION?
COME A LITTLE CLOSER. I'LL TELL YOU ALL YOU NEED TO KNOW.
EH?
YIIIEE!
CRA- ACK
I WILL NOT DECEIVE YOU, HUMAN. YOU ARE GOING TO DIE.
IT CAN BE FAST AND PAINLESS, OR I CAN PROCEED TO THE LARGER BONES.
ONCE AGAIN, WHERE HAVE THE OTHERS GONE?

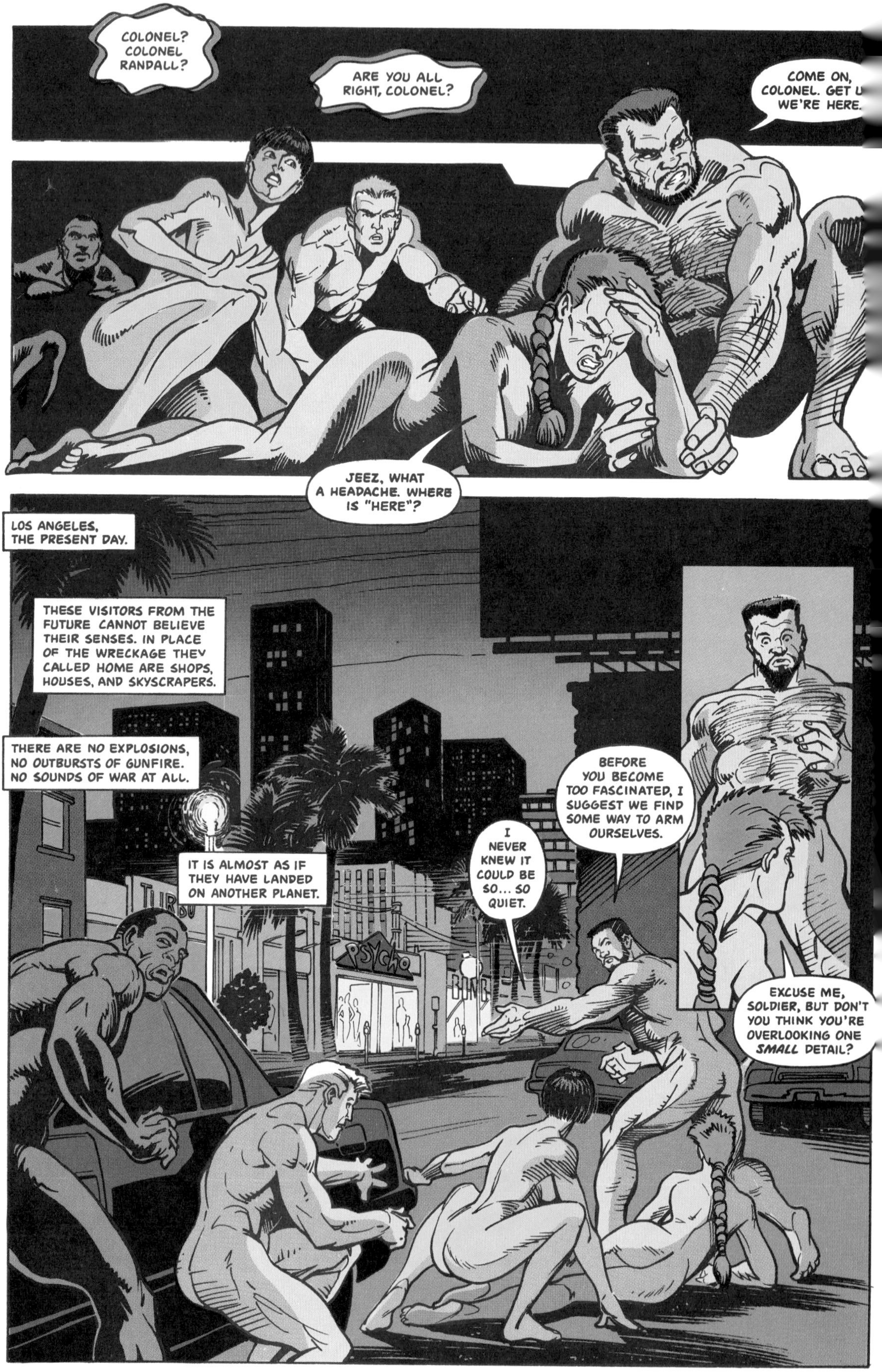
COLONEL? COLONEL RANDALL?
ARE YOU ALL RIGHT, COLONEL?
COME ON, COLONEL. GET U WE'RE HERE.
JEEZ, WHAT A HEADACHE. WHERE IS "HERE"?
LOS ANGELES, THE PRESENT DAY.
THESE VISITORS FROM THE FUTURE CANNOT BELIEVE THEIR SENSES. IN PLACE OF THE WRECKAGE THEY CALLED HOME ARE SHOPS, HOUSES, AND SKYSCRAPERS.
THERE ARE NO EXPLOSIONS, NO OUTBURSTS OF GUNFIRE. NO SOUNDS OF WAR AT ALL.
IT IS ALMOST AS IF THEY HAVE LANDED ON ANOTHER PLANET.
I NEVER KNEW IT COULD BE SO... SO QUIET.
BEFORE YOU BECOME TOO FASCINATED, I SUGGEST WE FIND SOME WAY TO ARM OURSELVES.
EXCUSE ME, SOLDIER, BUT DON'T YOU THINK YOU'RE OVERLOOKING ONE *SMALL* DETAIL?

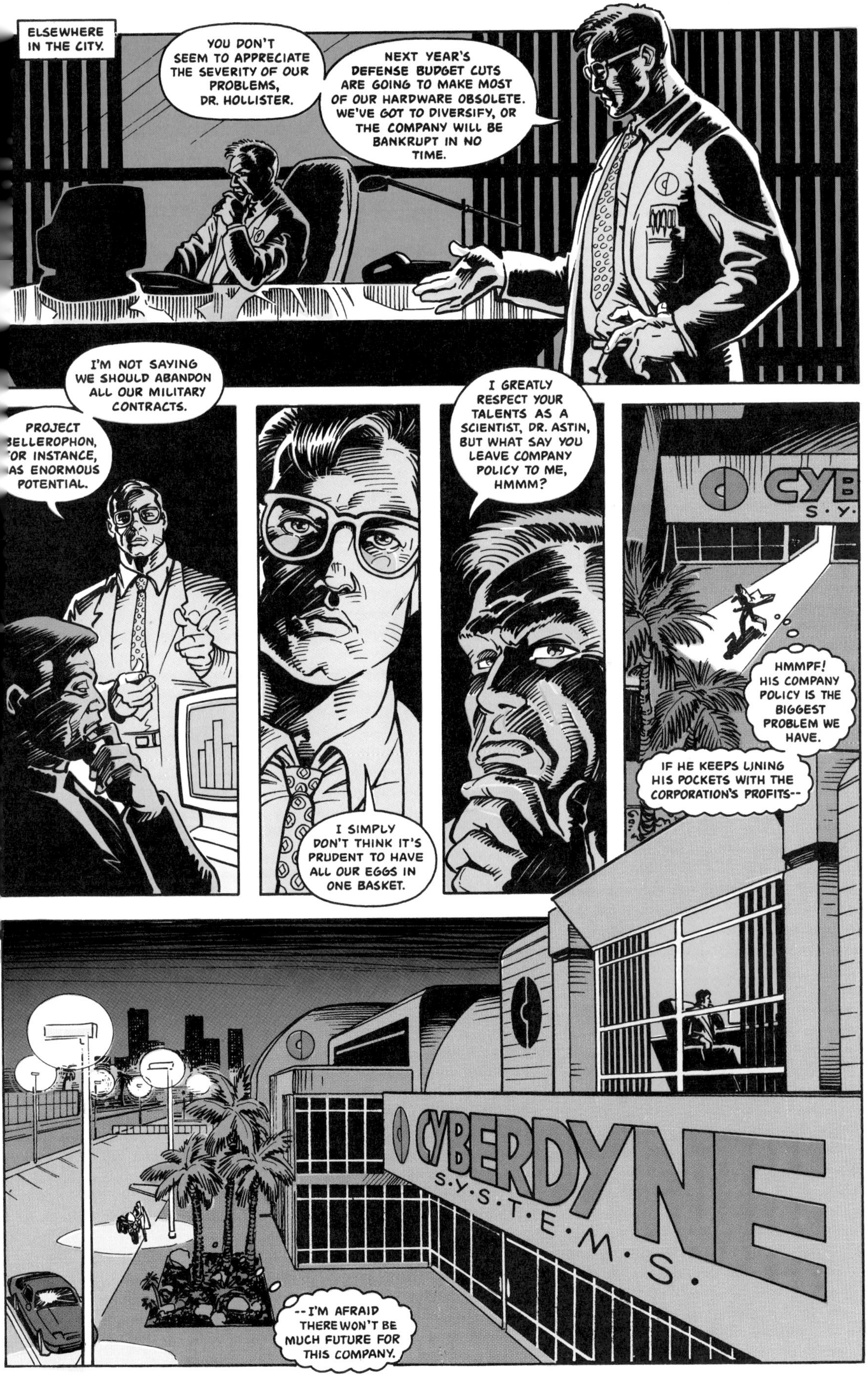
ELSEWHERE IN THE CITY.
YOU DON'T SEEM TO APPRECIATE THE SEVERITY OF OUR PROBLEMS, DR. HOLLISTER.
NEXT YEAR'S DEFENSE BUDGET CUTS ARE GOING TO MAKE MOST OF OUR HARDWARE OBSOLETE. WE'VE GOT TO DIVERSIFY, OR THE COMPANY WILL BE BANKRUPT IN NO TIME.
I'M NOT SAYING WE SHOULD ABANDON ALL OUR MILITARY CONTRACTS.
PROJECT BELLEROPHON, FOR INSTANCE, HAS ENORMOUS POTENTIAL.
I SIMPLY DON'T THINK IT'S PRUDENT TO HAVE ALL OUR EGGS IN ONE BASKET.
I GREATLY RESPECT YOUR TALENTS AS A SCIENTIST, DR. ASTIN, BUT WHAT SAY YOU LEAVE COMPANY POLICY TO ME, HMMM?
CYB
S·Y·
HMMPF! HIS COMPANY POLICY IS THE BIGGEST PROBLEM WE HAVE.
IF HE KEEPS LINING HIS POCKETS WITH THE CORPORATION'S PROFITS--
CYBERDYNE
S·Y·S·T·E·M·S·
--I'M AFRAID THERE WON'T BE MUCH FUTURE FOR THIS COMPANY.

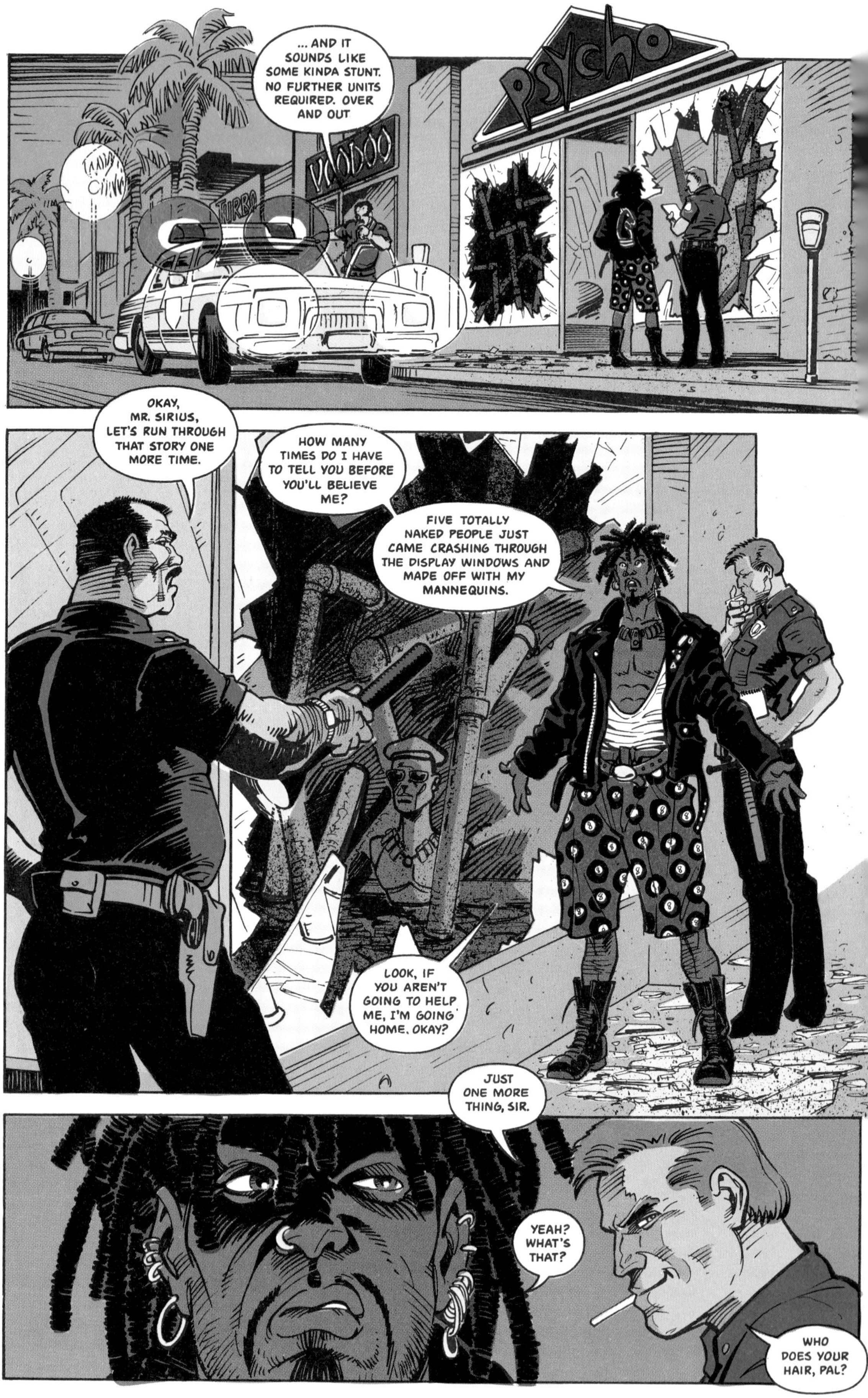
... AND IT SOUNDS LIKE SOME KINDA STUNT. NO FURTHER UNITS REQUIRED. OVER AND OUT
PSYCHO
VOODOO
TURBO
OKAY, MR. SIRIUS, LET'S RUN THROUGH THAT STORY ONE MORE TIME.
HOW MANY TIMES DO I HAVE TO TELL YOU BEFORE YOU'LL BELIEVE ME?
FIVE TOTALLY NAKED PEOPLE JUST CAME CRASHING THROUGH THE DISPLAY WINDOWS AND MADE OFF WITH MY MANNEQUINS.
LOOK, IF YOU AREN'T GOING TO HELP ME, I'M GOING HOME. OKAY?
JUST ONE MORE THING, SIR.
YEAH? WHAT'S THAT?
WHO DOES YOUR HAIR, PAL?

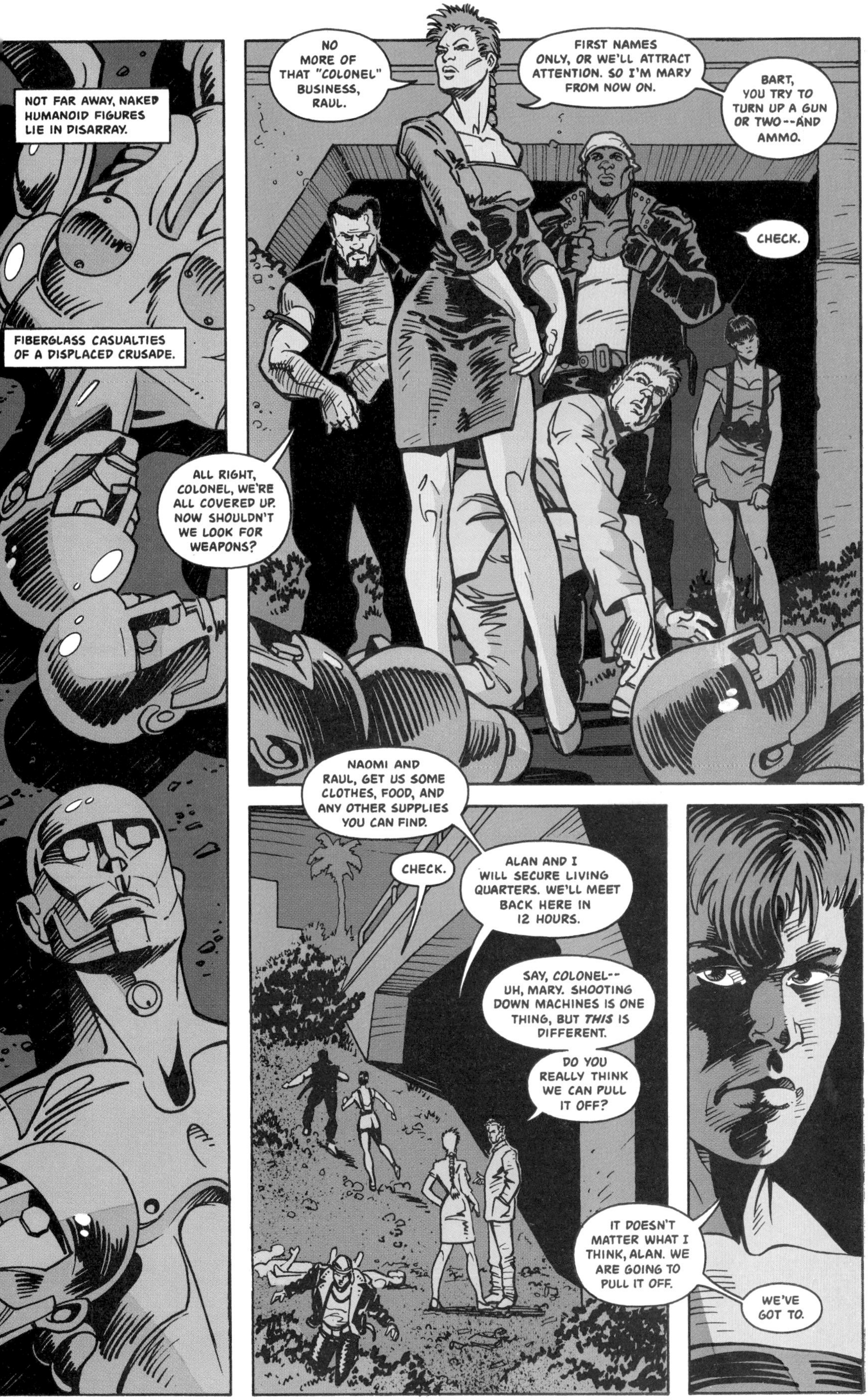
NOT FAR AWAY, NAKED HUMANOID FIGURES LIE IN DISARRAY.
FIBERGLASS CASUALTIES OF A DISPLACED CRUSADE.
NO MORE OF THAT "COLONEL" BUSINESS, RAUL.
FIRST NAMES ONLY, OR WE'LL ATTRACT ATTENTION. SO I'M MARY FROM NOW ON.
BART, YOU TRY TO TURN UP A GUN OR TWO--AND AMMO.
CHECK.
ALL RIGHT, COLONEL, WE'RE ALL COVERED UP. NOW SHOULDN'T WE LOOK FOR WEAPONS?
NAOMI AND RAUL, GET US SOME CLOTHES, FOOD, AND ANY OTHER SUPPLIES YOU CAN FIND.
CHECK.
ALAN AND I WILL SECURE LIVING QUARTERS. WE'LL MEET BACK HERE IN 12 HOURS.
SAY, COLONEL--UH, MARY. SHOOTING DOWN MACHINES IS ONE THING, BUT THIS IS DIFFERENT.
DO YOU REALLY THINK WE CAN PULL IT OFF?
IT DOESN'T MATTER WHAT I THINK, ALAN. WE ARE GOING TO PULL IT OFF.
WE'VE GOT TO.

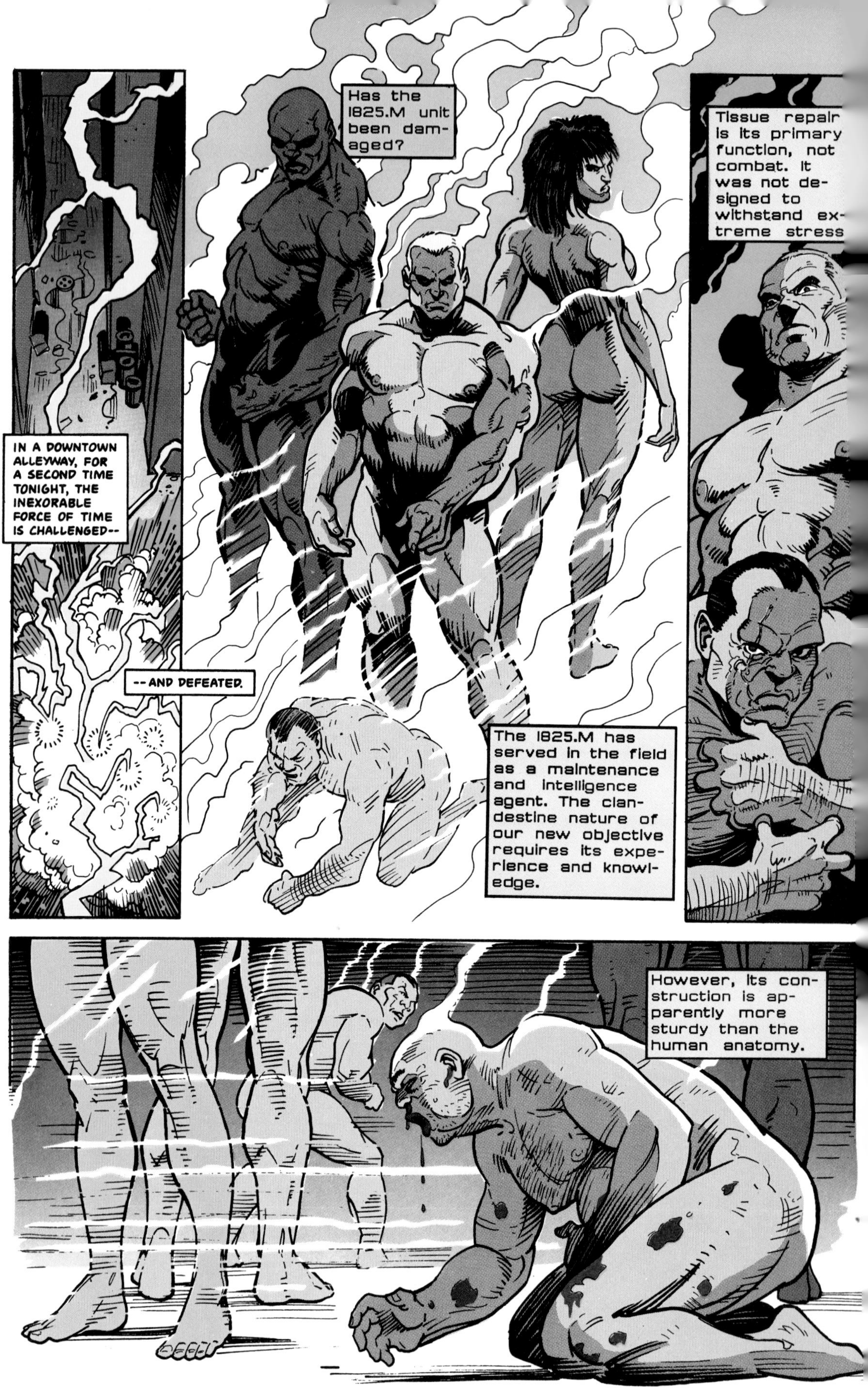
IN A DOWNTOWN ALLEYWAY, FOR A SECOND TIME TONIGHT, THE INEXORABLE FORCE OF TIME IS CHALLENGED--
--AND DEFEATED.
Has the 1825.M unit been damaged?
The 1825.M has served in the field as a maintenance and intelligence agent. The clandestine nature of our new objective requires its experience and knowledge.
Tissue repair is its primary function, not combat. It was not designed to withstand extreme stress
However, its construction is apparently more sturdy than the human anatomy.

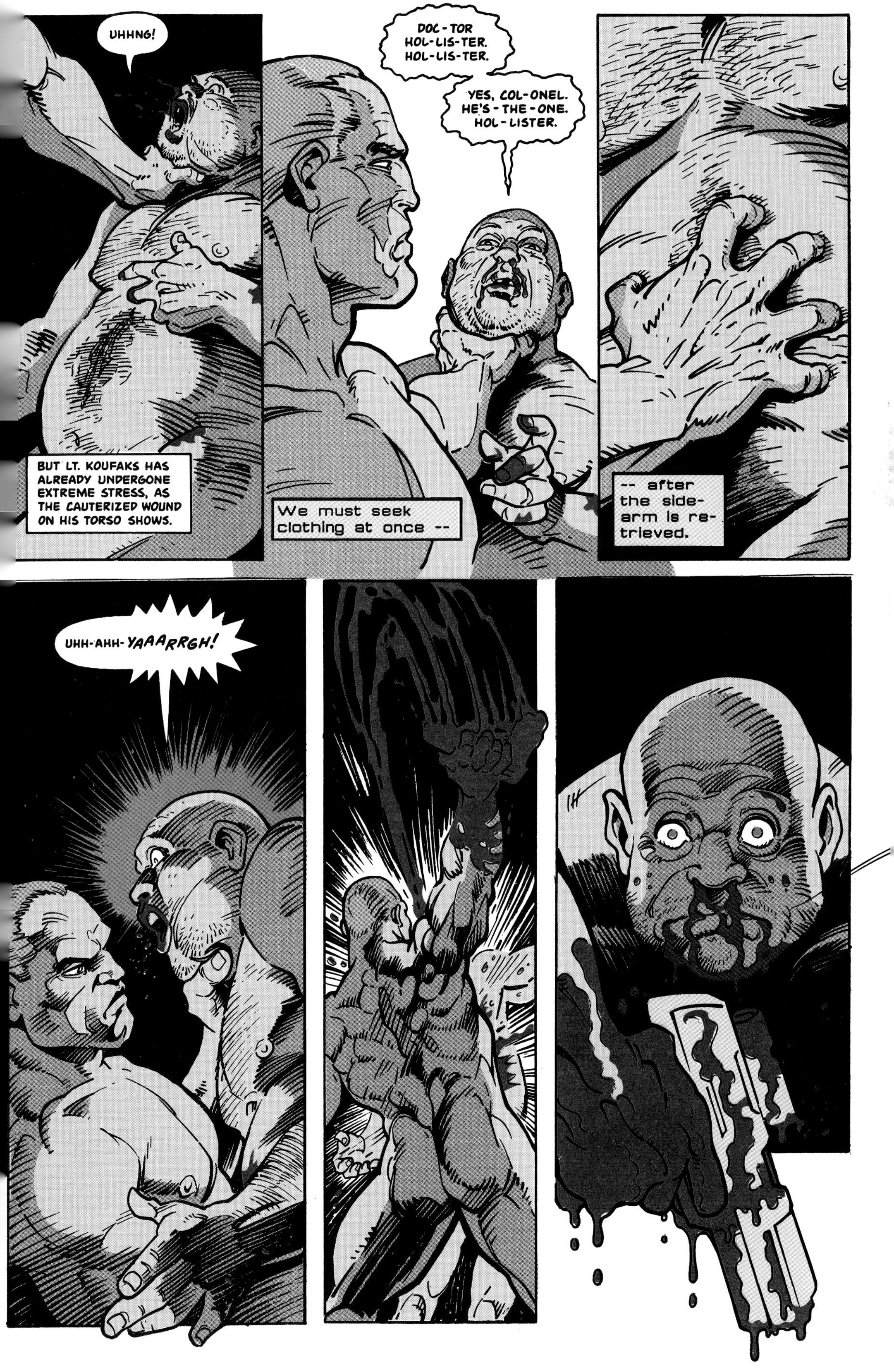
UHHNG!
BUT LT. KOUFAKS HAS ALREADY UNDERGONE EXTREME STRESS, AS THE CAUTERIZED WOUND ON HIS TORSO SHOWS.
DOC-TOR HOL-LIS-TER. HOL-LIS-TER.
YES, COL-ONEL. HE'S-THE-ONE. HOL-LISTER.
We must seek clothing at once --
-- after the side-arm is re-trieved.
UHH-AHH-YAAARRGH!

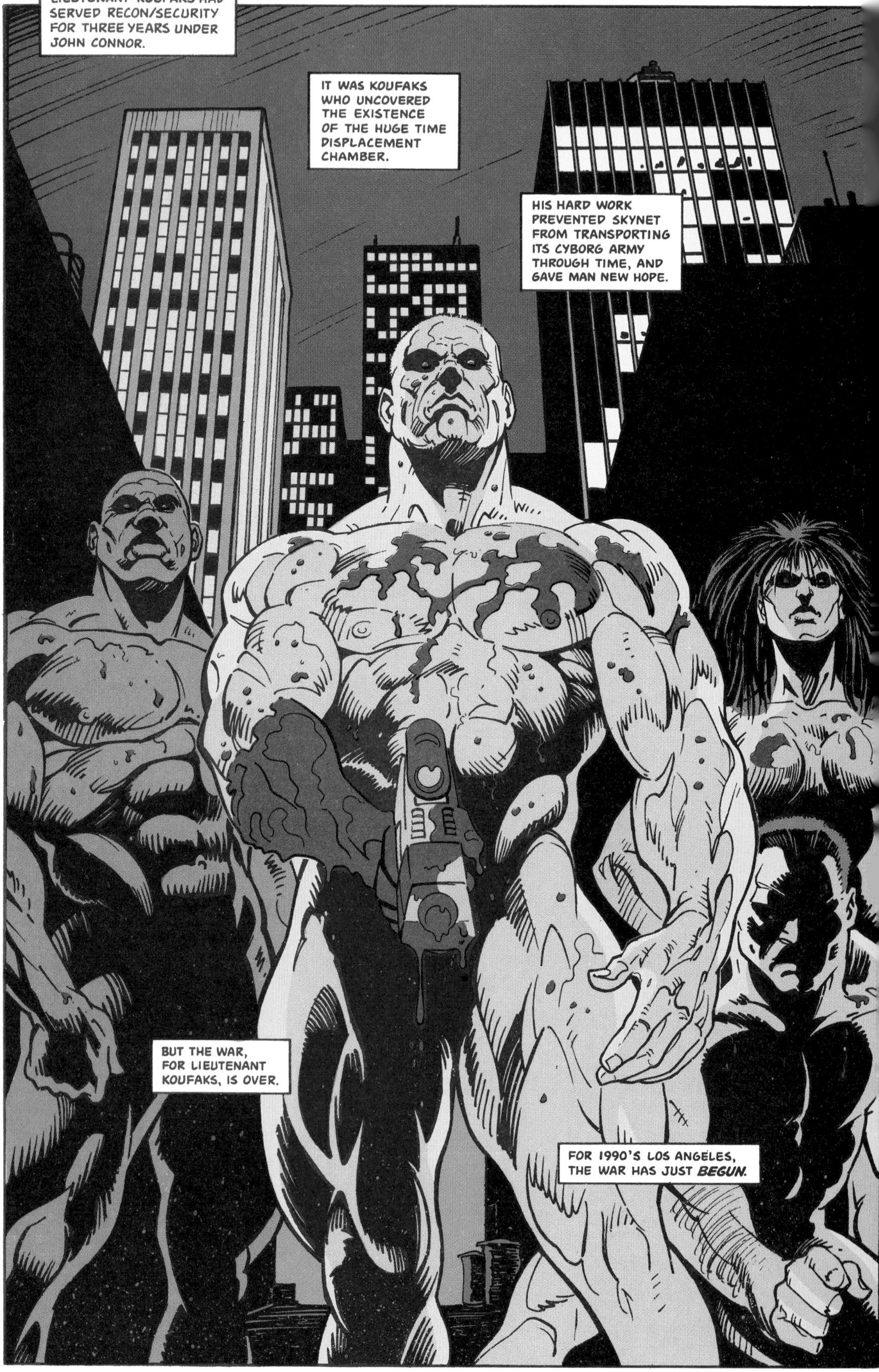
LIEUTENANT KOUFAKS HAD SERVED RECON/SECURITY FOR THREE YEARS UNDER JOHN CONNOR.
IT WAS KOUFAKS WHO UNCOVERED THE EXISTENCE OF THE HUGE TIME DISPLACEMENT CHAMBER.
HIS HARD WORK PREVENTED SKYNET FROM TRANSPORTING ITS CYBORG ARMY THROUGH TIME, AND GAVE MAN NEW HOPE.
BUT THE WAR, FOR LIEUTENANT KOUFAKS, IS OVER.
FOR 1990'S LOS ANGELES, THE WAR HAS JUST *BEGUN.*

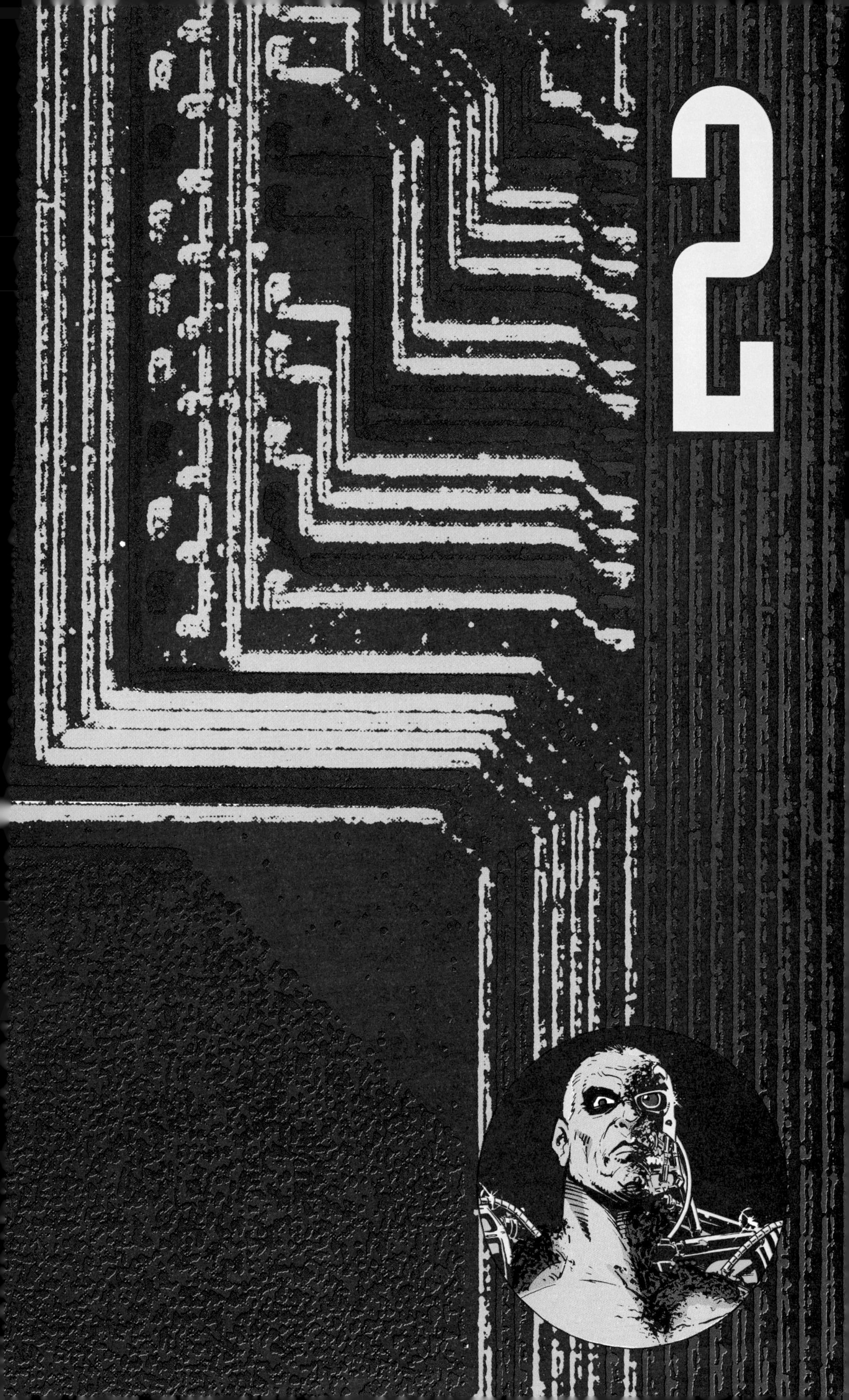
2

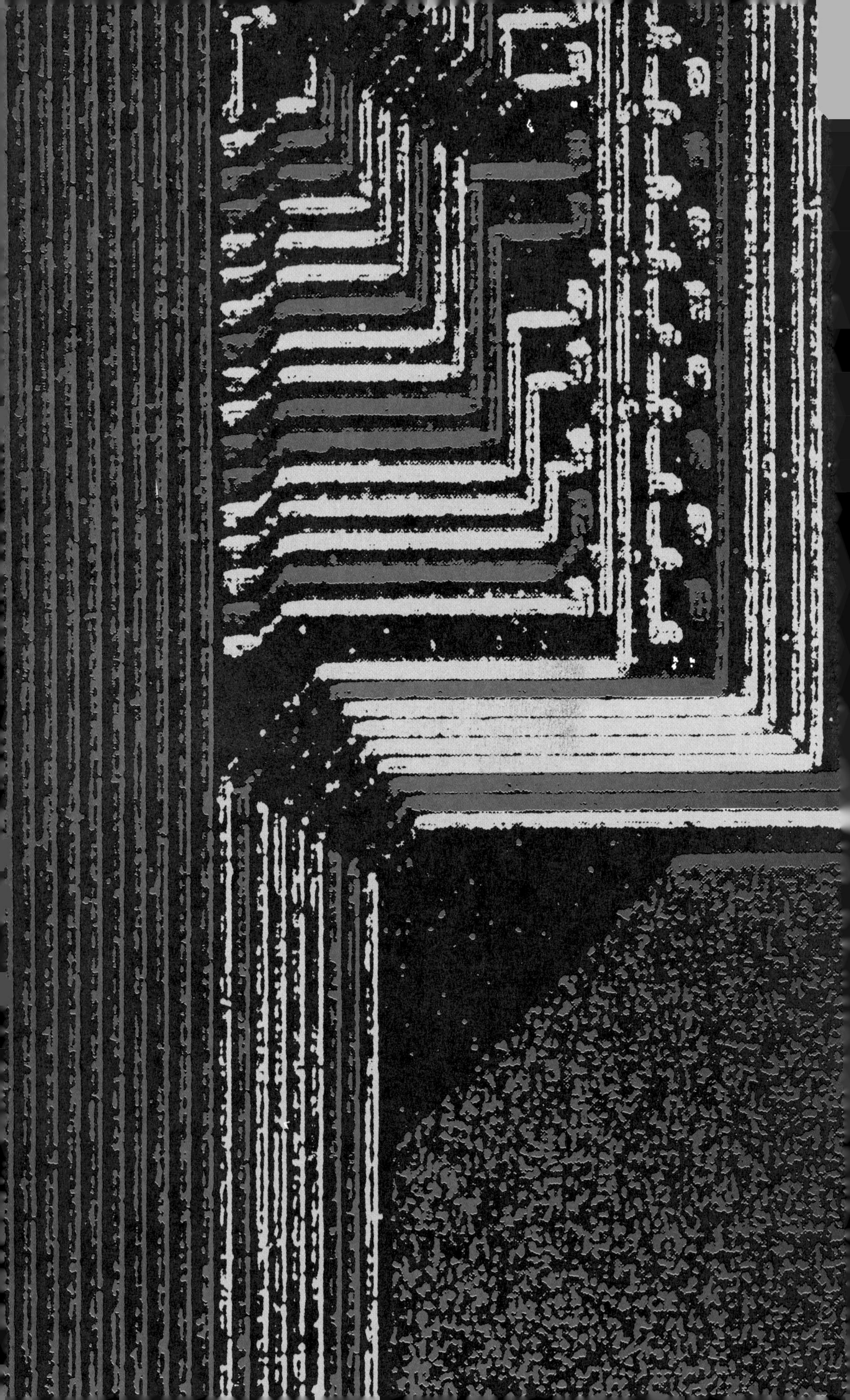

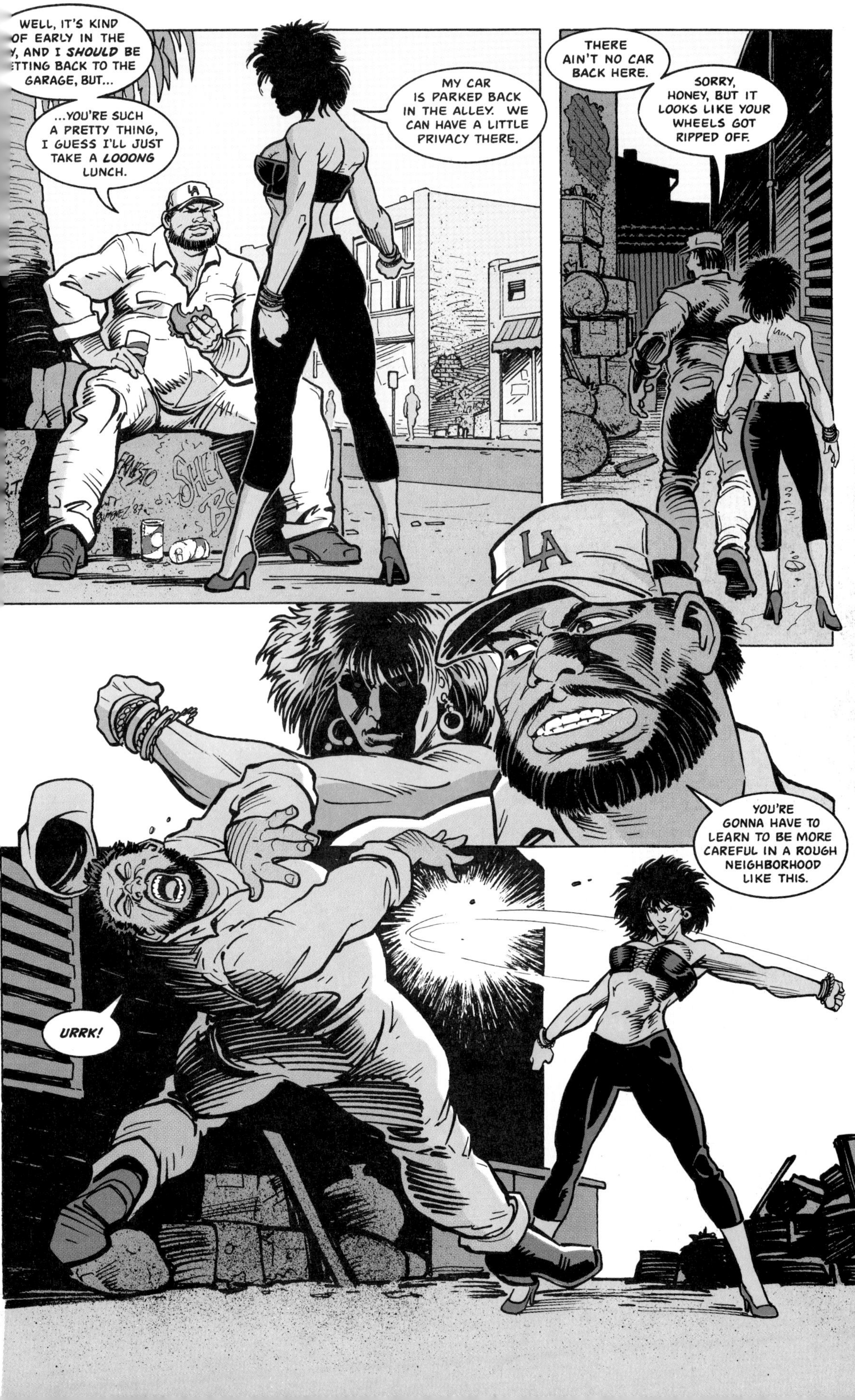
WELL, IT'S KIND OF EARLY IN THE Y, AND I *SHOULD* BE ETTING BACK TO THE GARAGE, BUT...
...YOU'RE SUCH A PRETTY THING, I GUESS I'LL JUST TAKE A *LOOONG* LUNCH.
MY CAR IS PARKED BACK IN THE ALLEY. WE CAN HAVE A LITTLE PRIVACY THERE.
THERE AIN'T NO CAR BACK HERE.
SORRY, HONEY, BUT IT LOOKS LIKE YOUR WHEELS GOT RIPPED OFF.
LA
YOU'RE GONNA HAVE TO LEARN TO BE MORE CAREFUL IN A ROUGH NEIGHBORHOOD LIKE THIS.
URRK!

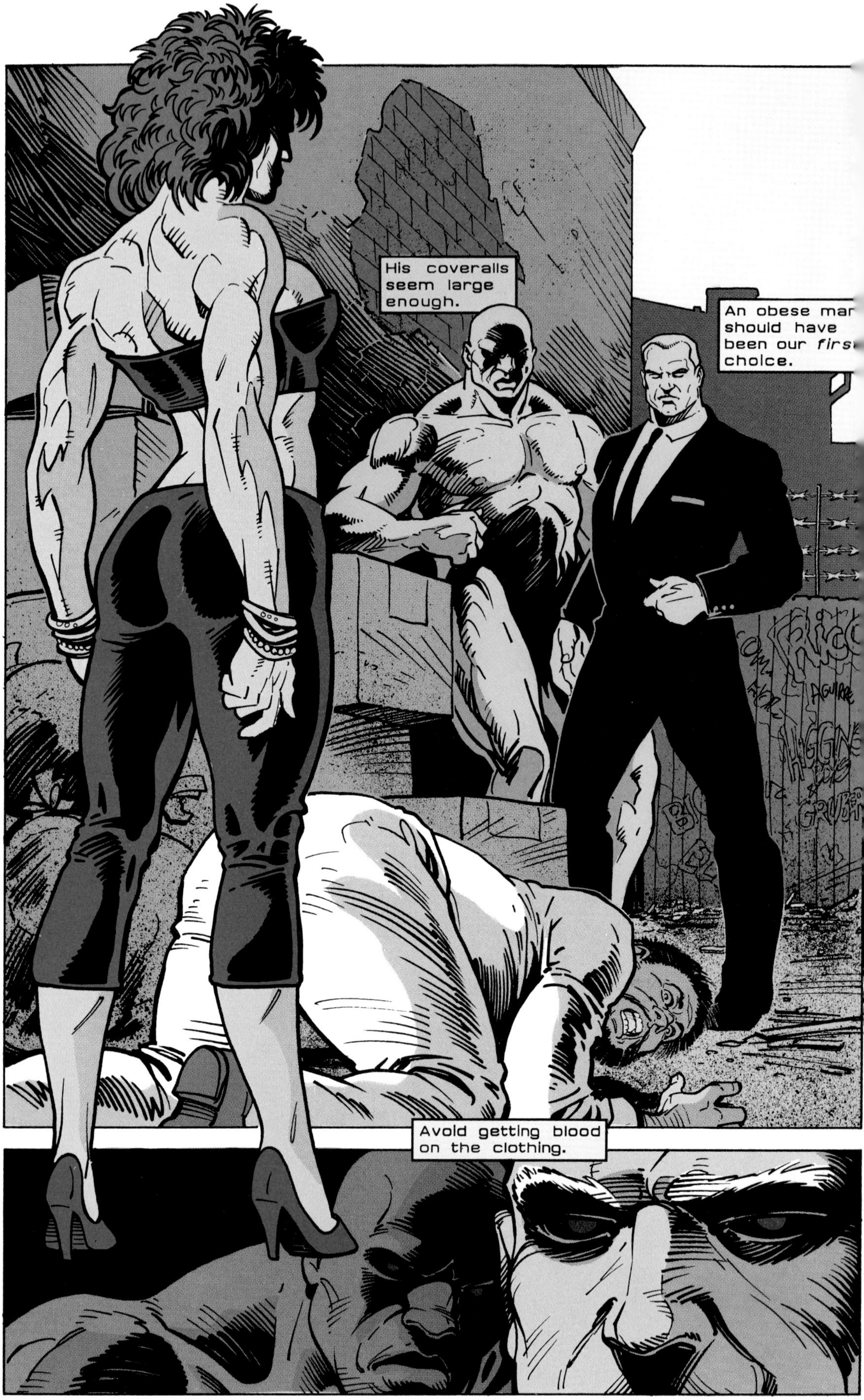
His coveralls seem large enough.
An obese mar should have been our firs choice.
Avoid getting blood on the clothing.

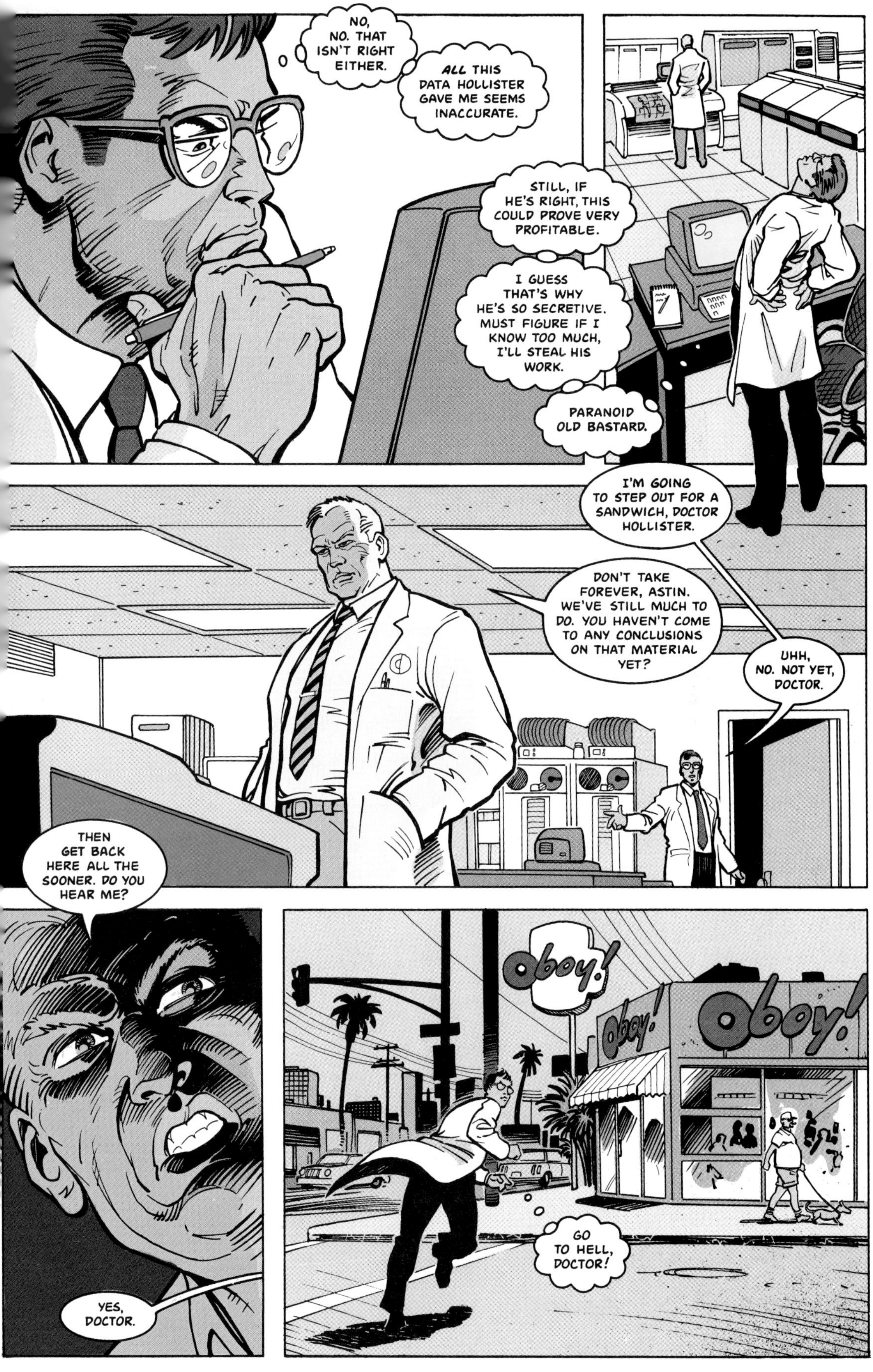
NO, NO. THAT ISN'T RIGHT EITHER.
ALL THIS DATA HOLLISTER GAVE ME SEEMS INACCURATE.
STILL, IF HE'S RIGHT, THIS COULD PROVE VERY PROFITABLE.
I GUESS THAT'S WHY HE'S SO SECRETIVE. MUST FIGURE IF I KNOW TOO MUCH, I'LL STEAL HIS WORK.
PARANOID OLD BASTARD.
I'M GOING TO STEP OUT FOR A SANDWICH, DOCTOR HOLLISTER.
DON'T TAKE FOREVER, ASTIN. WE'VE STILL MUCH TO DO. YOU HAVEN'T COME TO ANY CONCLUSIONS ON THAT MATERIAL YET?
UHH, NO. NOT YET, DOCTOR.
THEN GET BACK HERE ALL THE SOONER. DO YOU HEAR ME?
YES, DOCTOR.
Oboy!
Oboy!
Oboy!
GO TO HELL, DOCTOR!

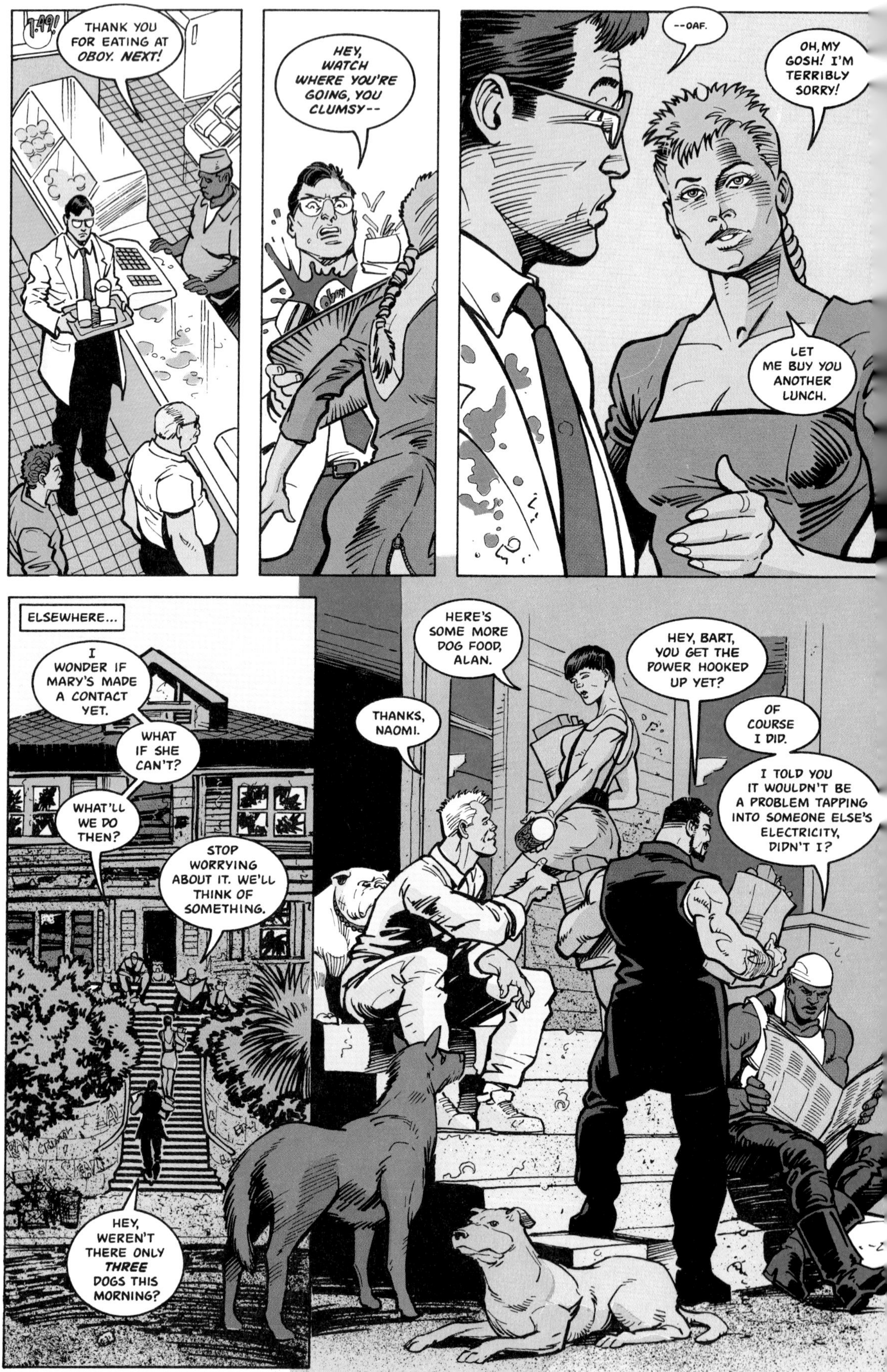
THANK YOU FOR EATING AT *OBOY*. ***NEXT!***
HEY, WATCH WHERE YOU'RE GOING, YOU CLUMSY--
--OAF.
OH, MY GOSH! I'M TERRIBLY SORRY!
LET ME BUY YOU ANOTHER LUNCH.
ELSEWHERE...
I WONDER IF MARY'S MADE A CONTACT YET.
WHAT IF SHE CAN'T?
WHAT'LL WE DO THEN?
STOP WORRYING ABOUT IT. WE'LL THINK OF SOMETHING.
HEY, WEREN'T THERE ONLY ***THREE*** DOGS THIS MORNING?
HERE'S SOME MORE DOG FOOD, ALAN.
THANKS, NAOMI.
HEY, BART, YOU GET THE POWER HOOKED UP YET?
OF COURSE I DID.
I TOLD YOU IT WOULDN'T BE A PROBLEM TAPPING INTO SOMEONE ELSE'S ELECTRICITY, DIDN'T I?

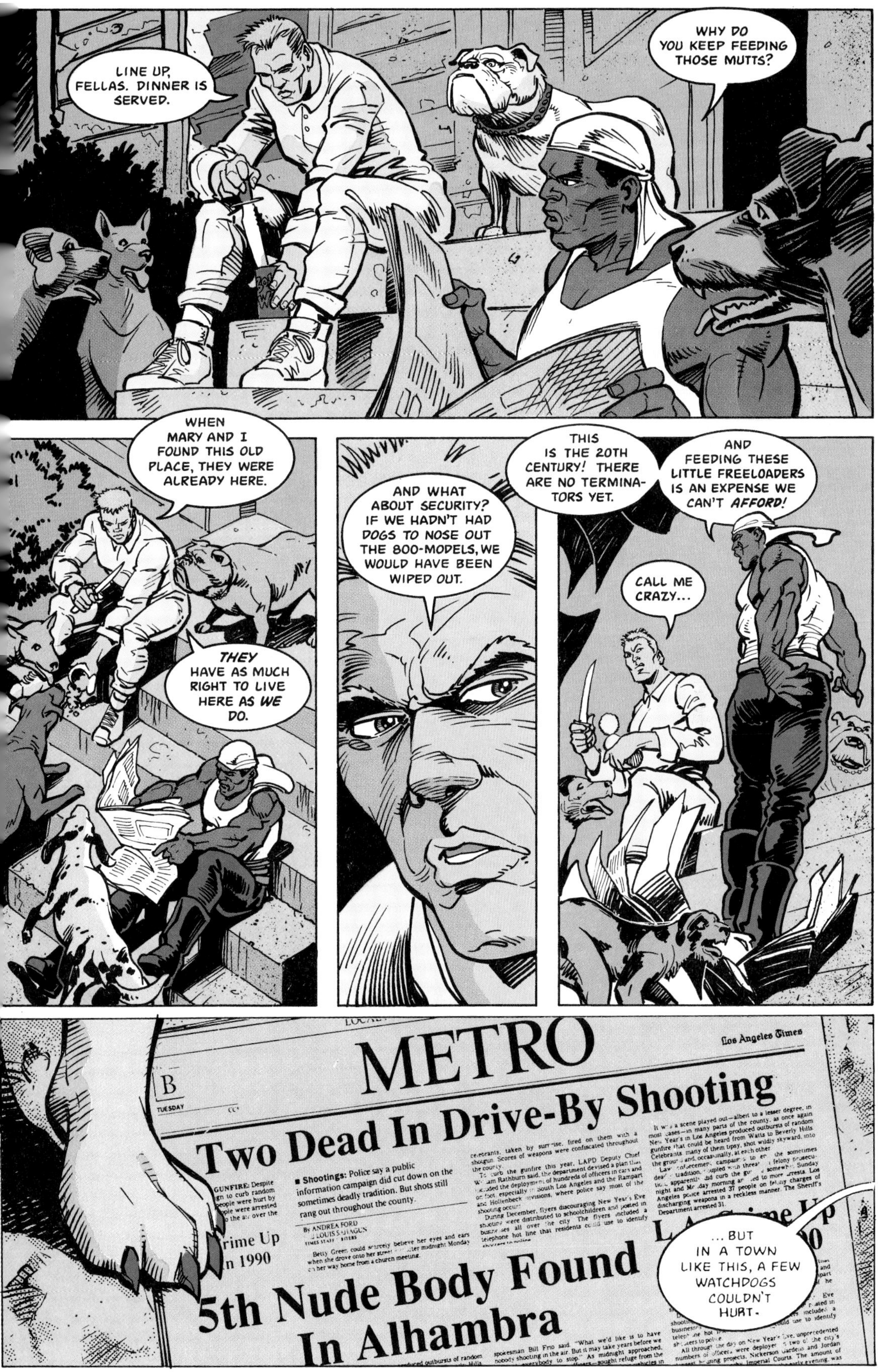
LINE UP, FELLAS. DINNER IS SERVED.
WHY DO YOU KEEP FEEDING THOSE MUTTS?
WHEN MARY AND I FOUND THIS OLD PLACE, THEY WERE ALREADY HERE.
THEY HAVE AS MUCH RIGHT TO LIVE HERE AS *WE* DO.
AND WHAT ABOUT SECURITY? IF WE HADN'T HAD DOGS TO NOSE OUT THE 800-MODELS, WE WOULD HAVE BEEN WIPED OUT.
THIS IS THE 20TH CENTURY! THERE ARE NO TERMINATORS YET.
AND FEEDING THESE LITTLE FREELOADERS IS AN EXPENSE WE CAN'T *AFFORD!*
CALL ME CRAZY...
METRO
Los Angeles Times
B
TUESDAY
Two Dead In Drive-By Shooting
■ Shootings: Police say a public information campaign did cut down on the sometimes deadly tradition. But shots still rang out throughout the county.
By ANDREA FORD
5th Nude Body Found In Alhambra
...BUT IN A TOWN LIKE THIS, A FEW WATCHDOGS COULDN'T HURT.

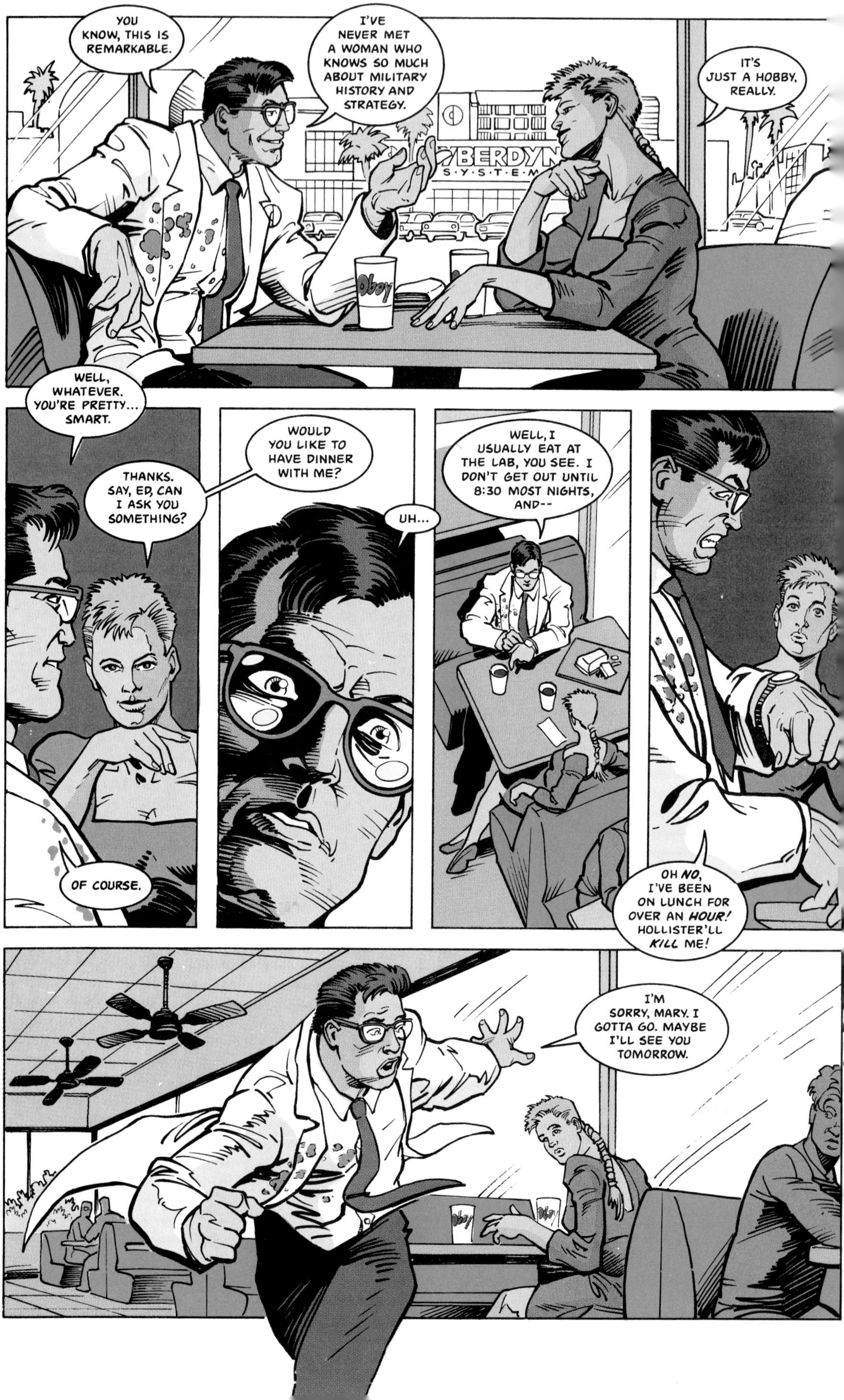
YOU KNOW, THIS IS REMARKABLE.
I'VE NEVER MET A WOMAN WHO KNOWS SO MUCH ABOUT MILITARY HISTORY AND STRATEGY.
IT'S JUST A HOBBY, REALLY.
CYBERDYNE SYSTEMS
WELL, WHATEVER. YOU'RE PRETTY... SMART.
THANKS. SAY, ED, CAN I ASK YOU SOMETHING?
OF COURSE.
WOULD YOU LIKE TO HAVE DINNER WITH ME?
UH...
WELL, I USUALLY EAT AT THE LAB, YOU SEE. I DON'T GET OUT UNTIL 8:30 MOST NIGHTS, AND--
OH *NO*, I'VE BEEN ON LUNCH FOR OVER AN *HOUR!* HOLLISTER'LL *KILL* ME!
I'M SORRY, MARY. I GOTTA GO. MAYBE I'LL SEE YOU TOMORROW.

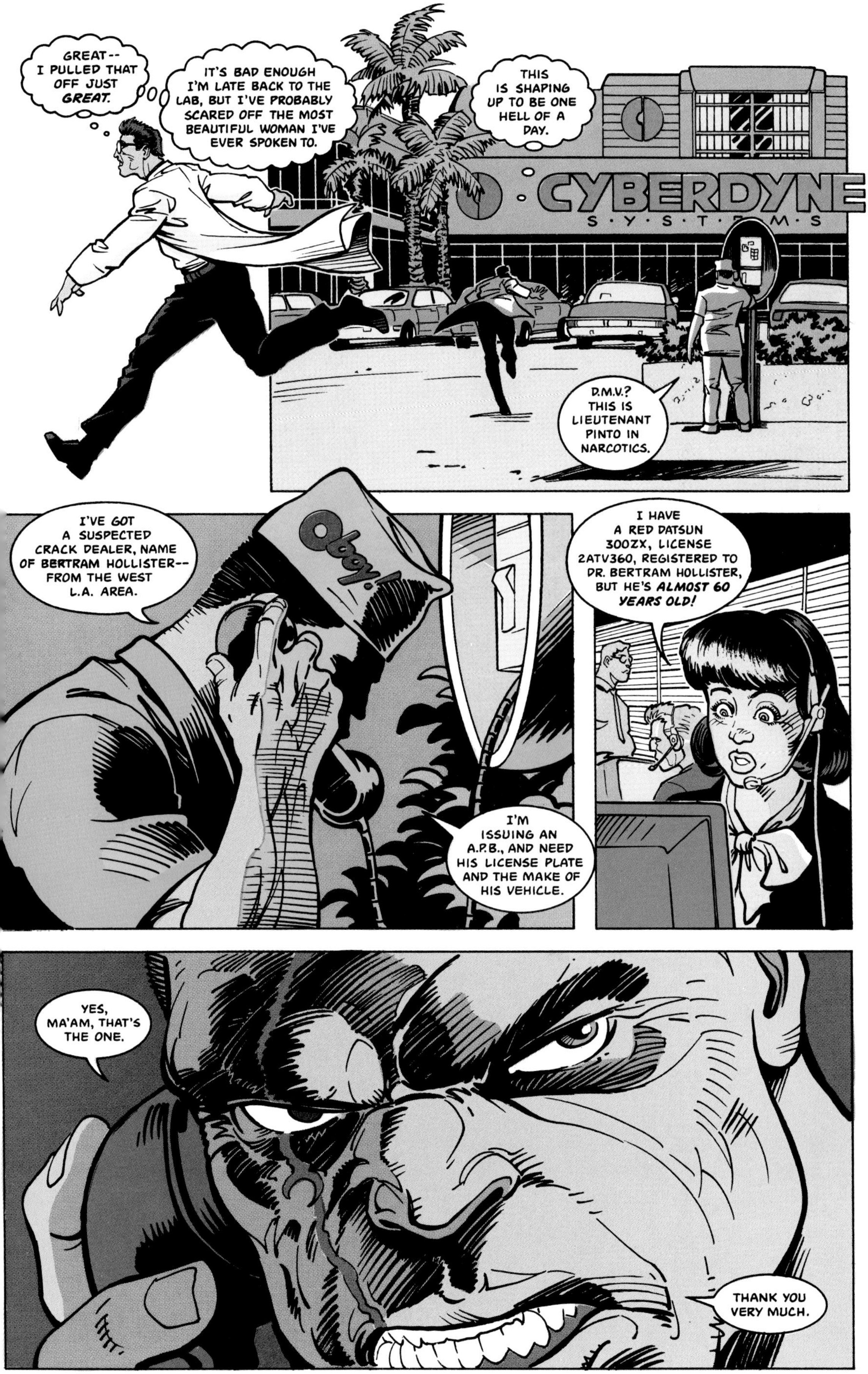
GREAT-- I PULLED THAT OFF JUST *GREAT.*
IT'S BAD ENOUGH I'M LATE BACK TO THE LAB, BUT I'VE PROBABLY SCARED OFF THE MOST BEAUTIFUL WOMAN I'VE EVER SPOKEN TO.
THIS IS SHAPING UP TO BE ONE HELL OF A DAY.
CYBERDYNE
S·Y·S·T·E·M·S
D.M.V.? THIS IS LIEUTENANT PINTO IN NARCOTICS.
I'VE GOT A SUSPECTED CRACK DEALER, NAME OF BERTRAM HOLLISTER-- FROM THE WEST L.A. AREA.
Oboy!
I'M ISSUING AN A.P.B., AND NEED HIS LICENSE PLATE AND THE MAKE OF HIS VEHICLE.
I HAVE A RED DATSUN 300ZX, LICENSE 2ATV360, REGISTERED TO DR. BERTRAM HOLLISTER, BUT HE'S *ALMOST 60 YEARS OLD!*
YES, MA'AM, THAT'S THE ONE.
THANK YOU VERY MUCH.

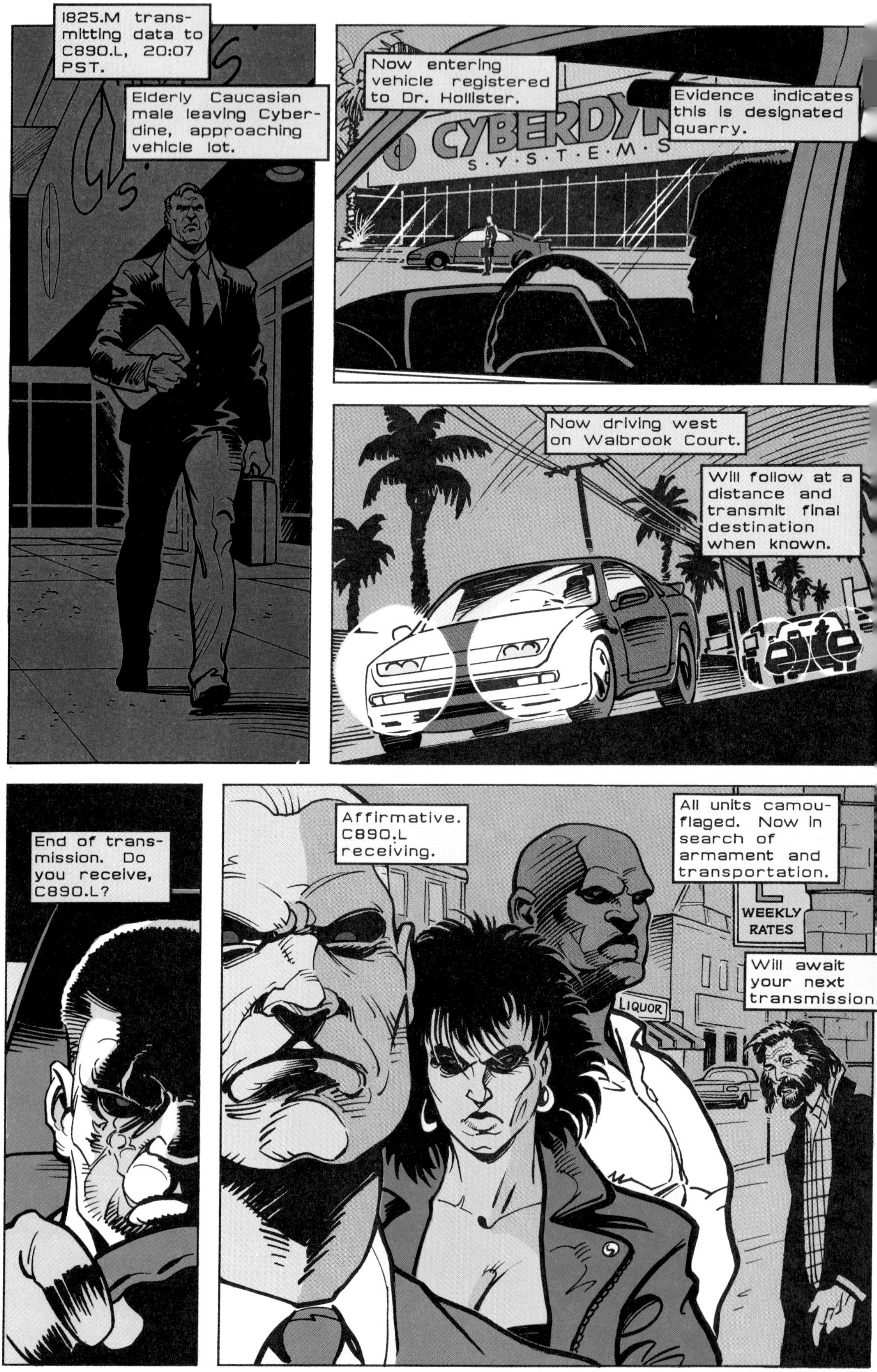

1825.M transmitting data to C890.L, 20:07 PST.
Elderly Caucasian male leaving Cyberdine, approaching vehicle lot.
Now entering vehicle registered to Dr. Hollister.
CYBERDYN S·Y·S·T·E·M·S
Evidence indicates this is designated quarry.
Now driving west on Walbrook Court.
Will follow at a distance and transmit final destination when known.
End of transmission. Do you receive, C890.L?
Affirmative. C890.L receiving.
All units camouflaged. Now in search of armament and transportation.
WEEKLY RATES
Will await your next transmission
LIQUOR

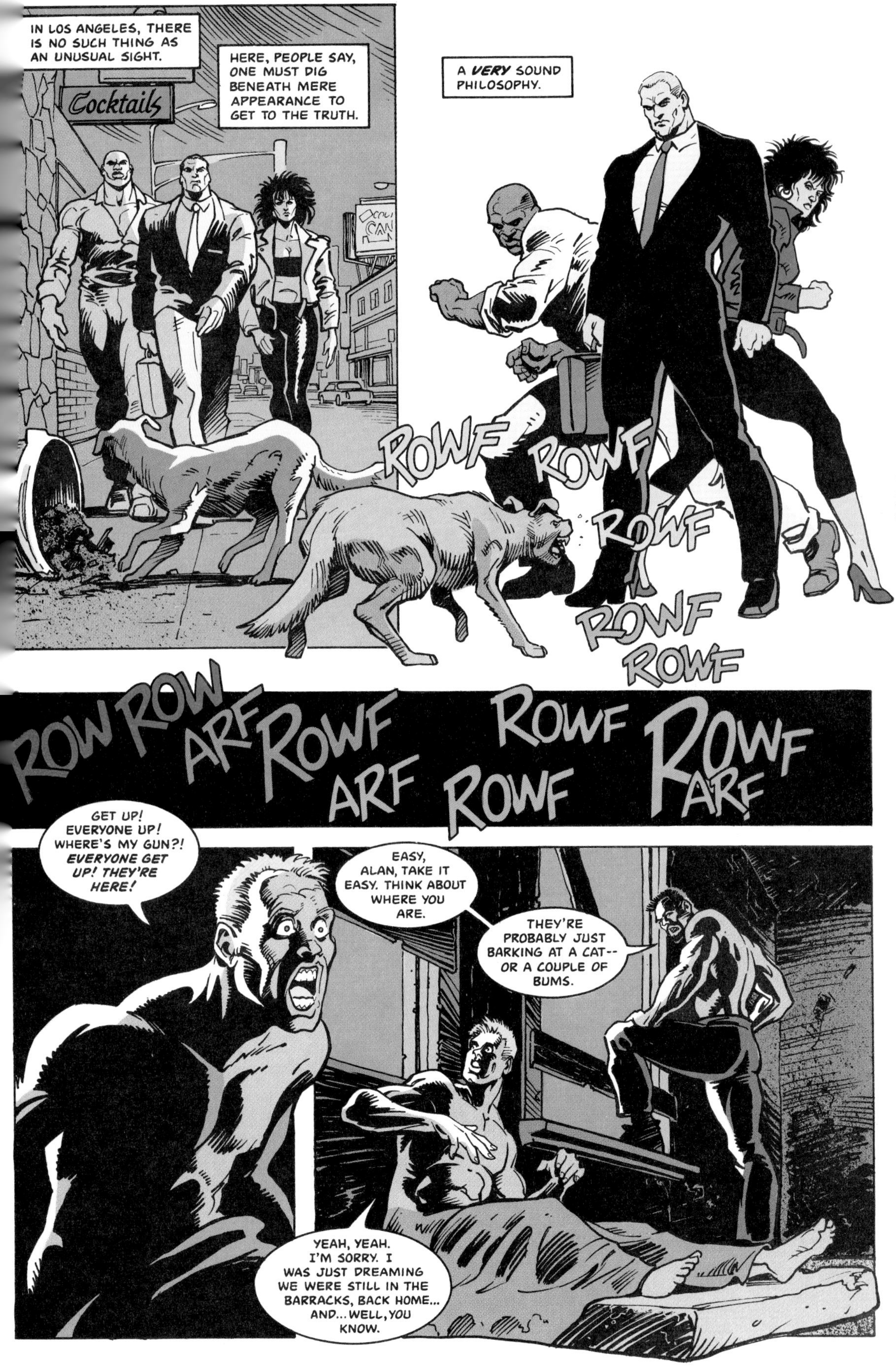

IN LOS ANGELES, THERE IS NO SUCH THING AS AN UNUSUAL SIGHT.
Cocktails
HERE, PEOPLE SAY, ONE MUST DIG BENEATH MERE APPEARANCE TO GET TO THE TRUTH.
A *VERY* SOUND PHILOSOPHY.
ROWF
ROWF
ROWF
ROWF
ROWF
ROW ROW
ARF
ROWF
ARF
ROWF
ROWF
ROWF
ARF
GET UP! EVERYONE UP! WHERE'S MY GUN?! *EVERYONE GET UP! THEY'RE HERE!*
EASY, ALAN, TAKE IT EASY. THINK ABOUT WHERE YOU ARE.
THEY'RE PROBABLY JUST BARKING AT A CAT-- OR A COUPLE OF BUMS.
YEAH, YEAH. I'M SORRY. I WAS JUST DREAMING WE WERE STILL IN THE BARRACKS, BACK HOME... AND...WELL, YOU KNOW.

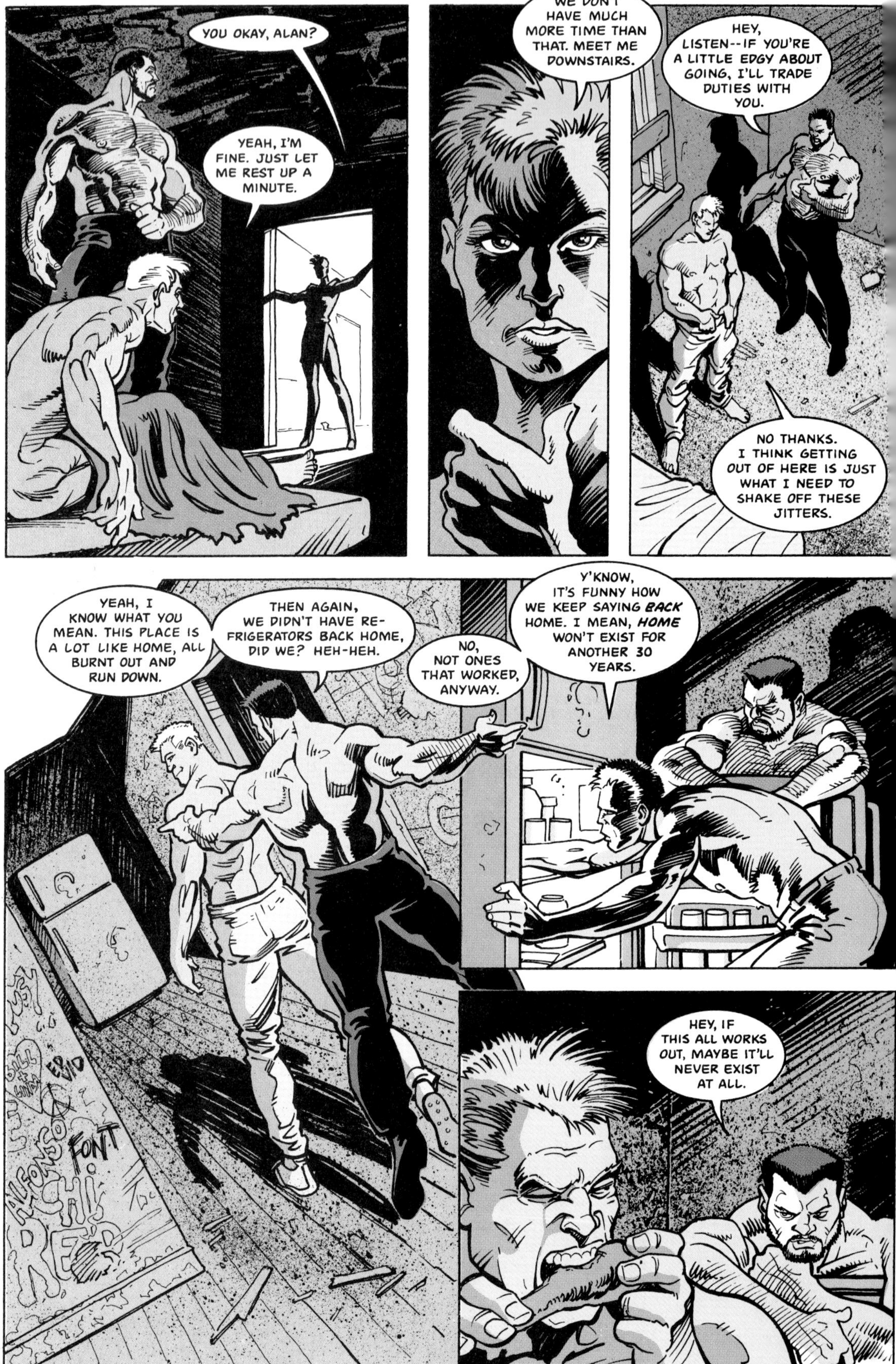
YOU OKAY, ALAN?
YEAH, I'M FINE. JUST LET ME REST UP A MINUTE.
WE DON'T HAVE MUCH MORE TIME THAN THAT. MEET ME DOWNSTAIRS.
HEY, LISTEN--IF YOU'RE A LITTLE EDGY ABOUT GOING, I'LL TRADE DUTIES WITH YOU.
NO THANKS. I THINK GETTING OUT OF HERE IS JUST WHAT I NEED TO SHAKE OFF THESE JITTERS.
YEAH, I KNOW WHAT YOU MEAN. THIS PLACE IS A LOT LIKE HOME, ALL BURNT OUT AND RUN DOWN.
THEN AGAIN, WE DIDN'T HAVE RE-FRIGERATORS BACK HOME, DID WE? HEH-HEH.
FONT
NO, NOT ONES THAT WORKED, ANYWAY.
Y'KNOW, IT'S FUNNY HOW WE KEEP SAYING ***BACK*** HOME. I MEAN, ***HOME*** WON'T EXIST FOR ANOTHER 30 YEARS.
HEY, IF THIS ALL WORKS OUT, MAYBE IT'LL NEVER EXIST AT ALL.

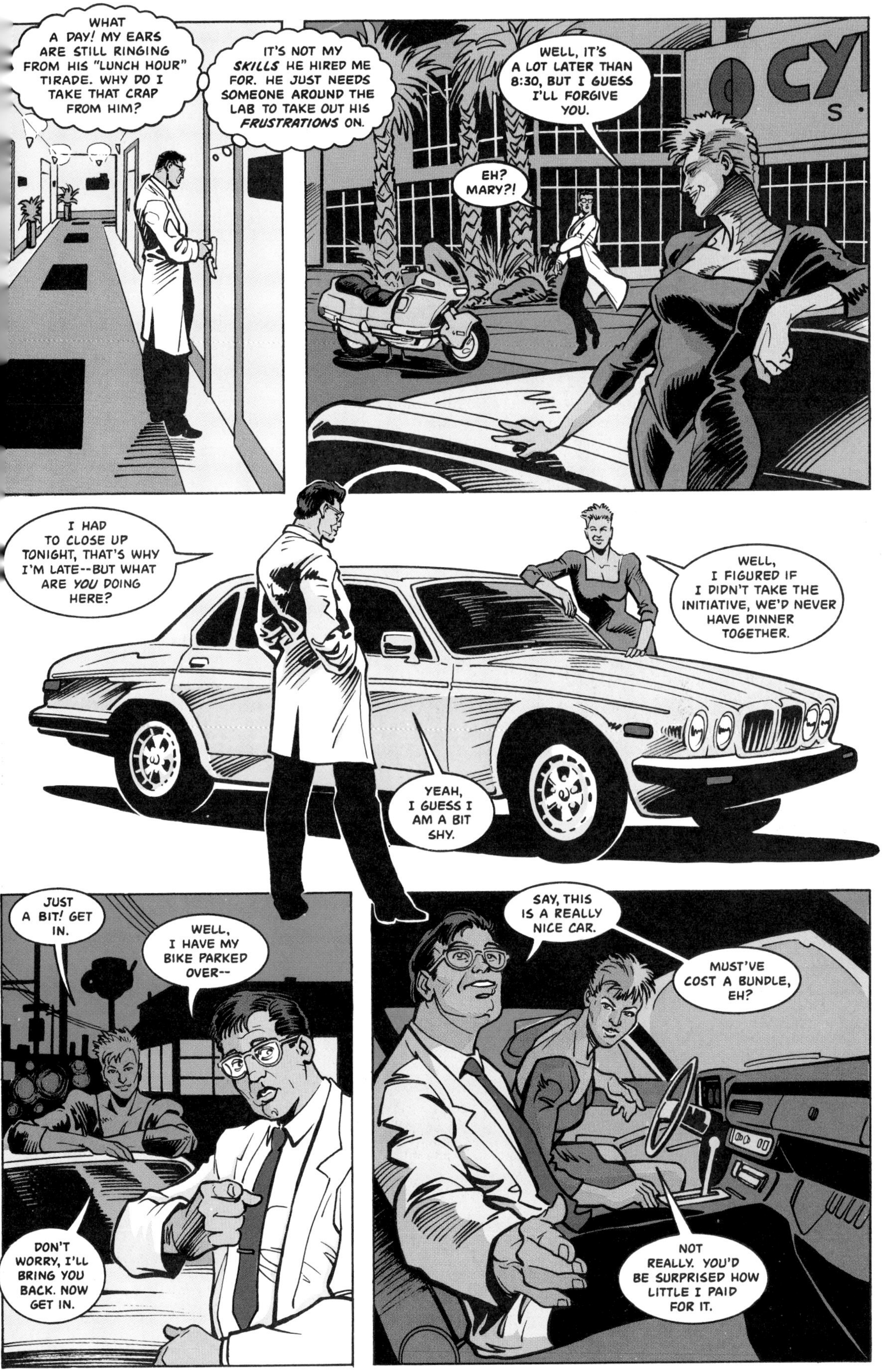
WHAT A DAY! MY EARS ARE STILL RINGING FROM HIS "LUNCH HOUR" TIRADE. WHY DO I TAKE THAT CRAP FROM HIM?
IT'S NOT MY SKILLS HE HIRED ME FOR. HE JUST NEEDS SOMEONE AROUND THE LAB TO TAKE OUT HIS FRUSTRATIONS ON.
WELL, IT'S A LOT LATER THAN 8:30, BUT I GUESS I'LL FORGIVE YOU.
EH? MARY?!
I HAD TO CLOSE UP TONIGHT, THAT'S WHY I'M LATE--BUT WHAT ARE YOU DOING HERE?
WELL, I FIGURED IF I DIDN'T TAKE THE INITIATIVE, WE'D NEVER HAVE DINNER TOGETHER.
YEAH, I GUESS I AM A BIT SHY.
JUST A BIT! GET IN.
WELL, I HAVE MY BIKE PARKED OVER--
DON'T WORRY, I'LL BRING YOU BACK. NOW GET IN.
SAY, THIS IS A REALLY NICE CAR.
MUST'VE COST A BUNDLE, EH?
NOT REALLY. YOU'D BE SURPRISED HOW LITTLE I PAID FOR IT.

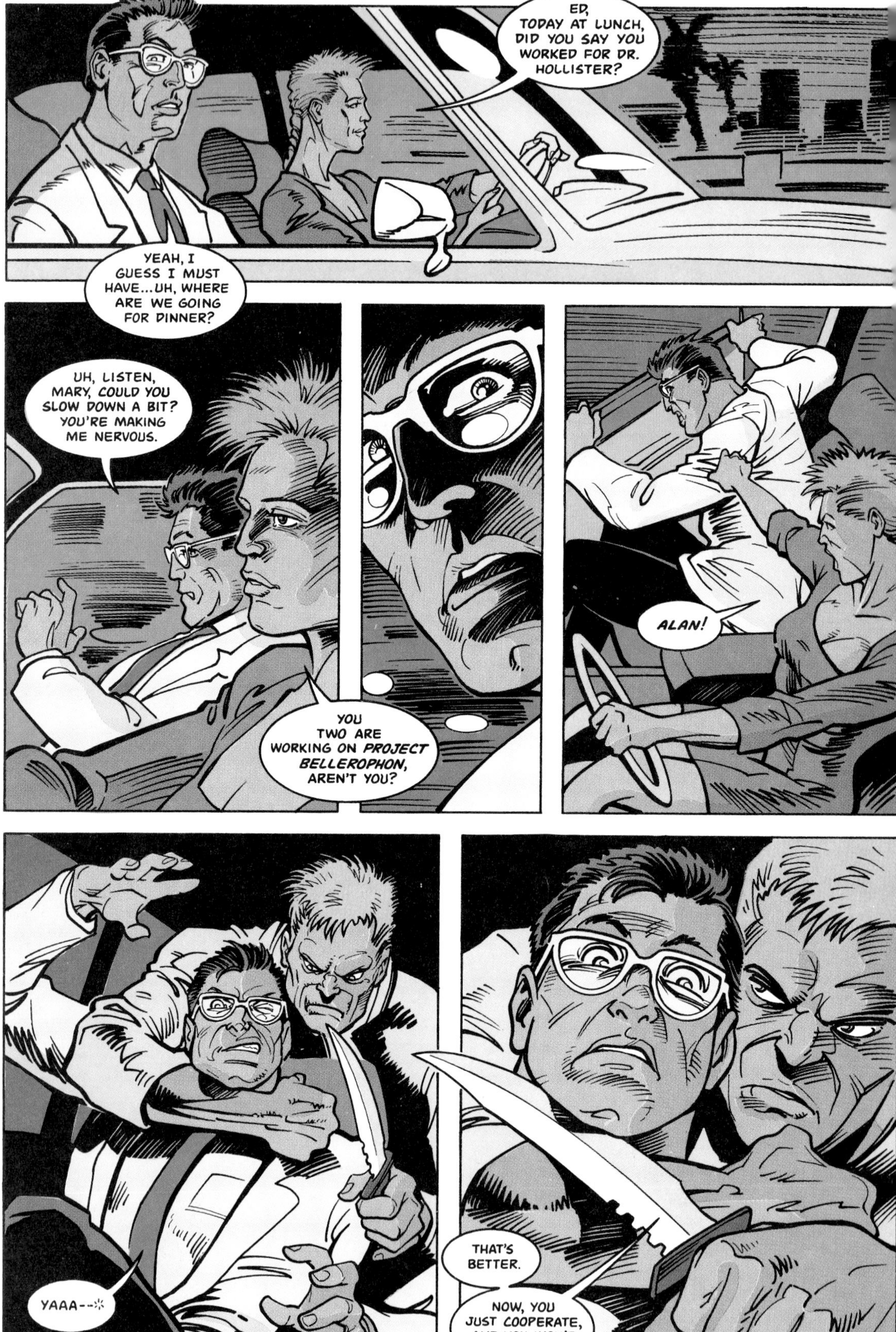
ED, TODAY AT LUNCH, DID YOU SAY YOU WORKED FOR DR. HOLLISTER?
YEAH, I GUESS I MUST HAVE...UH, WHERE ARE WE GOING FOR DINNER?
UH, LISTEN, MARY, COULD YOU SLOW DOWN A BIT? YOU'RE MAKING ME NERVOUS.
YOU TWO ARE WORKING ON PROJECT BELLEROPHON, AREN'T YOU?
ALAN!
YAAA--
THAT'S BETTER.
NOW, YOU JUST COOPERATE, AND YOU WON'T GET HURT.

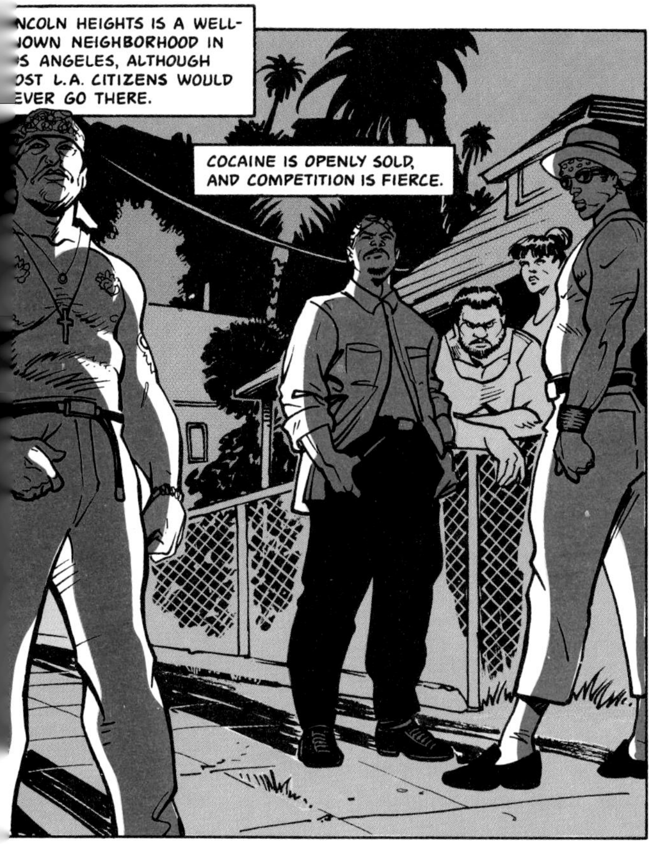
NCOLN HEIGHTS IS A WELL-
NOWN NEIGHBORHOOD IN
S ANGELES, ALTHOUGH
OST L.A. CITIZENS WOULD
EVER GO THERE.
COCAINE IS OPENLY SOLD,
AND COMPETITION IS FIERCE.

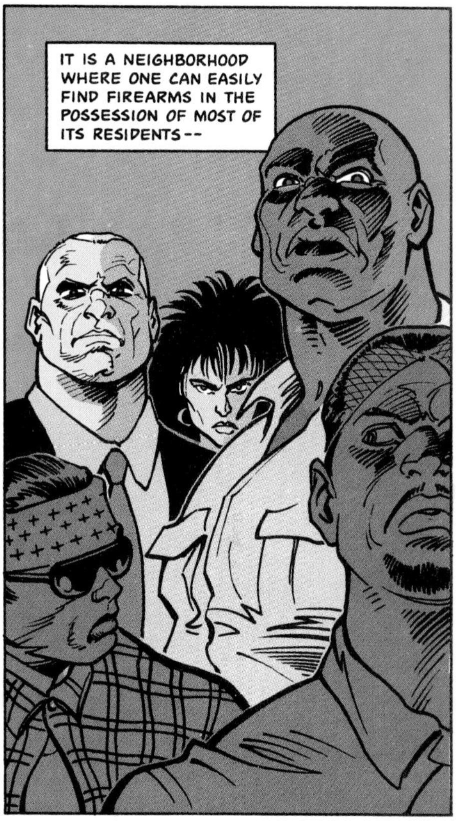
IT IS A NEIGHBORHOOD
WHERE ONE CAN EASILY
FIND FIREARMS IN THE
POSSESSION OF MOST OF
ITS RESIDENTS--

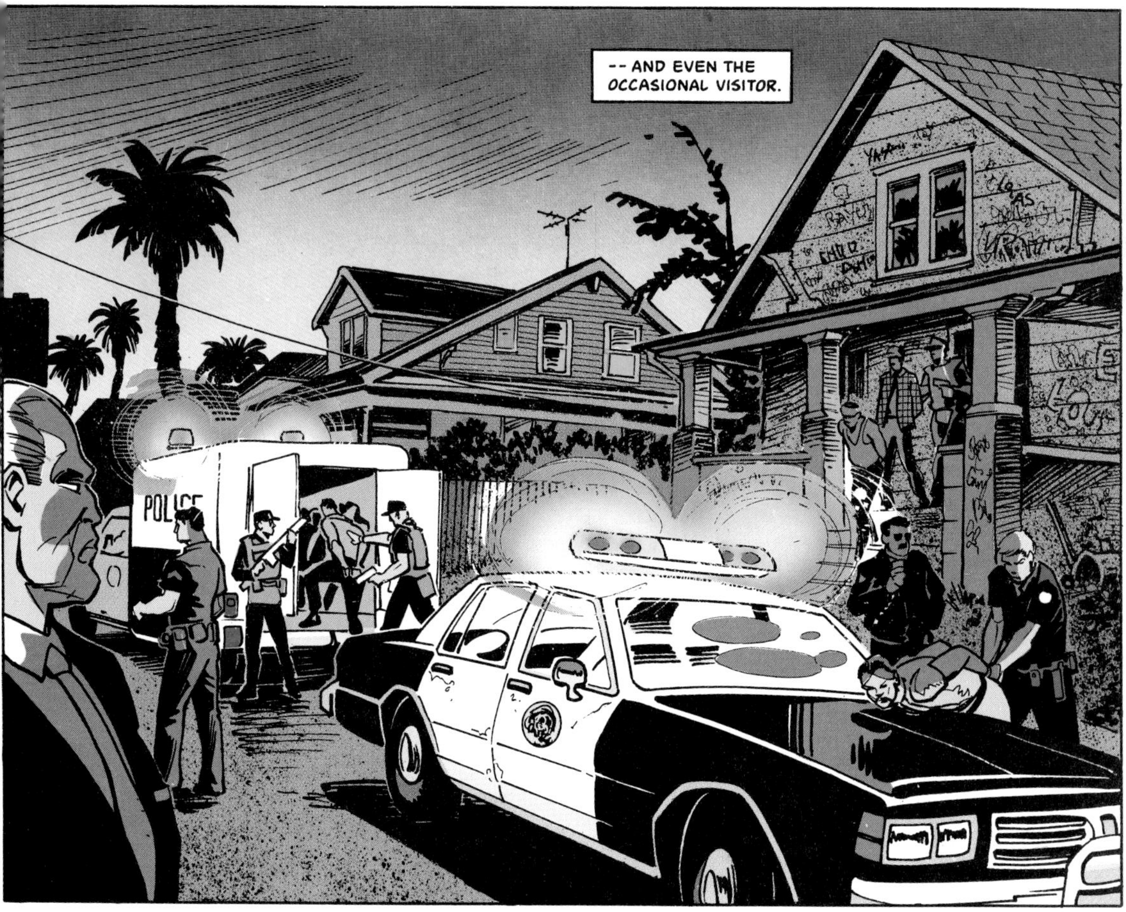
--AND EVEN THE
OCCASIONAL VISITOR.
POLICE

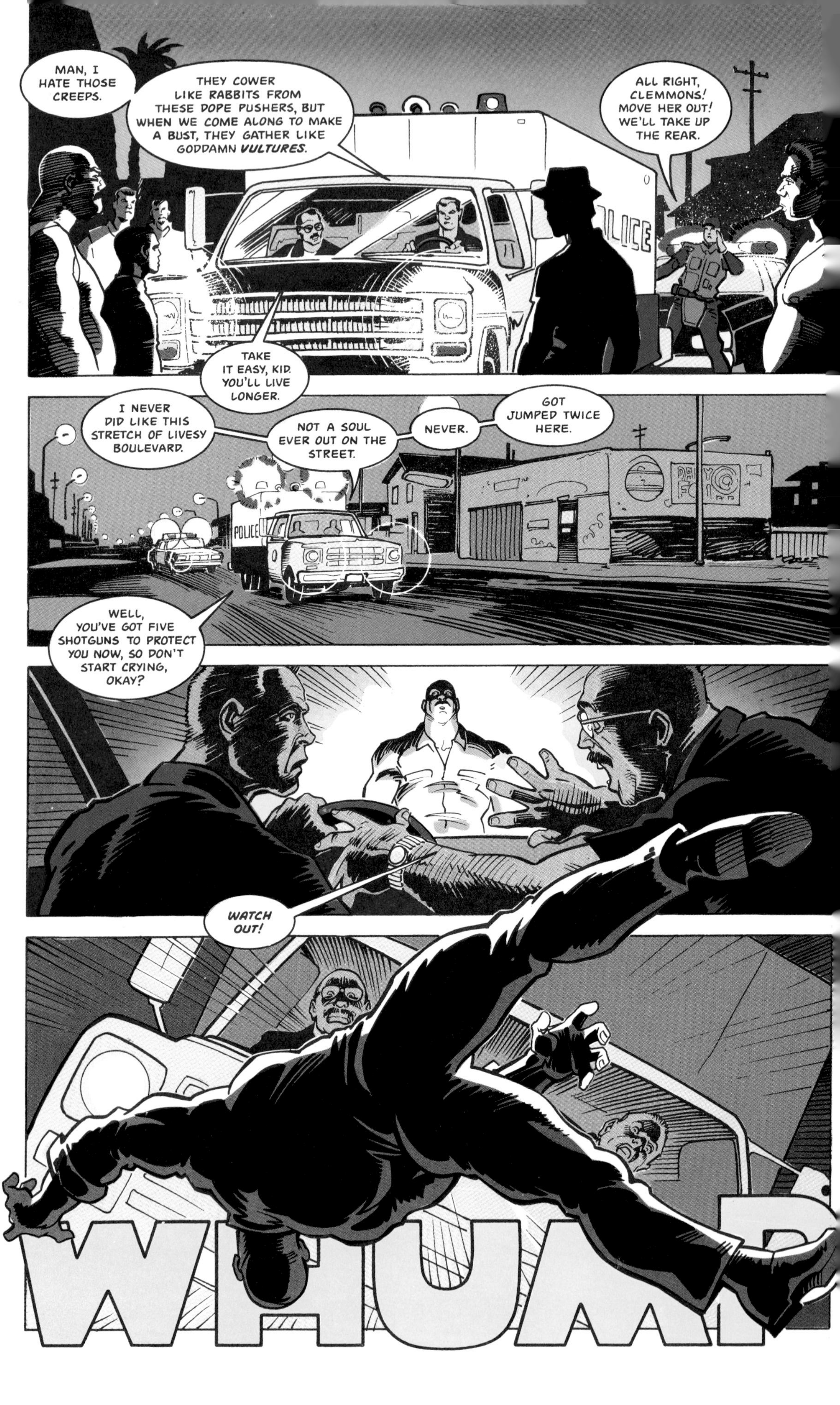
MAN, I HATE THOSE CREEPS.
THEY COWER LIKE RABBITS FROM THESE DOPE PUSHERS, BUT WHEN WE COME ALONG TO MAKE A BUST, THEY GATHER LIKE GODDAMN VULTURES.
TAKE IT EASY, KID. YOU'LL LIVE LONGER.
ALL RIGHT, CLEMMONS! MOVE HER OUT! WE'LL TAKE UP THE REAR.
POLICE
I NEVER DID LIKE THIS STRETCH OF LIVESY BOULEVARD.
NOT A SOUL EVER OUT ON THE STREET.
NEVER.
GOT JUMPED TWICE HERE.
POLICE
WELL, YOU'VE GOT FIVE SHOTGUNS TO PROTECT YOU NOW, SO DON'T START CRYING, OKAY?
WATCH OUT!
WHUMP

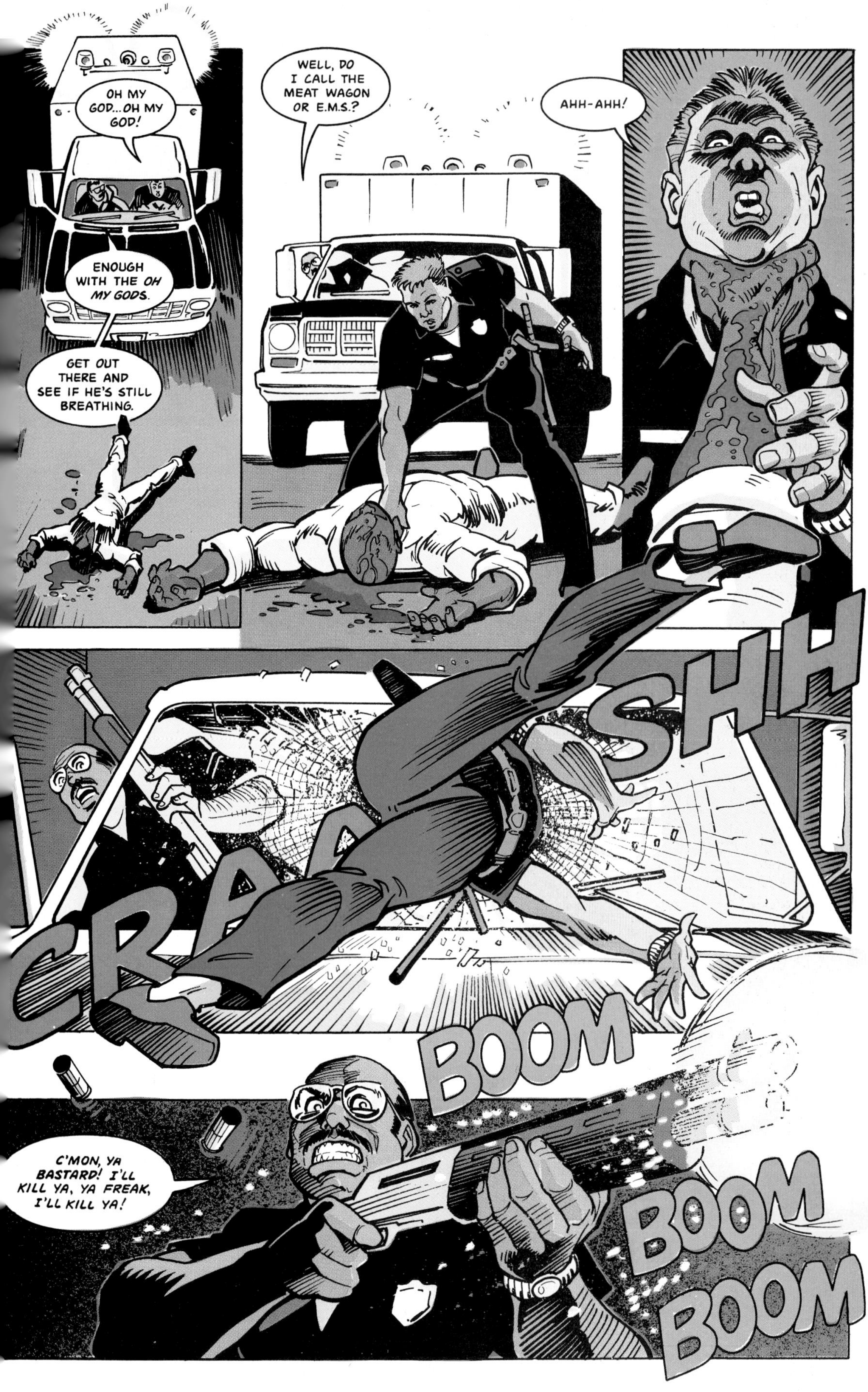

OH MY GOD...OH MY GOD!
ENOUGH WITH THE *OH MY GODS*.
GET OUT THERE AND SEE IF HE'S STILL BREATHING.
WELL, DO I CALL THE MEAT WAGON OR E.M.S.?
AHH-AHH!
CRAASHH
BOOM
C'MON, YA BASTARD! I'LL KILL YA, YA FREAK, I'LL KILL YA!
BOOM
BOOM

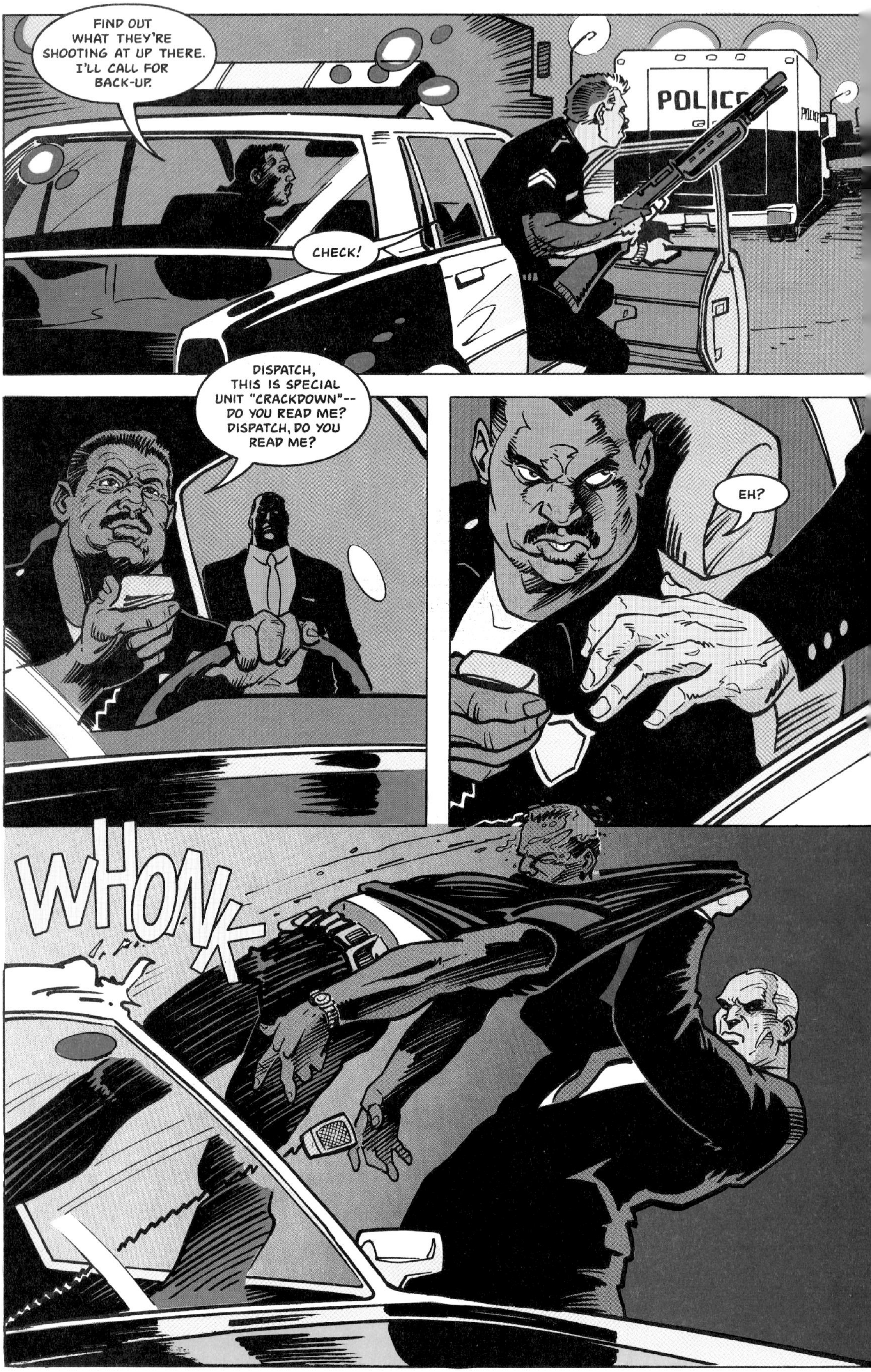
FIND OUT WHAT THEY'RE SHOOTING AT UP THERE. I'LL CALL FOR BACK-UP.
CHECK!
POLICE
DISPATCH, THIS IS SPECIAL UNIT "CRACKDOWN"-- DO YOU READ ME? DISPATCH, DO YOU READ ME?
EH?
WHONK

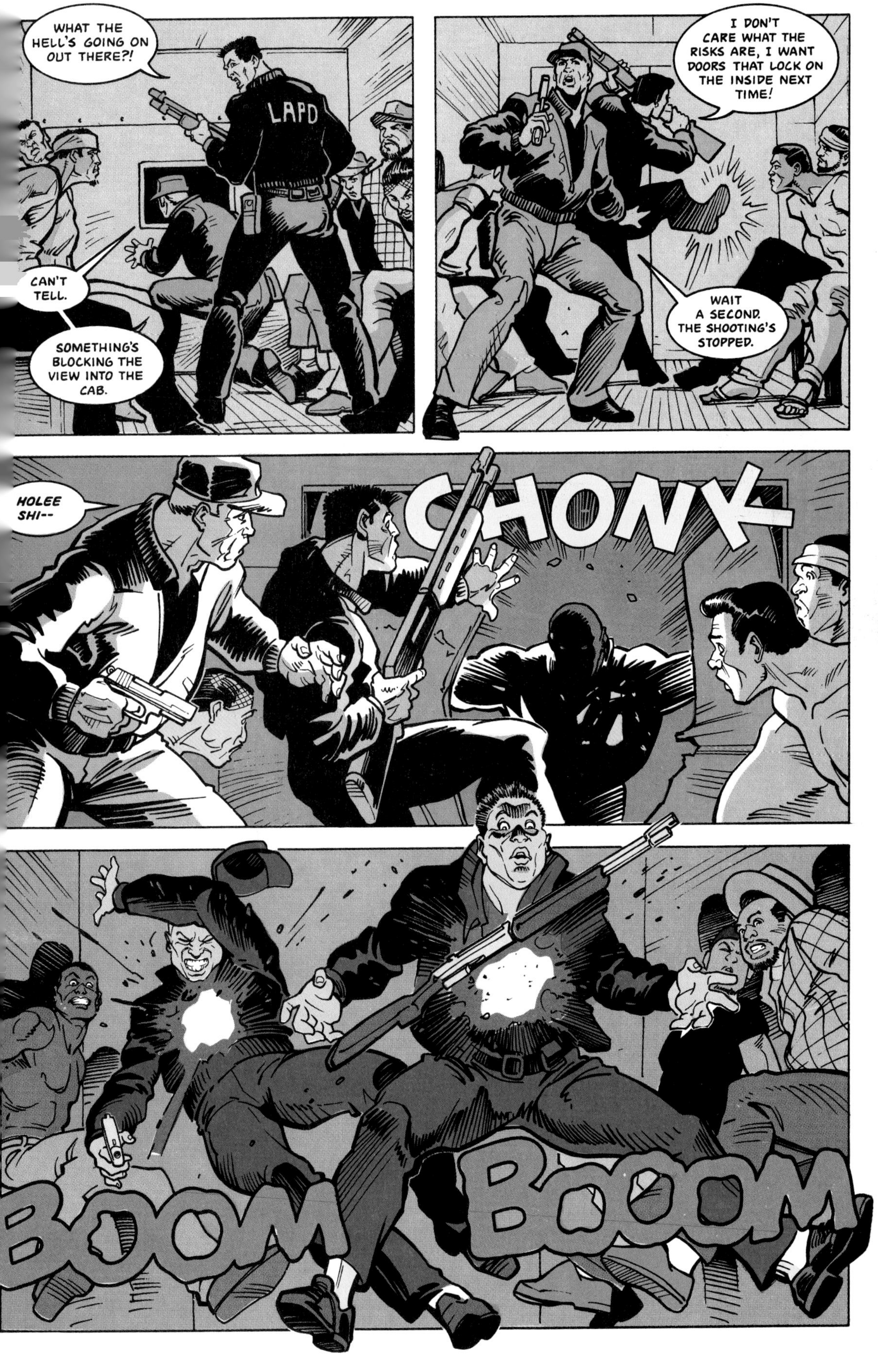
WHAT THE HELL'S GOING ON OUT THERE?!
CAN'T TELL.
SOMETHING'S BLOCKING THE VIEW INTO THE CAB.
I DON'T CARE WHAT THE RISKS ARE, I WANT DOORS THAT LOCK ON THE INSIDE NEXT TIME!
WAIT A SECOND. THE SHOOTING'S STOPPED.
HOLEE SHI--
CHONK
BOOOM
BOOOM

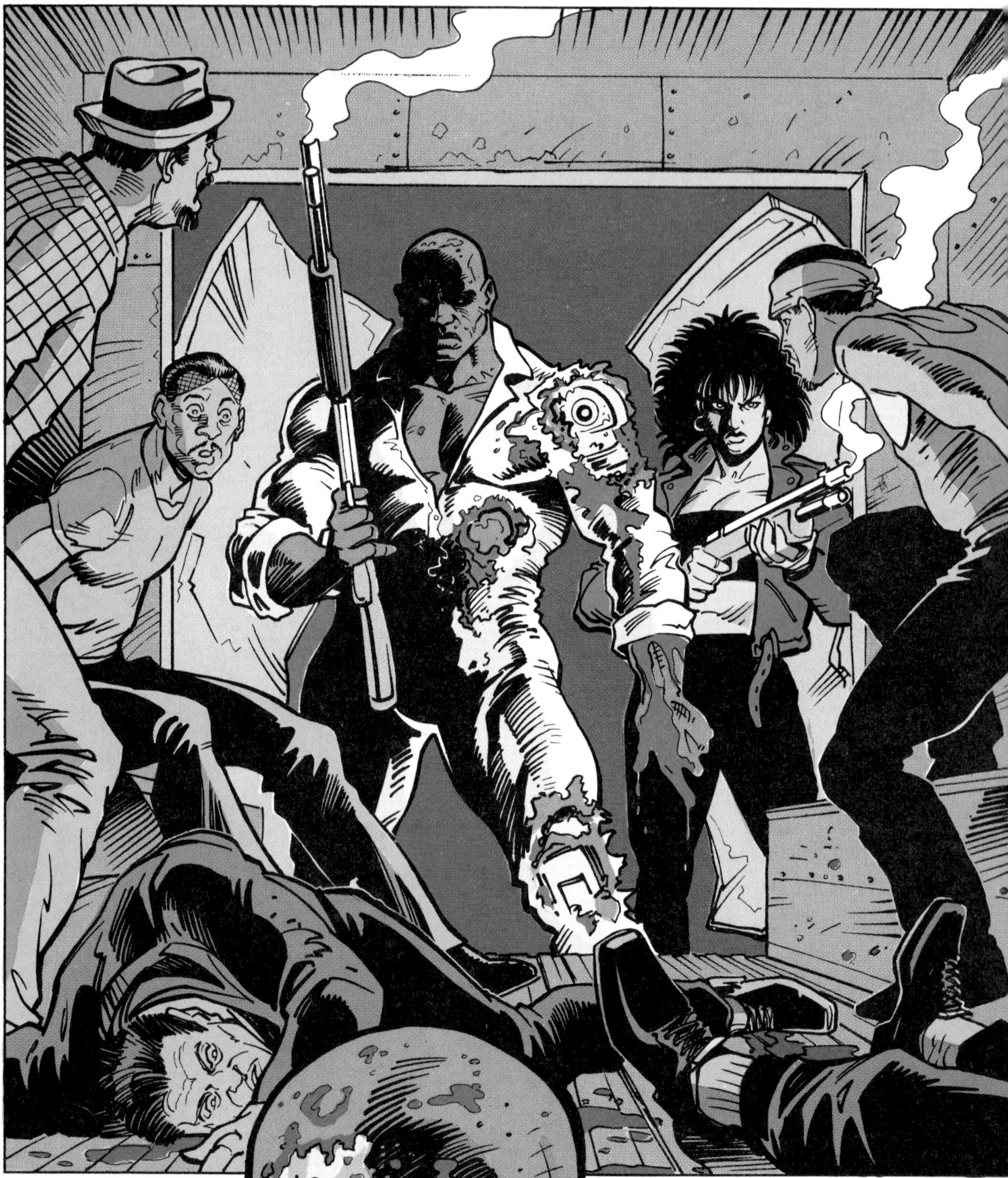

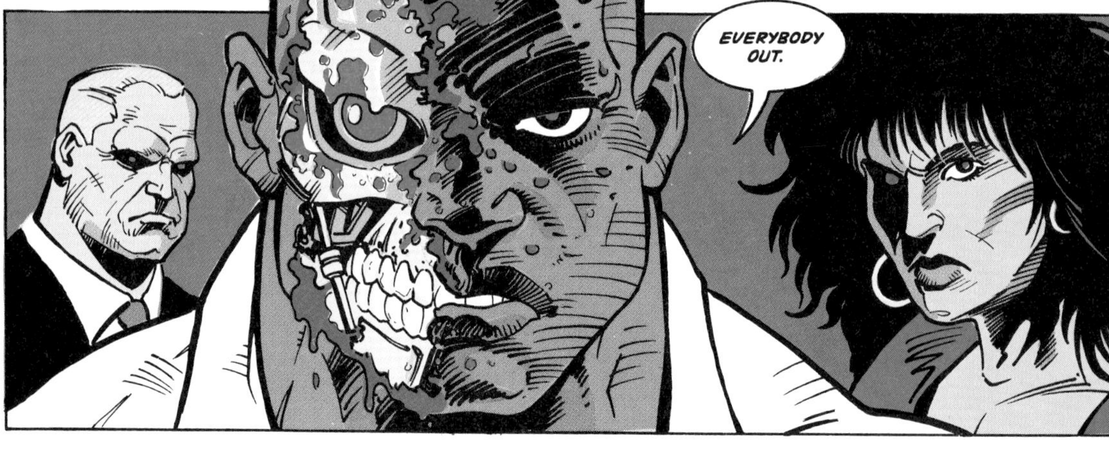
EVERYBODY OUT.

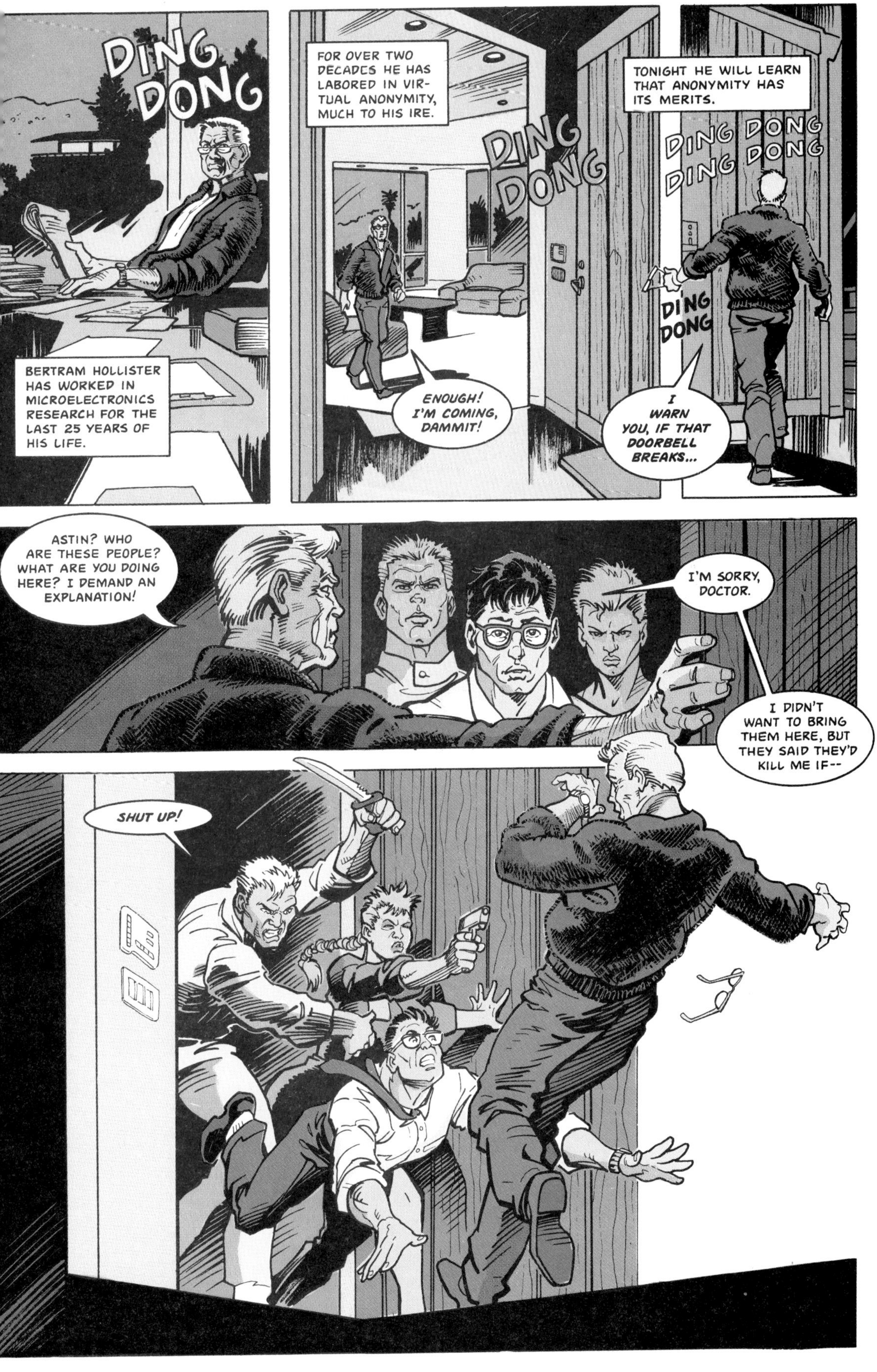
DING DONG
BERTRAM HOLLISTER HAS WORKED IN MICROELECTRONICS RESEARCH FOR THE LAST 25 YEARS OF HIS LIFE.
FOR OVER TWO DECADES HE HAS LABORED IN VIRTUAL ANONYMITY, MUCH TO HIS IRE.
DING DONG
ENOUGH! I'M COMING, DAMMIT!
TONIGHT HE WILL LEARN THAT ANONYMITY HAS ITS MERITS.
DING DONG DING DONG
DING DONG DING DONG
DING DONG
I WARN YOU, IF THAT DOORBELL BREAKS...
ASTIN? WHO ARE THESE PEOPLE? WHAT ARE YOU DOING HERE? I DEMAND AN EXPLANATION!
I'M SORRY, DOCTOR.
I DIDN'T WANT TO BRING THEM HERE, BUT THEY SAID THEY'D KILL ME IF--
SHUT UP!

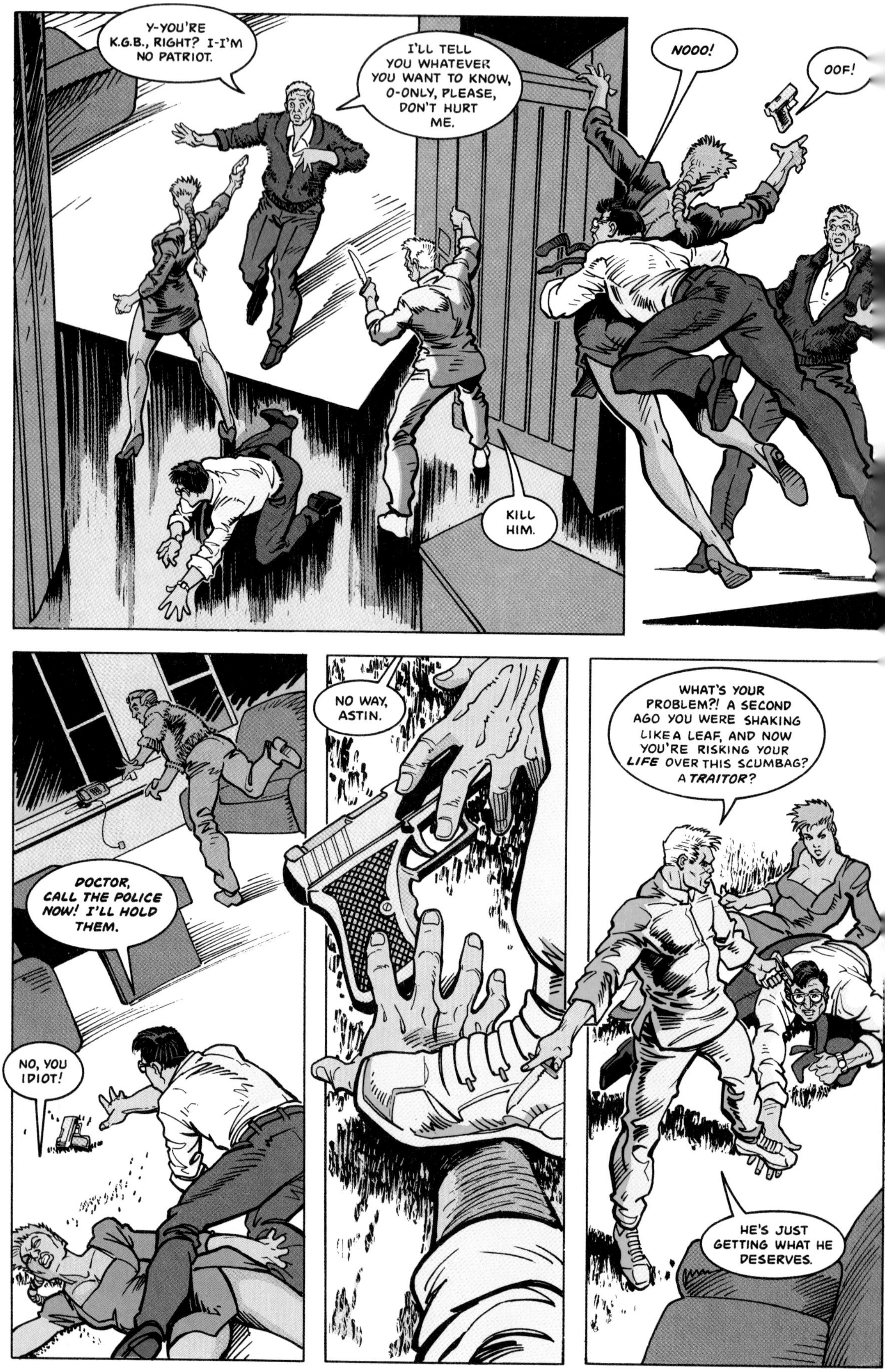
Y-YOU'RE K.G.B., RIGHT? I-I'M NO PATRIOT.
I'LL TELL YOU WHATEVER YOU WANT TO KNOW, O-ONLY, PLEASE, DON'T HURT ME.
KILL HIM.
NOOO!
OOF!
DOCTOR, CALL THE POLICE NOW! I'LL HOLD THEM.
NO, YOU IDIOT!
NO WAY, ASTIN.
WHAT'S YOUR PROBLEM?! A SECOND AGO YOU WERE SHAKING LIKE A LEAF, AND NOW YOU'RE RISKING YOUR LIFE OVER THIS SCUMBAG? A TRAITOR?
HE'S JUST GETTING WHAT HE DESERVES.

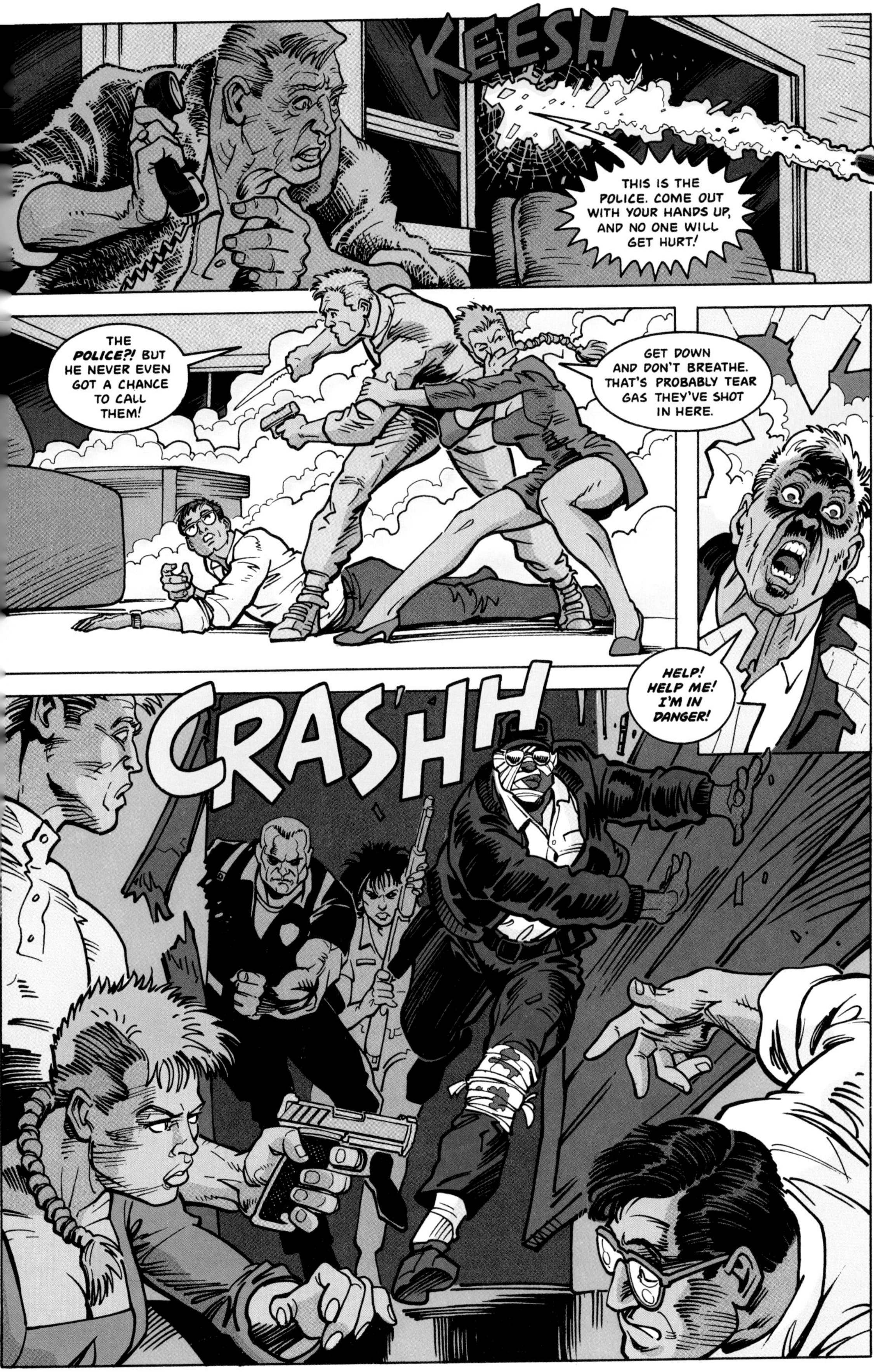
KEESH
THIS IS THE POLICE. COME OUT WITH YOUR HANDS UP, AND NO ONE WILL GET HURT!
THE POLICE?! BUT HE NEVER EVEN GOT A CHANCE TO CALL THEM!
GET DOWN AND DON'T BREATHE. THAT'S PROBABLY TEAR GAS THEY'VE SHOT IN HERE.
HELP! HELP ME! I'M IN DANGER!
CRASHH

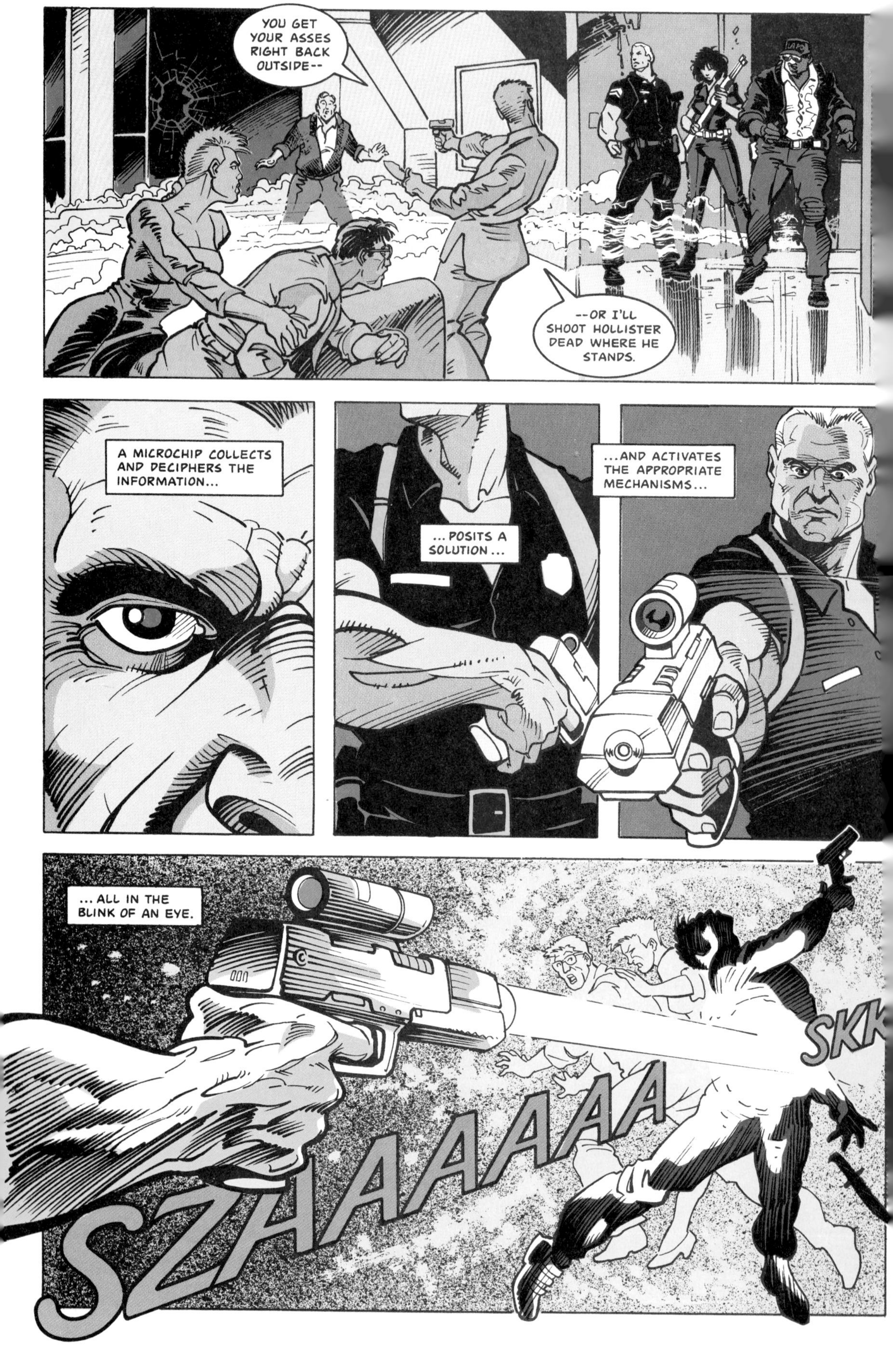
YOU GET YOUR ASSES RIGHT BACK OUTSIDE--
--OR I'LL SHOOT HOLLISTER DEAD WHERE HE STANDS.
A MICROCHIP COLLECTS AND DECIPHERS THE INFORMATION...
...POSITS A SOLUTION...
...AND ACTIVATES THE APPROPRIATE MECHANISMS...
...ALL IN THE BLINK OF AN EYE.
SZHAAAAAA
SKK

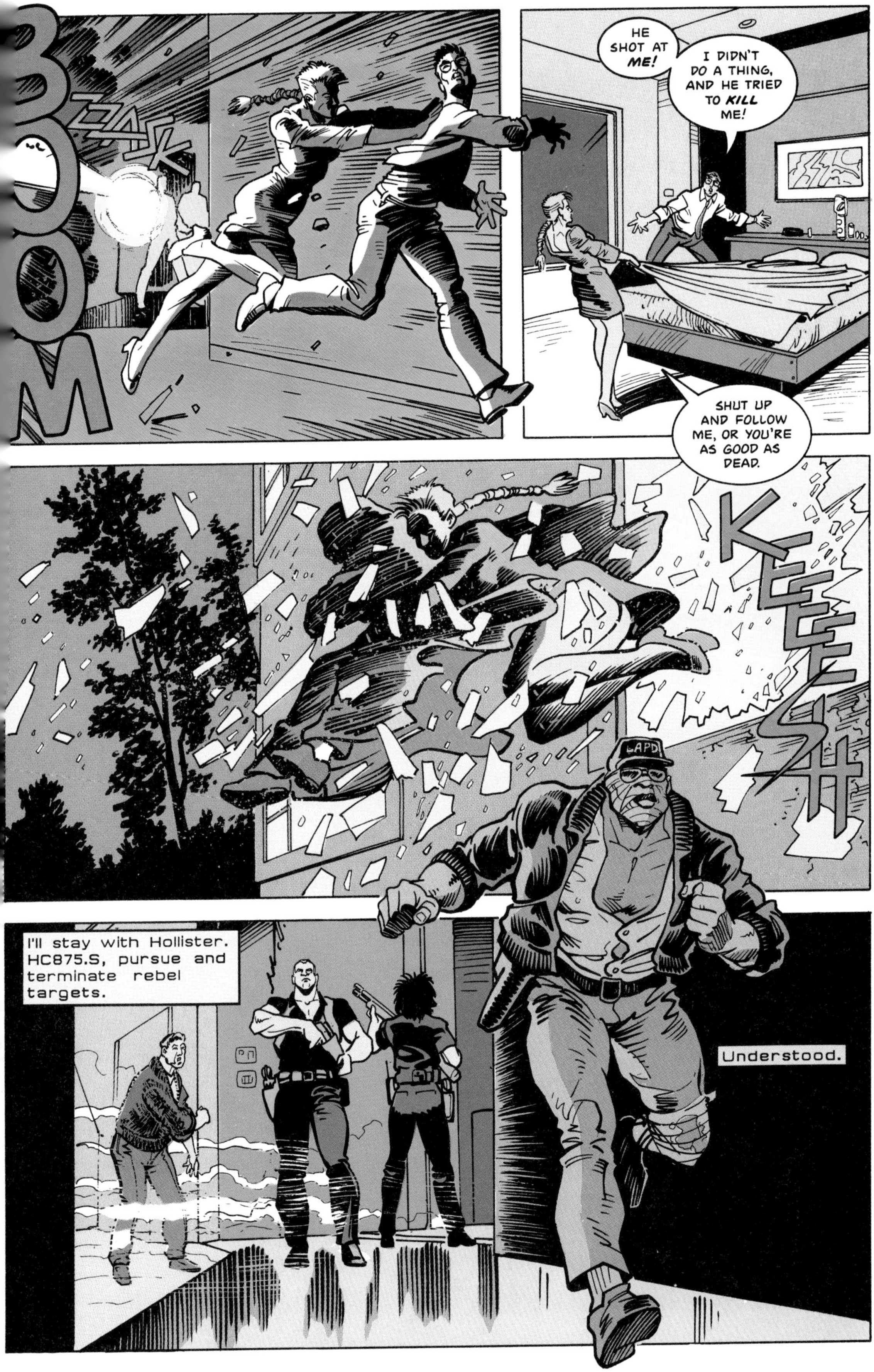
BOOM
ZZAK
HE SHOT AT ME!
I DIDN'T DO A THING, AND HE TRIED TO KILL ME!
SHUT UP AND FOLLOW ME, OR YOU'RE AS GOOD AS DEAD.
KEEEESH
LAPD
I'll stay with Hollister. HC875.S, pursue and terminate rebel targets.
Understood.

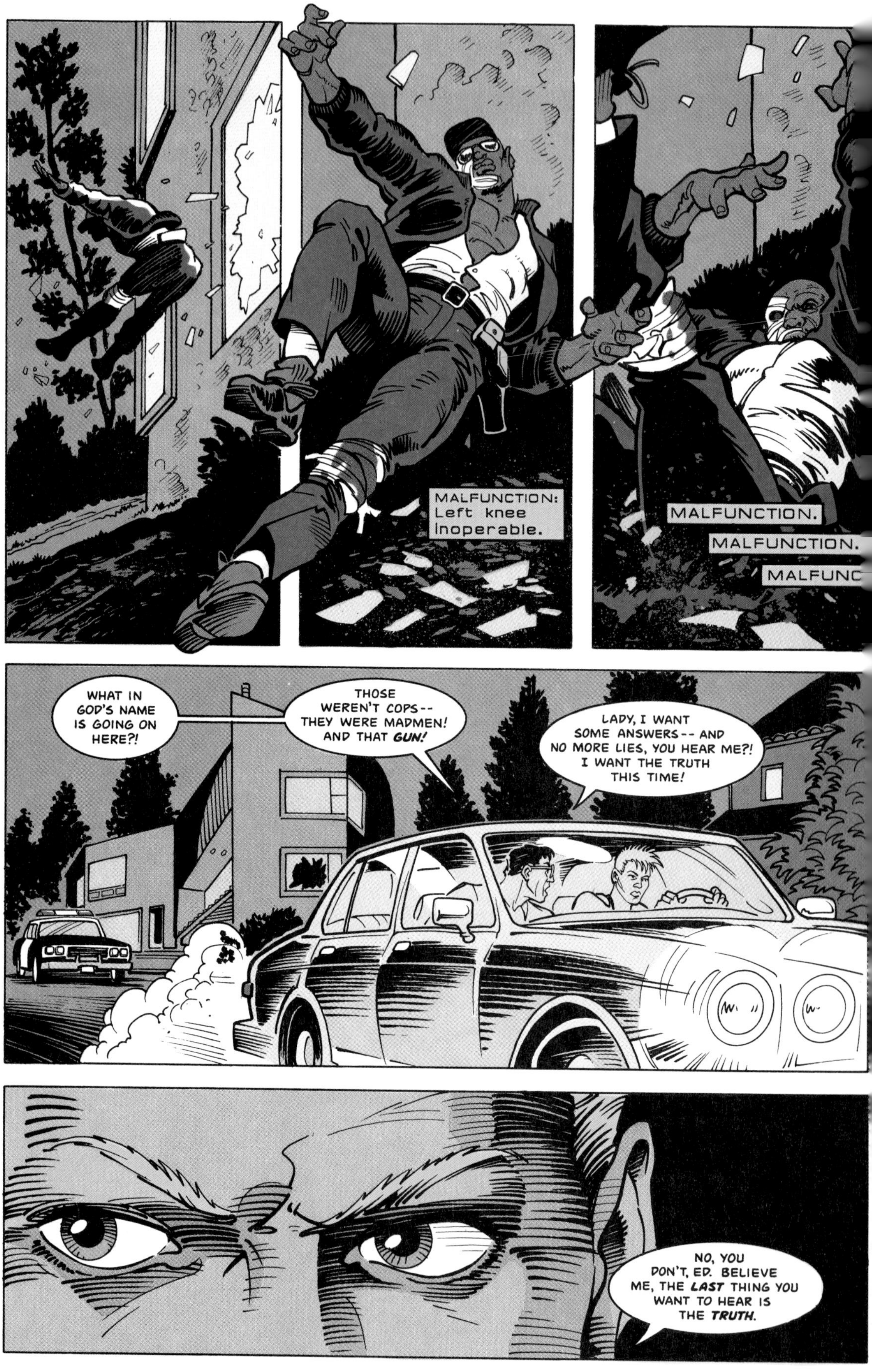
MALFUNCTION: Left knee Inoperable.
MALFUNCTION.
MALFUNCTION.
MALFUNC
WHAT IN GOD'S NAME IS GOING ON HERE?!
THOSE WEREN'T COPS-- THEY WERE MADMEN! AND THAT GUN!
LADY, I WANT SOME ANSWERS-- AND NO MORE LIES, YOU HEAR ME?! I WANT THE TRUTH THIS TIME!
NO, YOU DON'T, ED. BELIEVE ME, THE LAST THING YOU WANT TO HEAR IS THE TRUTH.

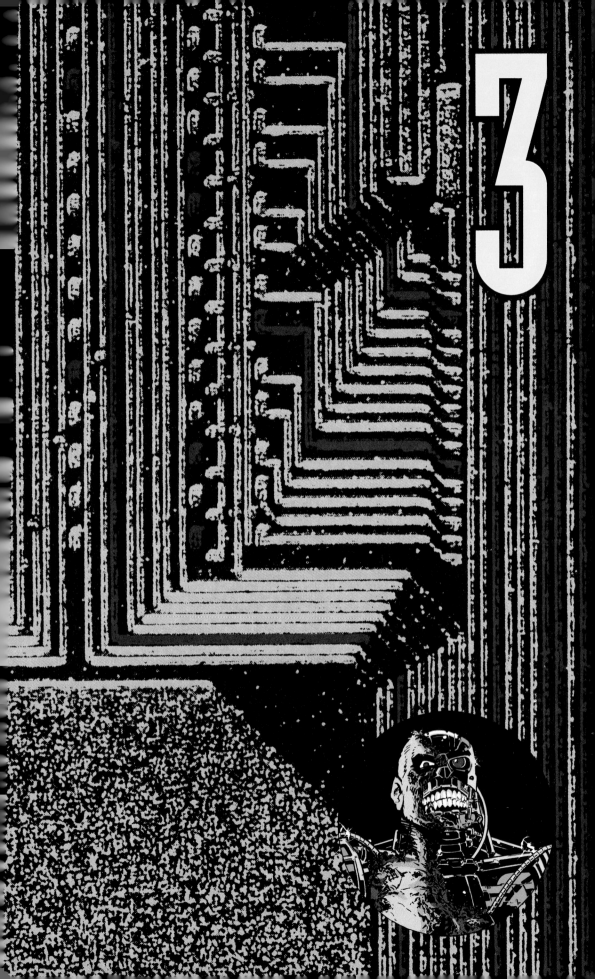

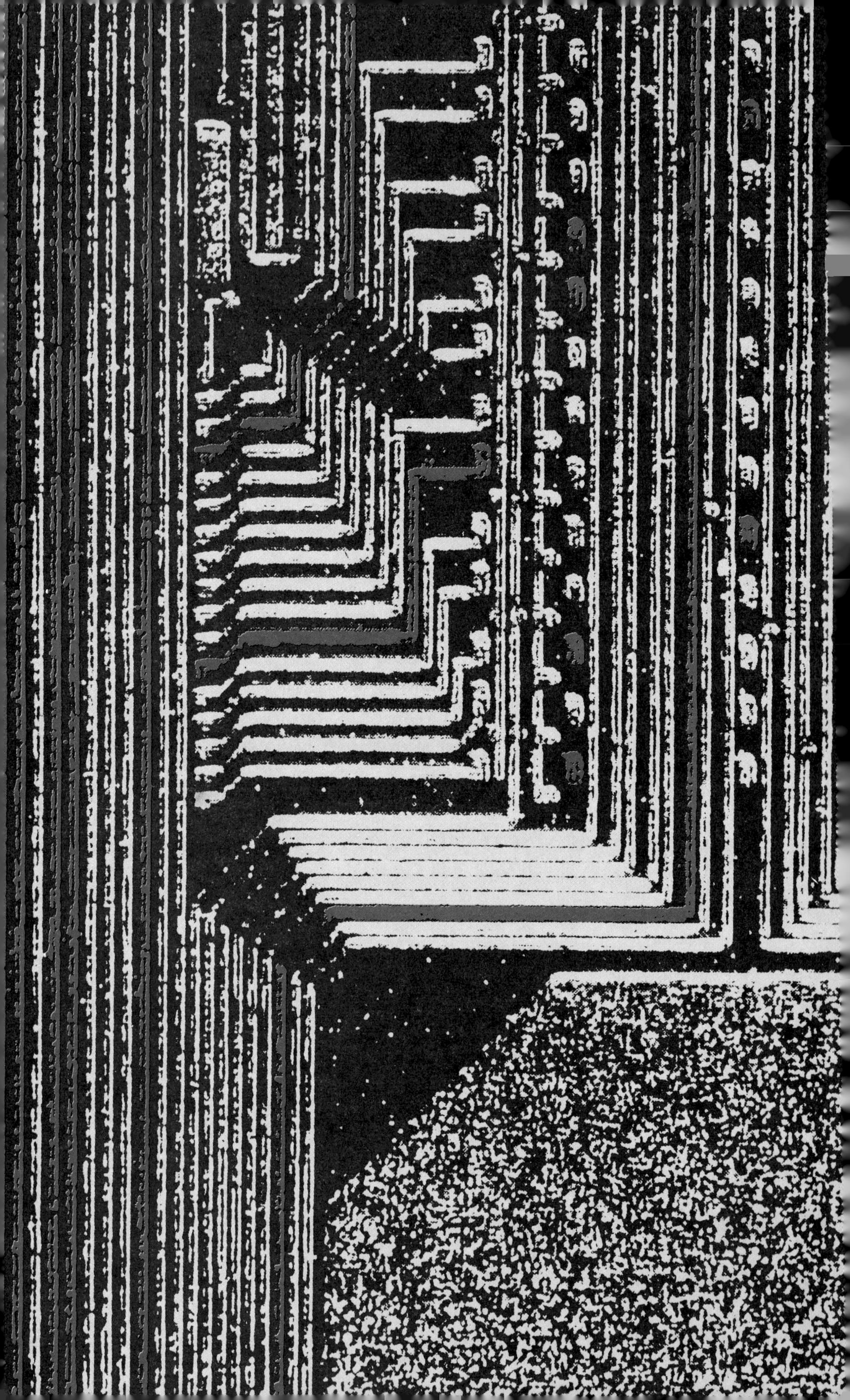

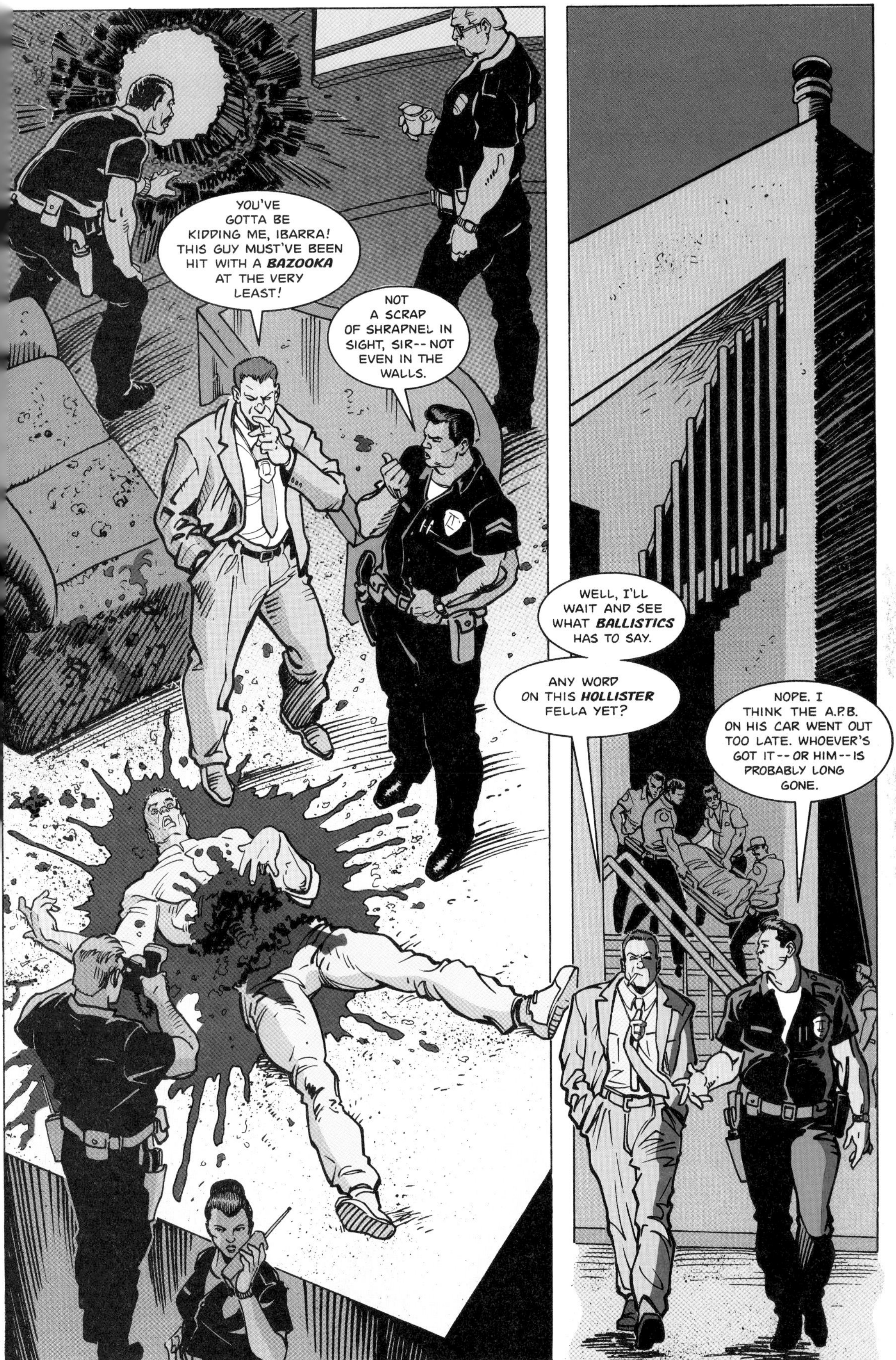
YOU'VE GOTTA BE KIDDING ME, IBARRA! THIS GUY MUST'VE BEEN HIT WITH A **BAZOOKA** AT THE VERY LEAST!
NOT A SCRAP OF SHRAPNEL IN SIGHT, SIR-- NOT EVEN IN THE WALLS.
WELL, I'LL WAIT AND SEE WHAT **BALLISTICS** HAS TO SAY.
ANY WORD ON THIS **HOLLISTER** FELLA YET?
NOPE. I THINK THE A.P.B. ON HIS CAR WENT OUT TOO LATE. WHOEVER'S GOT IT-- OR HIM-- IS PROBABLY LONG GONE.

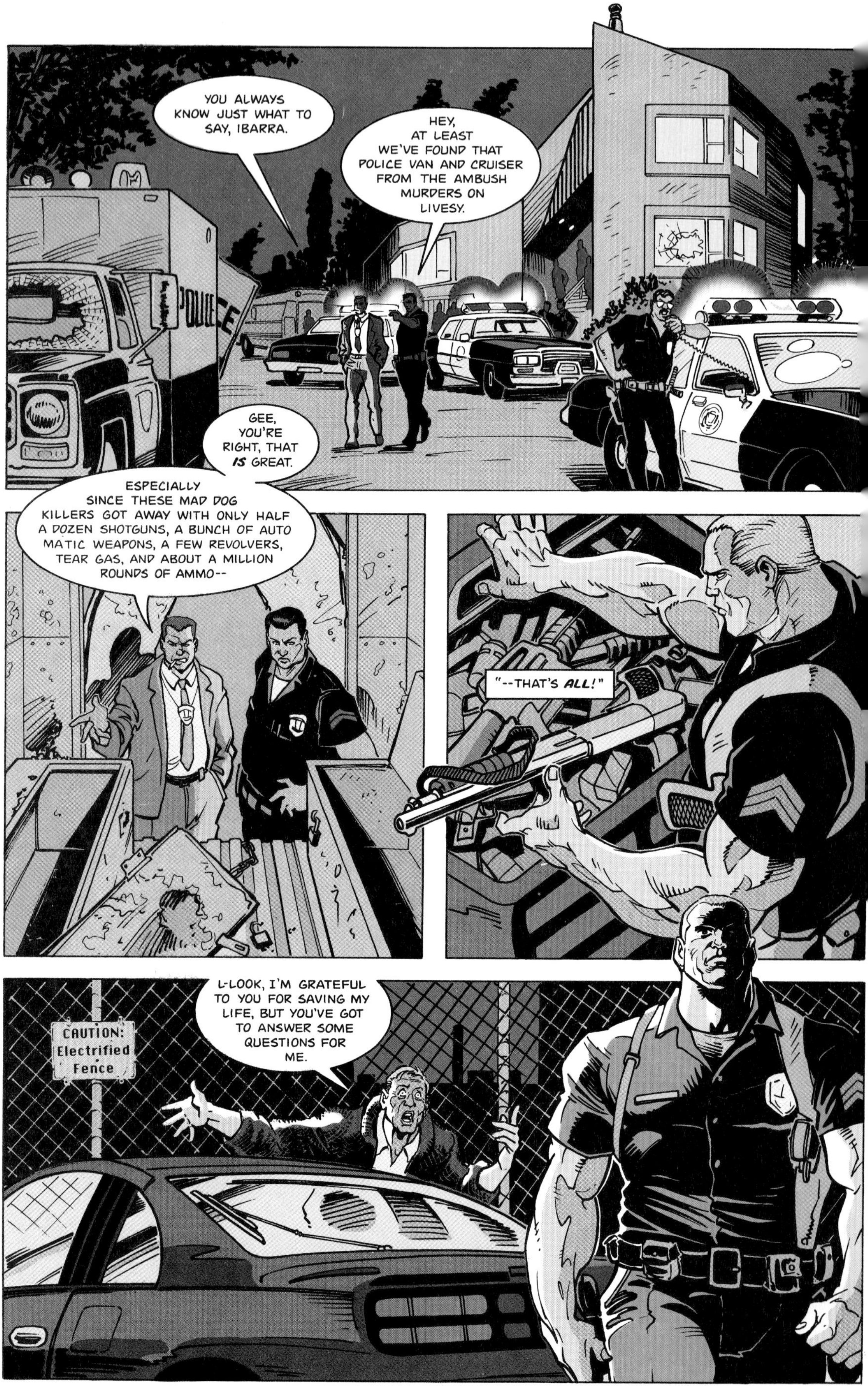
YOU ALWAYS KNOW JUST WHAT TO SAY, IBARRA.
HEY, AT LEAST WE'VE FOUND THAT POLICE VAN AND CRUISER FROM THE AMBUSH MURDERS ON LIVESY.
POLICE
GEE, YOU'RE RIGHT, THAT *IS* GREAT.
ESPECIALLY SINCE THESE MAD DOG KILLERS GOT AWAY WITH ONLY HALF A DOZEN SHOTGUNS, A BUNCH OF AUTO MATIC WEAPONS, A FEW REVOLVERS, TEAR GAS, AND ABOUT A MILLION ROUNDS OF AMMO--
"--THAT'S *ALL!*"
CAUTION: Electrified Fence
L-LOOK, I'M GRATEFUL TO YOU FOR SAVING MY LIFE, BUT YOU'VE GOT TO ANSWER SOME QUESTIONS FOR ME.

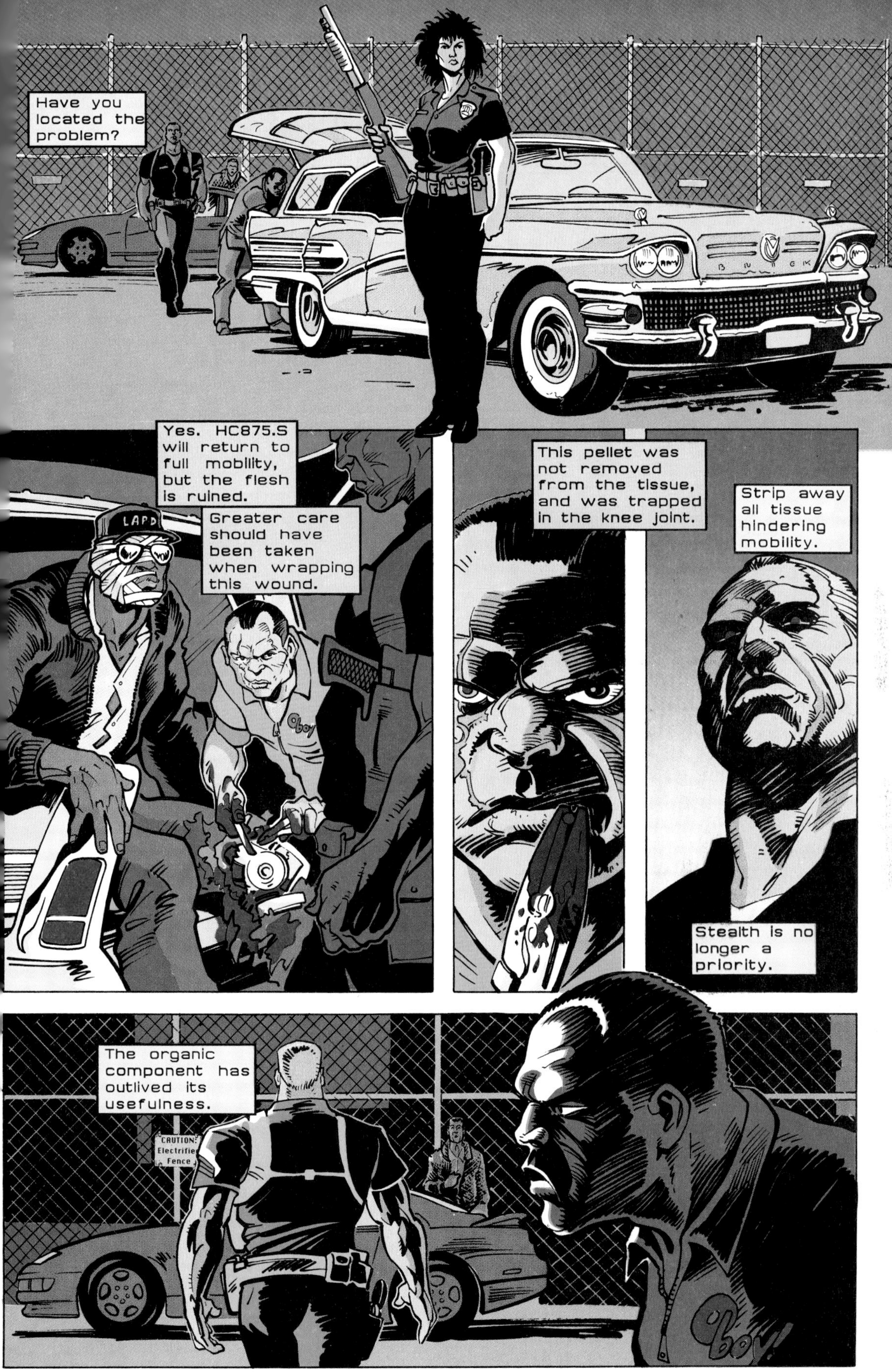
Have you located the problem?
Yes. HC875.S will return to full mobility, but the flesh is ruined.
Greater care should have been taken when wrapping this wound.
LAPD
This pellet was not removed from the tissue, and was trapped in the knee joint.
Strip away all tissue hindering mobility.
Stealth is no longer a priority.
The organic component has outlived its usefulness.
CAUTION
Electrifie
Fence

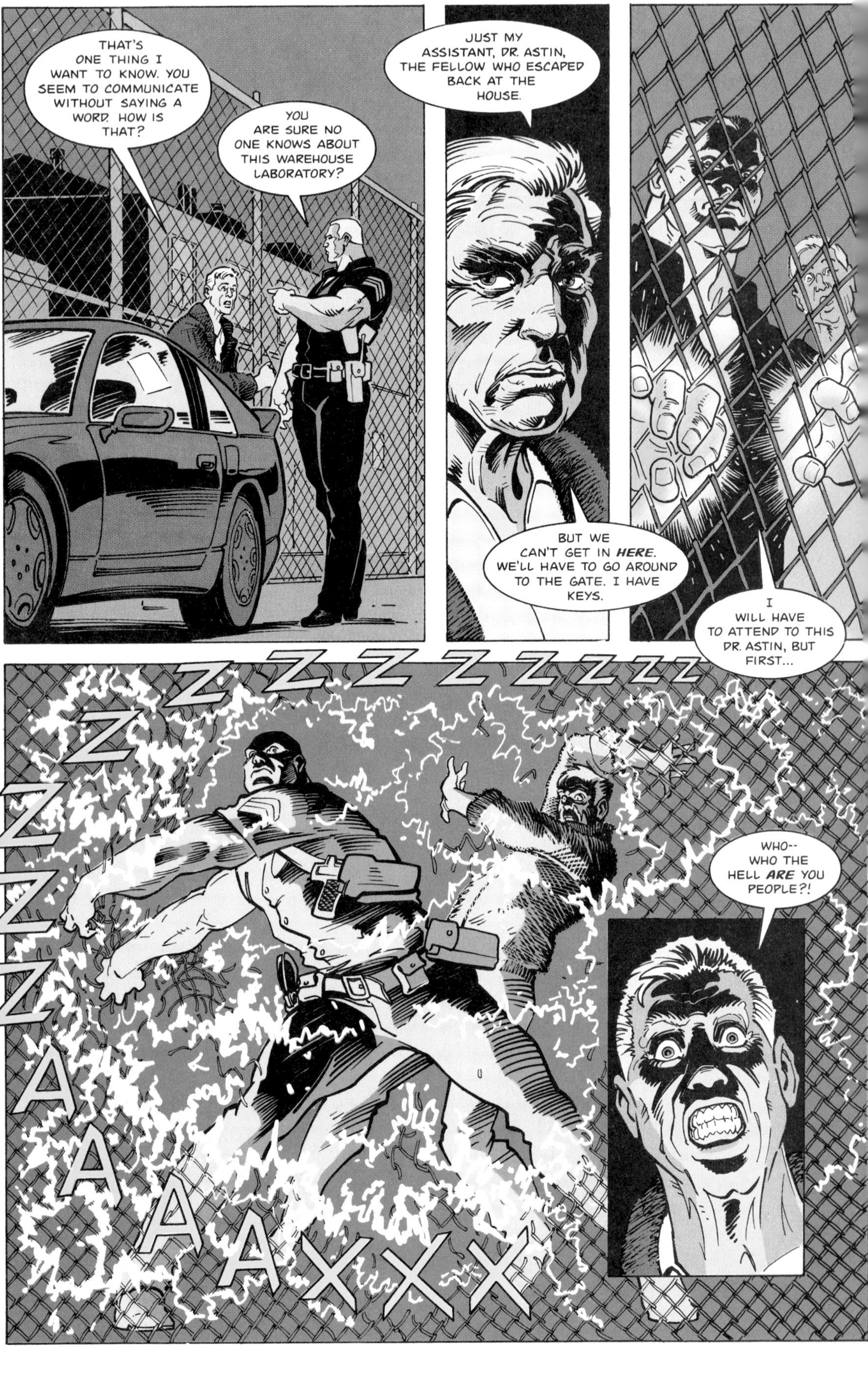
THAT'S ONE THING I WANT TO KNOW. YOU SEEM TO COMMUNICATE WITHOUT SAYING A WORD. HOW IS THAT?
YOU ARE SURE NO ONE KNOWS ABOUT THIS WAREHOUSE LABORATORY?
JUST MY ASSISTANT, DR. ASTIN, THE FELLOW WHO ESCAPED BACK AT THE HOUSE.
BUT WE CAN'T GET IN HERE. WE'LL HAVE TO GO AROUND TO THE GATE. I HAVE KEYS.
I WILL HAVE TO ATTEND TO THIS DR. ASTIN, BUT FIRST...
ZZZZZZZZZZZZZ
AAAAAXXX
WHO-- WHO THE HELL ARE YOU PEOPLE?!

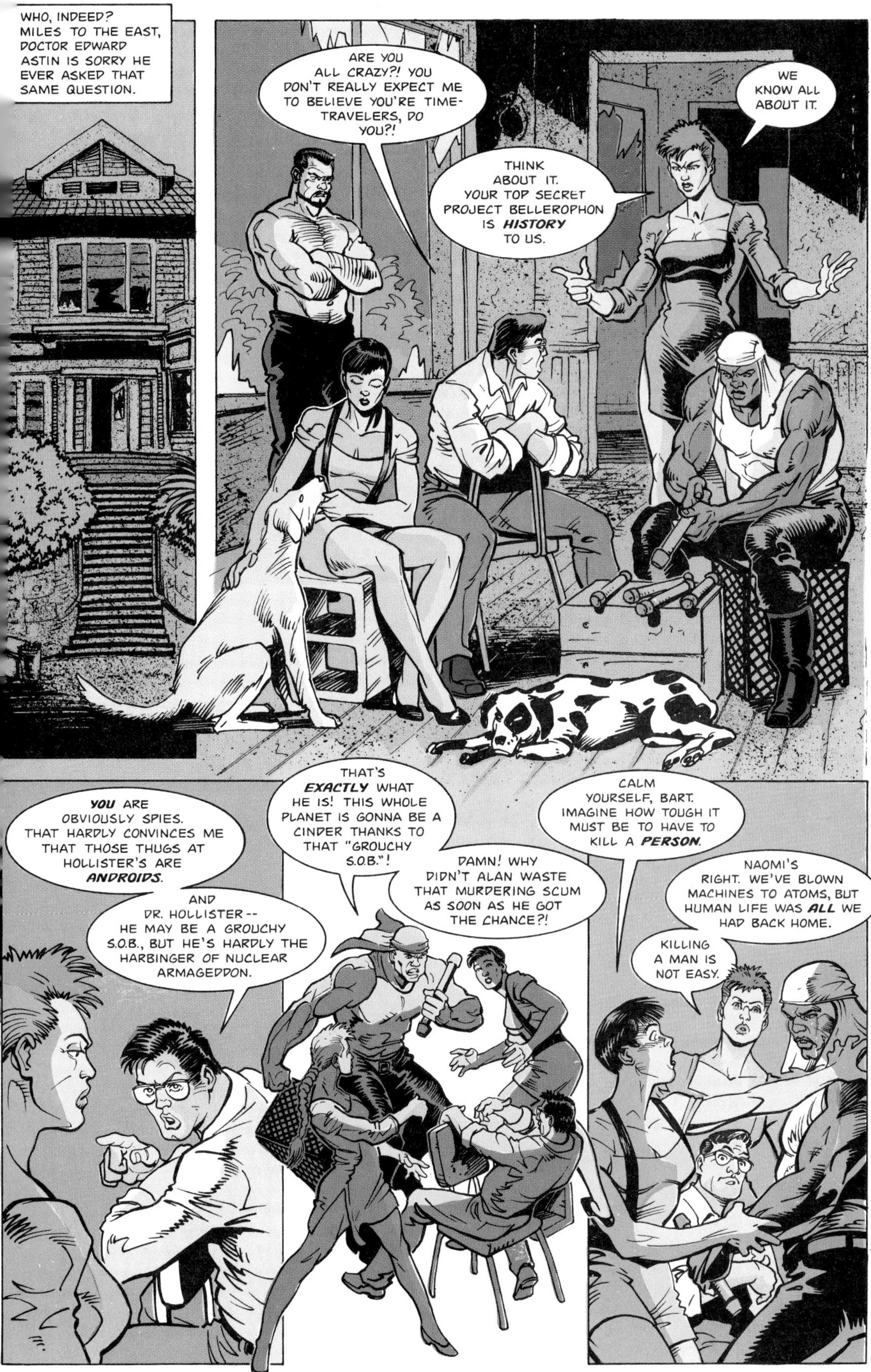
WHO, INDEED? MILES TO THE EAST, DOCTOR EDWARD ASTIN IS SORRY HE EVER ASKED THAT SAME QUESTION.
ARE YOU ALL CRAZY?! YOU DON'T REALLY EXPECT ME TO BELIEVE YOU'RE TIME-TRAVELERS, DO YOU?!
WE KNOW ALL ABOUT IT.
THINK ABOUT IT. YOUR TOP SECRET PROJECT BELLEROPHON IS ***HISTORY*** TO US.
YOU ARE OBVIOUSLY SPIES. THAT HARDLY CONVINCES ME THAT THOSE THUGS AT HOLLISTER'S ARE ***ANDROIDS***.
AND DR. HOLLISTER-- HE MAY BE A GROUCHY S.O.B., BUT HE'S HARDLY THE HARBINGER OF NUCLEAR ARMAGEDDON.
THAT'S ***EXACTLY*** WHAT HE IS! THIS WHOLE PLANET IS GONNA BE A CINDER THANKS TO THAT "GROUCHY S.O.B."!
DAMN! WHY DIDN'T ALAN WASTE THAT MURDERING SCUM AS SOON AS HE GOT THE CHANCE?!
CALM YOURSELF, BART. IMAGINE HOW TOUGH IT MUST BE TO HAVE TO KILL A ***PERSON***.
NAOMI'S RIGHT. WE'VE BLOWN MACHINES TO ATOMS, BUT HUMAN LIFE WAS ***ALL*** WE HAD BACK HOME.
KILLING A MAN IS NOT EASY.

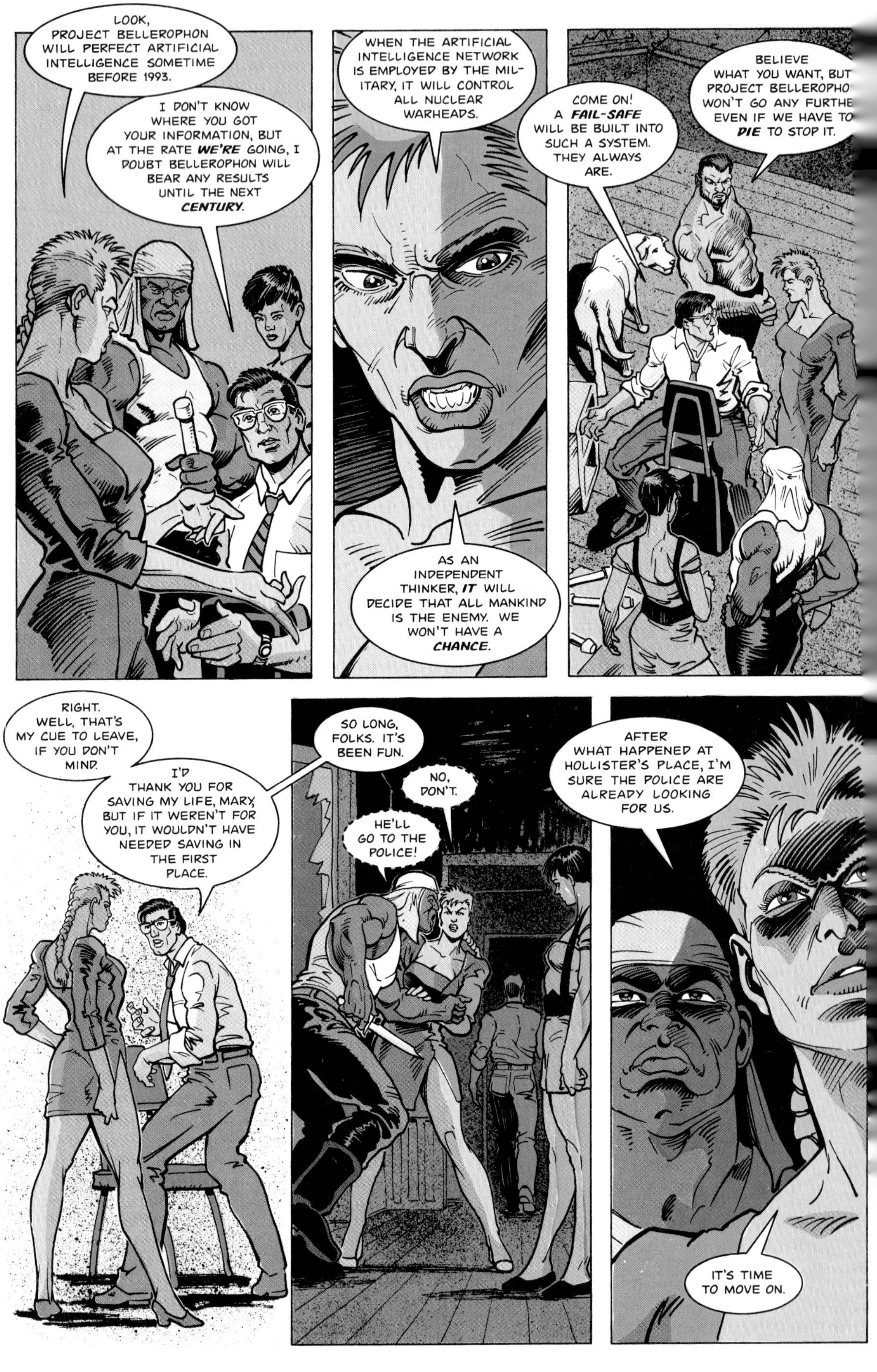
LOOK, PROJECT BELLEROPHON WILL PERFECT ARTIFICIAL INTELLIGENCE SOMETIME BEFORE 1993.
I DON'T KNOW WHERE YOU GOT YOUR INFORMATION, BUT AT THE RATE *WE'RE* GOING, I DOUBT BELLEROPHON WILL BEAR ANY RESULTS UNTIL THE NEXT *CENTURY*.
WHEN THE ARTIFICIAL INTELLIGENCE NETWORK IS EMPLOYED BY THE MIL-ITARY, IT WILL CONTROL ALL NUCLEAR WARHEADS.
AS AN INDEPENDENT THINKER, *IT* WILL DECIDE THAT ALL MANKIND IS THE ENEMY. WE WON'T HAVE A *CHANCE*.
COME ON! A *FAIL-SAFE* WILL BE BUILT INTO SUCH A SYSTEM. THEY ALWAYS ARE.
BELIEVE WHAT YOU WANT, BUT PROJECT BELLEROPHO WON'T GO ANY FURTHE EVEN IF WE HAVE TO *DIE* TO STOP IT.
RIGHT. WELL, THAT'S MY CUE TO LEAVE, IF YOU DON'T MIND.
I'D THANK YOU FOR SAVING MY LIFE, MARY, BUT IF IT WEREN'T FOR YOU, IT WOULDN'T HAVE NEEDED SAVING IN THE FIRST PLACE.
SO LONG, FOLKS. IT'S BEEN FUN.
NO, DON'T.
HE'LL GO TO THE POLICE!
AFTER WHAT HAPPENED AT HOLLISTER'S PLACE, I'M SURE THE POLICE ARE ALREADY LOOKING FOR US.
IT'S TIME TO MOVE ON.

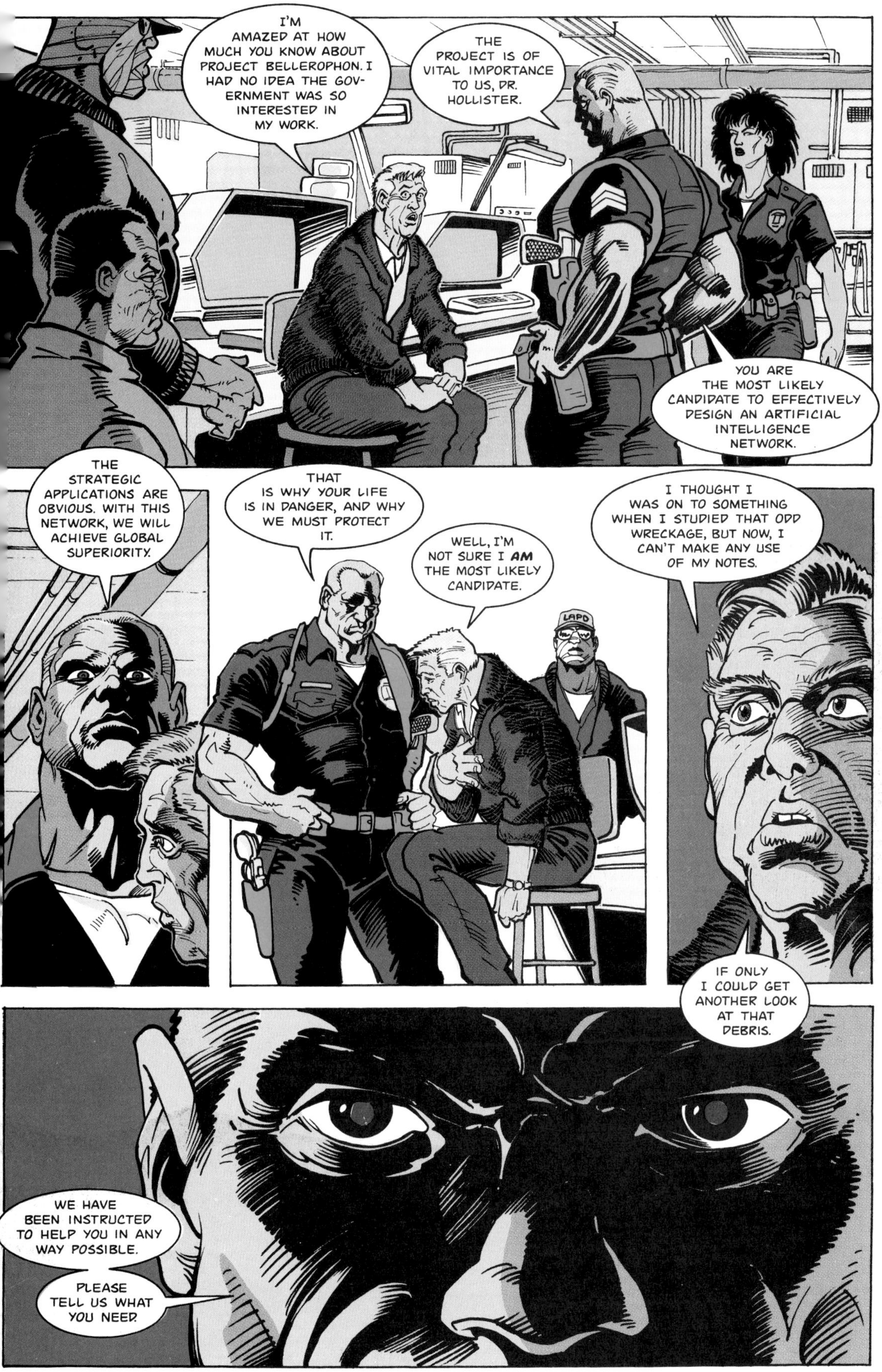
I'M AMAZED AT HOW MUCH YOU KNOW ABOUT PROJECT BELLEROPHON. I HAD NO IDEA THE GOVERNMENT WAS SO INTERESTED IN MY WORK.
THE PROJECT IS OF VITAL IMPORTANCE TO US, DR. HOLLISTER.
YOU ARE THE MOST LIKELY CANDIDATE TO EFFECTIVELY DESIGN AN ARTIFICIAL INTELLIGENCE NETWORK.
THE STRATEGIC APPLICATIONS ARE OBVIOUS. WITH THIS NETWORK, WE WILL ACHIEVE GLOBAL SUPERIORITY.
THAT IS WHY YOUR LIFE IS IN DANGER, AND WHY WE MUST PROTECT IT.
WELL, I'M NOT SURE I **AM** THE MOST LIKELY CANDIDATE.
LAPD
I THOUGHT I WAS ON TO SOMETHING WHEN I STUDIED THAT ODD WRECKAGE, BUT NOW, I CAN'T MAKE ANY USE OF MY NOTES.
IF ONLY I COULD GET ANOTHER LOOK AT THAT DEBRIS.
WE HAVE BEEN INSTRUCTED TO HELP YOU IN ANY WAY POSSIBLE.
PLEASE TELL US WHAT YOU NEED.

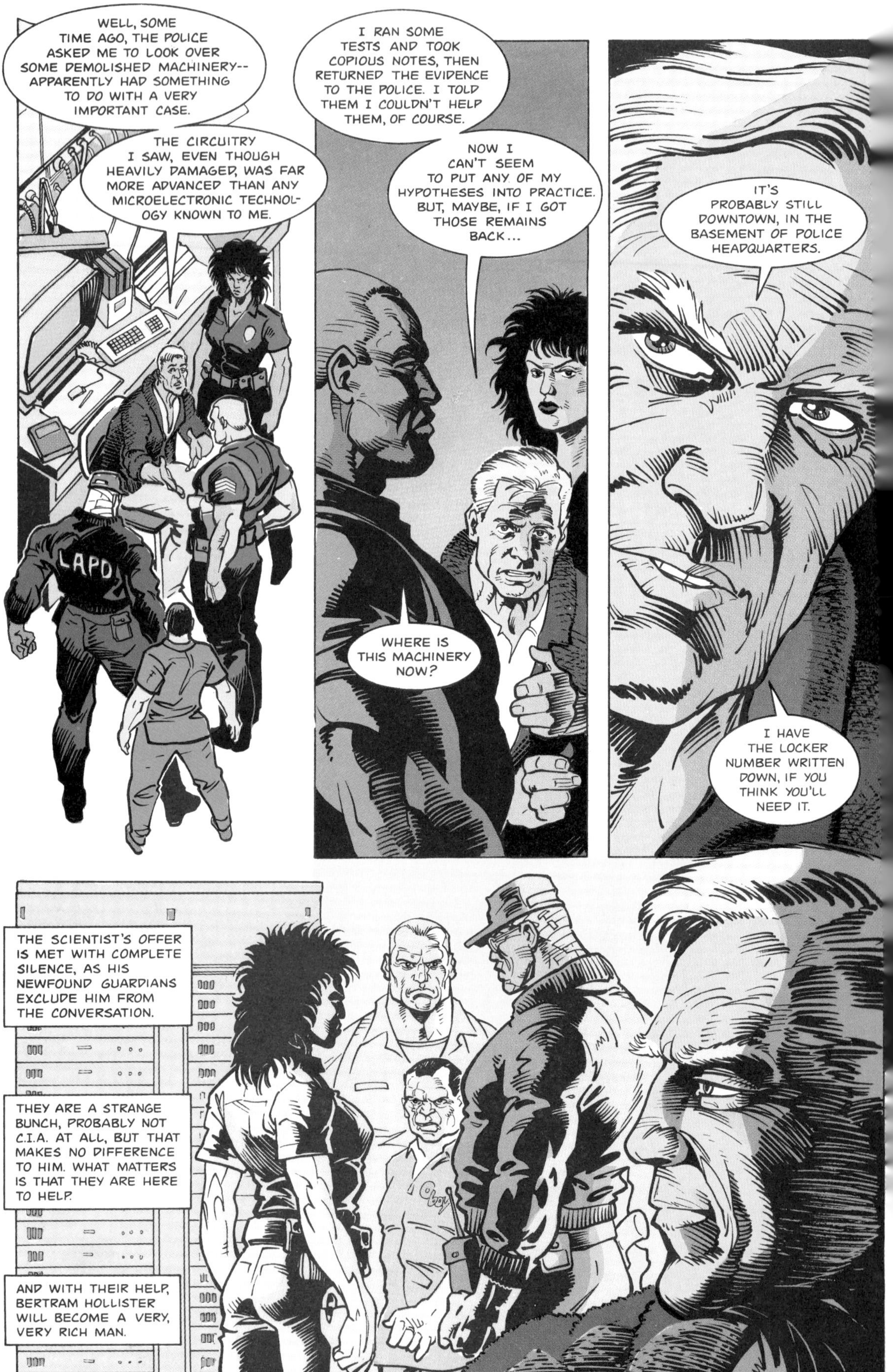
WELL, SOME TIME AGO, THE POLICE ASKED ME TO LOOK OVER SOME DEMOLISHED MACHINERY-- APPARENTLY HAD SOMETHING TO DO WITH A VERY IMPORTANT CASE.
THE CIRCUITRY I SAW, EVEN THOUGH HEAVILY DAMAGED, WAS FAR MORE ADVANCED THAN ANY MICROELECTRONIC TECHNOLOGY KNOWN TO ME.
LAPD
I RAN SOME TESTS AND TOOK COPIOUS NOTES, THEN RETURNED THE EVIDENCE TO THE POLICE. I TOLD THEM I COULDN'T HELP THEM, OF COURSE.
NOW I CAN'T SEEM TO PUT ANY OF MY HYPOTHESES INTO PRACTICE. BUT, MAYBE, IF I GOT THOSE REMAINS BACK...
WHERE IS THIS MACHINERY NOW?
IT'S PROBABLY STILL DOWNTOWN, IN THE BASEMENT OF POLICE HEADQUARTERS.
I HAVE THE LOCKER NUMBER WRITTEN DOWN, IF YOU THINK YOU'LL NEED IT.
THE SCIENTIST'S OFFER IS MET WITH COMPLETE SILENCE, AS HIS NEWFOUND GUARDIANS EXCLUDE HIM FROM THE CONVERSATION.
THEY ARE A STRANGE BUNCH, PROBABLY NOT C.I.A. AT ALL, BUT THAT MAKES NO DIFFERENCE TO HIM. WHAT MATTERS IS THAT THEY ARE HERE TO HELP.
AND WITH THEIR HELP, BERTRAM HOLLISTER WILL BECOME A VERY, VERY RICH MAN.

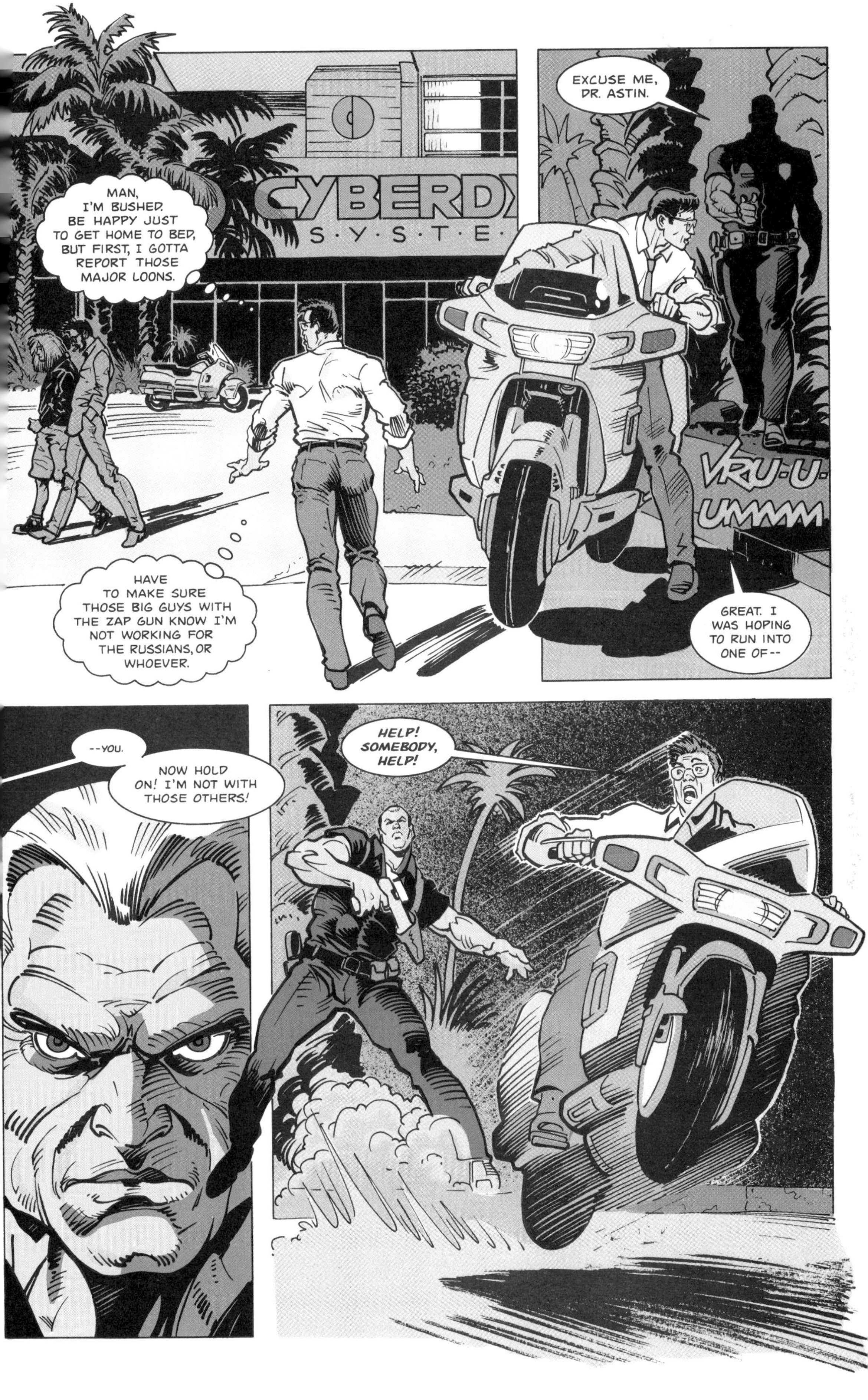
MAN, I'M BUSHED. BE HAPPY JUST TO GET HOME TO BED, BUT FIRST, I GOTTA REPORT THOSE MAJOR LOONS.
HAVE TO MAKE SURE THOSE BIG GUYS WITH THE ZAP GUN KNOW I'M NOT WORKING FOR THE RUSSIANS, OR WHOEVER.
EXCUSE ME, DR. ASTIN.
VRU-U-UMMM
GREAT. I WAS HOPING TO RUN INTO ONE OF--
--YOU.
NOW HOLD ON! I'M NOT WITH THOSE OTHERS!
HELP! SOMEBODY, HELP!

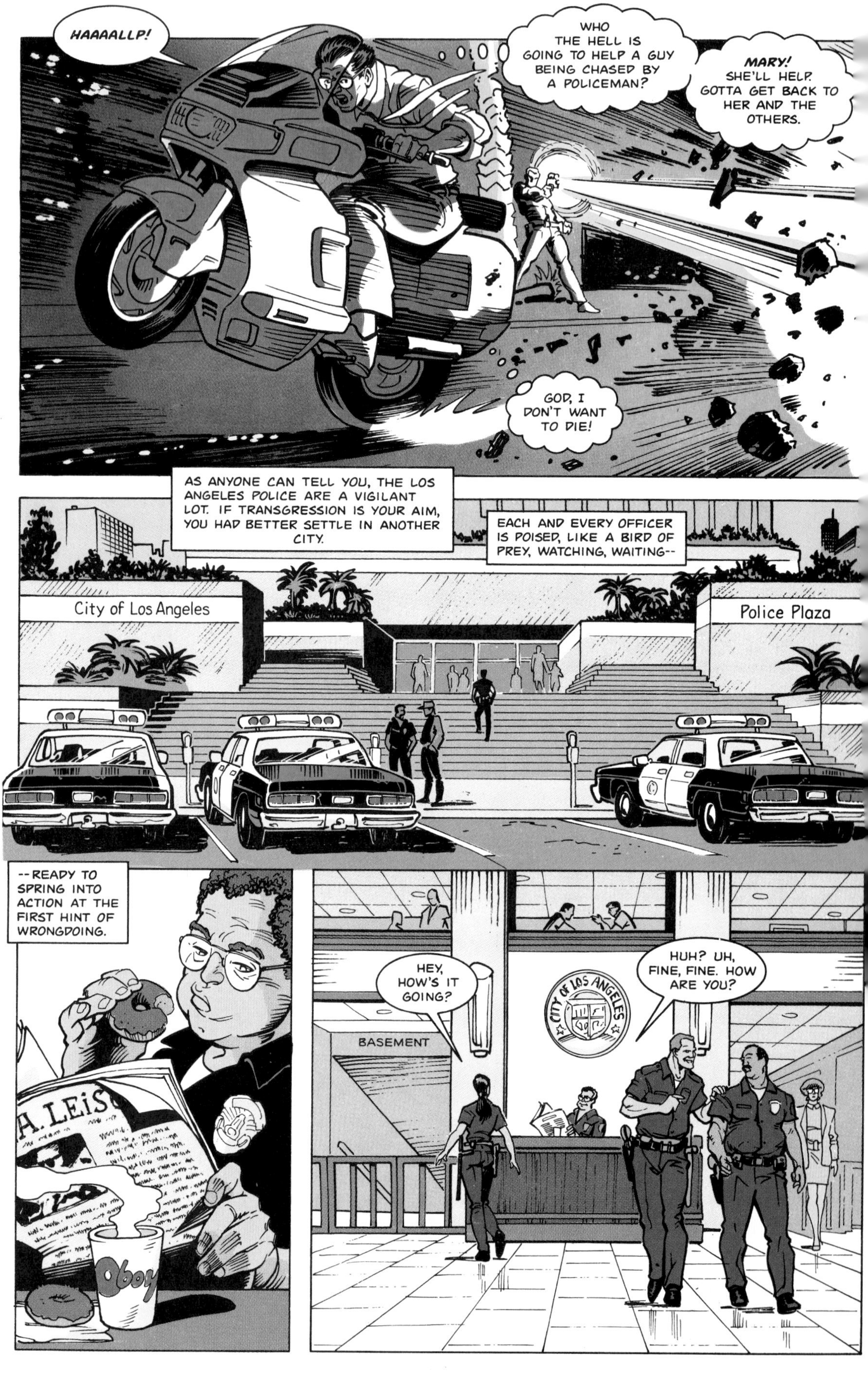

HAAAAALLP!
WHO THE HELL IS GOING TO HELP A GUY BEING CHASED BY A POLICEMAN?
MARY! SHE'LL HELP. GOTTA GET BACK TO HER AND THE OTHERS.
GOD, I DON'T WANT TO DIE!
AS ANYONE CAN TELL YOU, THE LOS ANGELES POLICE ARE A VIGILANT LOT. IF TRANSGRESSION IS YOUR AIM, YOU HAD BETTER SETTLE IN ANOTHER CITY.
EACH AND EVERY OFFICER IS POISED, LIKE A BIRD OF PREY, WATCHING, WAITING--
City of Los Angeles
Police Plaza
--READY TO SPRING INTO ACTION AT THE FIRST HINT OF WRONGDOING.
HEY, HOW'S IT GOING?
BASEMENT
CITY OF LOS ANGELES
HUH? UH, FINE, FINE. HOW ARE YOU?

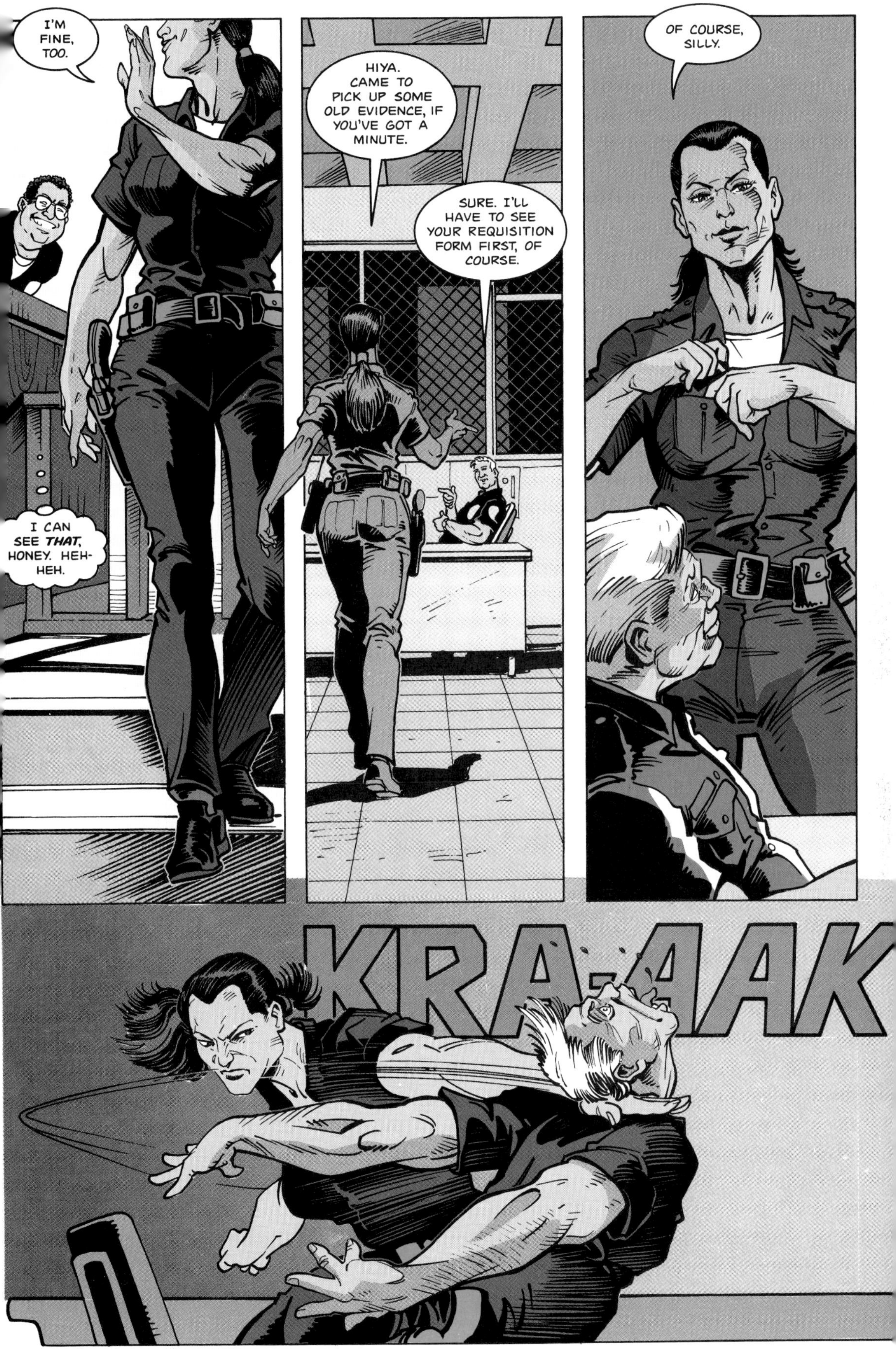
I'M FINE, TOO.
I CAN SEE THAT, HONEY. HEH-HEH.
HIYA. CAME TO PICK UP SOME OLD EVIDENCE, IF YOU'VE GOT A MINUTE.
SURE. I'LL HAVE TO SEE YOUR REQUISITION FORM FIRST, OF COURSE.
OF COURSE, SILLY.
KRA-AAK

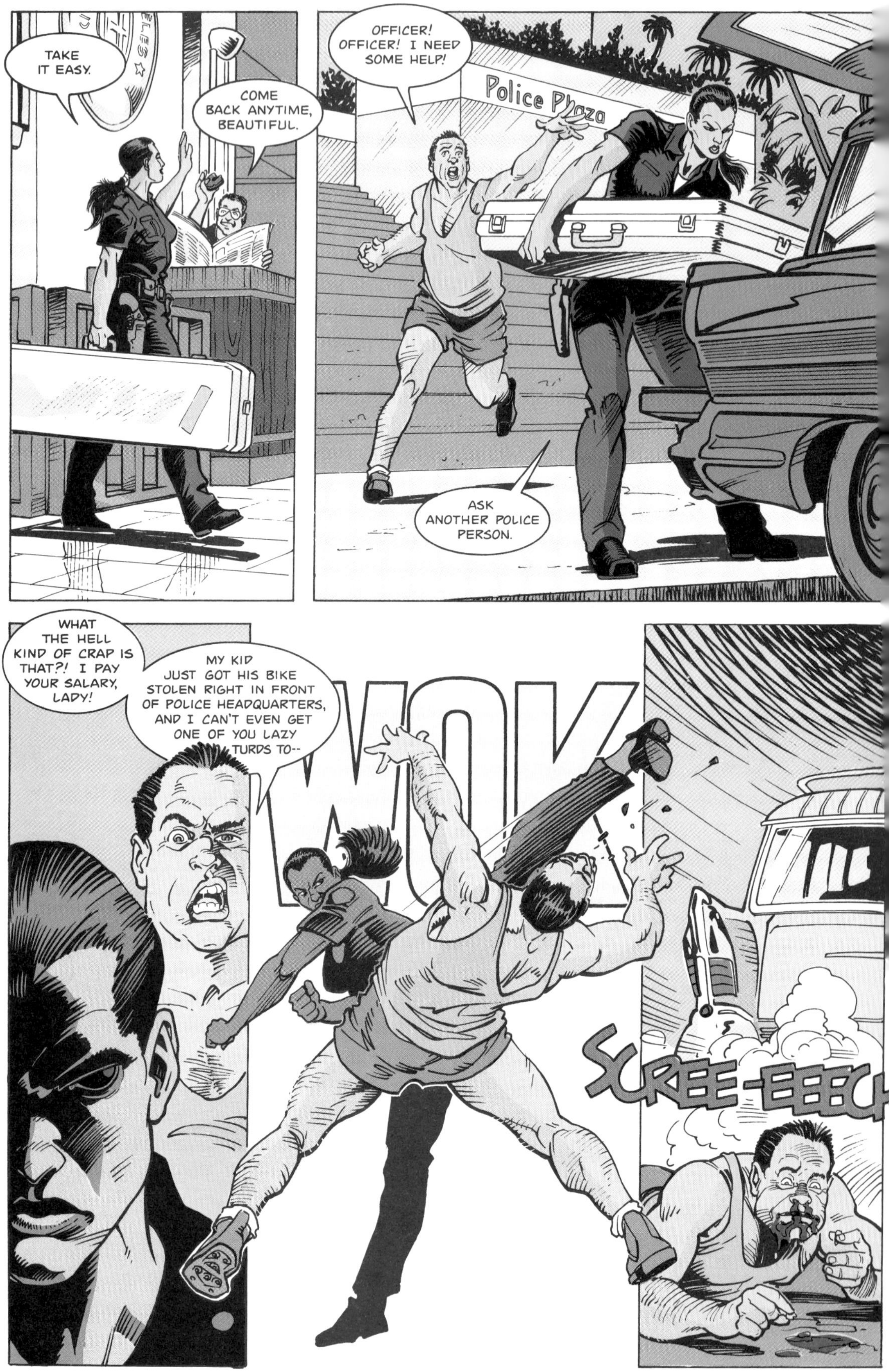
TAKE IT EASY.
COME BACK ANYTIME, BEAUTIFUL.
OFFICER! OFFICER! I NEED SOME HELP!
Police Plaza
ASK ANOTHER POLICE PERSON.
WHAT THE HELL KIND OF CRAP IS THAT?! I PAY YOUR SALARY, LADY!
MY KID JUST GOT HIS BIKE STOLEN RIGHT IN FRONT OF POLICE HEADQUARTERS, AND I CAN'T EVEN GET ONE OF YOU LAZY TURDS TO--
WOK
SCREE-EEECH

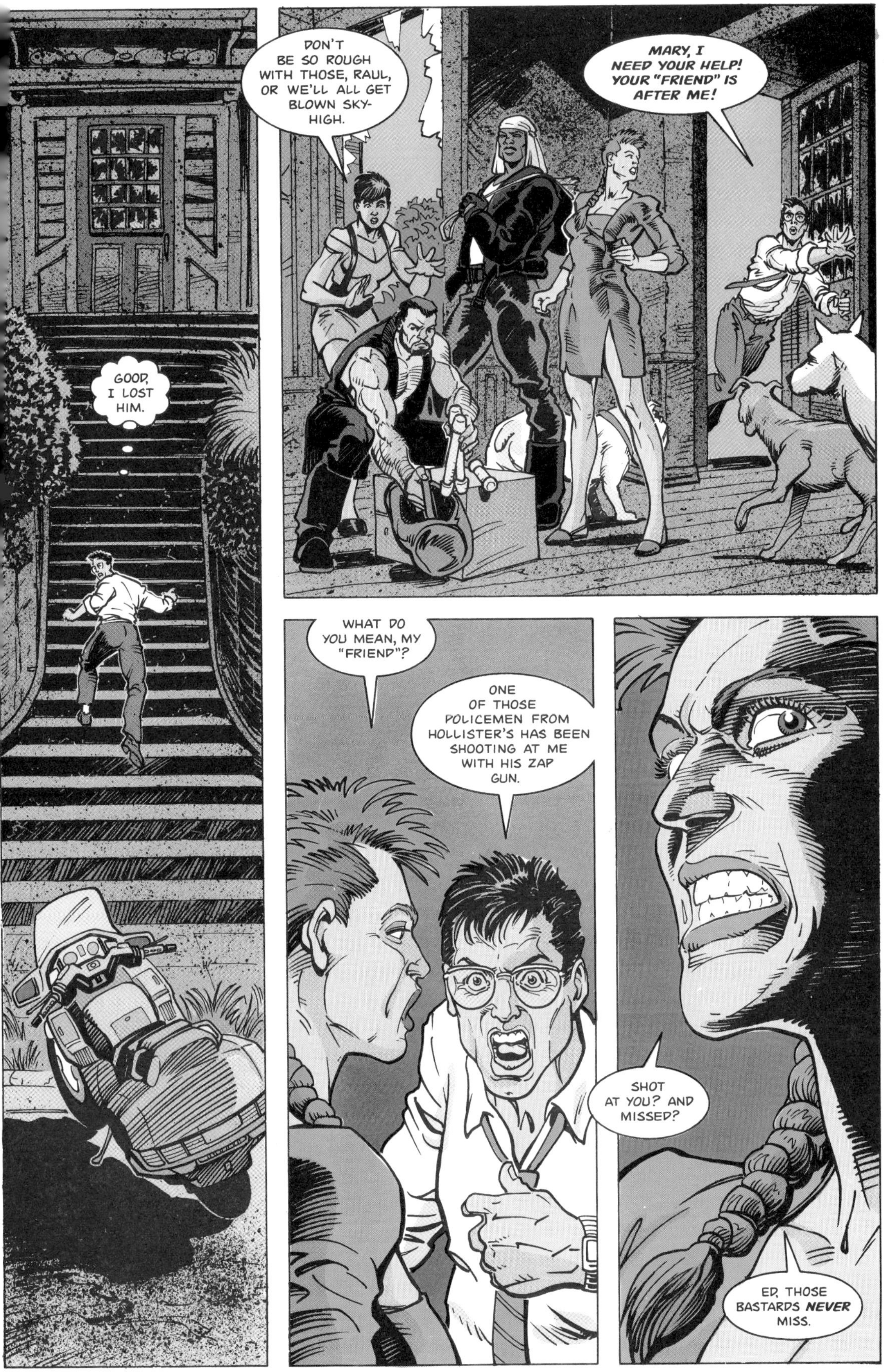
GOOD, I LOST HIM.
DON'T BE SO ROUGH WITH THOSE, RAUL, OR WE'LL ALL GET BLOWN SKY-HIGH.
MARY, I NEED YOUR HELP! YOUR "FRIEND" IS AFTER ME!
WHAT DO YOU MEAN, MY "FRIEND"?
ONE OF THOSE POLICEMEN FROM HOLLISTER'S HAS BEEN SHOOTING AT ME WITH HIS ZAP GUN.
SHOT AT YOU? AND MISSED?
ED, THOSE BASTARDS NEVER MISS.

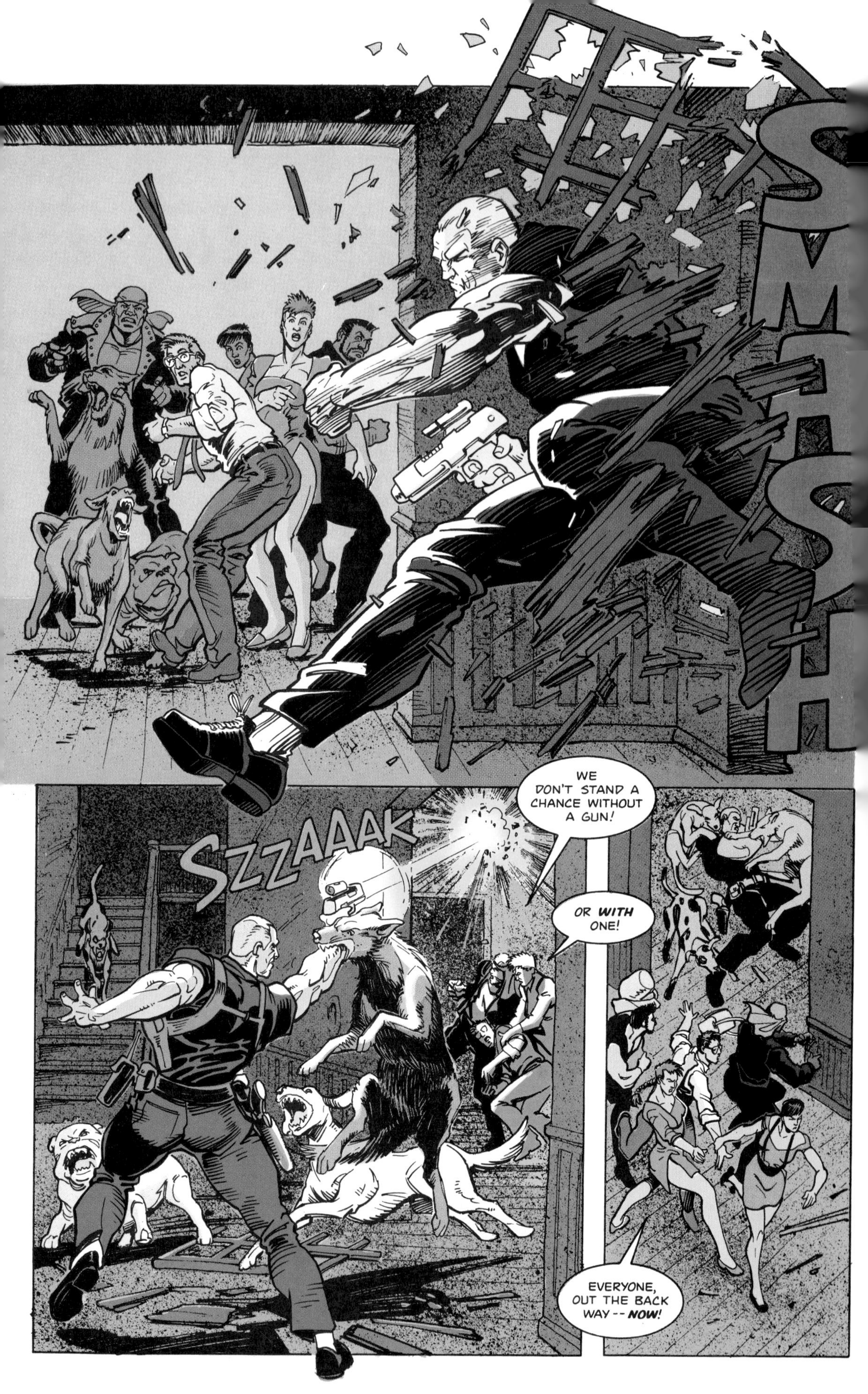
SMASH
SZZAAAK
WE DON'T STAND A CHANCE WITHOUT A GUN!
OR WITH ONE!
EVERYONE, OUT THE BACK WAY -- NOW!

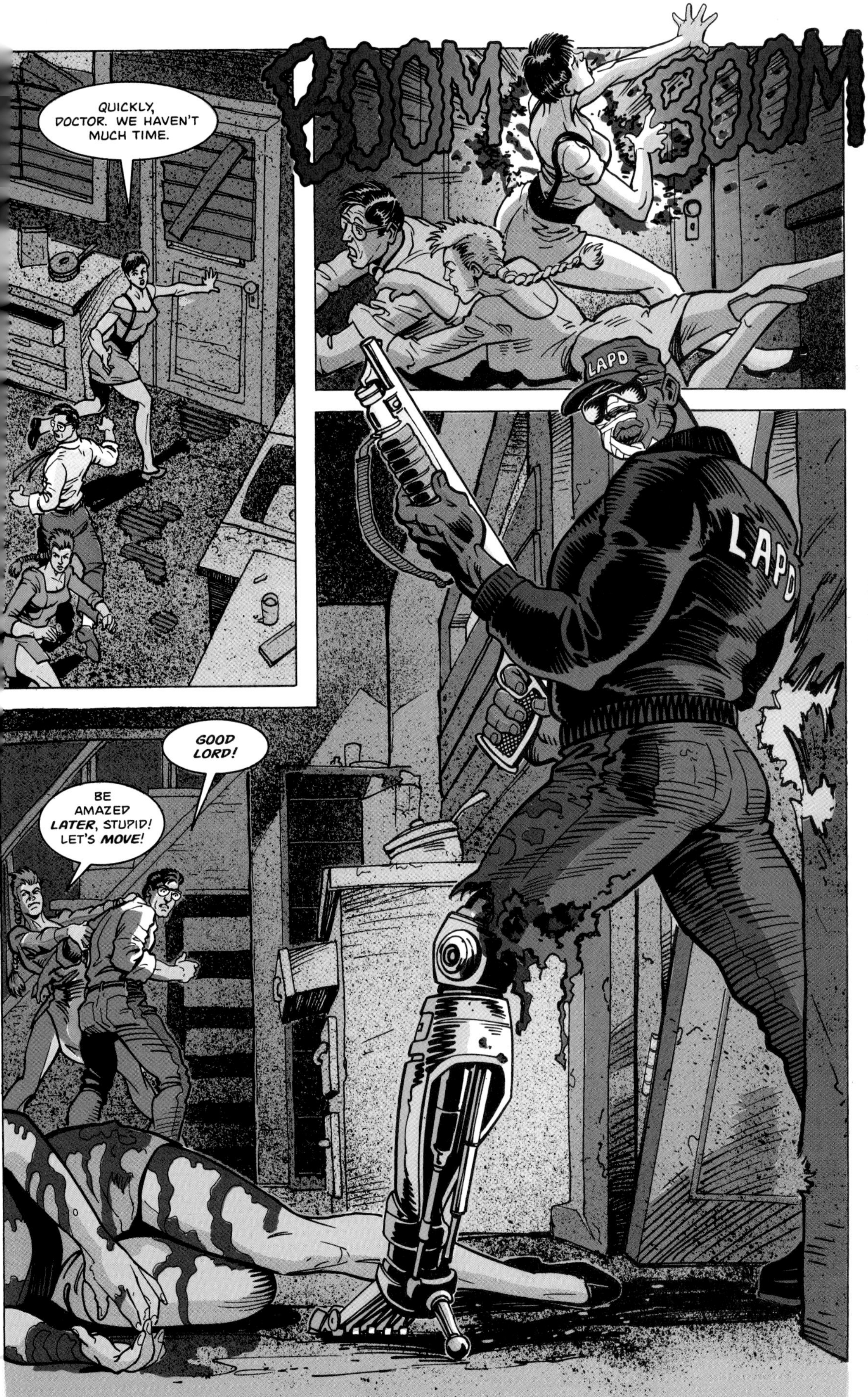
QUICKLY, DOCTOR. WE HAVEN'T MUCH TIME.
BOOM BOOM
LAPD
LAPD
GOOD LORD!
BE AMAZED *LATER*, STUPID! LET'S *MOVE*!

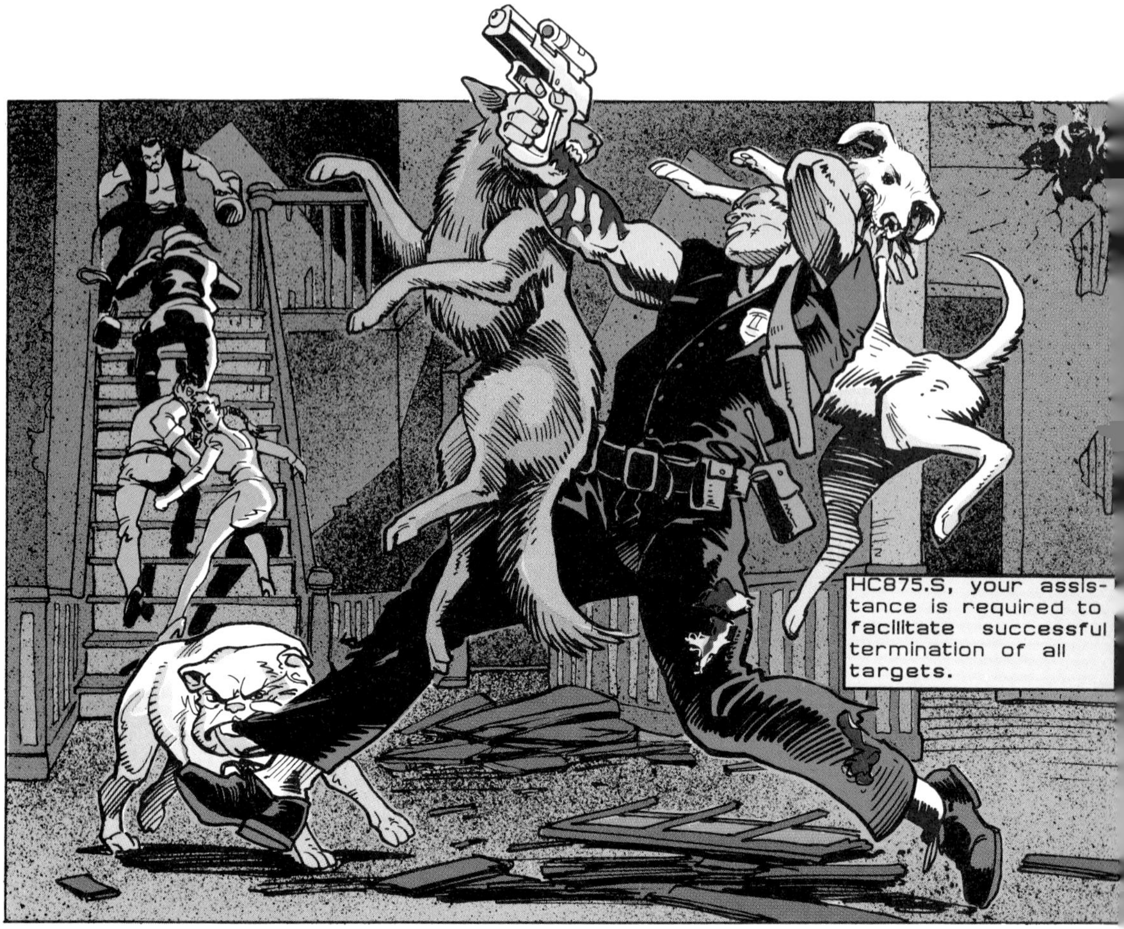
HC875.S, your assistance is required to facilitate successful termination of all targets.

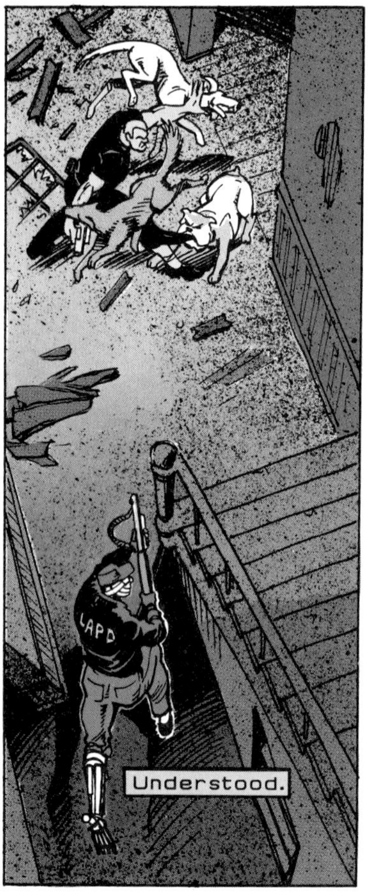
Understood.

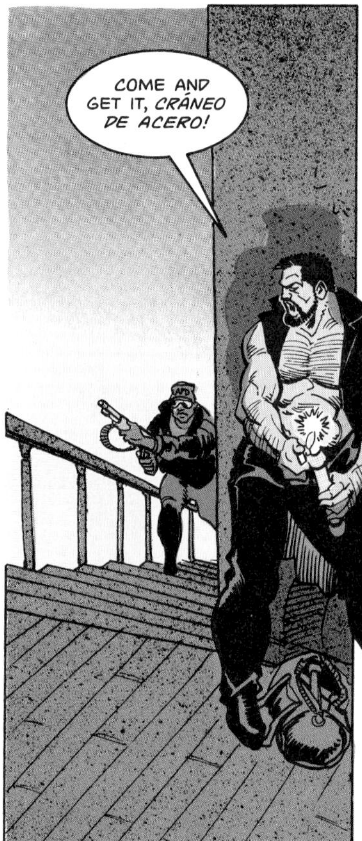
COME AND GET IT, CRÁNEO DE ACERO!

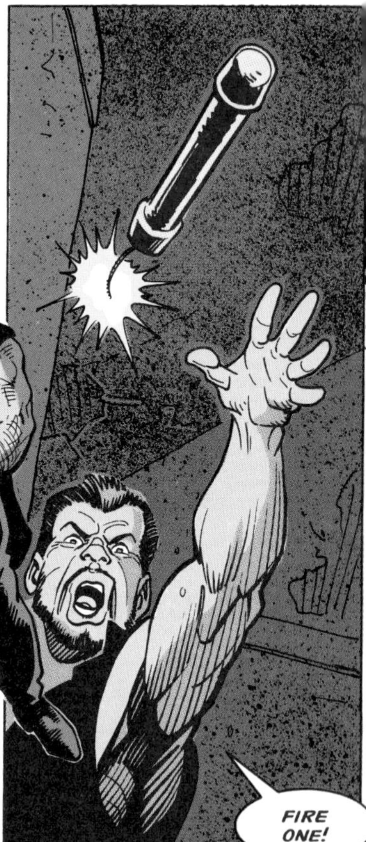
FIRE ONE!

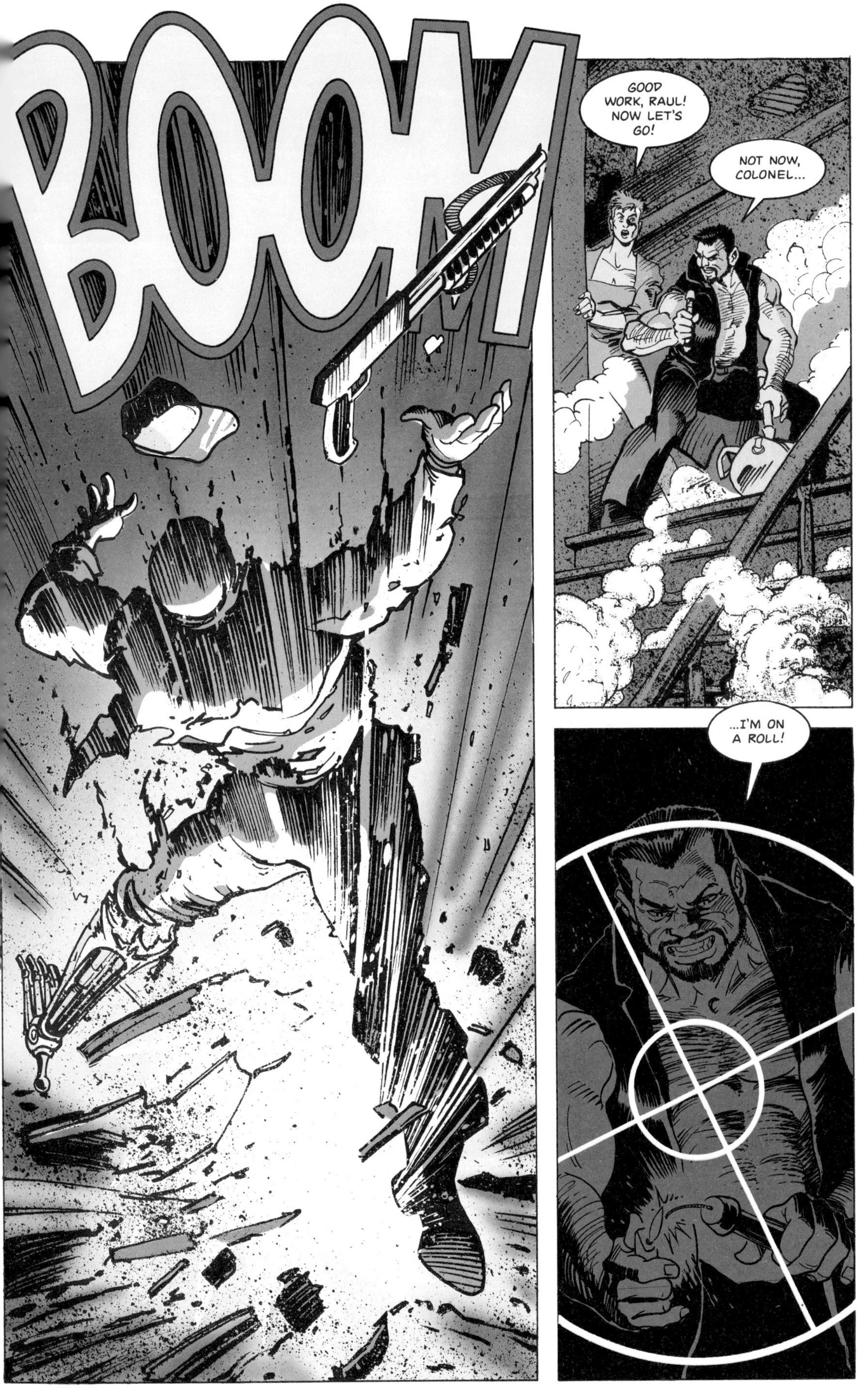
BOOM
GOOD WORK, RAUL! NOW LET'S GO!
NOT NOW, COLONEL...
...I'M ON A ROLL!

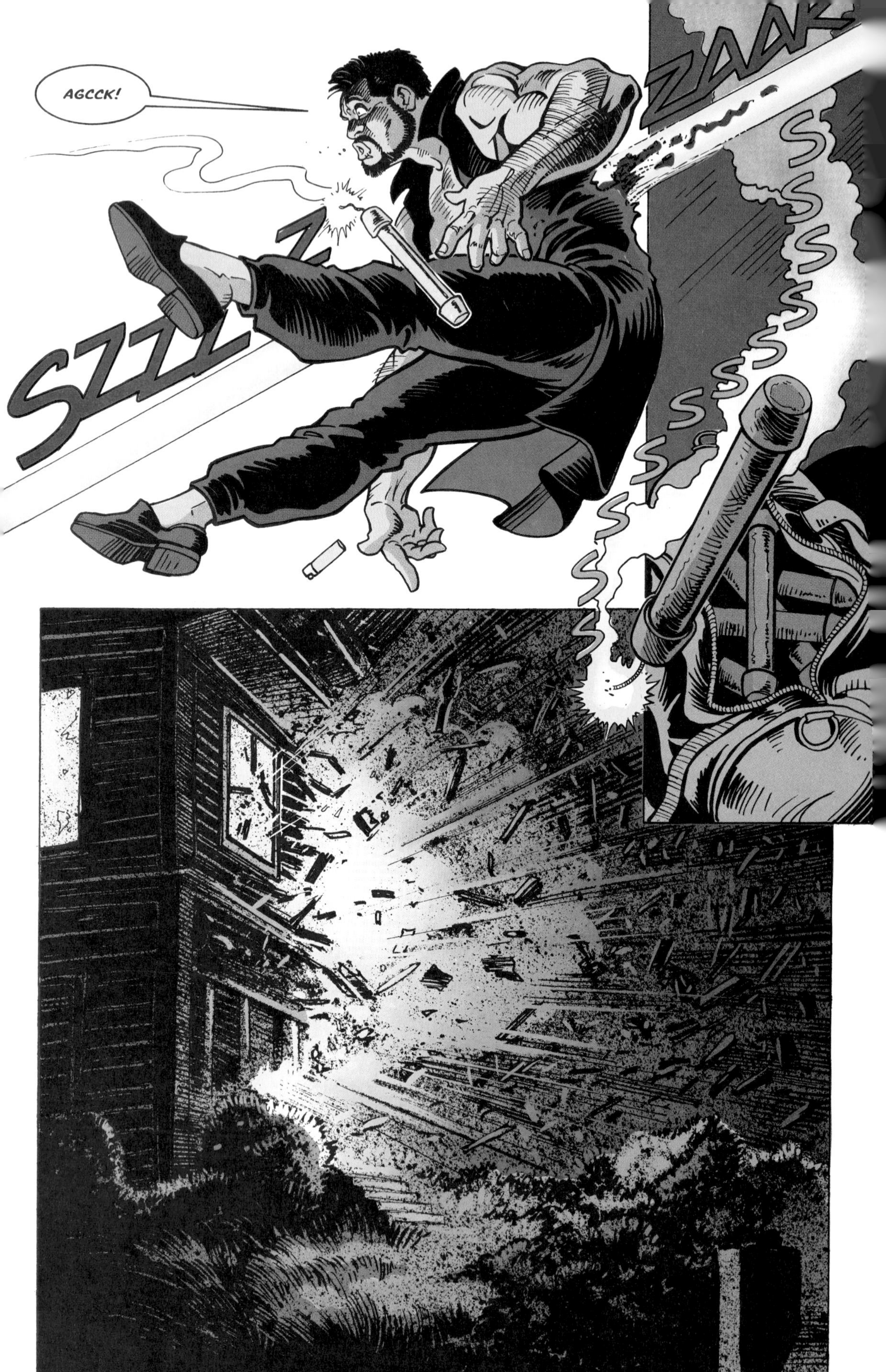
AGCCK!
SZZZZ
ZAAK

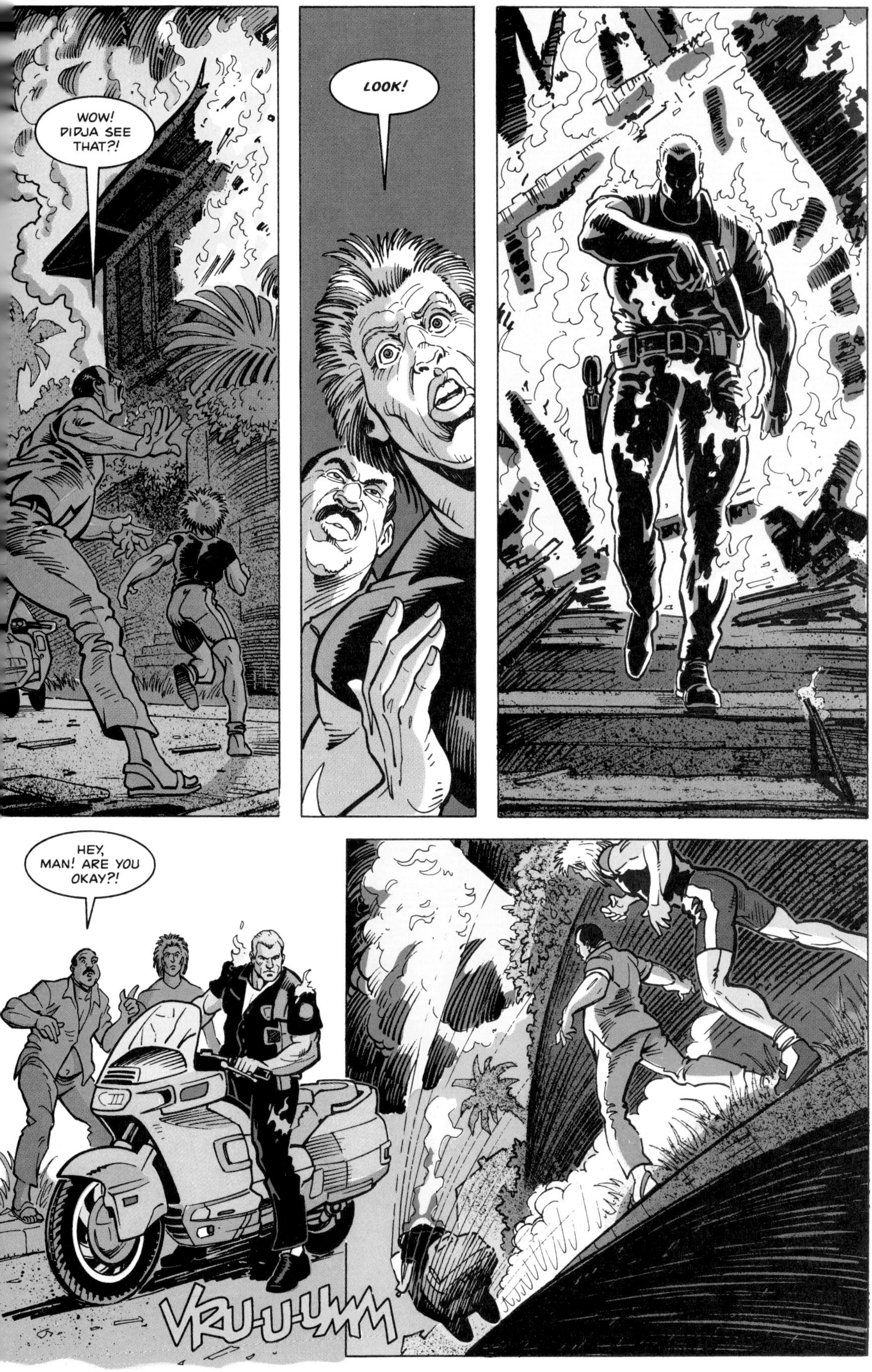
WOW! DIDJA SEE THAT?!
LOOK!
HEY, MAN! ARE YOU OKAY?!
VRU-U-UMM

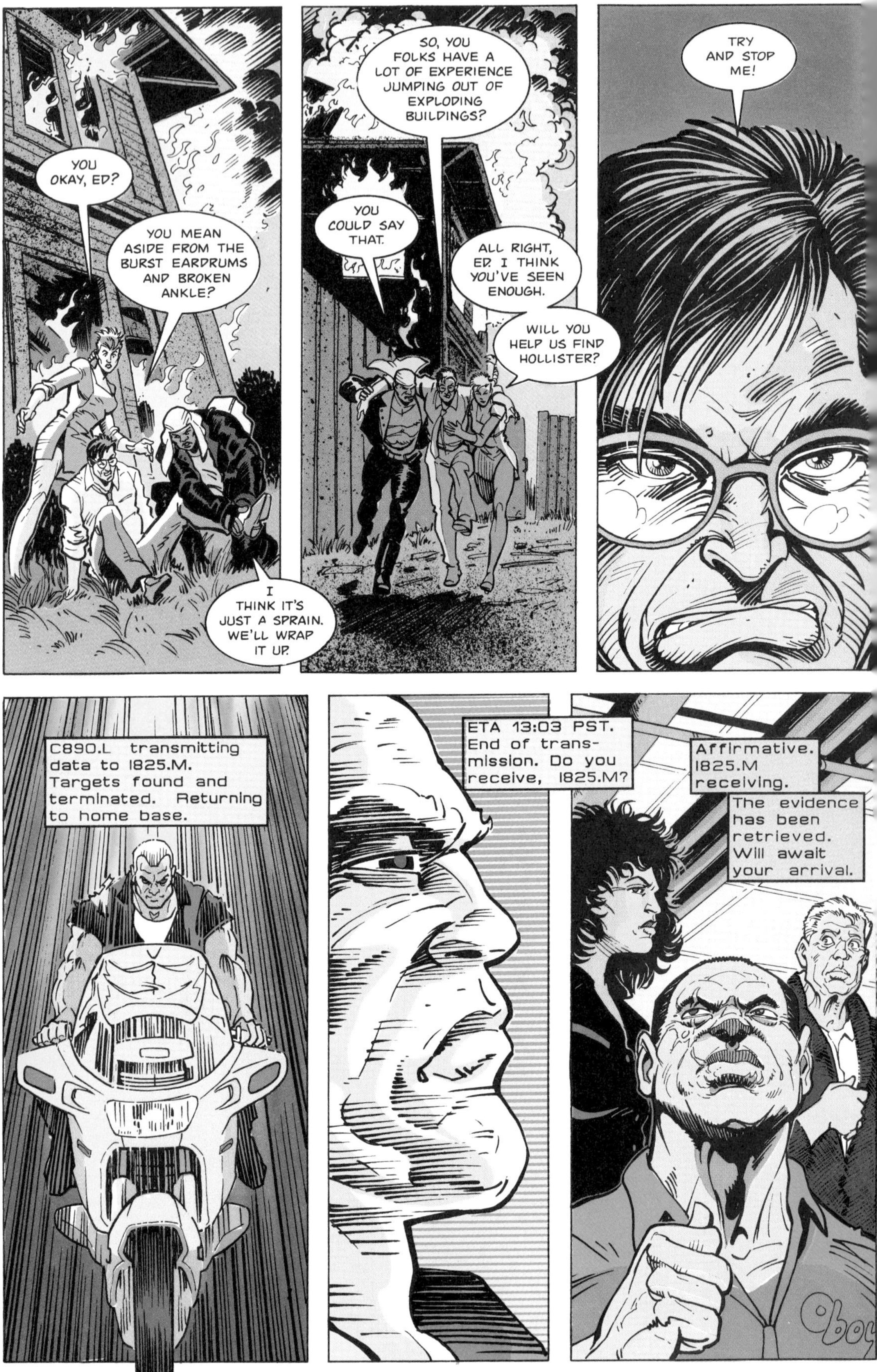
YOU OKAY, ED?
YOU MEAN ASIDE FROM THE BURST EARDRUMS AND BROKEN ANKLE?
I THINK IT'S JUST A SPRAIN. WE'LL WRAP IT UP.
SO, YOU FOLKS HAVE A LOT OF EXPERIENCE JUMPING OUT OF EXPLODING BUILDINGS?
YOU COULD SAY THAT.
ALL RIGHT, ED. I THINK YOU'VE SEEN ENOUGH.
WILL YOU HELP US FIND HOLLISTER?
TRY AND STOP ME!
C890.L transmitting data to 1825.M. Targets found and terminated. Returning to home base.
ETA 13:03 PST. End of transmission. Do you receive, 1825.M?
Affirmative. 1825.M receiving.
The evidence has been retrieved. Will await your arrival.

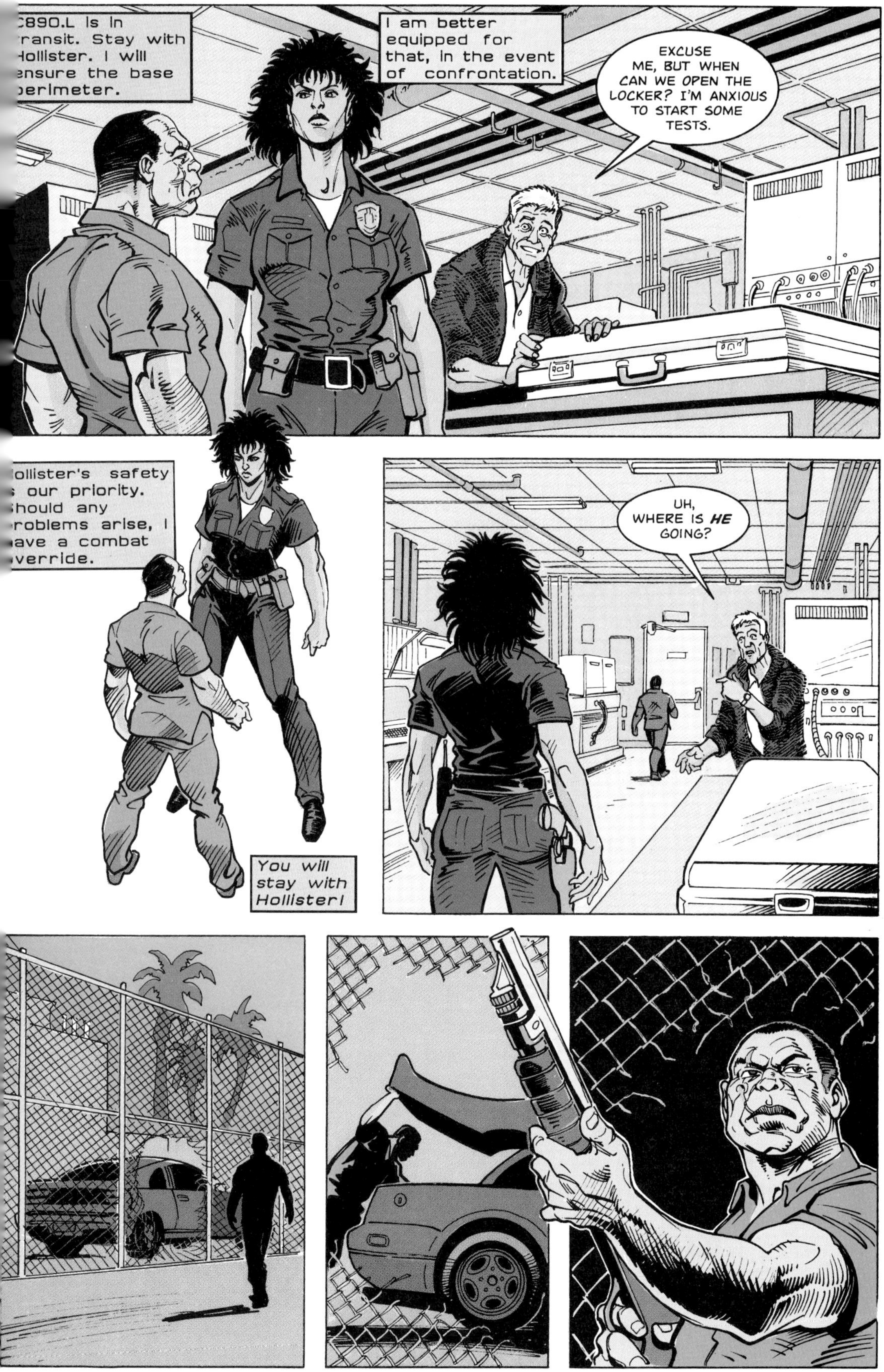
C890.L is in ransit. Stay with Iollister. I will ensure the base perimeter.
I am better equipped for that, in the event of confrontation.
EXCUSE ME, BUT WHEN CAN WE OPEN THE LOCKER? I'M ANXIOUS TO START SOME TESTS.
ollister's safety s our priority. hould any roblems arise, I ave a combat verride.
You will stay with Hollister!
UH, WHERE IS ***HE*** GOING?

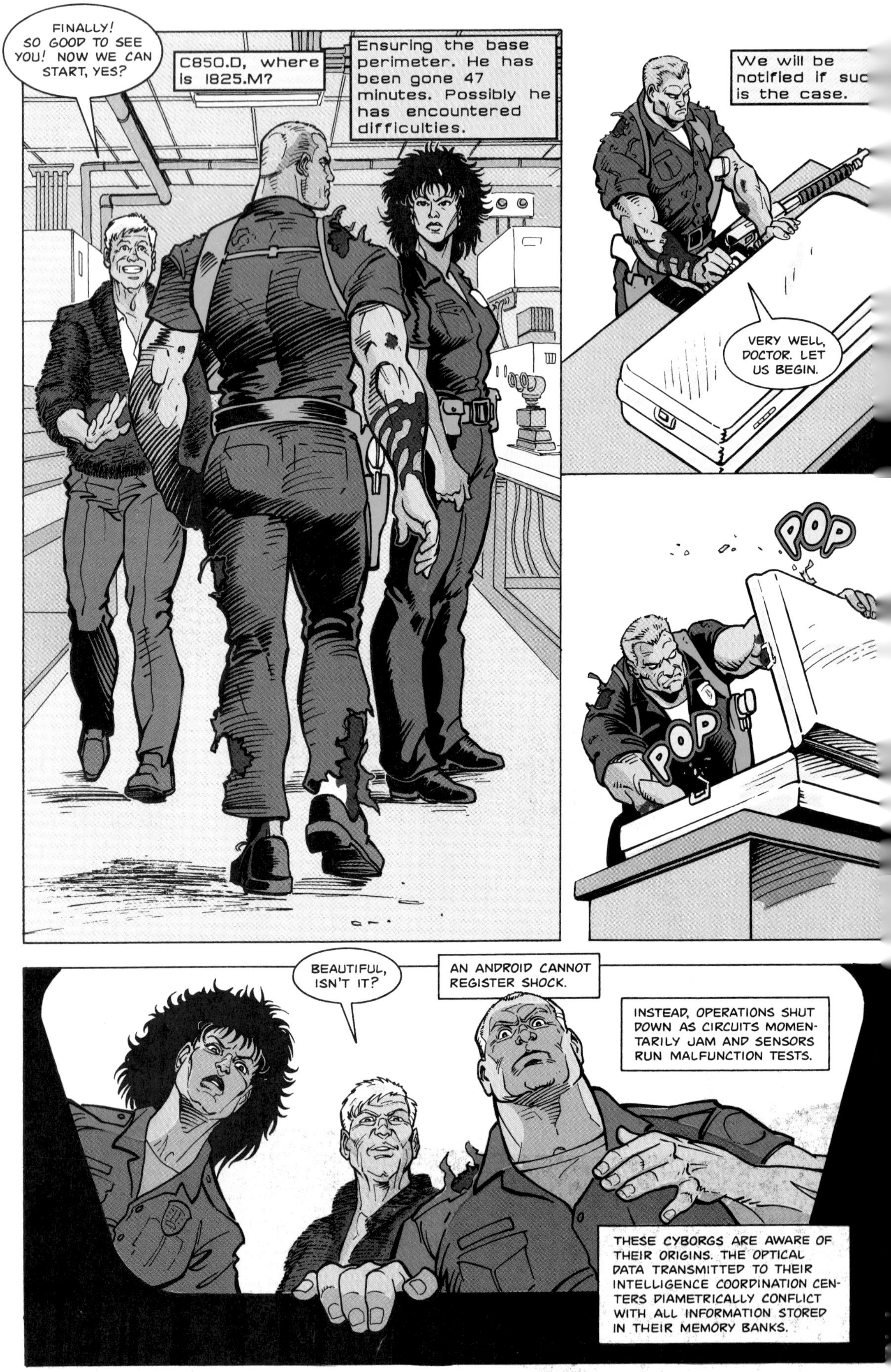
FINALLY! SO GOOD TO SEE YOU! NOW WE CAN START, YES?
C850.D, where is 1825.M?
Ensuring the base perimeter. He has been gone 47 minutes. Possibly he has encountered difficulties.
We will be notified if suc
is the case.
VERY WELL, DOCTOR. LET US BEGIN.
POP
POP
BEAUTIFUL, ISN'T IT?
AN ANDROID CANNOT REGISTER SHOCK.
INSTEAD, OPERATIONS SHUT DOWN AS CIRCUITS MOMENTARILY JAM AND SENSORS RUN MALFUNCTION TESTS.
THESE CYBORGS ARE AWARE OF THEIR ORIGINS. THE OPTICAL DATA TRANSMITTED TO THEIR INTELLIGENCE COORDINATION CENTERS DIAMETRICALLY CONFLICT WITH ALL INFORMATION STORED IN THEIR MEMORY BANKS.

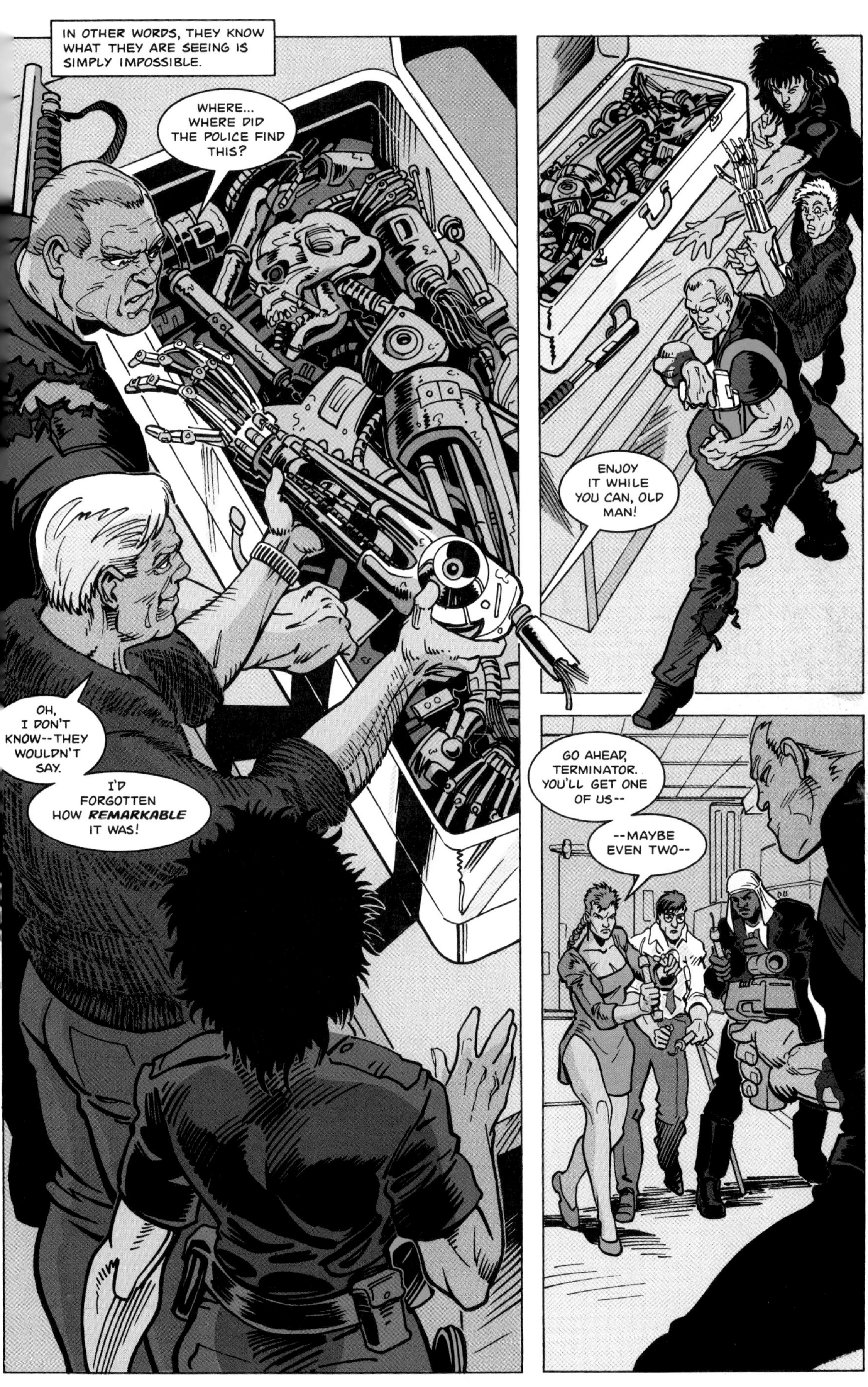
IN OTHER WORDS, THEY KNOW WHAT THEY ARE SEEING IS SIMPLY IMPOSSIBLE.
WHERE... WHERE DID THE POLICE FIND THIS?
OH, I DON'T KNOW--THEY WOULDN'T SAY.
I'D FORGOTTEN HOW **REMARKABLE** IT WAS!
ENJOY IT WHILE YOU CAN, OLD MAN!
GO AHEAD, TERMINATOR. YOU'LL GET ONE OF US--
--MAYBE EVEN TWO--

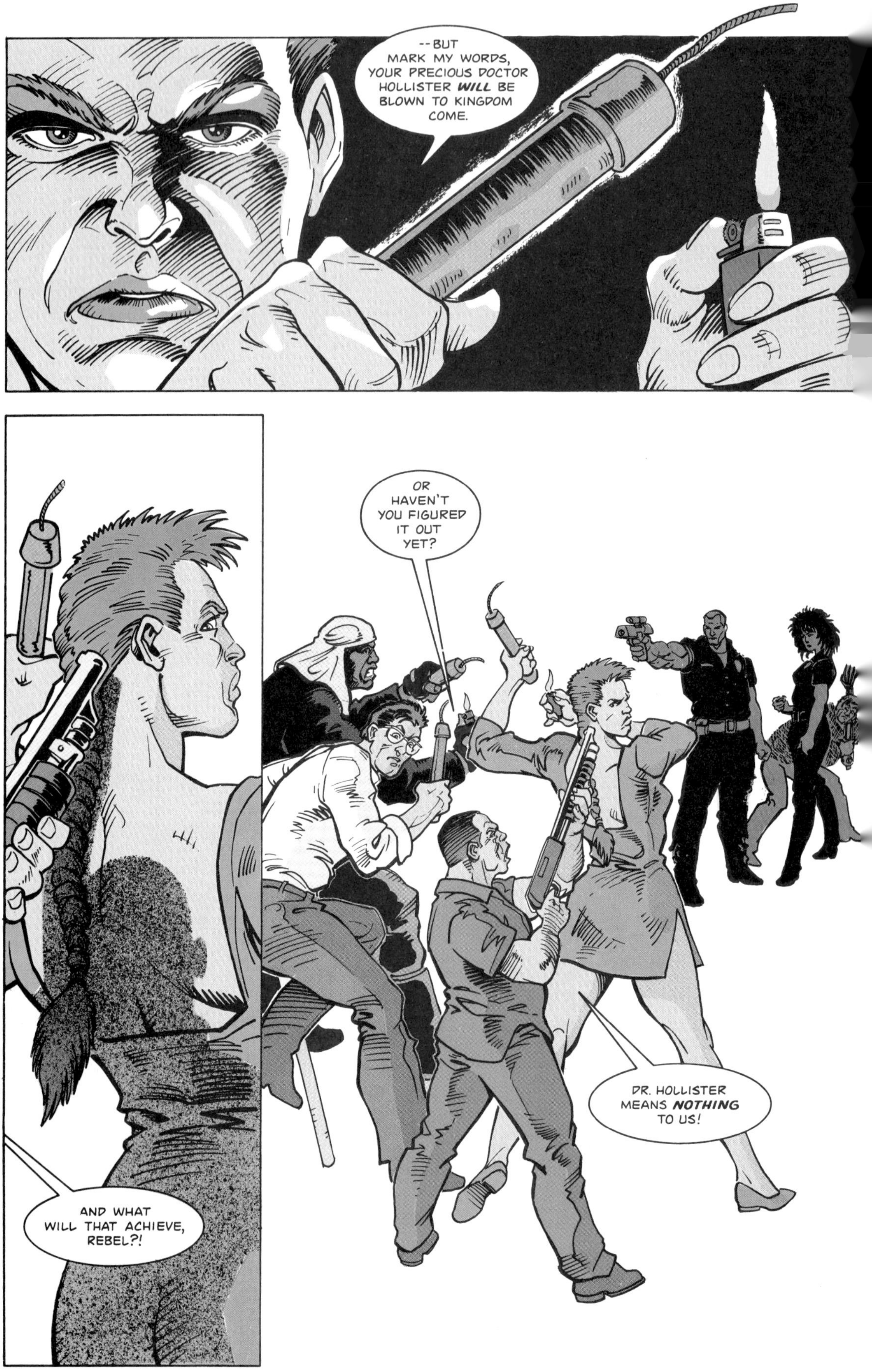
--BUT MARK MY WORDS, YOUR PRECIOUS DOCTOR HOLLISTER *WILL* BE BLOWN TO KINGDOM COME.
AND WHAT WILL THAT ACHIEVE, REBEL?!
OR HAVEN'T YOU FIGURED IT OUT YET?
DR. HOLLISTER MEANS *NOTHING* TO US!

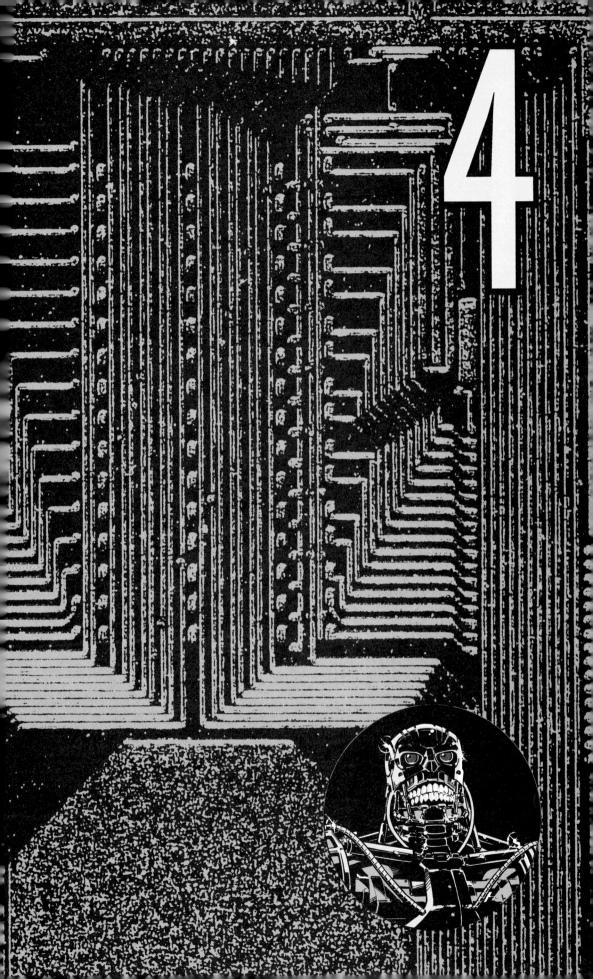

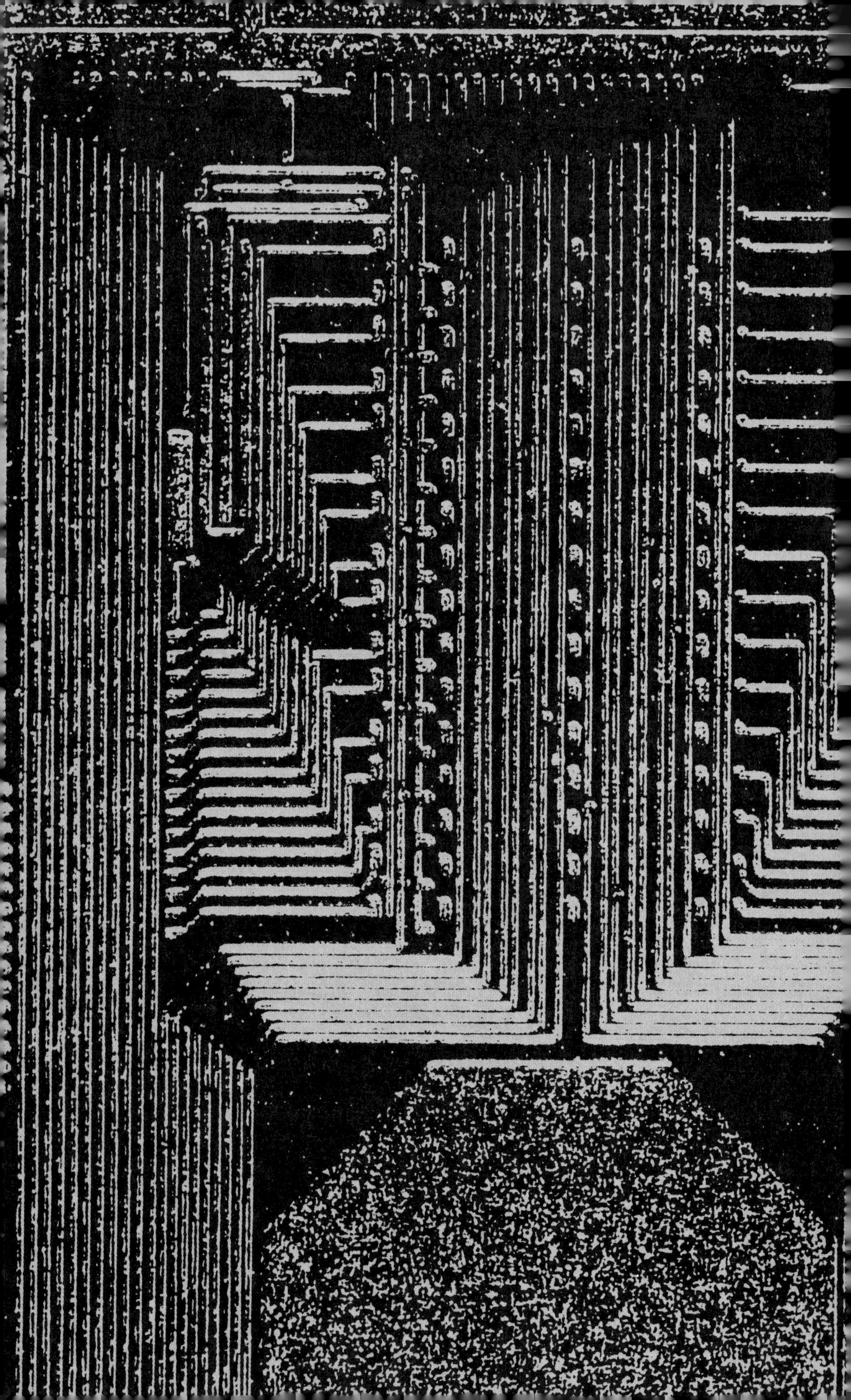

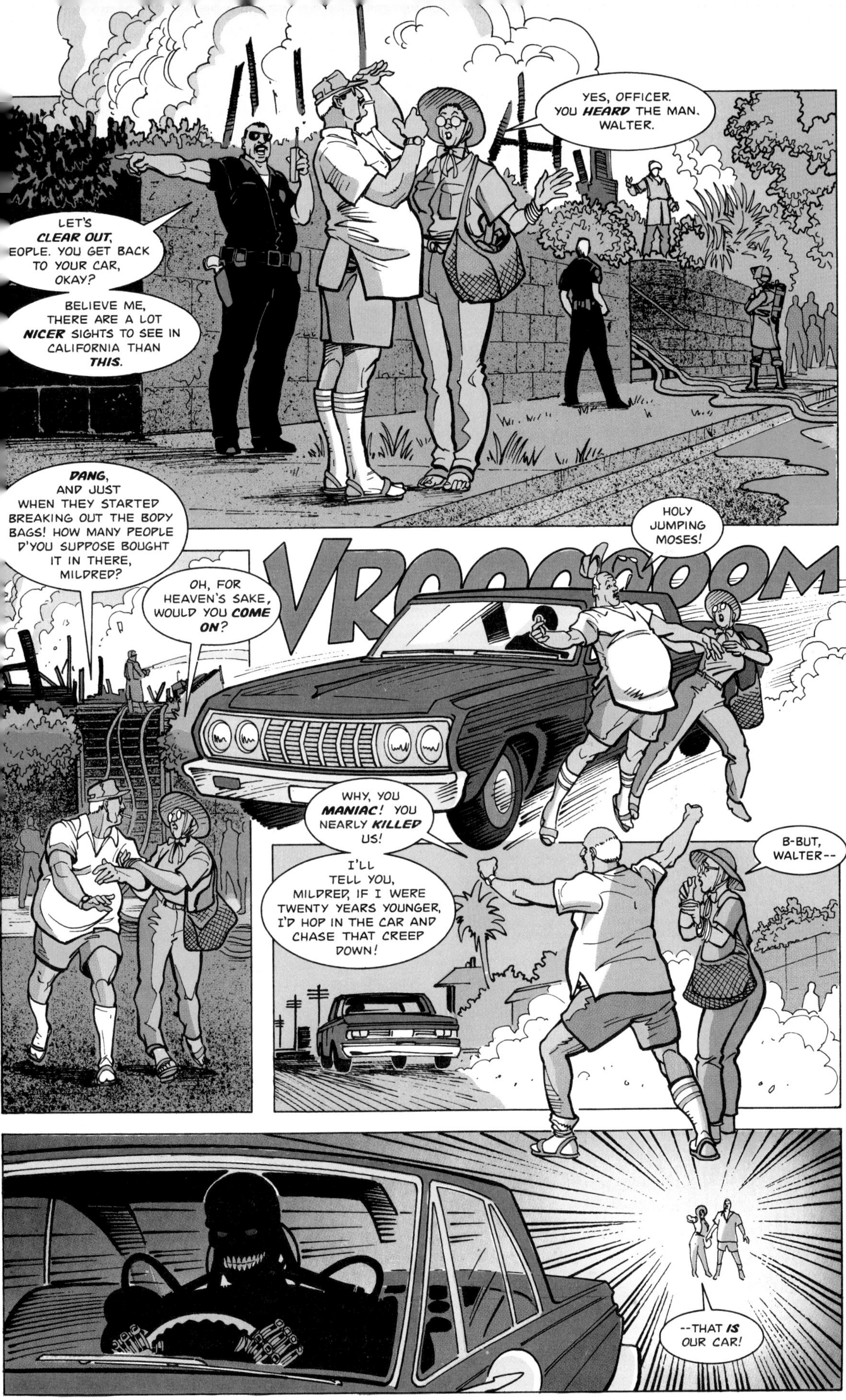

YES, OFFICER. YOU HEARD THE MAN. WALTER.
LET'S CLEAR OUT, EOPLE. YOU GET BACK TO YOUR CAR, OKAY?
BELIEVE ME, THERE ARE A LOT NICER SIGHTS TO SEE IN CALIFORNIA THAN THIS.
DANG, AND JUST WHEN THEY STARTED BREAKING OUT THE BODY BAGS! HOW MANY PEOPLE D'YOU SUPPOSE BOUGHT IT IN THERE, MILDRED?
OH, FOR HEAVEN'S SAKE, WOULD YOU COME ON?
VROOOOOOM
HOLY JUMPING MOSES!
WHY, YOU MANIAC! YOU NEARLY KILLED US!
I'LL TELL YOU, MILDRED, IF I WERE TWENTY YEARS YOUNGER, I'D HOP IN THE CAR AND CHASE THAT CREEP DOWN!
B-BUT, WALTER--
--THAT IS OUR CAR!

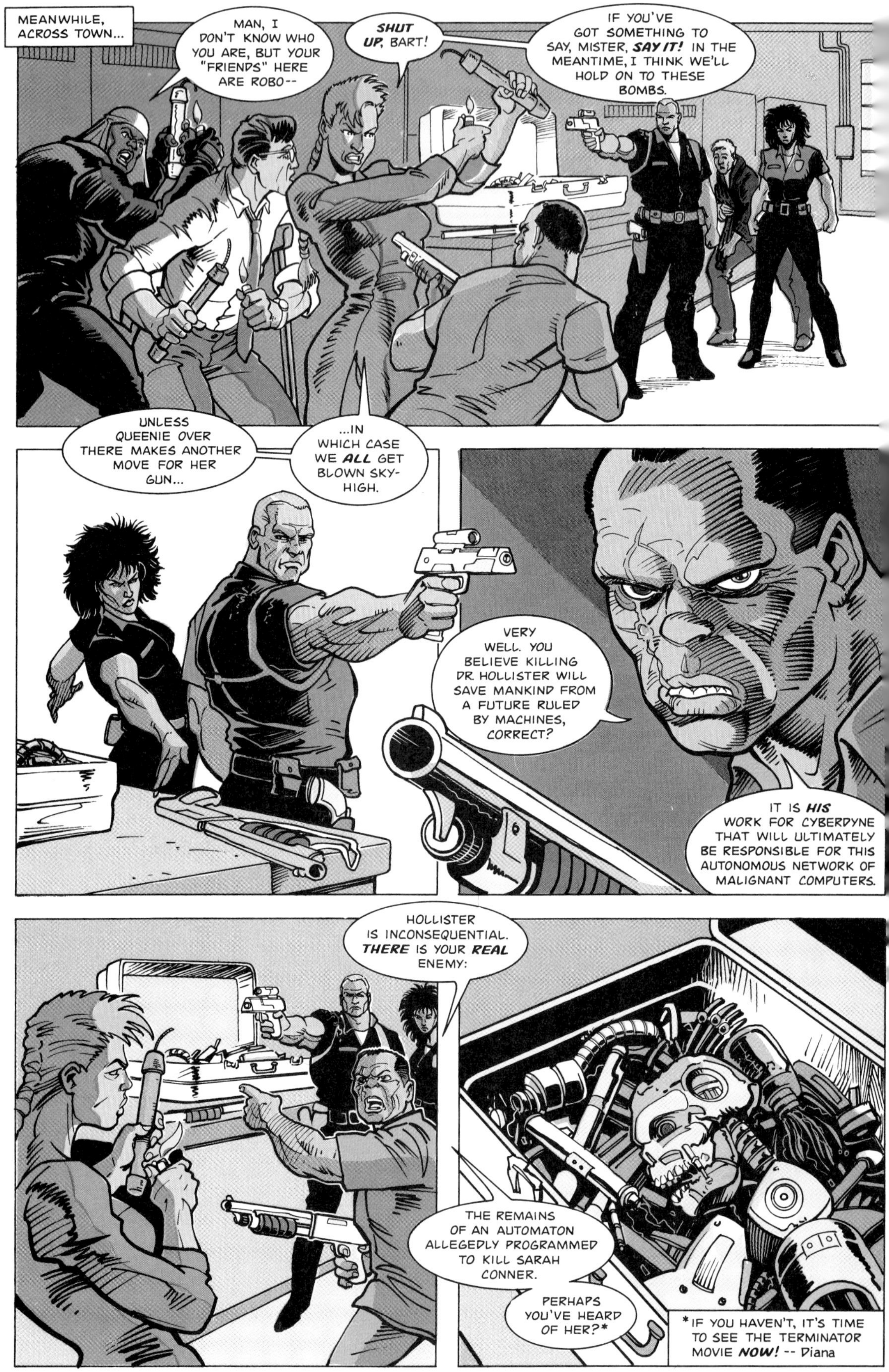
MEANWHILE, ACROSS TOWN...
MAN, I DON'T KNOW WHO YOU ARE, BUT YOUR "FRIENDS" HERE ARE ROBO--
SHUT UP, BART!
IF YOU'VE GOT SOMETHING TO SAY, MISTER, SAY IT! IN THE MEANTIME, I THINK WE'LL HOLD ON TO THESE BOMBS.
UNLESS QUEENIE OVER THERE MAKES ANOTHER MOVE FOR HER GUN...
...IN WHICH CASE WE ALL GET BLOWN SKY-HIGH.
VERY WELL. YOU BELIEVE KILLING DR. HOLLISTER WILL SAVE MANKIND FROM A FUTURE RULED BY MACHINES, CORRECT?
IT IS HIS WORK FOR CYBERDYNE THAT WILL ULTIMATELY BE RESPONSIBLE FOR THIS AUTONOMOUS NETWORK OF MALIGNANT COMPUTERS.
HOLLISTER IS INCONSEQUENTIAL. THERE IS YOUR REAL ENEMY:
THE REMAINS OF AN AUTOMATON ALLEGEDLY PROGRAMMED TO KILL SARAH CONNER.
PERHAPS YOU'VE HEARD OF HER?*
*IF YOU HAVEN'T, IT'S TIME TO SEE THE TERMINATOR MOVIE NOW! -- Diana

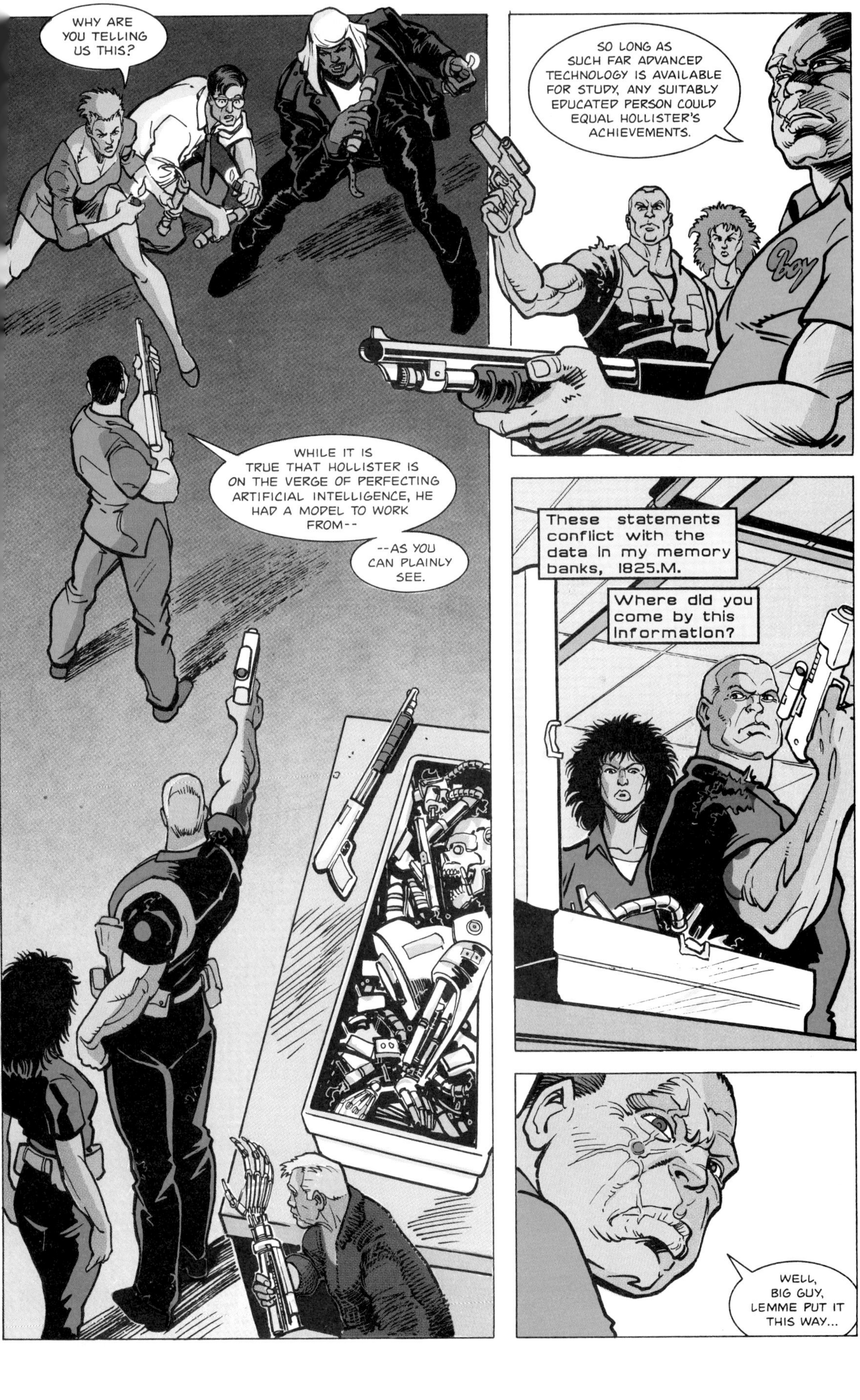
WHY ARE YOU TELLING US THIS?
WHILE IT IS TRUE THAT HOLLISTER IS ON THE VERGE OF PERFECTING ARTIFICIAL INTELLIGENCE, HE HAD A MODEL TO WORK FROM--
--AS YOU CAN PLAINLY SEE.
SO LONG AS SUCH FAR ADVANCED TECHNOLOGY IS AVAILABLE FOR STUDY, ANY SUITABLY EDUCATED PERSON COULD EQUAL HOLLISTER'S ACHIEVEMENTS.
These statements conflict with the data in my memory banks, 1825.M.
Where did you come by this information?
WELL, BIG GUY, LEMME PUT IT THIS WAY...

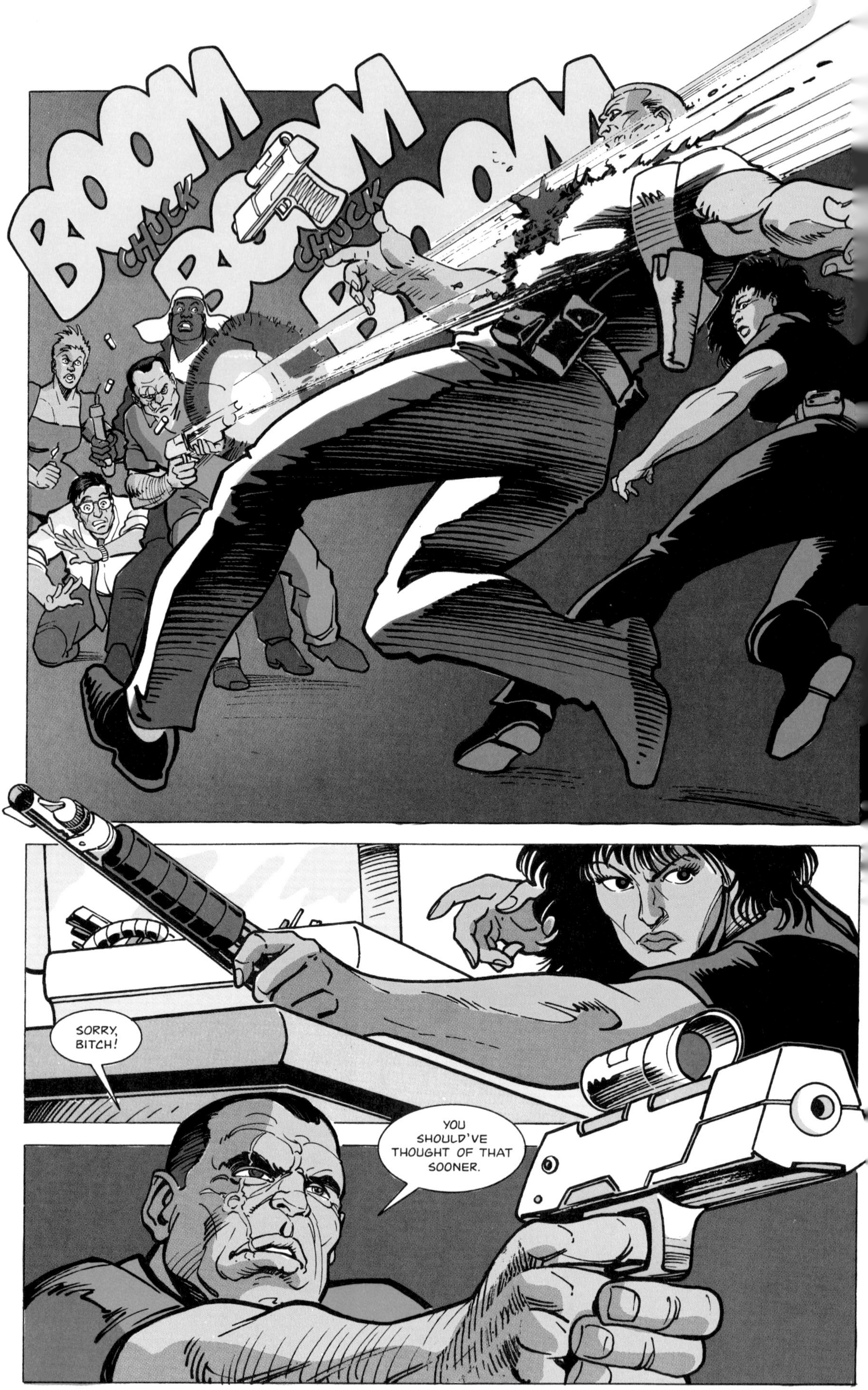
BOOM
CHUCK
BOOM
CHUCK
BOOM
SORRY, BITCH!
YOU SHOULD'VE THOUGHT OF THAT SOONER.

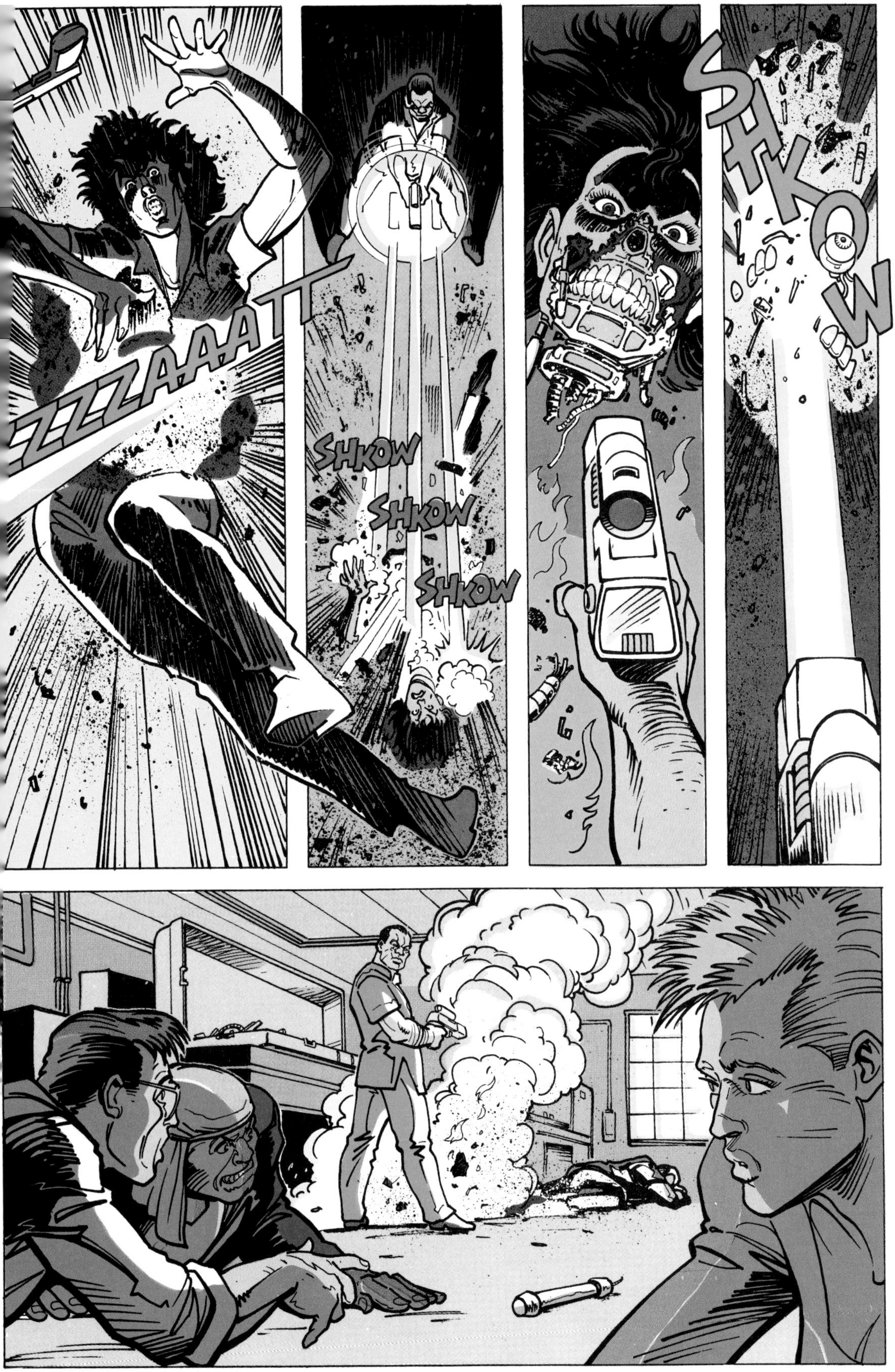
ZZZZAAAATT
SHKOW
SHKOW
SHKOW
SHKOW

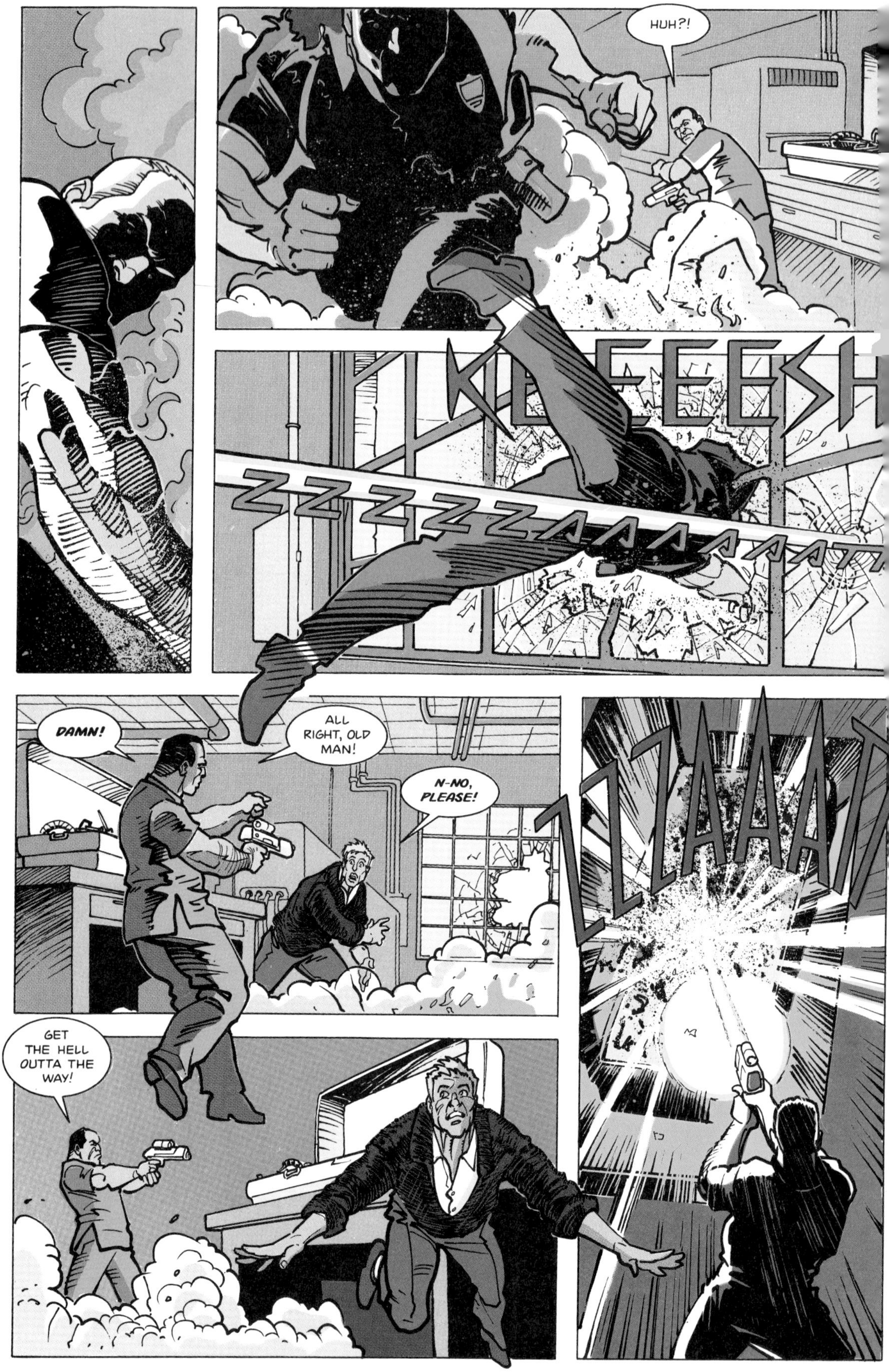
HUH?!
KRESSSH
ZZZZZAAAAAAAT
DAMN!
ALL RIGHT, OLD MAN!
N-NO, PLEASE!
ZZZAAAT
GET THE HELL OUTTA THE WAY!

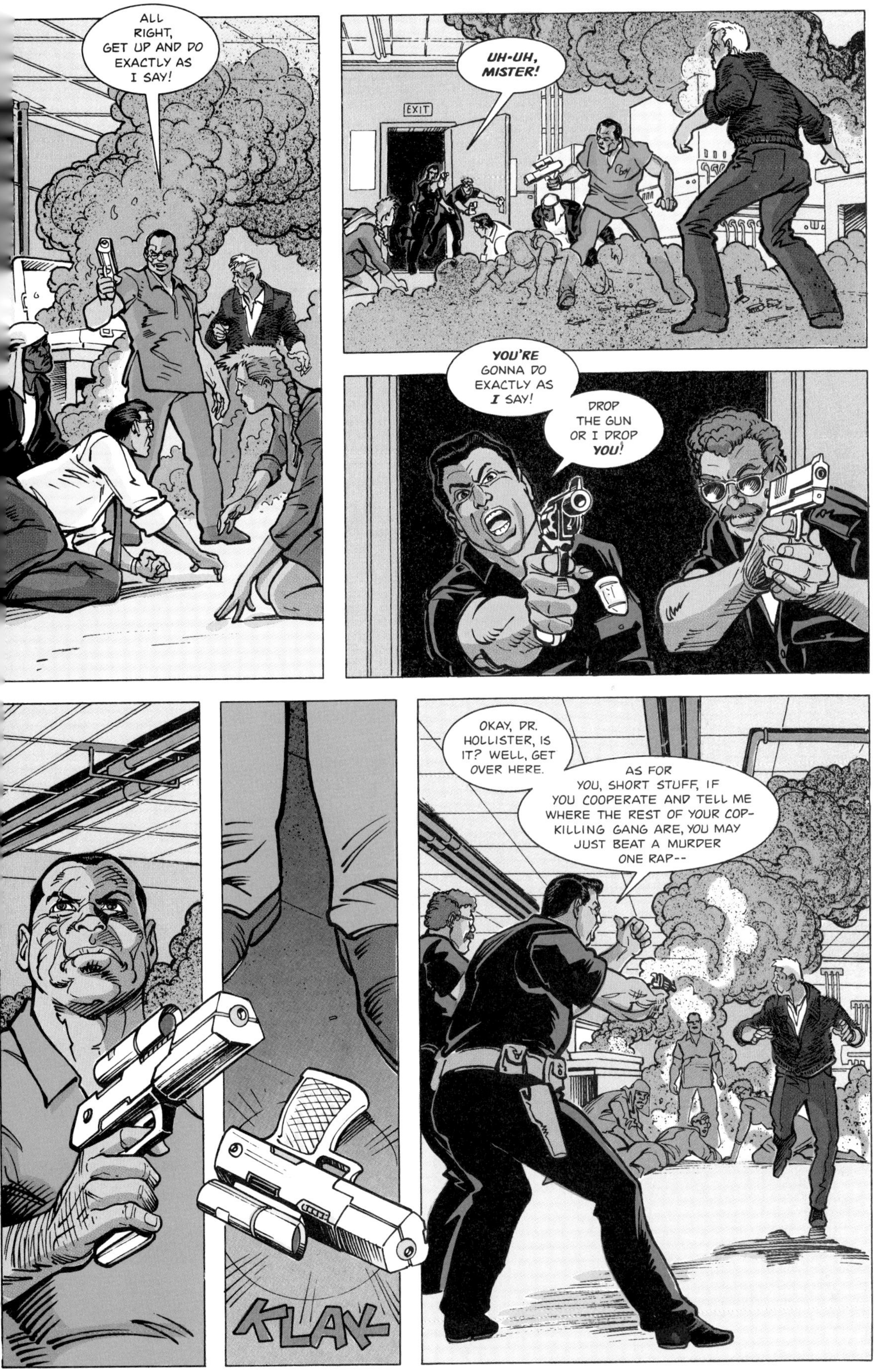
ALL RIGHT, GET UP AND DO EXACTLY AS I SAY!
UH-UH, MISTER!
EXIT
YOU'RE GONNA DO EXACTLY AS I SAY!
DROP THE GUN OR I DROP YOU!
KLAK
OKAY, DR. HOLLISTER, IS IT? WELL, GET OVER HERE.
AS FOR YOU, SHORT STUFF, IF YOU COOPERATE AND TELL ME WHERE THE REST OF YOUR COP-KILLING GANG ARE, YOU MAY JUST BEAT A MURDER ONE RAP--

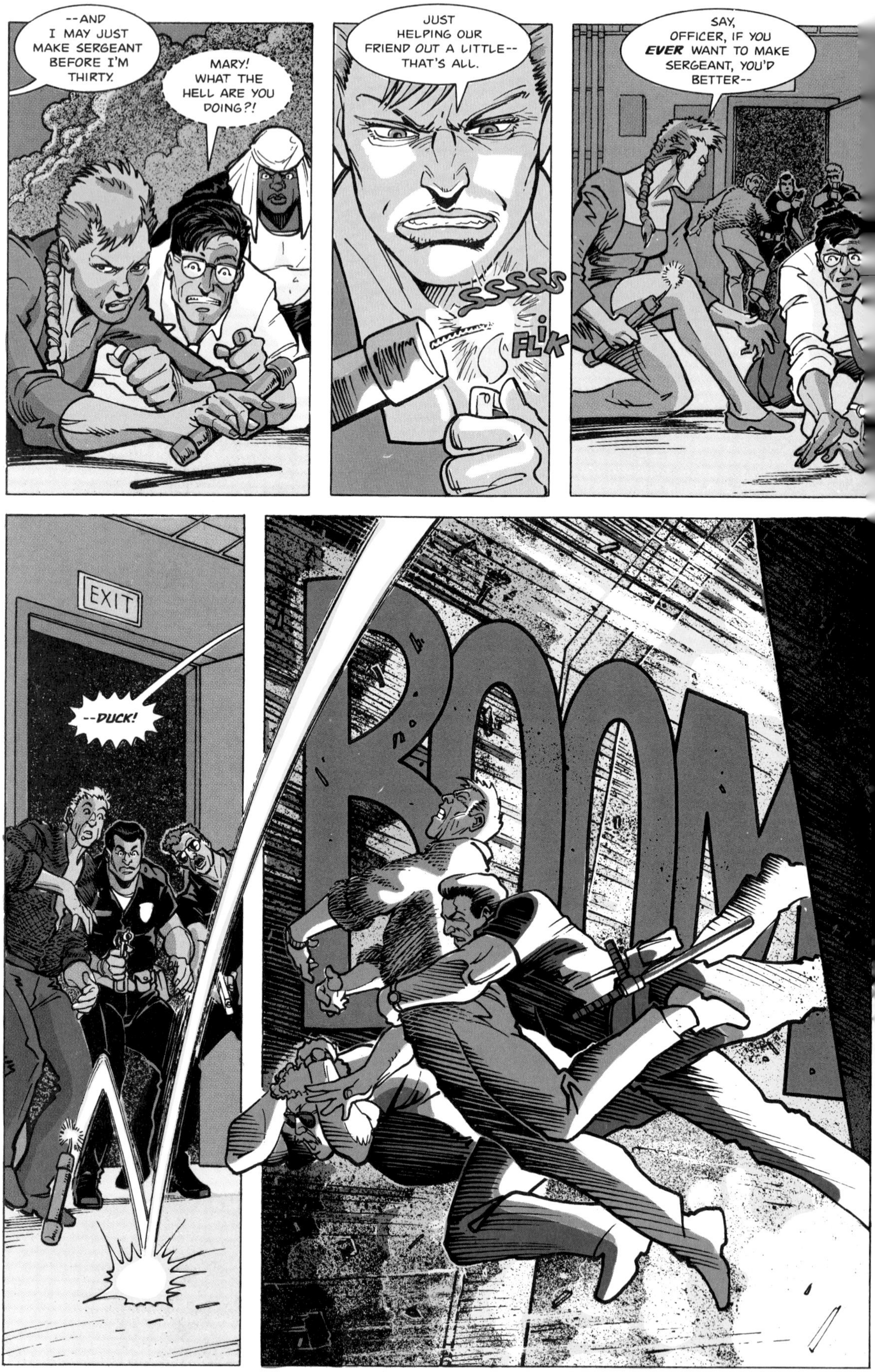
--AND I MAY JUST MAKE SERGEANT BEFORE I'M THIRTY.
MARY! WHAT THE HELL ARE YOU DOING?!
JUST HELPING OUR FRIEND OUT A LITTLE-- THAT'S ALL.
SSSSS
FLIK
SAY, OFFICER, IF YOU **EVER** WANT TO MAKE SERGEANT, YOU'D BETTER--
EXIT
--DUCK!
BOOM

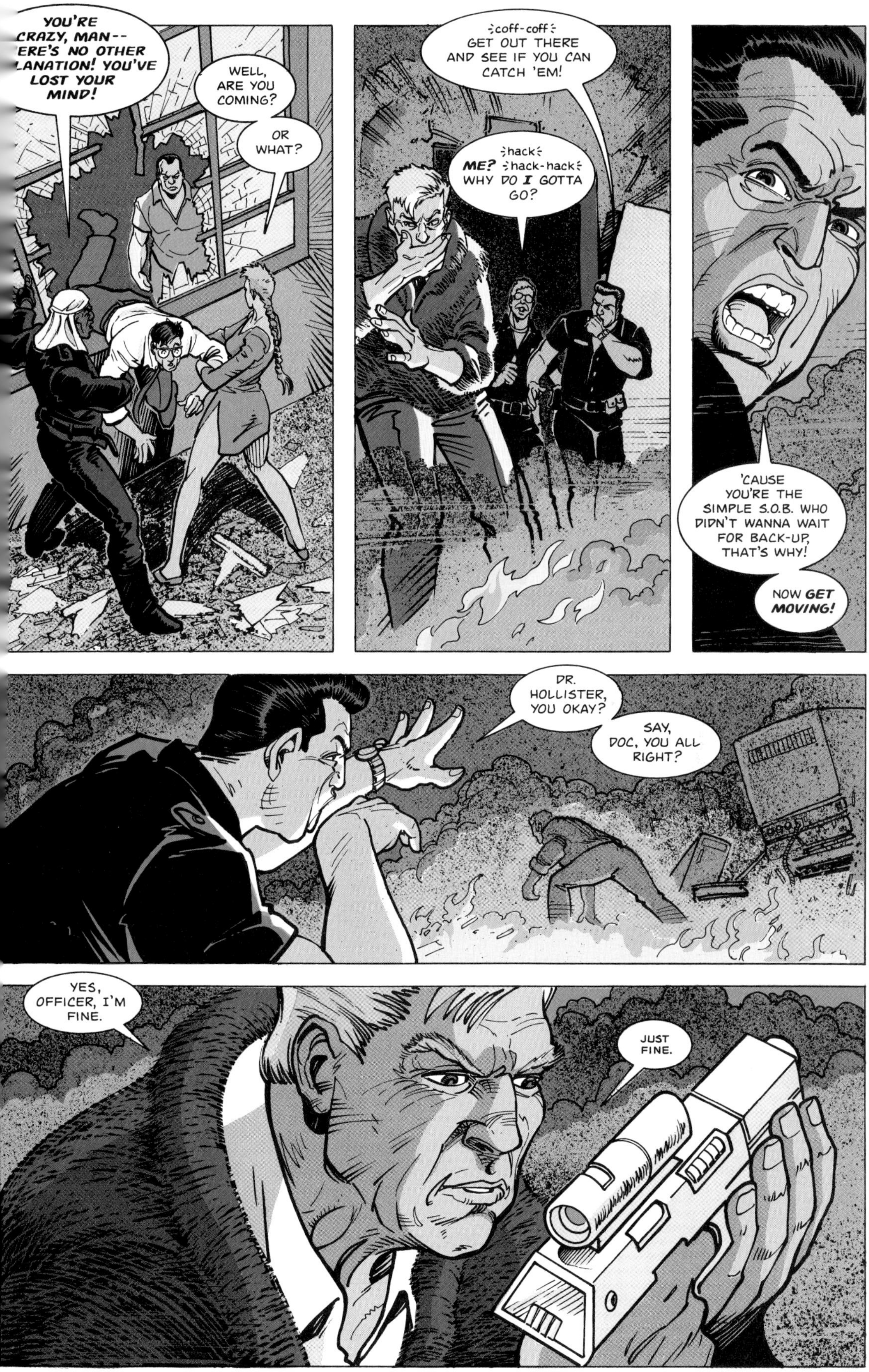
YOU'RE CRAZY, MAN-- ERE'S NO OTHER LANATION! YOU'VE LOST YOUR MIND!
WELL, ARE YOU COMING?
OR WHAT?
coff-coff GET OUT THERE AND SEE IF YOU CAN CATCH 'EM!
ME? hack hack-hack WHY DO I GOTTA GO?
'CAUSE YOU'RE THE SIMPLE S.O.B. WHO DIDN'T WANNA WAIT FOR BACK-UP, THAT'S WHY!
NOW GET MOVING!
DR. HOLLISTER, YOU OKAY?
SAY, DOC, YOU ALL RIGHT?
YES, OFFICER, I'M FINE.
JUST FINE.

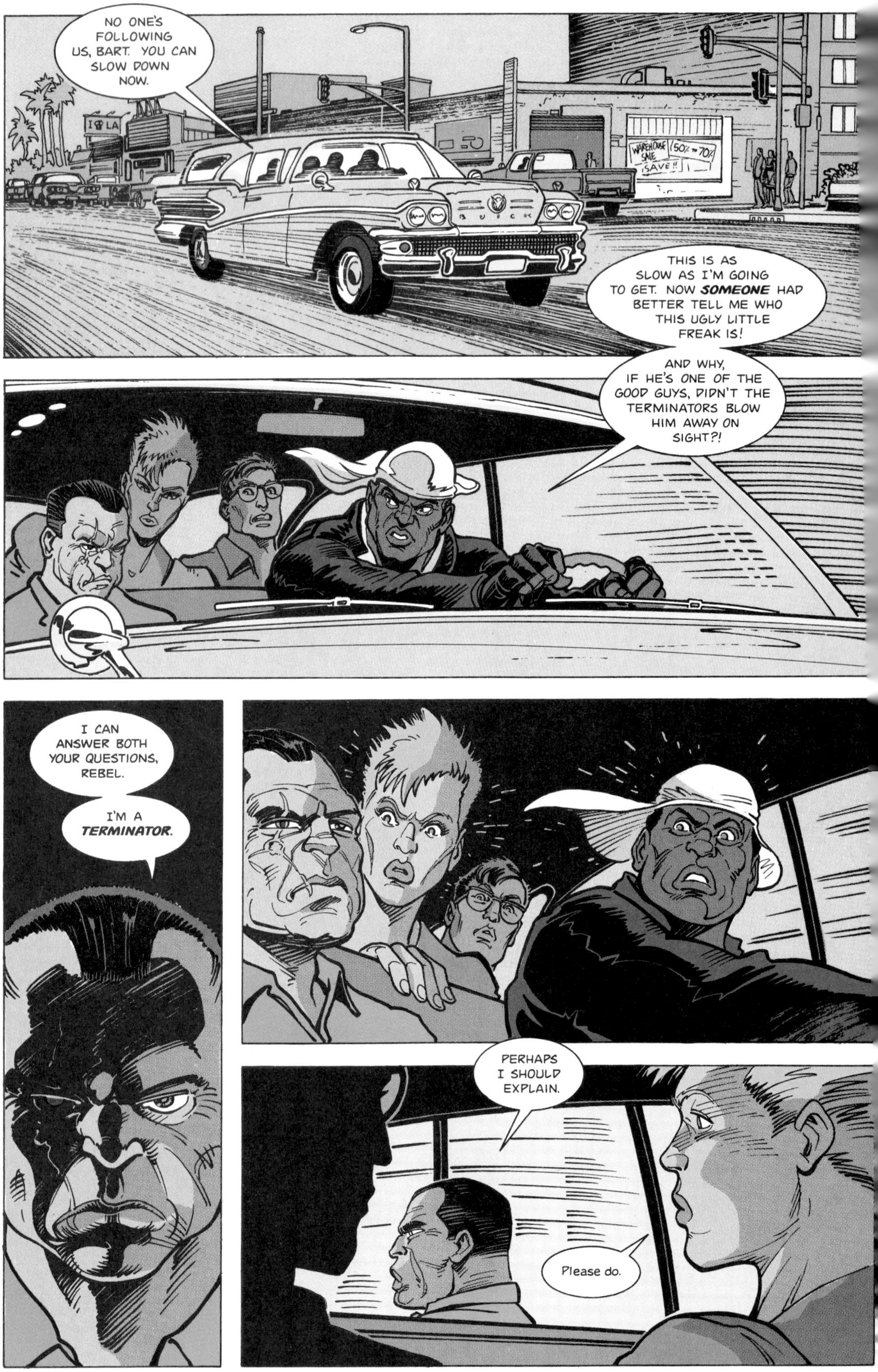
NO ONE'S FOLLOWING US, BART. YOU CAN SLOW DOWN NOW.
WAREHOUSE SALE
50% TO 70%
SAVE!!
THIS IS AS SLOW AS I'M GOING TO GET. NOW **SOMEONE** HAD BETTER TELL ME WHO THIS UGLY LITTLE FREAK IS!
AND WHY, IF HE'S ONE OF THE GOOD GUYS, DIDN'T THE TERMINATORS BLOW HIM AWAY ON SIGHT?!
I CAN ANSWER BOTH YOUR QUESTIONS, REBEL.
I'M A ***TERMINATOR***.
PERHAPS I SHOULD EXPLAIN.
Please do.

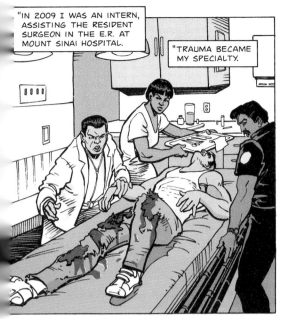

"IN 2009 I WAS AN INTERN, ASSISTING THE RESIDENT SURGEON IN THE E.R. AT MOUNT SINAI HOSPITAL.

"TRAUMA BECAME MY SPECIALTY.

"THEN SKYNET BOMBED THE WORLD TO HELL.

"NATURALLY, WHEN THE HUMAN INSURRECTION STARTED, I BECAME A MEDIC TREATING FIELD WOUNDS.

"UNFORTUNATELY, SKYNET DIDN'T OBSERVE THE GENEVA CONVENTION.

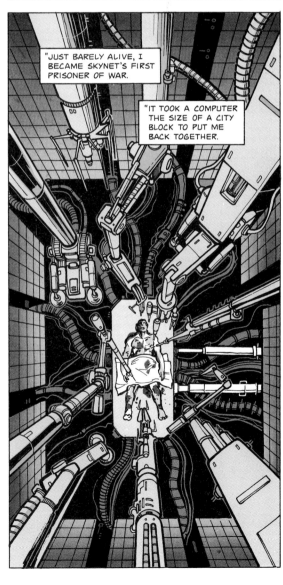

"JUST BARELY ALIVE, I BECAME SKYNET'S FIRST PRISONER OF WAR.

"IT TOOK A COMPUTER THE SIZE OF A CITY BLOCK TO PUT ME BACK TOGETHER.

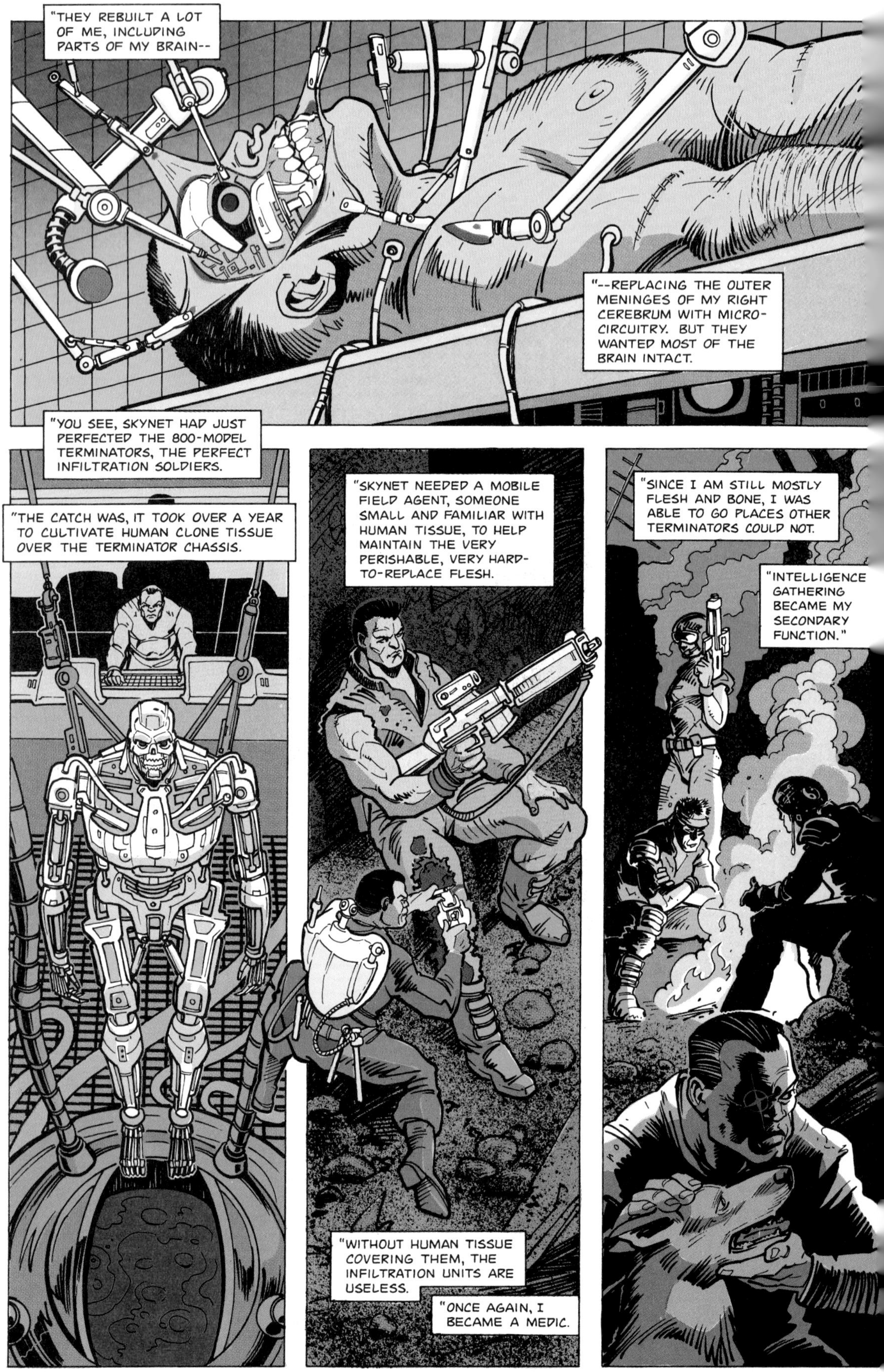
"THEY REBUILT A LOT OF ME, INCLUDING PARTS OF MY BRAIN--
"--REPLACING THE OUTER MENINGES OF MY RIGHT CEREBRUM WITH MICRO-CIRCUITRY. BUT THEY WANTED MOST OF THE BRAIN INTACT.
"YOU SEE, SKYNET HAD JUST PERFECTED THE 800-MODEL TERMINATORS, THE PERFECT INFILTRATION SOLDIERS.
"THE CATCH WAS, IT TOOK OVER A YEAR TO CULTIVATE HUMAN CLONE TISSUE OVER THE TERMINATOR CHASSIS.
"SKYNET NEEDED A MOBILE FIELD AGENT, SOMEONE SMALL AND FAMILIAR WITH HUMAN TISSUE, TO HELP MAINTAIN THE VERY PERISHABLE, VERY HARD-TO-REPLACE FLESH.
"WITHOUT HUMAN TISSUE COVERING THEM, THE INFILTRATION UNITS ARE USELESS.
"ONCE AGAIN, I BECAME A MEDIC.
"SINCE I AM STILL MOSTLY FLESH AND BONE, I WAS ABLE TO GO PLACES OTHER TERMINATORS COULD NOT.
"INTELLIGENCE GATHERING BECAME MY SECONDARY FUNCTION."

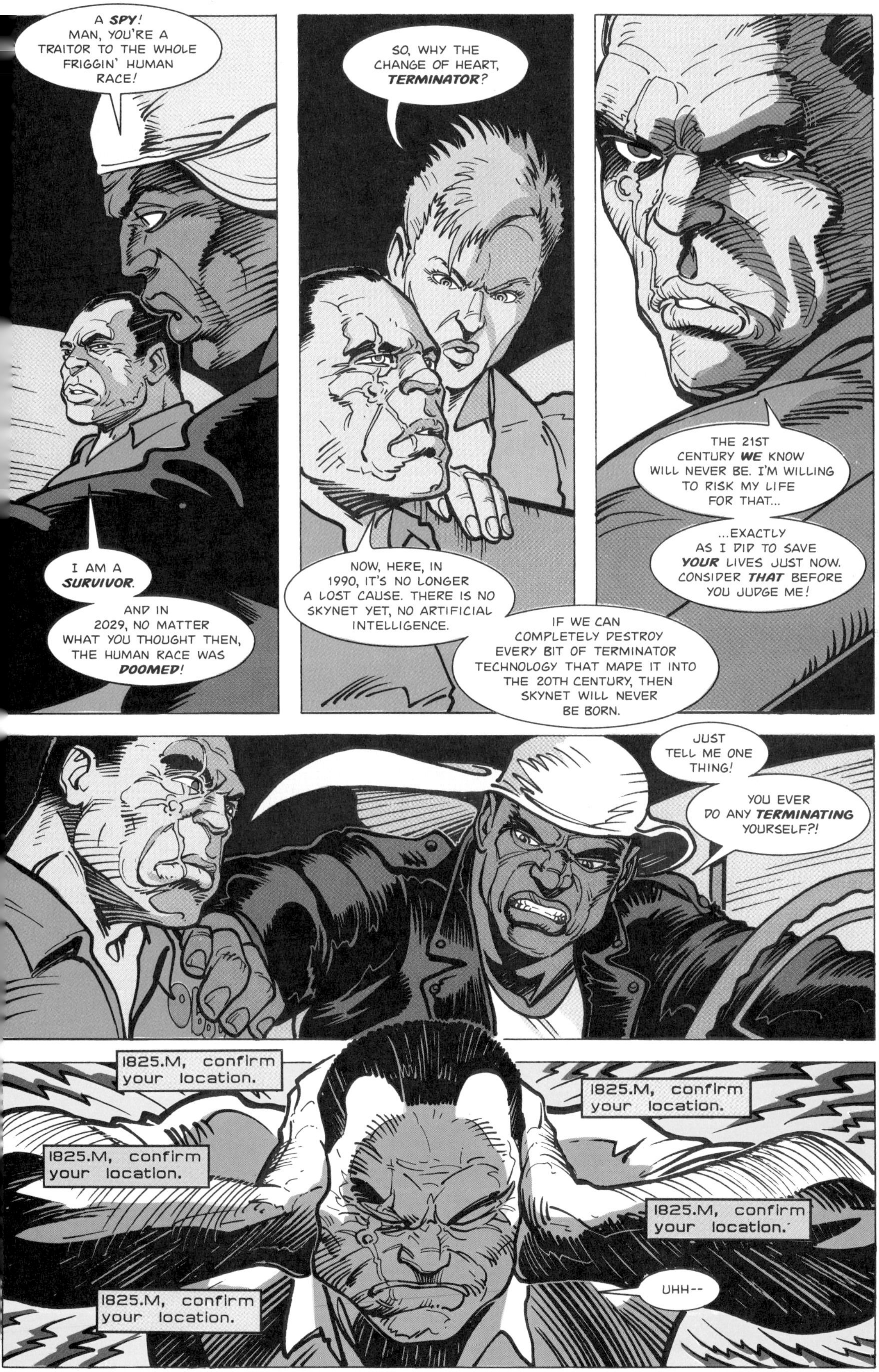
A SPY! MAN, YOU'RE A TRAITOR TO THE WHOLE FRIGGIN' HUMAN RACE!
I AM A SURVIVOR.
AND IN 2029, NO MATTER WHAT YOU THOUGHT THEN, THE HUMAN RACE WAS DOOMED!
SO, WHY THE CHANGE OF HEART, TERMINATOR?
NOW, HERE, IN 1990, IT'S NO LONGER A LOST CAUSE. THERE IS NO SKYNET YET, NO ARTIFICIAL INTELLIGENCE.
IF WE CAN COMPLETELY DESTROY EVERY BIT OF TERMINATOR TECHNOLOGY THAT MADE IT INTO THE 20TH CENTURY, THEN SKYNET WILL NEVER BE BORN.
THE 21ST CENTURY WE KNOW WILL NEVER BE. I'M WILLING TO RISK MY LIFE FOR THAT...
...EXACTLY AS I DID TO SAVE YOUR LIVES JUST NOW. CONSIDER THAT BEFORE YOU JUDGE ME!
JUST TELL ME ONE THING!
YOU EVER DO ANY TERMINATING YOURSELF?!
1825.M, confirm your location.
1825.M, confirm your location.
1825.M, confirm your location.
1825.M, confirm your location.
1825.M, confirm your location.
UHH--

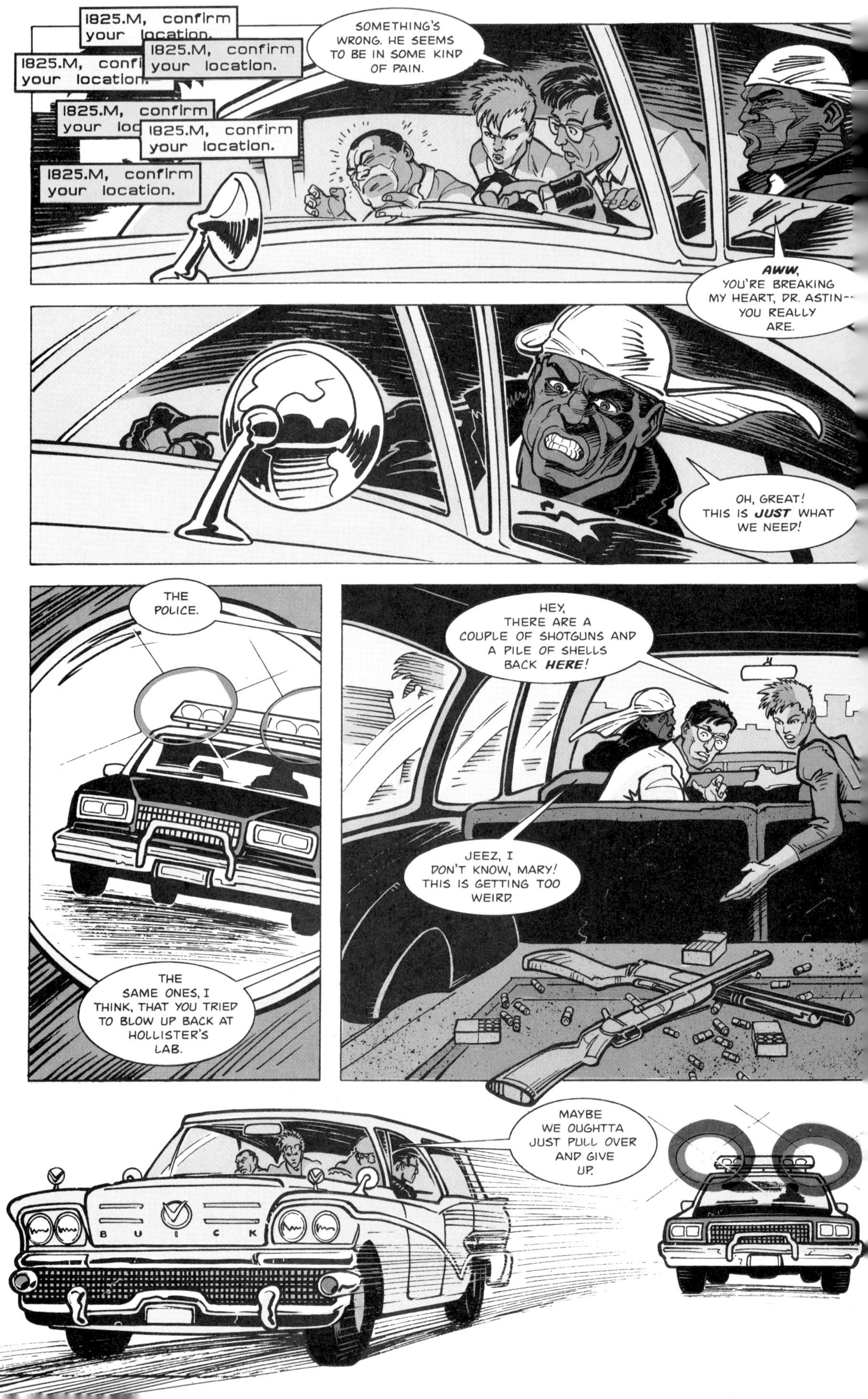
1825.M, confirm your location.
1825.M, confirm your location.
1825.M, confirm your location.
1825.M, confirm your location.
1825.M, confirm your location.
1825.M, confirm your location.
SOMETHING'S WRONG. HE SEEMS TO BE IN SOME KIND OF PAIN.
AWW, YOU'RE BREAKING MY HEART, DR. ASTIN-- YOU REALLY ARE.
OH, GREAT! THIS IS JUST WHAT WE NEED!
THE POLICE.
THE SAME ONES, I THINK, THAT YOU TRIED TO BLOW UP BACK AT HOLLISTER'S LAB.
HEY, THERE ARE A COUPLE OF SHOTGUNS AND A PILE OF SHELLS BACK HERE!
JEEZ, I DON'T KNOW, MARY! THIS IS GETTING TOO WEIRD.
BUICK
MAYBE WE OUGHTTA JUST PULL OVER AND GIVE UP.

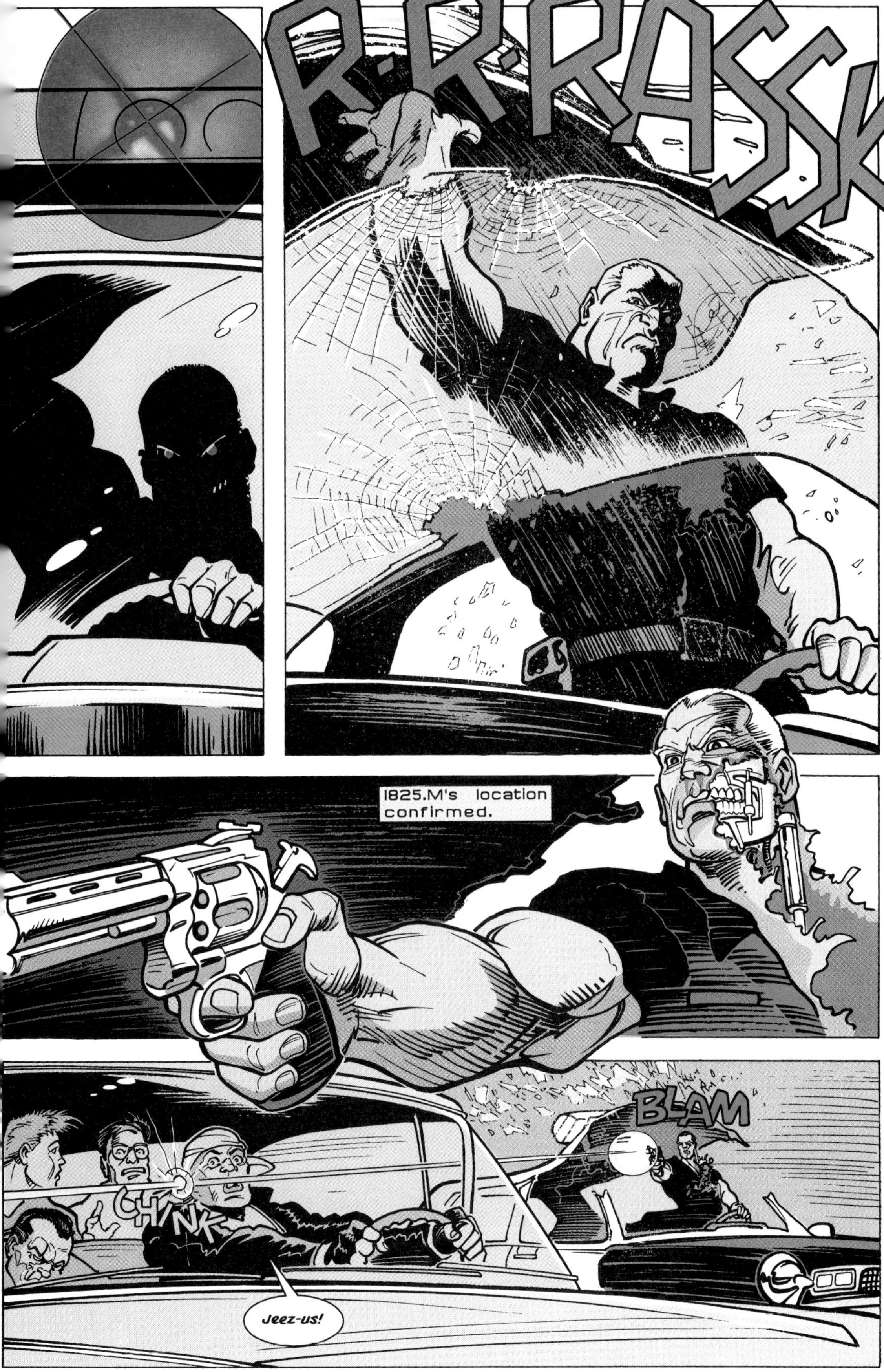
R-R-RASSK
1825.M's location confirmed.
CHINK
BLAM
Jeez-us!

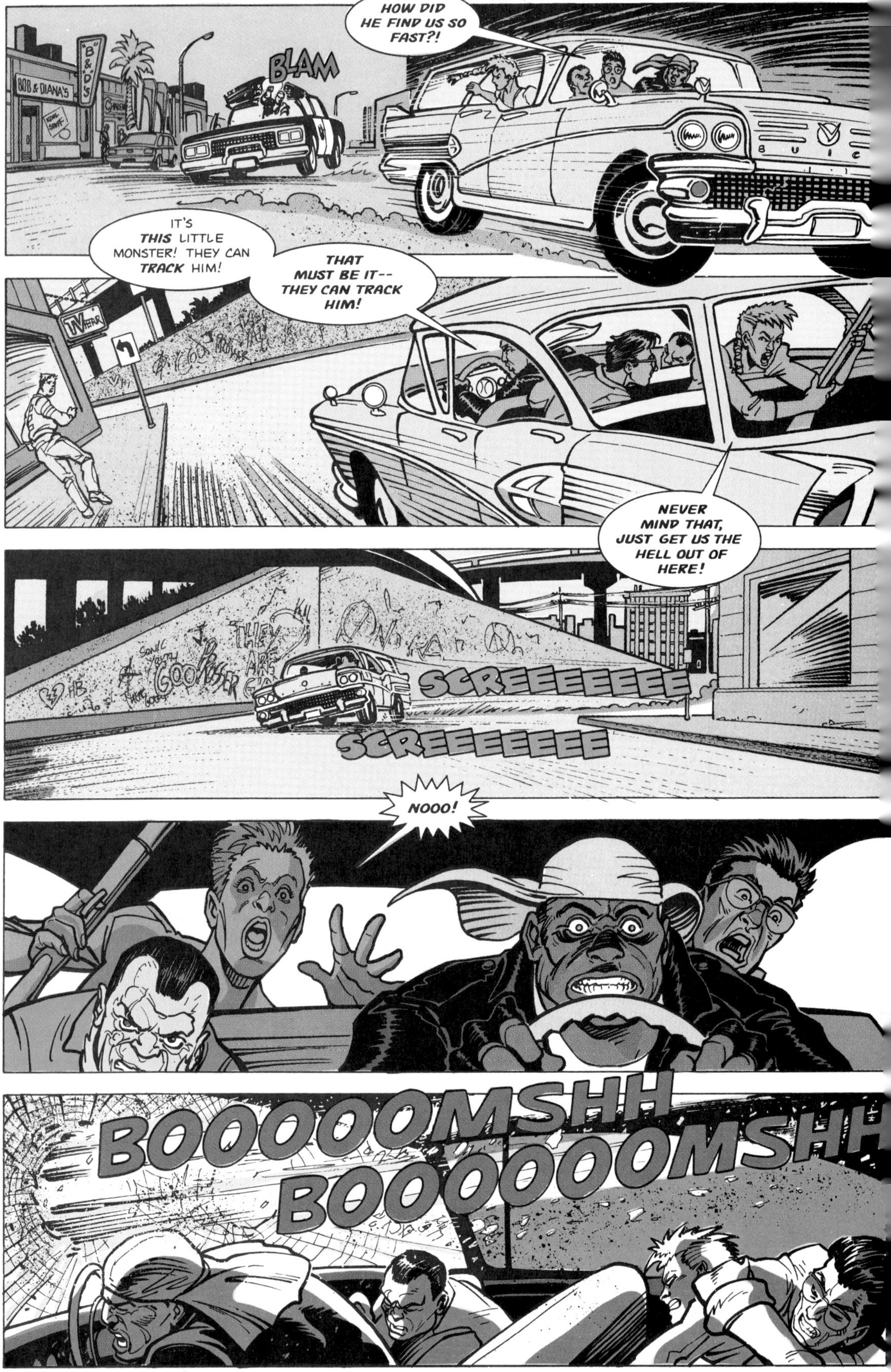
BOB & DIANA'S
"B" & "D"'S
BLAM
HOW DID HE FIND US SO FAST?!
IT'S THIS LITTLE MONSTER! THEY CAN TRACK HIM!
THAT MUST BE IT-- THEY CAN TRACK HIM!
NEVER MIND THAT, JUST GET US THE HELL OUT OF HERE!
THEY ARE
SCREEEEEEEE
SCREEEEEEEE
NOOO!
BOOOOOOMSHH
BOOOOOOOMSHH

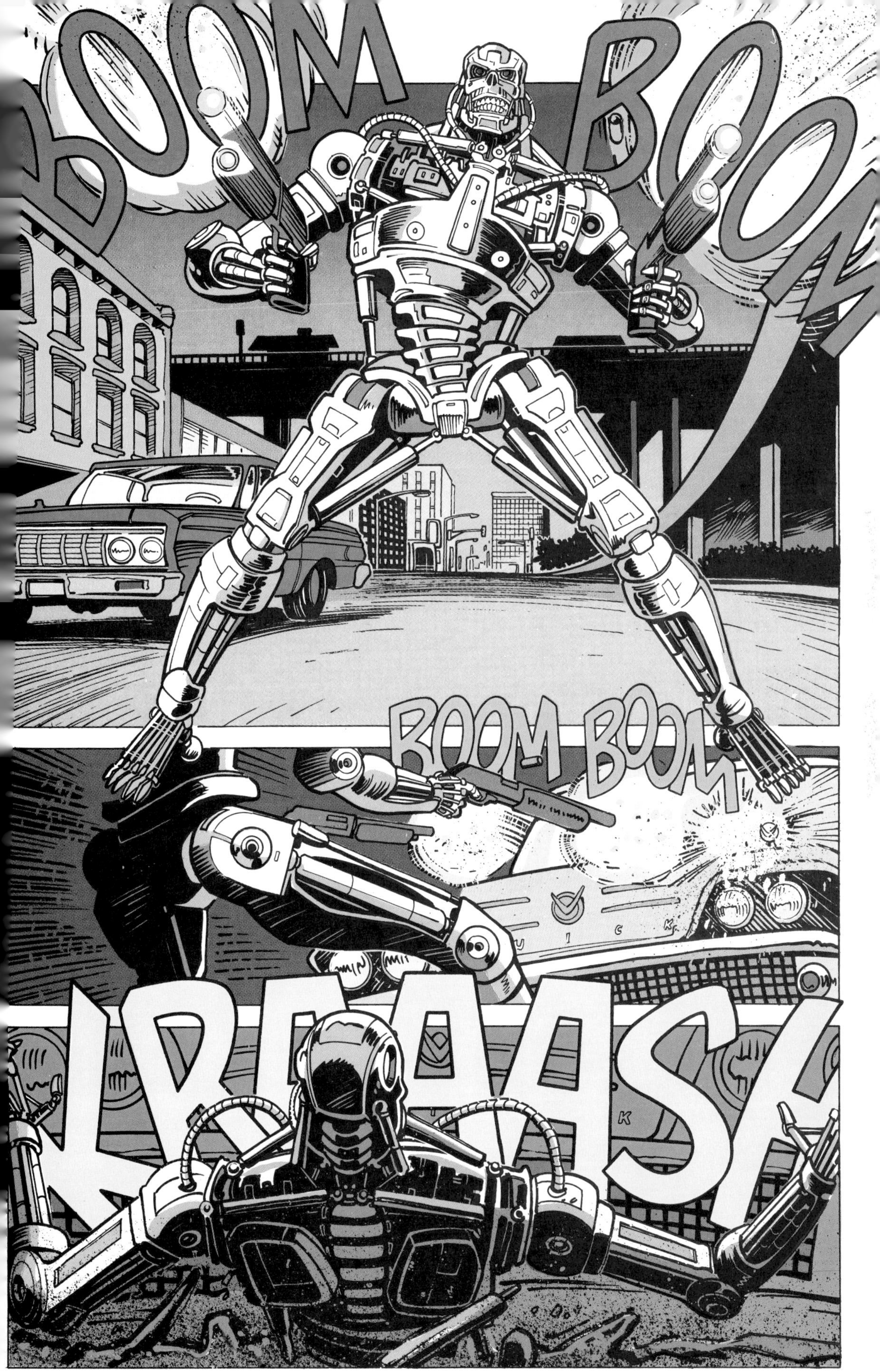
BOOM
BOOM
BOOM-BOOM

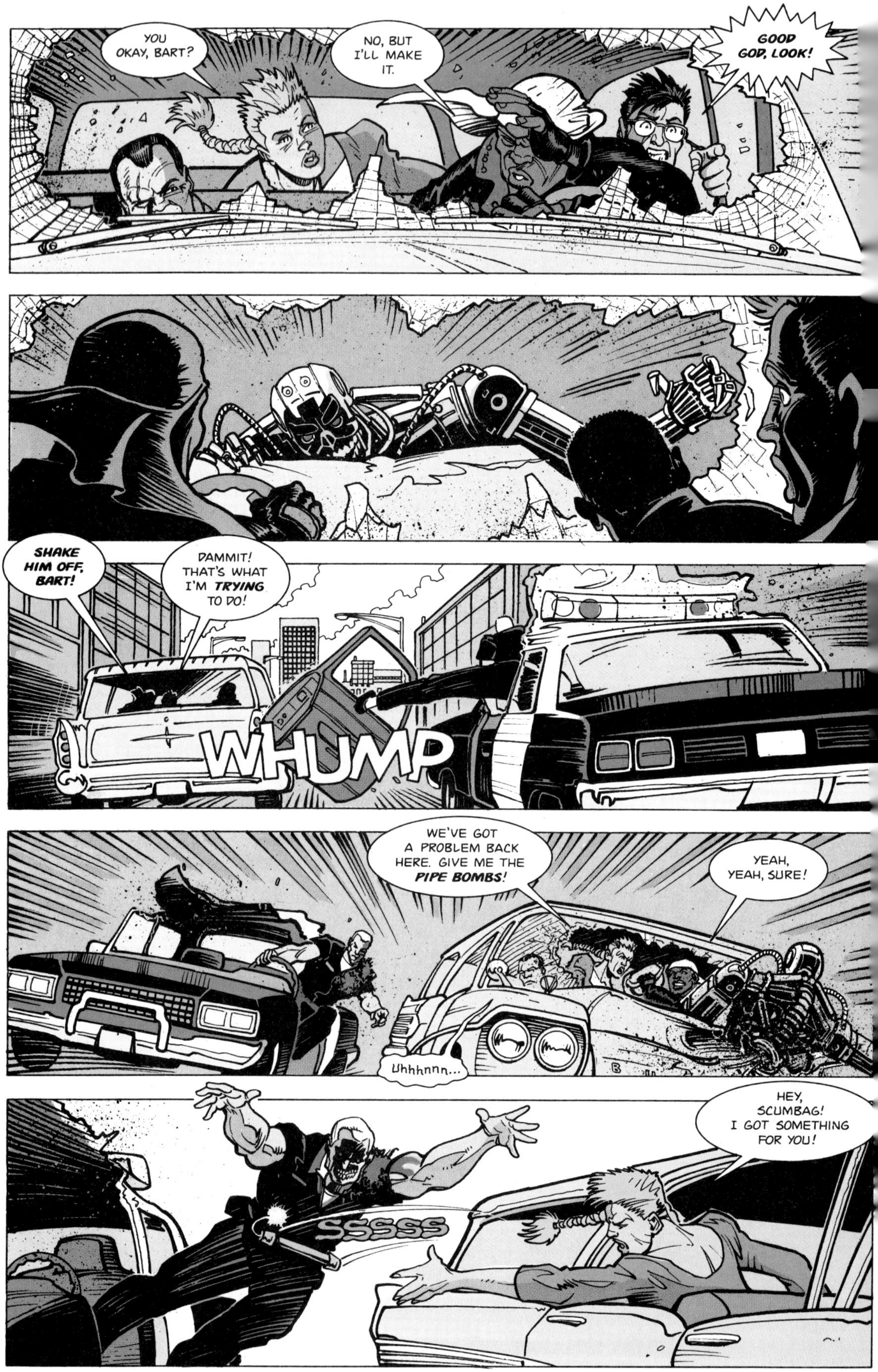
YOU OKAY, BART?
NO, BUT I'LL MAKE IT.
GOOD GOD, LOOK!
SHAKE HIM OFF, BART!
DAMMIT! THAT'S WHAT I'M TRYING TO DO!
WHUMP
WE'VE GOT A PROBLEM BACK HERE. GIVE ME THE PIPE BOMBS!
YEAH, YEAH, SURE!
Uhhhnnn...
HEY, SCUMBAG! I GOT SOMETHING FOR YOU!
SSSSSS

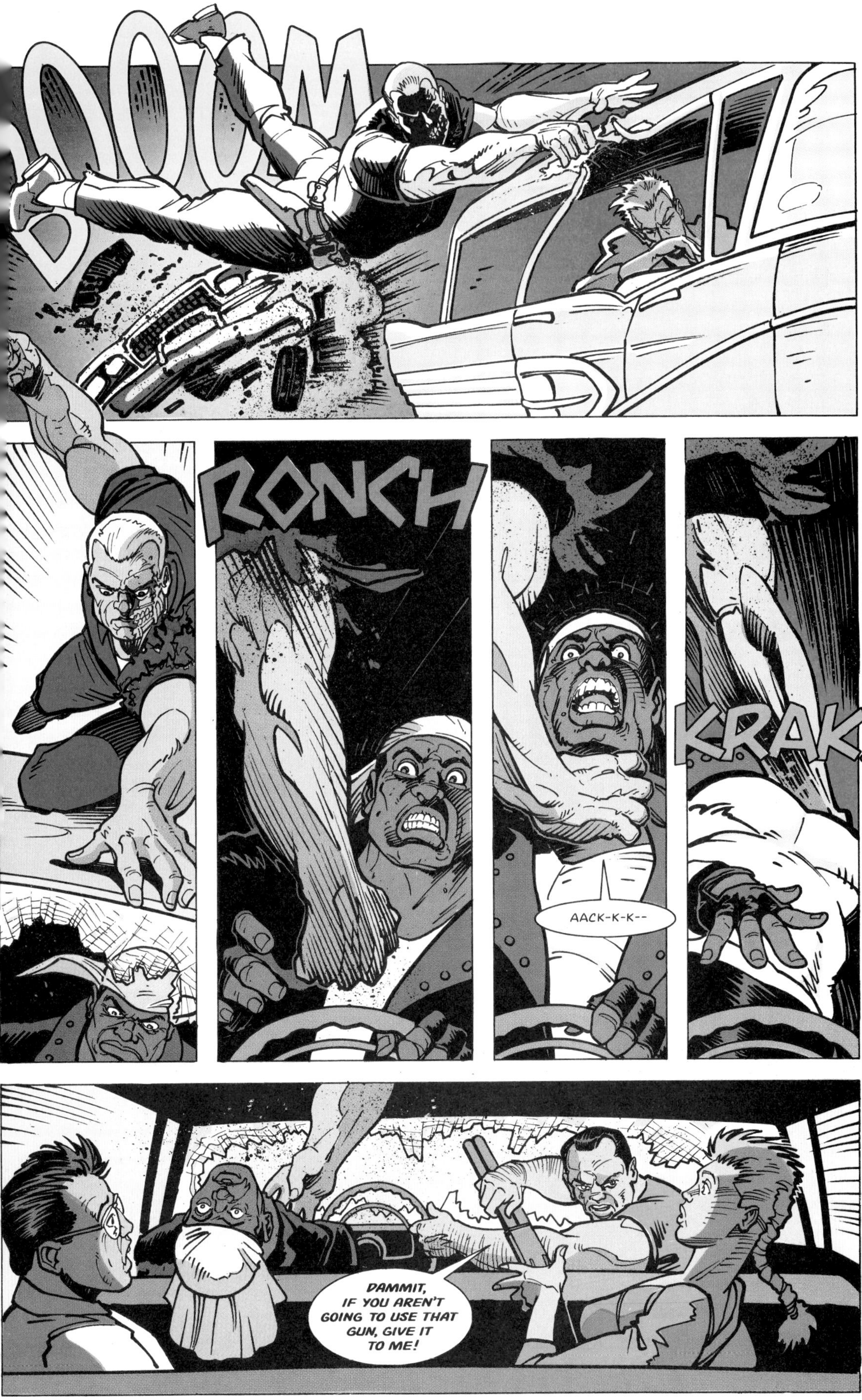
BOOOOM
RONCH
AACK-K-K--
KRAK!
DAMMIT, IF YOU AREN'T GOING TO USE THAT GUN, GIVE IT TO ME!

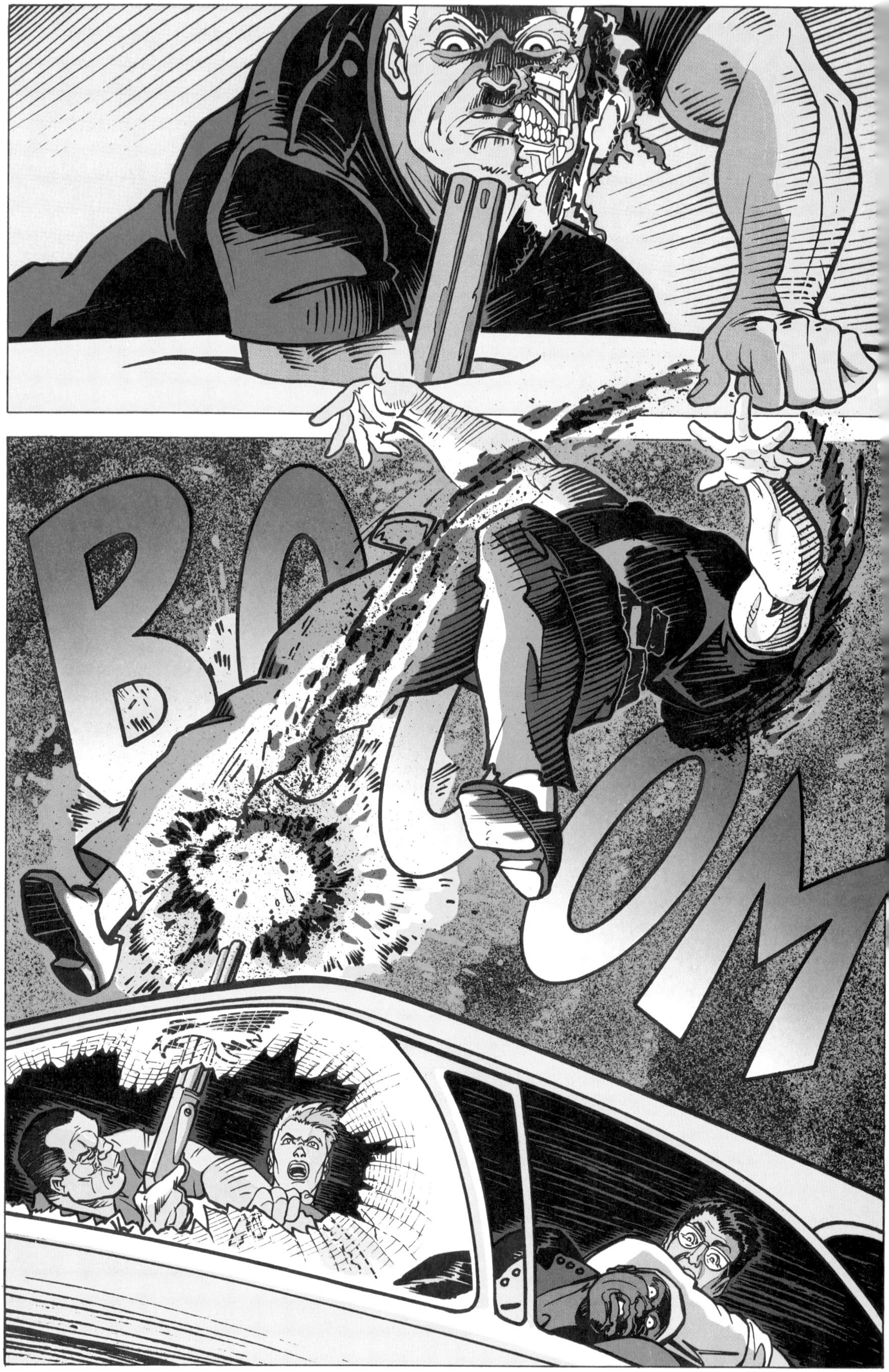
BOOM

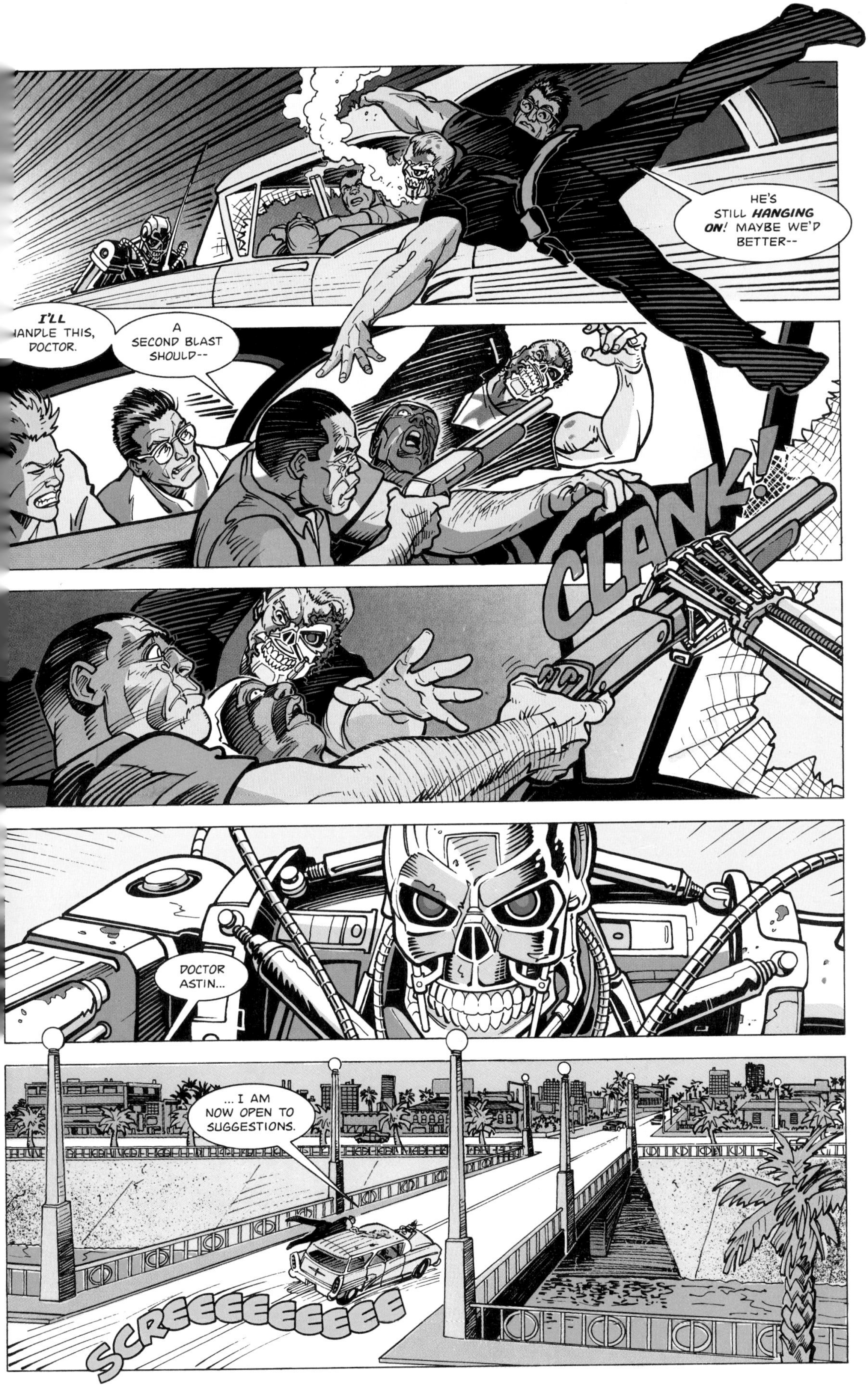
HE'S STILL **HANGING ON!** MAYBE WE'D BETTER--
I'LL HANDLE THIS, DOCTOR.
A SECOND BLAST SHOULD--
CLANK!
DOCTOR ASTIN...
...I AM NOW OPEN TO SUGGESTIONS.
SCREEEEEEEEEE

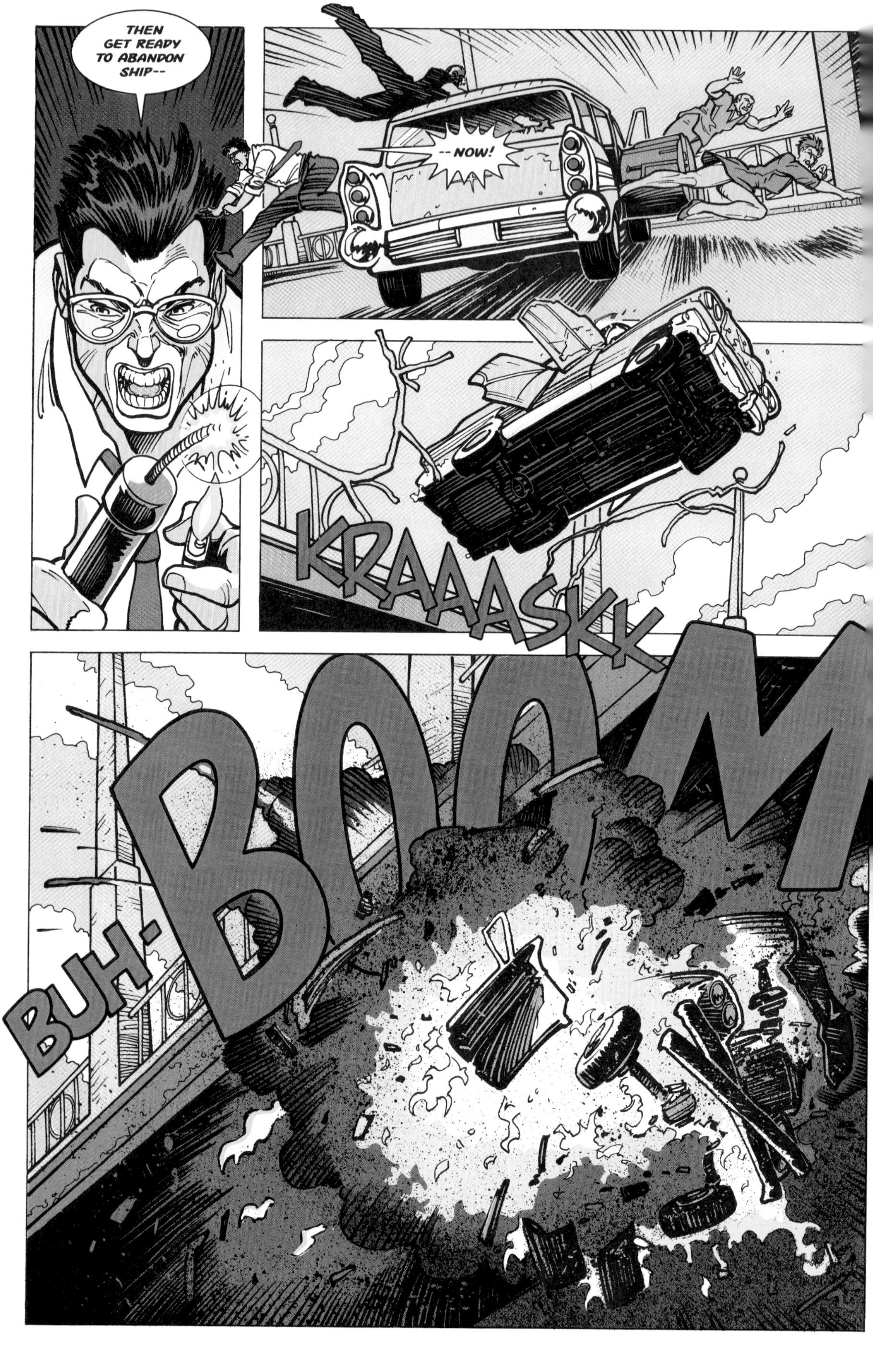
THEN GET READY TO ABANDON SHIP--
--NOW!
KRAAASKK
BUH-BOOM

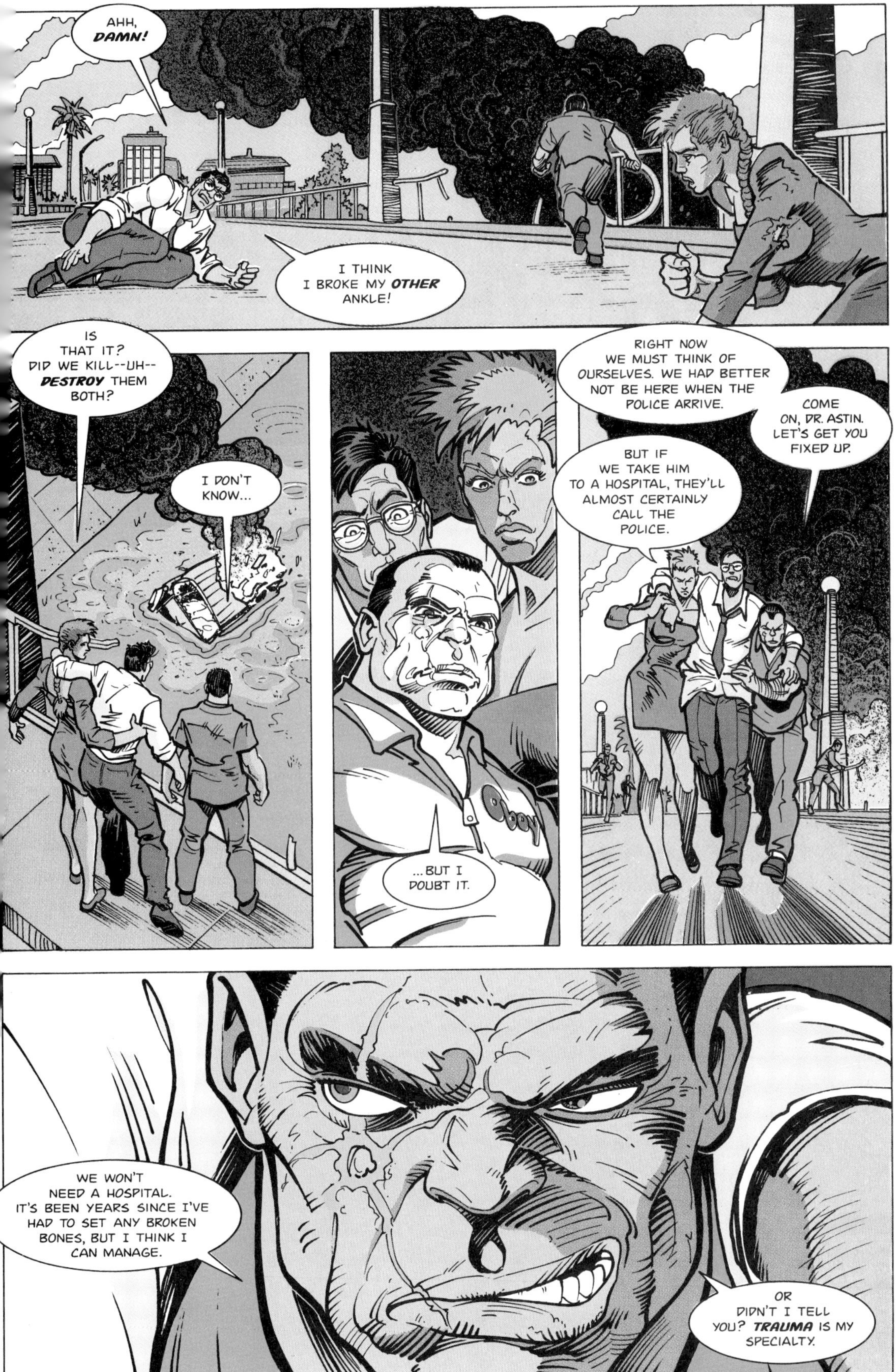
AHH, **DAMN!**
I THINK I BROKE MY **OTHER** ANKLE!
IS THAT IT? DID WE KILL--UH-- **DESTROY** THEM BOTH?
I DON'T KNOW...
...BUT I DOUBT IT.
RIGHT NOW WE MUST THINK OF OURSELVES. WE HAD BETTER NOT BE HERE WHEN THE POLICE ARRIVE.
COME ON, DR. ASTIN. LET'S GET YOU FIXED UP.
BUT IF WE TAKE HIM TO A HOSPITAL, THEY'LL ALMOST CERTAINLY CALL THE POLICE.
WE WON'T NEED A HOSPITAL. IT'S BEEN YEARS SINCE I'VE HAD TO SET ANY BROKEN BONES, BUT I THINK I CAN MANAGE.
OR DIDN'T I TELL YOU? **TRAUMA** IS MY SPECIALTY.

EPILOGUE:

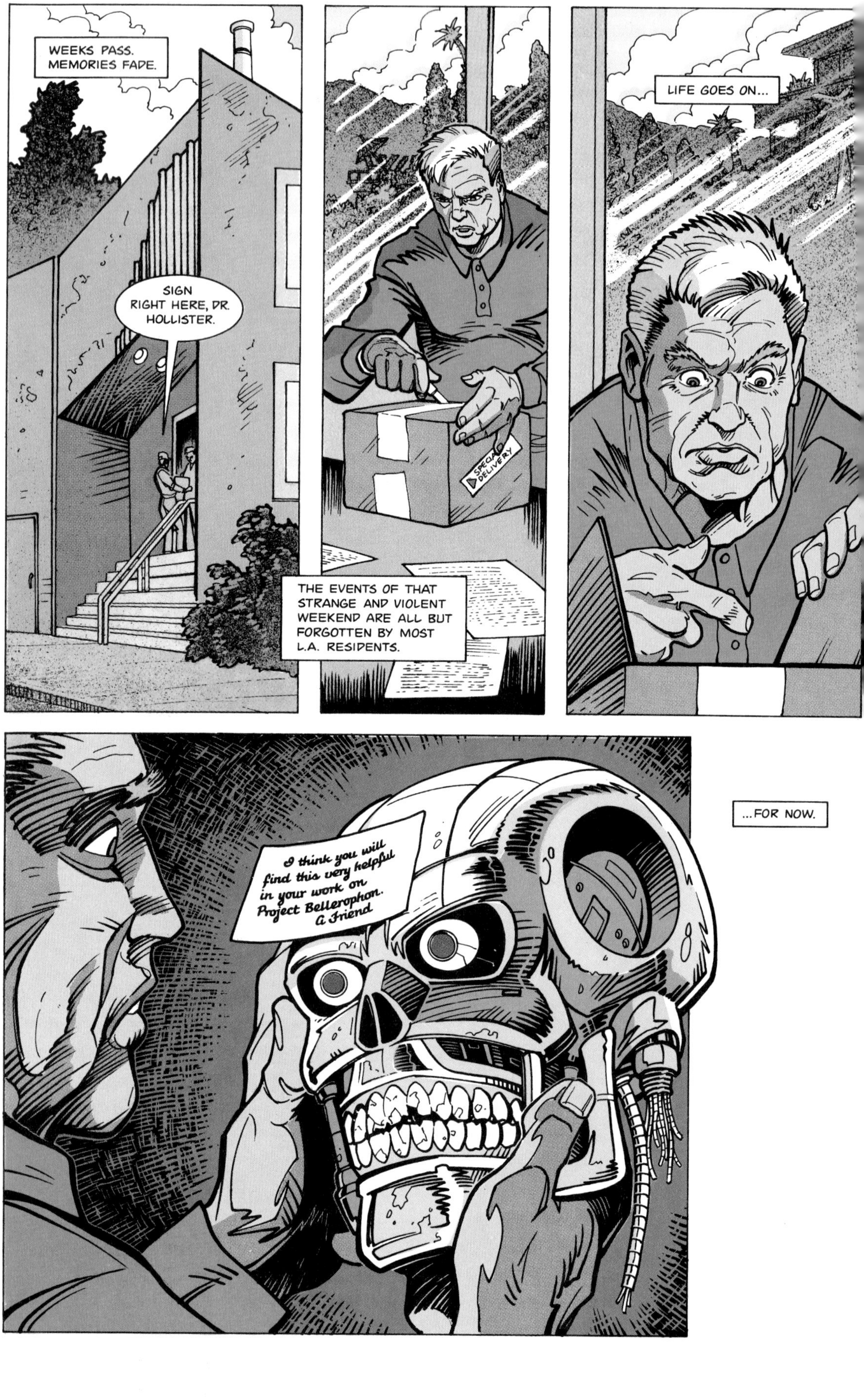
WEEKS PASS. MEMORIES FADE.
SIGN RIGHT HERE, DR. HOLLISTER.
SPECIAL DELIVERY
THE EVENTS OF THAT STRANGE AND VIOLENT WEEKEND ARE ALL BUT FORGOTTEN BY MOST L.A. RESIDENTS.
LIFE GOES ON...
I think you will find this very helpful in your work on Project Bellerophon. A Friend
...FOR NOW.

ABOUT THE CREATORS

JOHN ARCUDI

John's work came to the attention of Dark Horse fans through his *Homicide* stories which have run in *Dark Horse Presents* and in the *Homicide Special*. John's lean writing style will also excite fans in his upcoming work: *Aliens: Genocide*, *The Mask*, and *Predator: Big Game*.

CHRIS WARNER

Well known for his dynamic illustrations on popular titles such as *Predator*, *Terminator*, and *The American*, Chris is developing a color graphic novel featuring *Black Cross*, one of the most requested characters at Dark Horse.

PAUL GUINAN

Besides his stylish inking on *Terminator: Tempest*, Paul is known for his distinctive art on the *Heartbreakers* series, co-created with Anina Bennett. *Heartbreakers* often appears in the anthology *Dark Horse Presents*.

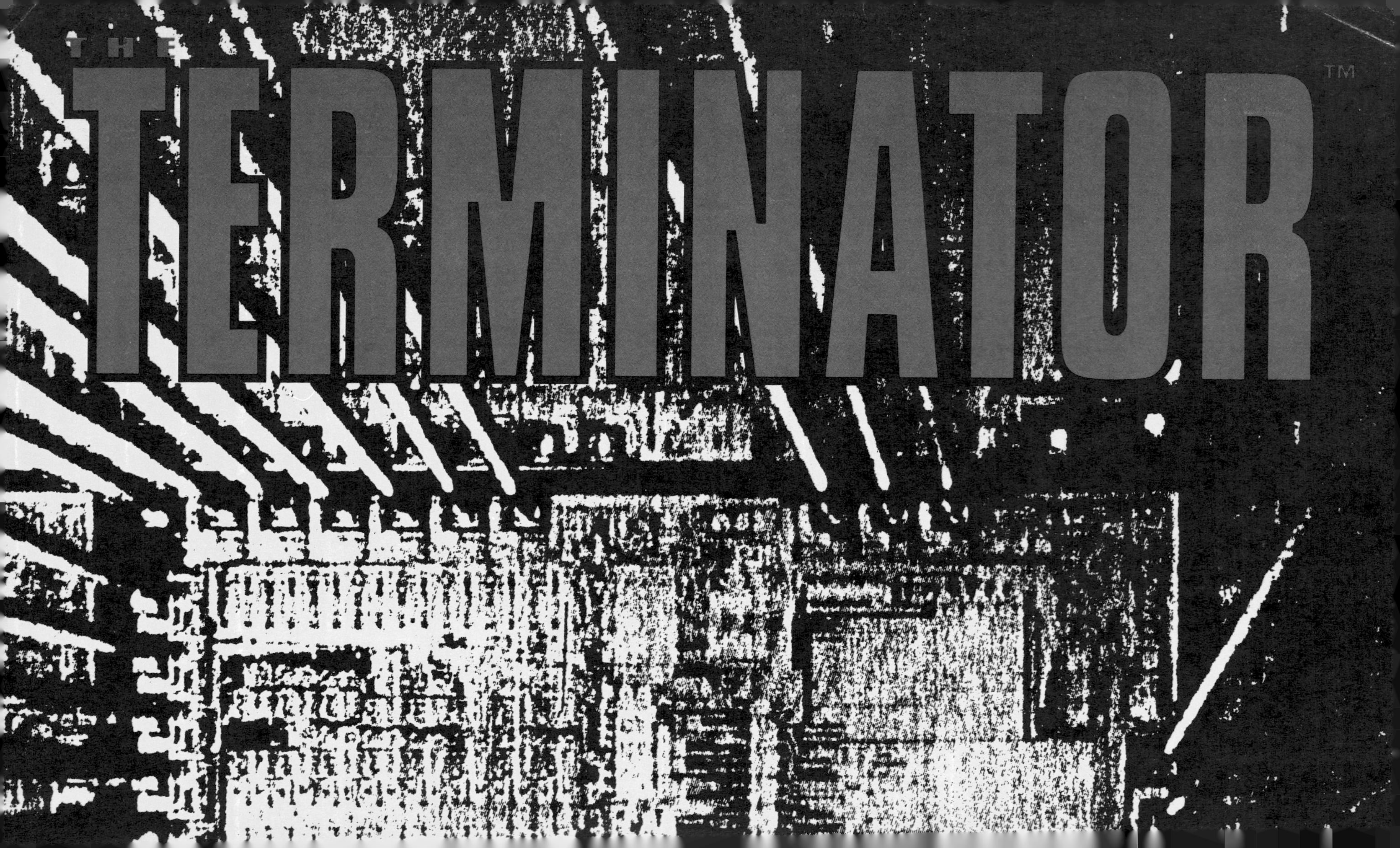
THE
TERMINATOR™